The Coal Killer

The Coal Killer

Trevor Negus

© Trevor Negus, 2016

Published by Bathwood Manor Publishing

A CIP catalogue record for this book is available from the British Library.

ISBN 978-0-9955737-0-3

Book layout by Clare Brayshaw

Prepared and printed by:

York Publishing Services Ltd
64 Hallfield Road
Layerthorpe
York YO31 7ZQ

Tel: 01904 431213

Website: www.yps-publishing.co.uk

PROLOGUE

Newstead Colliery Village, Nottinghamshire 1970

The scruffy blonde boy sat on the dusty concrete floor of the yard, behind the terraced house where he lived with his elderly grandparents. He was wondering what to do. It was the last week of the school summer holidays and he was totally bored, having already exhausted every fun thing there was to do.

He was wearing a dirty Leeds United football shirt and red shorts that didn't match the shirt. He had black plimsolls on with no socks. His dirty feet felt uncomfortable, sweating in the heat.

Lethargically, he dragged himself to his feet and kicked the deflated football that sat on the concrete of the yard.

The ball scuffed noisily across the floor and landed in the corner, it was useless.

Ignoring the ball, the boy slouched over to the small brick outhouse in the corner of the yard. Opening the latch of the door he found the cool darkness appealing after sitting in the baking hot sun.

Looking on the shelves in the small shed, his eyes latched onto a magnifying glass. Taking the magnifying glass, he stepped back out into the sunshine, scanning the concrete, he soon spotted movement.

Over by the back door of the house, he could see a column of ants.

He wore a very serious expression as he used the magnifying glass to focus the sun's rays on the line of ants that were purposefully marching across the yard.

Suddenly he felt enthused again. He was now an alien from Mars, circling planet Earth in his space ship. The magnifying glass became the space ship's death ray wiping out whole populations below.

He grinned as the ants popped, fried alive by the sun's rays.

Eventually, after twenty minutes, he bored of the game. After surveying the rows of burned ants, that were now twisted into macabre shapes, with a satisfied grin he slouched down into the corner of the yard.

The boy looked along the row of red brick terraced houses.

The red bricks had become discoloured over time and were now almost black. The mortar in between the bricks had been stained by decades of smoke, soot and grime. The grey slates on the roof shimmered in the bright sunlight and the boy could see the heat haze bouncing off the tiles.

The houses had been built just after the turn of the century to house miners working at the local coal mine. Every house was identical, traditional two up, two down terraces.

All the back yards were small, with an outhouse in one corner and an outside toilet in the other. The wooden fences separating the yards were only three feet high, standing up the boy looked over the fences at the different coloured clothes on the washing lines.

It was roasting hot, a perfect wash day.

Squatting down on the concrete, the boy began thinking about the local grammar school he was due to start at next week. He wasn't looking forward to it. He didn't make friends easily and had heard tales of vicious bullying.

It came as no surprise to the boy's doting grandmother that he had sailed through his eleven plus exam, she was always quick to point out to anyone who would listen, that he was a 'gifted child'.

Gifted he may have been; strange he definitely was.

The boy had no friends, he was happiest when left with his head buried in a book. He was considered a bookworm and a swot by the other kids. Adult neighbours considered him to be aloof and sullen, almost weird.

Six months ago, just prior to his eleventh birthday, a group of neighbours had rounded on the boy, accusing him of harming their children's pets. Two rabbits and a cat had been stolen from nearby gardens. All the animals were later found mutilated after being throttled by wire nooses.

His grandmother had vehemently defended the boy. She had quickly lied to the group of neighbours, saying her grandson had spent the last day or two ill in bed with a cold.

The gathering of angry neighbours didn't go as far as involving the local police as there was no hard proof of the boy's involvement. The boy had smirked at the gathered neighbours from behind his grandmothers back.

He really couldn't understand what all the fuss was about. The cat had scratched his hand, surely it was only fair that he made it suffer. The rabbits were just plain stupid and deserved to be tormented.

Killing the pets was the thing he had enjoyed most, through the entire boring holidays.

In her heart his grandmother knew the boy was odd, but she felt it was her duty to protect him after the harsh start in life he had endured.

The boy had never known his own father. His mother had only just turned seventeen when she fell pregnant following a brief affair with a foreign businessman.

The young woman had become infatuated with the tall blonde Norwegian who she met while working as a chamber maid at the Royal Hotel in Nottingham. The Norwegian businessman used her for sex. As soon as his business in the city was completed he left immediately, returning to Oslo. He had left the young chambermaid without a moment's hesitation. He had also left her very pregnant.

Shortly after his third birthday the boy's mother moved out of the family home in Newstead, to start a new life on the East Coast working at a holiday camp near Great Yarmouth.

It was easy for her to leave behind a son she had never really wanted. It was then left to the grandparents to raise the boy.

The boy never asked after his mother, and his grandmother did her best to provide everything he needed, within the meagre budget they lived on.

The sun was getting hotter now, the boy was being plagued by a troublesome wasp that continually flew around his face.

He moved nearer to the outhouse, as it caused the only parcel of shade on the yard. He didn't want to sit inside as the smell of creosote and old paint tins gave him a headache. The back door to the house itself was locked and both grandparents were out at the shops.

The grandfather now insisted the boy was not to be left alone in the house, after he had caught him smoking his cigarettes.

Before going out to the shops his grandparents had left strict instructions with the boy, ordering him not to stray from the yard. They knew that relations with some of the neighbours were still quite raw and strained.

Suddenly he heard a door bang a few houses along the street. He immediately stood up and looking over the fence he saw his neighbour, Mrs Daines, coming out of her back gate pulling on the arm of her young son Billy.

The family had only moved into the terrace about three months before and Mrs Daines didn't yet know many of her new neighbours. Since the family arrived in Newstead, the only person she had spent any time chatting to was the boy's grandmother.

Mrs Daines was now dragging Billy along by his arm.

'Come along Billy I haven't got time for any of your nonsense today.'

The small boy said nothing, he just dragged along behind her like a dead weight.

Mrs Daines walked up to the boy's gate.

'Hello Jimmy is your Grandma home?'

'No she's at the shops with my Grandad.'

'Are they going to be home soon?'

'I reckon so. They've been gone a couple of hours already, so I don't think they'll be long. Why?'

Mrs Daines looked worried, she shifted her weight from one foot to the other before taking a deep breath.

'Jimmy, could you do me a huge favour and watch young Billy for a while, just until your Grandma gets home. My bloke's had an accident at the pit, I've got to go and meet him at the General Hospital over in Mansfield and I don't want to drag Billy down there as well.'

The boy looked over the gate at young Billy who was now sitting at the feet of his harassed mother.

The youngster looked even more bored than the older boy felt.

Billy was about seven years old, with a mop of unruly red hair, a short, plump child. He was also an only child and his parents doted on him, dressing him immaculately. Today was no different, the young boy was dressed in a blue and white striped T-shirt, matching blue shorts, blue sandals and white ankle socks.

The boy opened the gate to the yard.

'No problem Mrs. I'll watch Billy, it'll be fun.'

Mrs Daines shooed her young son into the yard and the boy closed the gate.

As she walked hurriedly away Mrs Daines looked back and shouted, 'Don't go wandering off Billy, be good for Jimmy and do what he tells you.'

Both boys played in the yard for about half an hour, before once again boredom set in. There was only so much to do in such a small space with no toys. Even frying the ants soon became tedious.

The boy suddenly stood up and turned to Billy.

'Shall we go for an adventure Billy? There's a small pond just over the fields, I saw a huge pike in there the other day. Do you want to see it?'

'What's a pike?'

'A pike's a massive fish with huge teeth, it can eat other fish and even ducklings. It's amazing Billy.'

'Ok', said Billy his eyes widening.

The boys then left the haven of the yard and set off walking through the maze of terraced houses, known locally as the Newstead Rows.

The terraces were criss-crossed with narrow alleyways, that ran in front of tiny postage stamp front gardens and rear yards. The boy knew the alleyways like the back of his hand.

The boys walked quickly through the Rows, eventually passing Newstead Miners Welfare and crossing the disused railway line.

Billy whined as his podgy little legs struggled to keep pace.

'How far is it Jimmy?'

'It's not far now Billy, we're nearly there.'

Having crossed the overgrown railway tracks, the boys walked into a field of nearly ripe wheat, that was almost the same height as Billy.

The youngster was getting agitated because of the heat and the dust from the high wheat.

'I'm tired, I want to go back Jimmy.'

The boy bent down so he was looking straight into Billy's eyes.

'Look Billy. Can you see those bushes and trees over there? That's where the pond is, come on.'

The older boy grabbed Billy's hand and almost pulled him along.

'Ok, I'm coming, there's no need to drag me.'

The boys reached the bushes and sure enough there was a small pond. It was completely surrounded by vegetation and couldn't be seen from the fields. It was a small irrigation pond that had been dug years before by a farmer who had previously owned the land and who raised a few cattle.

The field hadn't been used to raise cattle for over twenty years, everything was now geared towards raising crops. It was difficult for the current farmer to plough right to the edge of the pond and that was the reason the bushes and small trees had flourished.

'Come on Billy, come and see the big fish.'

Billy looked very apprehensive, almost scared.

'I'm frightened of the pike Jimmy. You said it's got huge teeth, will it eat me?'

'No Billy, course not. You're way too big, but if you're lucky you might see it grab a smaller fish and eat that.'

Feeling a little bolder Billy grinned and walked through the bushes until he stood right at the side of the pond.

'Where is it?' he said

'You've got to look a little closer Billy.'

Billy edged ever closer to the water's edge until he was on his knees bending right over the dark brackish water.

'I still can't see it', he said

Suddenly the boy grabbed Billy by his shoulders and rammed his face down into the water.

Frantically, the youngster twisted, trying to escape the older boy's grip. All Billy succeeded in doing was to twist over, so he was lying on his back in the water with the older boy standing astride him.

The pond was quite shallow near the edge, but was still up to the knees of the older boy who slowly exerted more pressure on the youngster's shoulders forcing his face down under the water.

Billy started to scream but clamped his mouth and eyes shut as his head was forced under the brackish water.

The boy held Billy just below the surface of the water

until suddenly he saw the young child's eyes open. There was now a panicked expression on the youngster's face. The older boy was fascinated and stared into Billy's eyes. As the seconds passed he watched closely as the expression in the youngster's eyes went from panicked to pleading to nothing.

Eventually, after several minutes, there was nothing in the eyes except a blank lifeless stare.

The boy suddenly realised that everywhere was now deathly quiet. The splashing that had been made by Billy's arms and legs had stopped.

The youngster was lifeless and floppy.

The boy slowly stood up and finally released his grip on Billy's shoulders.

He remained standing astride the dead boy, who was now lying just below the surface of the dirty brown water. He peered intently into the water and saw tiny bubbles escaping from the partially open mouth of the dead child.

After a couple of minutes, he stepped out of the pond and looked at the drowned child.

He didn't know what he felt.

It was a toxic mixture of excitement, fear and pleasure. He had no idea why he drowned the child, it just felt right. When he had looked into the youngster's eyes, the boy knew it was something he had to do.

His brain was now going into overdrive, he felt panicked and his breathing was shallow.

He sat down in his wet clothes on the bank of the pond to think.

A bright green dragon fly skimmed across the surface of the pond and birds had started to sing in the bushes around him.

Life had resumed its normal course.

After a few minutes everything became clear, he knew what to do. He turned his back on the pond and walked out from the bushes, back into the harsh sunlight. He stopped and began forcing himself to cry. Eventually there were real tears streaming down his face, carving track marks in the dusty grime caked on his cheeks.

Then suddenly he began to run as fast as he could, back towards Newstead Village.

He smashed his way through the high ripening wheat and sped over the railway line until he could see the Miners Welfare. As he raced towards the Welfare, he saw a group of four men standing outside chatting, drinking and smoking.

The boy ran straight up to them, shouting for help at the top of his voice.

'Calm down lad, what's up? You're soaking wet, what's tha' been doing?' said one of the younger miners.

Breathless the boy tried to speak between sobs.

'It's Billy Daines, I'm supposed to be looking after him but he ran off! He's fallen into the Farmers Pond and I can't get him out!'

One of the men bent down to the anguished boy.

'Stay here with George, we'll go and see what's happened.'

The three younger men threw down their cigarettes and ran off in the direction of the Farmers Pond. The older miner who had stayed with the boy took a long pull on his cigarette and quaffed a mouthful of cold beer.

'Don't thee worry lad, it'll be alright. You're not to blame. Have you tried to get him out? Is that why you're wet?'

The boy sobbed and nodded.

'He wasn't moving, there's something wrong with Billy, I know there is.'

'There, there lad, it's not your fault, you tried to get him out', said the old man gently, trying to comfort the boy.

'Aren't you young Jimmy Wade? Brian Wade's grandson', the old miner asked.

The boy nodded again.

'Come on then Jimmy, I'll walk you back to your house. I know it's hot but you need to get out of those wet clothes.'

Just as they were about to set off, one of the men came sprinting back to the Welfare.

He shouted to the older miner standing with the boy.

'It looks bad George; I reckon the young kid's drowned. We've got him out of the pond, I need to call the police and an ambulance.'

The young miner then ran inside the Welfare to call the emergency services.

The boy standing with George started to sob even harder.

'Don't worry lad, I've already told you it's not your fault. It was an accident, you tried to get him out. You're only a kid yourself, stop crying now lad. Come on let's get you home to your granddad's house.'

The old miner put his gnarled bony hand on the shoulder of the boy and together they walked through the Newstead Rows back to his grandparents' house.

As they walked, the old miner didn't see the sparkle in the boy's eyes or the sly smirk spreading slowly across his mouth.

CHAPTER 1

Wembley, North London – March 1984

'For God's sake woman, will you give it a bloody rest!'

The voice belonged to Mick Reynolds, who at thirty-eight years of age was totally sick of his life, well his married life anyway.

Reynolds was an ugly man, short and squat with a large nose and bad skin. His teeth were uncared for and rotting. His black hair was chopped short in no apparent style and he had a permanent five o'clock shadow.

He had married Rita late in life when he was thirty-four. The last four years had been a living hell. He regretted the marriage almost from the first week they had lived together.

His wife never missed an opportunity to slag him off. It was either his lack of ambition to attain promotion at work, his lack of handyman skills or most telling of all his lack of prowess in bed.

Throughout his life Mick Reynolds had always struggled with the opposite sex. Unfortunately, Mick wasn't blessed down below, his penis was very small and he could rarely raise or sustain an erection.

When they first got together his lack of sexual prowess didn't seem to trouble Rita, who seemed far more interested in the material things in life. At the time they met she was living in a very small bedsit in one of the roughest parts of the East End. The area was frequented by prostitutes and criminals. Understandably she jumped at the chance to live with Mick in his relatively new and spacious three bedroomed semi-detached house in suburban Wembley, about half a mile from the famous football stadium.

Mick was a hardworking man with a responsible job that paid well and had the prospect of a very good pension. Whether Rita went out to work or not, there was always plenty of money to spend.

As the months of virtually no sex of any kind turned into years, Rita blatantly embarked on a series of squalid affairs that really rubbed Mick's nose in it. As well as deliberately flaunting her own promiscuity with a string of different men, Rita never missed an opportunity to ridicule him for his lack of prowess in satisfying her needs.

As a result, the couple now lived virtually separate lives.

Mick had grown to physically loathe his wife and dreamed how much better his life would be if Rita wasn't in it. He constantly fantasised about killing her, replaying various plots and schemes over and over in his mind, both during the day and at night. Especially at night, as he lay awake in bed and Rita snored loudly next to him.

Mick had never laid a finger on a woman in his life, but recently he found himself getting the urge to physically assault her, to shut that poisonous mouth for one second so he could get some peace and quiet.

Finally, after his last shouted plea Rita had finally stopped goading him.

The front door of the house slammed shut and he heard her tarty heels clipping up the front path of his house.

'At last', he breathed quietly to himself.

It was getting on for eight o'clock at night, Mick knew if he hurried he would still be able to get there, before he started work at ten o'clock.

'Bloody nights again already!' he mumbled to himself.

He grabbed his bomber jacket and lunch box and after switching the lights off in the house he walked through the interior door that led to the garage.

He switched on the light in the garage and smiled as he saw his pride and joy, a very new Ford Sierra.

Mick opened the garage door, then drove the car out of the garage onto the sloping drive. He quickly jumped out, closed the garage door and locked it.

Getting back in he smiled and revved the powerful engine.

He really did love his car.

One of the only good things about Rita was that she had failed her driving test. The last thing he needed was the expense of buying the bitch her own car.

When Rita stormed out of the house earlier he had no idea where she was going. Now, as he drove away from the house he found himself wishing she would fall under the knife or hammer of some sadistic serial killer.

'If only!', he muttered aloud before switching on the cassette player in the car.

As he listened to Depeche Mode belting out their latest track, he replayed the brutal slaughter of his wife over and over again in his mind.

A quick drive across town and fifteen minutes later he was cruising slowly along one of the roads in a well-known red light district near the centre of London. The cassette player in the car was now switched off.

Mick knew this place like the back of his hand, for the past two years he had sought company with various working girls who were only too pleased to lavish him with a bit of false admiration and sexual fulfilment in exchange for cash. The women were happy to exchange sexual favours for his money so they could get the next fix of whatever drug they were abusing.

As he drove slowly along the long road he saw a young girl standing alone, leaning backwards against the large wall.

The young prostitute had long straggly blonde hair, that was wet and plastered to her head due to the very fine drizzle that was falling. She was wearing a plastic looking pink top that was left open revealing a tight white vest covering her ample breasts. Her short skirt was fake leather and more like a belt. The whole look was finished off with white plastic, knee length boots.

She was hard faced with dark rimmed eyes and looked about twenty-five years old.

The woman was not the type he would normally choose to go with, but the cold and the drizzle had kept most of the working girls off the street.

He parked the car at the side of the road, thirty yards away from where the prostitute was standing. He let the wipers move the drizzle from the screen and squinted trying to get a better look at her. As the blades moved silently from side to side displacing the water on the windscreen he could momentarily see her features clearly, then the drizzle on the screen distorted them again.

He remained in the car watching her like that for five minutes.

'God she looks rough!' he grumbled.

However rough she looked, Mick was desperate for some relief. He checked his mirrors for other vehicles that could be the Vice Squad, before driving his car along the road until he was directly in line with the woman leaning on the wall.

As soon as he stopped the car the prostitute heaved herself away from the wall and sauntered over swaying her large hips in an over exaggerated sexy walk.

As the prostitute walked towards the car Mick leaned over and wound down the front passenger window. She leaned in the open window of the Sierra and as she did so her ample breasts, accidentally on purpose, spilled out of the vest top and Mick was treated to a free full frontal.

'All right darling', she said breathily. Before fluttering her false eyelashes and saying, 'Are you gonna let this girl spend some time out of the rain?'

'How much for a hand job?' Mick said abruptly.

'Blimey you don't mess about do you mate, hand relief's ten quid, full relief's thirty. Either way you're wearing a condom no arguments, I don't want my new clothes messing up.'

'Ok get in', stammered a now breathless Mick.

The car door opened and the woman got in.

Immediately the car was filled with the smell of her cheap perfume and cigarettes. He glanced over and saw that she had made no attempt to put her breasts back inside her vest top. They were big, far bigger than Rita's. The cold wet weather had made her nipples erect.

Staring at the breasts, Mick could feel himself getting aroused already.

The prostitute pointed along the dark road, 'Just drive straight on for about a hundred yards, there's an alleyway on the left. Pull in there and we won't be disturbed.'

Mick did as he was asked and a minute later was sitting in complete darkness with the prostitute.

The only sound was that of the steadily falling rain drumming on the car roof. The passenger window of the car was still open.

Mick reached over and wound the window back up, brushing his hand against the prostitute's large fleshy breasts as he did so. He felt himself shudder as he felt her bare skin against his hand.

As he leant over to wind the window back up she breathed into his ear.

'What can I do for you love?'

'Hand relief, here's your tenner', he stammered as he passed her the note.

Immediately the prostitute reached for the zip on his trousers, she swiftly slid open the fly, then unfastened his belt and undid the button of his trousers. She then yanked them down slightly and moved his boxer shorts to one side.

His pitifully small penis was already erect and he could feel himself nearing a climax. The woman quickly removed a foil packet from her pink Kagoul pocket. She tore open the packet and expertly flicked the condom onto his diminutive manhood, it was just in time and he ejaculated with a loud groan.

The prostitute giggled.

'Jesus Christ in a hand cart! That didn't take long did it mate!'

Mick could feel a rage building within him that he'd never felt before.

He quickly removed the now full condom and adjusted his clothing. He opened the driver's side window and threw out the condom before finally doing himself up.

He looked at the prostitute and hissed menacingly, 'What do you mean by that comment darling?'

Still feeling confident she said, 'I don't mean anything by it ducks, it's just that little Peter seemed anxious to get everything off his chest, so to speak.'

She smiled a nervous smile.

Mick glared at her.

'What did you call my cock?' he said in a low menacing whisper.

She giggled nervously.

'Little Peter, let's face it he ain't exactly Big John is he darling!'

Suddenly and without warning, Mick smashed his fist straight into the woman's face causing her nose to explode in a torrent of blood and mucus.

The punch was so hard it smacked the woman's head back onto the passenger door window.

'Fucking 'ell you lunatic you've smashed my nose, let me out this fucking car', she screamed.

Mick reached across and opened the car door. He then forcefully pushed her out of the car sending her sprawling across the wet pavement.

Desperate to get away from a further assault, she shuffled back from the car. Her short skirt rode up exposing her buttocks, they felt cold and wet on the rain soaked pavement. Blood dripped from her damaged nose onto her still exposed breasts. She whimpered as she dragged herself further away from the car over the rough pavement.

Mick slammed the door. Leaving the car lights off he reversed quickly out of the alleyway.

Try as she might, the dazed prostitute could not make out the registration number of the car. Slowly she staggered to her feet and wandered off further down the alley, away from the direction the car had sped off in.

'Fucking nutter!', she screamed after the car.

She tried to clean herself up with a couple of tissues from her pocket, before thrusting the bloodied ten pound note into the elastic of her wet knickers.

Mick drove for about four hundred yards before he risked putting the cars lights on.

'Damn, that felt good!' he shouted.

As he drove he switched the car stereo back on.

The loud reggae beat of a UB40 hit thumped out increasing his euphoric state, he felt exhilarated and his hands drummed on the steering wheel in time to the music.

When he had punched the tart, it was Rita's face he had seen. Now he imagined repeating that punch over and over again until he couldn't recognise Rita's poisonous features.

He looked at himself in the rear view mirror, he was smiling like a Cheshire cat.

A short ten-minute drive later and Mick arrived at work. He parked his car and walked into the old building. He went straight into the locker room to get his kit.

Some of his colleagues were already there getting changed. As he took off his jacket one of them looked across at him with a worried expression.

'What you staring at?' asked Mick in an indignant tone.

'Are you alright Mick? You've got blood on your hand and the cuff of your shirt.'

Feeling a moment of panic, Mick looked down and saw that his hand was indeed covered in the blood of the prostitute.

Regaining his composure, he quickly said, 'It's nothing, there was a dog in the road that had been hit by a car, it was stone dead but a bit of a mess. I dragged it away from the middle of the road into the gutter. It was dark and I didn't realise there was blood on my hand. Get yourself into the briefing room, I'll give my hands a quick wash then come and brief you on for the night shift.'

Police Sergeant Mick Reynolds then walked calmly off to the gents' toilets to wash the blood of the prostitute from his hands.

He had just finished washing off the blood when the duty Inspector walked in.

'How's it going Mick? I'm glad I've caught you before you start the briefing. Your nightshifts might be somewhat curtailed this week; we've had a request for at least twenty Police Support Units to travel as mutual aid to Nottinghamshire at any time this week. It looks like this coal miner's strike that's been threatening all over the news is going to happen. The Notts force is expecting the shit to hit the fan big time when it starts. You go and sort out the guys who make up your PSU and I'll brief the remainder of your shift. Once you and your men have got all your gear together just stand by in the canteen. I'm sure it won't be long before you get the order to go.'

'Will do sir.'

'Are you alright Mick?' he said. 'You look a bit flushed, you know, red in the face.'

'I'm fine sir. Actually I've never felt better, I'm just loving life at the moment', he replied grinning broadly.

CHAPTER 2

Mansfield Woodhouse – March 1984

Jimmy Wade was getting ready for his first shift of the week, he was on early turn at the colliery and his alarm clock had gone off just after four thirty that morning. It had been a real struggle to drag himself out of bed, he was awake most of the night studying for the exam he hoped would see him through to getting his Deputies papers. It was his ambition to be a Deputy at Warsop Main Colliery by the time he was twenty-five years of age.

Wade had entered the mining industry straight from leaving school, much to the dismay of his teachers who wanted him to further his education at university. After the death of his devoted grandmother, just before he left school in 1975, he made the decision to leave education and start work so he could earn a wage and look after his elderly grandfather, whose health was also failing.

The other reason that helped him make the decision to leave school and not pursue further education, was the realisation, at around fourteen years of age, that he was different from the rest of the pupils at his school.

It wasn't just that he was different from the other pupils, Jimmy knew he was different from everybody.

Ever since the incident from his childhood at the Farmers Pond in Newstead when young Billy Daines was drowned he had fought hard to suppress the emotions and feelings he felt on a daily basis.

The involvement of the police and subsequent Coroners Inquest into the boys drowning had taken its toll on him. So many times he had wanted to try and explain to the police and the coroner that it wasn't an accident, and that it wasn't wrong either as what happened at the pond just came naturally to him.

Eventually, after the Coroner's Inquest ruled that the death was an accidental drowning, Mr and Mrs Baines left the village. They couldn't accept that their beautiful little red haired child had been snatched from them. Mr Baines never believed the verdict of accidental death, and prior to him leaving the village, he twice made allegations to the police that Jimmy Wade was responsible for his son's death. On each occasion the police made brief enquiries, then decided that no blame could be apportioned to the boy. The grieving parents left the village to move back to the Kent coalfields and over time sentiments in the village settled down again, the incident at the pond was generally forgotten.

Some of the neighbours in the village continued to point the finger at Jimmy, refusing to rule out that he had some sinister involvement in the youngster's death.

It was this constant mudslinging that began to affect his grandmother's health. As a child he noticed how she dramatically lost weight and developed a constant, stuttering cough.

Even when doctors diagnosed that his grandmother was suffering from lung cancer, he still believed the real reason she became so ill was because of the poisonous gossips in that small minded village. After her death, he lost all interest in school and left at the first opportunity. He immediately applied for a job in the thriving coal industry and was accepted into the training centre for mining near Bevercotes village.

He enjoyed working at the mine, it helped to give him the cloak of normality and invisibility that he craved. He knew some people regarded him as strange, even weird and he tried hard to blend in as normal. As soon as he was down the pit and once the dust and grime had settled on his face, he knew that in his works clothes and helmet he looked the same as everyone else.

Fourteen years had passed since Billy Daines had died at the pond, in that time Jimmy Wade had developed from being a child into a man and had encountered all the changes that puberty brought, both physically and mentally.

He had matured into a strong good looking man, over six feet tall with golden blonde hair and piercing blue eyes, a reminder of his Nordic genes. As he grew into manhood women were drawn to him, he had a confident attitude which women generally found alluring. There were several girlfriends but they all found him impossible to get close to.

Physically he was a brilliant lover, but icy cold with it.

Passion was not within him; he could make love energetically, but to him it was like running an 800 metre race. It was purely physical exertion to him, there was no emotion. Eventually all the women he dated grew tired of this, and although they said the sex was great they wanted more.

They were looking for someone to love them, and the only person Jimmy truly loved was himself.

His grandfather died just before Christmas in 1982 after suffering briefly from pneumonia, he had succumbed to the deadly illness very quickly. In November he developed an irritating cough and quickly lost his appetite. He was taken into hospital on the 3rd December and died two weeks later.

The old man, ignoring his wayward daughter, left Jimmy everything. The house in Newstead and his beloved pristine Ford Cortina car.

Jimmy passed his driving test in 1980 but had never owned a car, now he could drive this beautiful, if not dated, car. His grandfather had always lavished time on the vehicle and it was literally in mint condition. It was only ever taken out from under the protective covers when the weather was fine. As a result, the mileage on the car was next to nothing.

With the passing of his grandfather there was nothing to keep Jimmy in Newstead any more. He had come to despise the village and the people in it for the way they had ostracised his grandmother.

He immediately sold his grandfather's two bedroomed terraced house in Newstead and purchased a fairly new three-bedroom, semi-detached house with attached garage on Marples Avenue at Mansfield Woodhouse in May 1983.

He had been living alone in the house on Marples Avenue for just under a year now. He liked the tree lined street with its well-kept manicured gardens.

He had lavished time and money on the house and the garden, it was now a very smart house in a lovely quiet neighbourhood. He also respected his neighbours for the way they kept themselves to themselves.

He was very well paid as a face worker at Warsop Main Colliery, so he was able to decorate the house well, inside and out. He had more than enough money to buy a brand new car but he insisted on driving the dark green Ford Cortina that was his grandfather's legacy to him.

All in all, life was good for Jimmy Wade.

The only problem for Jimmy was that over the last three months, long suppressed feelings and urges were once again pushing their way to the surface and they were extremely disturbing to him.

They didn't manifest themselves as manic voices in his head urging him to kill, or as messages from God telling him to purge the unclean from the earth.

The feelings and urges he felt came to him in a very strange manner. He would find himself looking directly into people's eyes, staring, unblinking at them. He knew something inside him was making a calculated assessment asking the same question silently in his head, 'Is this the one?'

The last time he felt urges this strong was the day he had stared into young Billy Daines eyes, before drowning him.

Jimmy knew already that he was losing the battle to keep the feelings and urges in check and that it was only a matter of time before he would need to placate them and kill again.

Today, as he ate his breakfast and got ready for work he felt in control. He switched on the small television in his kitchen. The news was dominated once again by the president of the National Union of Mineworkers, Arthur Scargill, stating he would call a national strike by the end of the week unless he received assurances from the conservative Prime Minister Margaret Thatcher that the programme for pit closures would be re assessed.

Listening to the news report he was shocked when he heard Scargill insisting that this tory government and Margaret Thatcher in particular, were hell bent on destroying the coal industry of Great Britain.

Jimmy had always believed that a job in the coal industry, was a job for life.

Scargill continued to rant into the camera, pointing angrily with his index finger as he was interviewed. He was standing outside one of the pits destined for closure in the Yorkshire coalfield. Heavy on the rhetoric, he claimed the pit closure would not only mean the death of the industry in that area but also the demise of the close knit community that relied on the mine for employment.

Jimmy quickly bored of Scargill's impassioned rhetoric and switched off the television. They might close a few uneconomic pits up in Yorkshire but Jimmy felt strongly that the cuts wouldn't impact on the more profitable Nottinghamshire pits. He grabbed his black Reefer coat and made his way out of the house.

He started up the Cortina and began the short drive along the main A60 road into Warsop, before turning left and dropping down to Church Warsop. Finally turning into the large car park of Warsop Main Colliery.

During the drive his thoughts were concentrated on the television news bulletin. The impending strike was sure to be the main topic of conversation again at work. It had been for weeks. He knew that most of his colleagues were reluctant to strike. They all knew the financial hardship such a strike would bring to their families. Nottinghamshire collieries were some of the best in the country, producing the most coal and more importantly the best coal to fire power stations.

Not many of his colleagues truly believed the vitriolic, working class struggle, rhetoric coming from Scargill and Mick McGahey, the leader of the Scottish miners, that the whole industry was at risk from Thatcher and her tory government. There were some that believed Scargill was speaking the truth, there had been several heated arguments about the merits of a strike, the divisions were already starting to show.

Jimmy personally thought that a few uneconomic pits, probably in Yorkshire, would close and that would be it, business as usual.

He was worried though. If the Union called a national strike he knew that there would be enormous pressure across all the coal fields to comply. The divisions between men used to working together would get wider, families would be deeply affected. Brother against brother, father against son. The strike, if and when it came, would only be bad news.

Having parked his car and with these thoughts racing around his head he walked into the busy pit canteen where he drank a mug of strong tea while chatting with workmates.

Finishing his tea, he walked into the clean side locker room and stripped off completely, hanging his clothes in the locker. He glanced around him at his now naked colleagues. It never ceased to amaze him how unfit and fat some of them were. Jimmy was naturally very strong and although slim was extremely muscular. He couldn't help but strut a little as he walked naked passed the huge communal showers towards the dirty side locker room.

He got dressed into the grey vest and pants supplied by the mine and then slipped on football shorts and socks before putting on the orange overalls, heavy boots and leather work belt. Finally, he removed the dirty coal stained helmet from the locker.

Once dressed he followed other miners and walked into the Deployment Office where an overman informed him and the other men where they would be working that shift. While waiting in the queue he joined in the talk of the impending strike with his workmates, once again there were varied opinions that were expressed strongly, each man trying to impress that his opinion was the correct one. Jimmy ignored the arguments and made his way to the Lamp Cabin, where he obtained his lamp and the large battery which clipped onto his belt. The man in the cabin then issued him with a self-rescuer which he also clipped onto his belt. Finally, he was given two brass tags stamped with a number.

The queue of miners then made their way slowly down to the cage. Jimmy stepped into the cage after handing over one of the brass tags to the Banksman. As always he stepped over to the far side of the cage.

He always liked to stand in the same place if he could.

As he waited for the cage to fill up he looked to his right and saw that the man standing alongside him was sixty-four-year-old Albie Jones.

Albie was a short man, his dirty orange overalls were open to the waist and his huge belly was straining to burst out of the grimy vest he was wearing.

Jimmy smiled and said, 'How do Albie, there can't be many more of these rides left for you, old lad? '

In a broad Welsh accent, Albie replied, 'No boy, finished next week I have, ready to put my feet up, me', laughing as he finished his sentence.

Another voice chimed up, 'If Scargill has his way boyo you'll be finished sooner than that.'

This comment was met with mutterings of agreement and disapproval in equal measure.

Albie said at the top of his booming Welsh voice, 'Just do

what the Union tells you and you'll be fine. You can't trust this Thatcher woman boys, she'll have all your jobs if she gets her way.'

Jimmy found himself staring into the old Welshman's watery blue eyes.

The realisation hit Jimmy like a hammer blow.

This was it, he had found him, Albie Jones was to be the next one. Instantly he knew what he had to do. The eyes were telling him it was the old man's destiny.

Jimmy quickly turned away to avoid staring into the old man's eyes, but it was too late. The fate of Albie Jones was already sealed.

With a small jerk the cage began its rapid descent, seconds later they were plummeting down towards the pit bottom.

Jimmy knew that initially this period was always one of silence, hard men said silent prayers to themselves that everything was going to be ok. There aren't many jobs where even the mere process of getting to work was death defying. One flaw in the machinery was all it would take for the entire cage to hurtle all the men crashing to their deaths at the bottom of the shaft. This brief silence was always quickly filled with general chat and laughter as the men hurtled towards their days' work underground.

All too soon the men were emerging from the cage and out into the relatively wide area of the gate at the pit bottom.

Jimmy was soon setting off along the gate with the other miners, making the long walk to the coal face.

As they walked along the loader gate they passed the freshly hewn coal hurtling past on the automated belts. One of the first lessons learned at the mine was to keep well clear of these belts. They could easily drag an inattentive man in crushing them to death on the rollers in an instant. Many a collier had lost his job for jumping on the belt to hitch a ride instead of walking.

Jimmy found himself walking directly behind old Albie.

'You working at the face today Albie?' he asked.

'Nah lad, my time at the face has long since passed. I'm on a button just up here a way.'

Being on the button was one of the most soul destroying and lonely jobs at the pit. It was monitoring a button to stop the belt. Basically, if instructed by the men working on the face, you pressed the button and stopped the belt, for whatever reason.

At certain parts along the loader gate, the belt would reach a junction where the coal would drop from one belt onto another. If the debris or dust got too great around the working parts of the belt it would need to be cleaned off to prevent a jam. This was also the responsibility of the button man. By rights the belt should be stopped and the covers taken off for the working parts to be cleaned. This invariably never happened and the working parts were always cleaned while the belts were moving. Every time the belt stopped it meant cutting coal on the face had to stop too and that meant a loss of money for the face workers.

In reality the hardest thing about being the button man was staying awake in the darkness.

As they walked along the loader gate Albie said, 'I don't mind the button now Jimmy, it's about all I'm good for', he chuckled before saying loudly above the noise of the passing belt so everyone could hear, 'While you boys are all sweating your bollocks off, I'll be sitting with my helmet off and my feet up reading the paper!'

The Deputy in charge of the men, Dave Smedley, heard

the shouted remark and shouted back to Albie, 'You'd better not let me catch you reading the bloody paper Jones, and keep your fucking helmet on! Some of the cover tins in that area have slipped and we haven't had time to send a haulage team in to fix them yet. There's been a couple of large chunks down from the walls and the roof already. If one of them hits you on the head you're gonna need more than a Disprin owd lad.'

The men reached the location of Albie's button.

Albie settled down for his battle against boredom, while the rest of the miners continued on the remaining three hundred yard walk to the face.

After three hours working at the coal face Jimmy sought out the Deputy.

'Sorry Dave, I've got a problem mate. I've got the biggest load of muck in my left eye, it doesn't matter what I do, I can't fucking shift it. I reckon I need to get to the medical centre, topside and get it flushed out properly.'

'Fucking hell Jimmy! We're just about to bang a new stint in. I can't afford to take anyone off the face to take you back to the pit bottom. It's gonna have to wait I'm afraid, just wash the fucker out.'

'I've tried that already Dave, nothing I'm doing is shifting it. I don't need anyone to walk me back Dave, I'll be fine, I can see ok out of my right eye. If I don't get it cleaned out properly it's just gonna end up scratching my eyeball and then I'll be forced off work for a week or two.'

It was against best practice for an injured man to take himself out of the pit and Jimmy knew this.

'Bloody hell Jimmy you pick your moments. Alright, I'll walk with you the first hundred yards or so and then you can just fuck off out of it, but If any of this lot asks you later I walked you all the way to the pit bottom, got it?'

'Yeah, got it Dave. Cheers mate.'

Jimmy immediately set off with Dave, they walked past the Stage Loader and continued along the loader gate and after a hundred yards or so Dave said, 'Off you go then Wade and remember what I said, I walked you all the way to the pit bottom, got it?'

'No problem Dave, I'll be fine thanks'.

Jimmy now set off alone along the loader gate back to where they had left Albie Jones earlier. There was a bend just before the junction where Albie was, Jimmy could now see the glow from Albie's lamp.

He reached up and dimmed his own lamp before covering it with a hessian rag from his pocket. This made the beam from his lamp barely visible.

As he rounded the bend he could see the old man sitting on the floor facing away from him and leaning sideways against one of the rings. Sure enough he had taken his helmet off and his legs were stretched out in front of him. Jimmy walked silently until he stood directly behind the old man, he was so close he could see the long rhythmic breathing of the man as his chest rose and fell slowly.

Albie Jones was asleep.

Jimmy quickly looked around and in the light cast from Albie's lamp on the floor, he saw a large rock below the belt. He knelt down and with some effort removed the huge rock from its resting place. Carrying the rock in both hands he crept silently behind the old man once again. Albie was still dozing and his mouth was wide open, he would have been snoring loudly but any noise was drowned out by the clatter of the coal filled belt rushing past.

Using all his strength Jimmy raised the large rock high

above his head before bringing it down with tremendous force straight onto the top of the old man's head.

He saw instantly that the head injury the rock caused was catastrophic. Albie's head had split wide apart and he could literally see brain below the huge crack in his balding head, blood was starting to pour out of the massive head wound.

It was obvious the old man had been killed instantly, a red frothy mucus was bubbling from his mouth and his nostrils.

Taking the oily rag from his lamp he turned his lamp up to full beam and surveyed the scene of the carnage properly.

Nobody would survive a head wound of such devastation, especially not an old man. The force of the blow had caused Albie to roll sideways out into the middle of the loader gate. He was now on his back and his lifeless eyes were wide open and staring up at the roof of the gate. The life force had gone, the eyes were blank, expressionless. The bright blue eyes that once sparkled in life were now dull.

Jimmy regretted that he had not been able to see the life force leave the eyes, he knew it was a special moment to watch and enjoy.

Once again he felt that familiar mixture of excitement and achievement. He noted this time there was no fear, just a real sense of release and a feeling that was almost pleasure.

Staging the large rock carefully at the side of the body, Jimmy removed two more cover tins directly above where Albie now lay, sliding them down the side of the gate. Satisfied the scene was set correctly he then made his way along the gate eventually arriving at the pit bottom.

Once at the pit bottom he used the telephone to contact

the Banksman and arranged to be taken in the cage back to the surface as a medical emergency. After a twenty minute wait he was once again top side. He made his way directly to the Medical Centre where the muck and grime he had rubbed into his left eye was washed out.

The accident book was filled in by the attending nurse and Jimmy knew by the time Albie was discovered, he would already be at home.

After undressing he checked his overalls and boots for any spatters of blood. He then showered and got changed before having a cup of tea and a cheese roll in the canteen.

As he drove home he found himself smiling. He was acutely aware now that his destiny was not to suppress the urges, but to act on them when he knew it was right.

He had killed again and this time he felt fulfilled and totally at peace.

CHAPTER 3

Mansfield Woodhouse – March 1984

The banging on his front door was getting more insistent.

'Alright I'm coming', yelled Jimmy.

Getting to the front door he paused, it was nearly eleven o'clock at night.

'Who is it?' he shouted.

'It's me Dave Smedley, open the door I need to talk to you now!'

Jimmy had a small rush of panic but composing himself quickly, he opened the door to the Pit Deputy.

'What the fucks the matter Dave? Don't tell me there's a problem about me coming out the pit today? Has old Albie fucking blabbed mate.'

'It's not that, but I have come about Albie, yes. What was he like when you walked past him on the gate?'

'He was like Albie always is, he was sitting with his feet up whistling when I went by. He offered to walk me to the pit bottom, he was surprised you'd let me come out alone but said he'd seen it a thousand times. I told him he'd better stay on his button. Why what's he said?'

'He hasn't said anything; he's fucking dead Jimmy!'

'What do you mean he's dead, he's retiring next week? What the fuck happened?'

'Oh believe me, he's dead alright, it must've been sometime after you went by, the roof came in and smashed his head in, the silly bastard had ignored what I told him and taken his helmet off. Was his helmet on when you saw him?'

'I reckon it was, yeah. Who found him Dave?'

'Some of the haulage lads. They put a call topside saying there'd been a large roof fall and that a number of the cover tins had slipped out of place leaving the roof exposed and that it was too dangerous for them to recover his body.'

'Fucking hell, they called out the Mines Rescue team?'

'Yes they fucking did. The shit has well and truly hit the fan Jimmy. Did you say he did have his helmet on?'

'I'm pretty sure he was wearing it Dave, yeah.'

'Thank fuck for that. I told the Inspectorate boys that he was fine when I walked back from taking you to the pit bottom and that when we went passed him he was wearing his helmet. You've got to stick to that when they come asking you at work tomorrow, otherwise we'll both be in the shit. You for walking out alone and me for letting you. Sorry to bother you so late tonight but I thought I'd better let you know what's happened.'

'That's ok Dave.'

'How's the eye now Jimmy?'

'It's fine now, I'll be back at work in the morning, if I wake up that is after getting no sleep.'

With a grin at Dave he opened the front door.

Dave took the hint and left saying, 'Alright Jimmy, see you at work tomorrow. Just stick to the story when they talk to you and we'll both be fine.'

'No problem Dave', he chuckled.

He closed the front door and let a smile develop across his face, it was great when a plan came together, he thought.

As Dave Smedley walked back to his car he was feeling

troubled. Why had Wade immediately assumed it was Albie Jones he had come to see him about?

He also noticed that there wasn't a shred of sympathy offered by Wade when he told him that Jones was dead.

It all felt a bit strange.

Smedley got in his car and started the engine. As he drove the car away he pondered whether to tell the truth, tell the Inspectorate that Wade had walked from the face to the pit bottom alone and that he was the last person to see Albie Jones alive not him.

'Fuck it!' he said aloud, there was nothing he could say that would change anything, Albie Jones would still be dead. All he would achieve by speaking out was losing his Deputy status and a massive drop in his take home pay.

He would stick to the story.

CHAPTER 4

Mansfield – March 1984

The week he had taken as annual leave had passed way too quickly and for Detective Inspector Danny Flint that meant another seven days of shifts at Mansfield Police Station, dealing with whatever crimes the people of the North Nottinghamshire market town could throw at him.

Danny was just under six feet tall and broad shouldered. Even though he was now nearly forty, he was still slim and extremely fit.

His short black hair was just starting to grey a little at the temples.

Danny had always taken a pride in his appearance, wearing smart suits and ties.

Today was no different and as he carefully tied a smart Windsor knot in his tie he thought about the consequences of a strike by the National Union of Mineworkers.

There was a strange atmosphere and palpable tension around the town as all the talk of a long drawn out strike by the miners became more and more likely.

The implications of such an action by the Union would be felt strongly by the town.

Mansfield was a town surrounded by coal mines.

The vast majority of men in the town and the surrounding areas were employed by British Coal. The local economy relied heavily on the income generated and spent by those mineworkers.

Danny also knew that in any strike action there would be some who would follow the Union doctrine and come out on strike and others who would defy the Union and continue to work.

In this area that would mean pitting neighbour against neighbour, even family member against family member.

It would be a recipe for conflict on a grand scale.

Danny was well aware that if and when the strike did happen it would herald an extremely busy time for the police.

The transistor radio in his kitchen was on as he ate breakfast and got ready for work. He shook his head in dismay as he listened to the latest updates on the news.

Once again Arthur Scargill was doing his best to rally the miners to hold a national strike, citing the fact that the livelihood of every working miner in the land was at risk if they did not stand up to pit closures now.

Danny sighed as he listened to the arguments put forward by the union's charismatic firebrand leader. It looked a done deal that a strike of some description was coming.

He thought to himself how easy it would have been for him to have followed his own father down the mine. He still had an uncle working at Thorseby Colliery in nearby Ollerton.

A life underground had never appealed to Danny and after leaving school he worked in one of the local furniture stores, helping out with deliveries.

He joined the Police Force quite late at twenty years of age in 1964. Right from the outset he had always leaned towards the investigation of crime and he joined the CID four years later in 1968.

Danny quickly achieved a reputation as a dedicated thief taker with a meticulous approach to the investigation of crime.

It was no surprise when he was promoted initially to Detective Sergeant and subsequently to Detective Inspector, remaining on the CID both times. He had not worn a uniform since 1968 and this suited him down to the ground.

He had been in his current post as the Detective Inspector at Mansfield CID for the last three years.

It had been a tough couple of years for Danny, he lost his mother eighteen months before to chronic heart failure.

Just over a year before her death he had been offered promotion to Detective Inspector. This was followed only days later, by his wife of nine years issuing him with an ultimatum. Spend less time at work or get a divorce.

Danny took the decision to accept the promotion, and the inevitability of the marriage breakdown came soon after.

Following the break up Danny moved back to live with his mother Jean and his father Frank in the original family home at High Oakham in Mansfield. His estranged wife had remained in the marital home until selling it quite soon after the break up.

Moving back to his parents' house had only ever been intended as a short term arrangement. Firstly, he had needed to stay on to help his father cope with his ailing mother and then afterwards when his mother passed away he stayed to help his father, whose own health had suffered as a result of his wife's illness.

His father Frank, although still working at nearby Silverhill Colliery just outside Sutton in Ashfield, suffered badly from depression and needed constant assistance with the running of the house.

Danny's estranged wife left the area shortly after the sale of their marital home and moved back to Rotherham, her home town, in order to "rebuild her life".

The only constants in Danny's life were his work, and his love of football. He had harboured dreams of carving out a professional career in the sport after being signed by Derby County as a youngster.

A serious knee injury had put paid to this ambition when he was nearing his eighteenth birthday.

After recovering from the injury he was fortunate that the medical into the Police Force wasn't too stringent. He managed to pass the medical and as the years went by his knee got stronger. Even now he regularly indulged in a game of five a side with some of the younger lads from the uniform section.

His real enjoyment, was accompanying his father to watch the local team, Mansfield Town, at their Field Mill ground, a short ten-minute walk from his father's house.

It was the one time his father could forget his troubles and lose the black dog depression that plagued his life. Win, lose or draw it didn't matter to his father, he was happy just watching his beloved Mansfield Town play football.

Switching the radio off Danny grabbed his coat.

He decided to make the fifteen-minute walk into work today rather than take the car. It wasn't raining and Danny found that the walk in to the police station helped to focus his mind on the days' work ahead.

It was still dark when he left the house.

The walk into town was an easy one, downhill all the way from the house on Garth Road to the police station.

It was a foggy morning and there was a cold chill in the air, there wasn't another soul about.

As he walked down the hill in the quiet darkness with the mist swirling in front of him, the town took on a foreboding

30

look. He sensed a feeling of real menace lurking below the surface, but pulling his coat a little tighter into his neck he shrugged off the feeling as being just one of returning to work blues.

Arriving at the station he made his way into the CID office. The first person he saw was his friend and colleague, Detective Sergeant Rob Buxton.

Rob Buxton had joined his team two years ago after transferring to Nottinghamshire from South Yorkshire upon promotion to Detective Sergeant.

He arrived with glowing references, not always the case with transferees.

Rob had settled in really quickly and easily overcame the petty resentments some of the other detectives already in the office felt. A few of them had also applied for the vacancy for Detective Sergeant, Rob quickly got them onside by his demeanour and attitude to hard work. It didn't take long for the other applicants to accept that he hadn't taken their job.

Rob's wife was local to the Mansfield area and this was the reason he had applied for the transfer, so his wife could be nearer her family.

He was a bubbly character always willing to help, a very fit and tough looking man who in his youth suffered a badly broken nose playing schoolboy rugby.

The battered face together with the shaved head gave him the look of a squat powerful boxer which he often used to his advantage. The truth was very different, he was a doting father and husband and would spend every minute the job allowed with his young family.

This was something that Danny himself envied a little, the ease with which Rob achieved that work life balance staggered him.

'Good morning boss, had a good holiday?'

'Yes thanks Rob, raring to go now though. Not!'

Both men laughed.

'Let me grab a brew Rob, then you can brief me on what's been happening. I'd better catch up on what I've missed last week.'

'No problem. I'll go and check today's tele printer messages to make sure nothing else has come in since I left yesterday.'

Danny walked into his small office and took off his coat, hanging it on a peg at the back of the door. His office was a small room added onto the large open plan office used by the rest of the CID.

As well as Det Sgt Buxton there were four other detective constables working the office at that time, with a further Det Sgt and three other detective constables working the late shift.

Danny tried to split himself between the two shifts as much as possible but tended to work more with Rob Buxton and his team.

He walked back into the main office and made himself a mug of coffee from the small area set aside to make hot drinks.

Taking the steaming hot coffee, he then returned to his office and sat down heavily in the chair behind his old dark wood desk placing the mug onto his Mansfield Town coaster.

He picked up the first report from the pile that sat in the In-Tray and started to read. He was still reading the first paragraph of the report when someone entered the room.

Expecting to see Rob Buxton, Danny was surprised to see Superintendent Ken Jackson standing there. The senior officer was unshaven and dressed in civilian clothes.

He looked like he had just got up.

Danny said, 'Bloody hell boss it's not seven o'clock yet what the hell are you doing here?'

'Don't worry Danny once I've spoken to you I'm going home for some more shut eye. I wanted to give you the heads up with this news in person rather than over the phone.'

'Christ, I don't like the sound of that. Grab a seat Ken, what's so urgent that it's dragged you here at this time of the day.'

'You've obviously been watching the news about the miners' strike, well we got word last night that it's definitely happening. It's starting tomorrow night. The government are going ahead with the pit closures up in Yorkshire as scheduled and Scargill will call a national strike straight away, no doubt starting at midnight tomorrow.'

'I thought they were going to hold a ballot first?' said Danny.

'No they're not and that's the rub. Our information suggests that some of the Notts miners are claiming the call for them to strike without a ballot is not in the Union rules and are refusing to join the call to strike.'

Danny let out a slow whistle, 'Jesus the shit will really hit the fan if the only mines not on strike are here in Notts. We'll have pickets descending from everywhere, they'll cause mayhem.'

Jackson continued, 'It's not a given by any means that none of the Notts miners will strike. Initially at least, I would expect that the vast majority of mines in this area will be brought to a standstill.'

'But that won't stop British Coal trying to get the stockpiles of coal from the pits to the power stations', said Danny.

'Exactly right Danny and with that in mind the Chief Constable has ordered that we ready all Police Support Units, even the emergency ones.'

The reason for the face to face meeting now became apparent to Danny.

'You're taking my staff aren't you, for fucking PSU duty!'

'I've no choice Danny, this order has come from the top, the very top in London. Our Chief Constable has no say in this whatsoever, the political masters at the Home Office are calling the shots here.'

'What staff are you leaving me with?'

'As well as yourself you'll have one Detective Sergeant and two Detective Constables.'

'You're joking Ken, how am I supposed to run a viable Criminal Investigation Department with those numbers. It's impossible for the size of the area we cover?'

'Like I said Danny, this is already a done deal. I've not come here for a debate.'

Sighing heavily and leaning back in his chair Danny said, 'Do I at least get to choose my own staff?'

'They've sort of selected themselves really Danny. DS Buxton, DC Andy Wills and DC Rachel Moore are the only officers who aren't PSU trained. I'm sorry Danny and obviously we'll monitor it constantly. If your men aren't needed on this fucking strike they'll be back with you straight away. Oh, one other thing Danny, there's no limit on overtime, work whatever hours you have to, it will get paid. That little gem has also come direct from the Home Office.'

'Marvellous, the four of us will be like zombies within four weeks. I know it's not down to you Ken and I do appreciate you getting up to tell me face to face, I'd better start ringing around to let them all know.'

'Sorry, Danny. I rang them all last night as soon as I knew what was happening. The only person I didn't speak to last night was Detective Sergeant Buxton.'

At that very moment Rob tapped on the door carrying a large bundle of papers.

The Superintendent opened the door allowing Rob to enter the office, 'Did I hear my name being used in vain Sir?' he said with a smile on his face.

Ignoring the comment and the smile, Jackson turned back to Danny and said, 'Your other two detectives will be here for eight o'clock Danny, I'm off home now. Any problems and you know where to reach me.'

'Yeah, thanks Sir', said Danny as the Superintendent closed the door.

'What have I missed boss, are we getting more staff?'

Danny grimaced, 'You couldn't be more wrong my little Yorkshire friend.'

Pointing at the other chair in the office Danny indicated for Rob to sit down, he then relayed the conversation he had just had with the Superintendent.

'Bloody hell, I'd better give my Mrs a quick ring and tell her to expect me when she sees me.'

He smiled and added, 'I tell you one thing boss, the Yorkshireman in me is loving the overtime bit though, might get that holiday to the Algarve yet.'

'I thought you might like the sound of that. Anyway down to business Rob, Is there anything startling on the briefing sheet this morning?'

Rob let a grim smile play across his features and said, 'Looks like this one's down to you and me now then boss, there was a death underground at Warsop Main Colliery last night. A sixty-four-year-old miner was killed after a roof fall.

Silly bugger had taken his helmet off according to the Mines Rescue Team that brought him out. The Mines Inspectorate turned out with the MRT and did all the necessary underground. Photos of the scene will be coming over later. There were no suspicious circumstances so no police officers were requested to go underground to the scene. Apparently the deceased was alone watching a button for the conveyor belt when part of the roof came down. It says there'd already been a number of roof falls logged at that location recently. They've asked that the police attend the post mortem first thing this morning to confirm no foul play and to provide the evidence of the injuries that caused the death once they have been identified at the post mortem examination, ready for the Coroner's Inquest.'

'Marvellous', sighed Danny, 'This day just keeps getting better, what time's the PM scheduled for?'

'It says here, Mansfield Mortuary at a quarter to eight this morning.'

'Ok Rob, we'll finish this drink and get down there. Leave a note on the briefing board for Rachel and Andy telling them where we are and not to go out. Tell them there'll be a meeting at eleven o'clock back here. If we're going to be able to function as a credible CID office with just the four of us, we need to get organised and fast.'

CHAPTER 5

Mansfield – March 1984

Having finished their coffees, Danny and Rob headed for the public mortuary.

The building was only a short five-minute walk from the Police Station.

From outside, the mortuary building looked like a small bungalow that was surrounded on three sides by high walls.

A driveway led to the rear of the building where there was double door access for vehicles to deposit the recently deceased.

The two detectives headed for the front door of the building and were met at the door by a very tall, skinny man. Stewart Henson had been the Coroners Officer since he retired from the Force two and a half years ago.

Stewart had been a police officer for thirty years before adopting the role of Coroners Officer. He spent most of his day either at the mortuary assisting the pathologists or in his small office at Mansfield Police Station helping officers prepare files for an inquest.

He was well liked by all the cops, uniform and plain clothes alike, as he was always helpful and brought a respectful joviality to an unpleasant but very necessary part of police work.

Unbeknown to Stewart, he was affectionately known by some of the younger constables as Dr Death.

Stewart opened the door for Danny and Rob, 'Good morning gents, sorry for the early start this morning but Professor Haynes is the on call pathologist today. He's got a full workload starting at Newark from ten o'clock today. He'll be here shortly. Do you want to see what we've got?'

'Ok Stew lead on', said Danny

Walking through a couple of doors the three men passed the public viewing area where loved ones had the awful task of identifying their next of kin. Through one more door and the detectives were standing in the large room where the post mortem examinations were carried out.

There were two stainless steel benches in the centre of the room.

On one side of the room were rows of floor to ceiling drawers where the dead were kept under refrigeration. On the other side wall were further drawers where the dead would be kept in a state of deep freeze. These were only used where the police under instruction from the Coroner could not release a body for burial or cremation due to ongoing criminal investigations.

Along the wall, opposite the door they had entered by, were long benches that had various sinks and scales as well as all the tools used by the pathologists.

Underneath these benches were cupboards that contained the green surgical suits, masks and overshoes used by pathologists and police officers alike, to protect their clothes.

The room was stark white and brightly lit, smelling strongly of disinfectant.

Lying on one of the stainless steel benches was the naked body of Albie Jones.

'Here we are then gents', said Stewart before continuing, 'This is the body of Albert Jones otherwise known as Albie, born 30th March 1919. He was identified last night by his wife and daughter in law. His son is a serving soldier in the Parachute Regiment, he's currently on exercise in West Germany. He has been notified of his father's death and is travelling home, he's expected back some time tomorrow.'

He continued, 'Mr Jones was brought here by the Mines Rescue Team who extracted his body from Warsop Main Colliery late yesterday evening. His body was found on the Loader gate between the pit bottom and the Harley Face.

He was found by the afternoon shift haulage team as they went into the pit to relieve the morning shift. It would appear on face value to be an accident pure and simple. He was found lying on his back with this massive head wound next to a large chunk of the roof, his helmet had been placed to one side of the gate as though he'd removed it himself.'

Danny and Rob both leaned forward to inspect the massive wound at the top of the dead miners' head.

'Jesus!' exclaimed Rob, 'That must've been a large piece of the roof to cause that mess'?

'I can't help you with that Rob', said Stewart, 'I haven't seen the photos they took of the scene yet.'

A doorbell that sounded like it should be fitted in a house rang twice, abruptly disturbing the silence.

'That bloody doorbell! I must get it changed. Every time it goes off it jars right through me, it's totally inappropriate!' exclaimed Stewart before making for the door.

'That'll be the Prof gents, we can get started shortly', he added before leaving the room.

The two detectives remained in the room examining the head wound on the body of Albie Jones.

It was Rob who broke the silence, 'This is all a bit weird Boss, when I was a Dc up in South Yorkshire I went to a couple of pit deaths that had happened down the mine near Dinnington. One of them was a roof fall, well two roof falls to be precise. The first fall had been enough to knock the helmet off the guy and the second more devastating one killed the man. He had very severe trauma to his head but it looked nothing like this. Mr Jones looks like he's literally had his head smashed in.'

'I know what you mean Rob, it looks like his head has been hit with tremendous force, we'll know better shortly anyway once the Professor does his stuff.'

Professor Gerard Haynes entered the room and offered a perfunctory greeting to the detectives before saying, 'Right let's get straight on shall we, I've got a busy day ahead.'

The professor, a Home Office pathologist, looked every inch his title. He was in his late fifties, quite overweight and wearing an ill-fitting suit. He had grey receding hair and wore spectacles that sat on the very tip of his large florid nose.

He quickly removed his jacket and put on a green protective gown, overshoes and gloves finally adding a face mask similar to that worn by surgeons. This was the cue for the detectives and Stewart to also get into protective gowns.

As this was not a criminal investigation yet, neither of the officers would be carrying out the evidence gathering that would be required in a murder case. They were there purely to observe at this stage, and to note anything out of the ordinary or anything that the pathologist identified as a probable cause of death ready for the Coroner's Inquest.

With a flourish of his arms that was almost theatrical the professor said in a loud voice, 'Right gents, let's begin shall we.'

The professor then began the process of the post mortem examination. He started at the massive head wound and instructed Stewart to take photographs as he progressed. The scalp was peeled away to reveal the glistening bone of the skull which glared white under the harsh lights.

There was a huge crack in the skull that led from a point at the top of the head, both forward down as far as the bridge of the nose and back as far as the top of the spinal cord.

The skull appeared almost cleaved in two, as though it had been struck by some medieval weapon such as a battle axe or a claymore sword.

When the full extent of the injury was apparent and grey matter of the brain was visible below the split the professor spoke, 'Well that's as plain as a pike staff for cause of death. Jot this down please Stewart, "Massive injury to the cranium causing numerous heavy bleeds to the underlying brain tissue" I've kept it in laymen's terms for you gents, but basically this wound is the primary cause of death and is conducive to being hit by a heavy piece of rock from above.'

The professor was in full flow now and continued rapidly, 'Close examination of the area around the wound reveals traces of mineral content that when analysed I suspect will match the offending piece of rock.'

Turning to the two detectives the professor said, 'Gentlemen there really is no need for you to stay and watch the rest of the examination, Stewart and I can finish up here. I will contact you if I find anything abnormal with the toxicology or bloods. Any questions?'

Rob immediately spoke up, 'Just one question Sir, how come the wound and the fracture of the skull itself is so huge? I've seen head injuries from rock falls at the pit before that were fatal and they looked nothing like this one.'

'Was the victim of the rock fall you saw a younger man detective?'

'Yes Sir, he was. As I recall he was only in his late twenties.'

The professor took a deep breath and pointed at the skull of Albie Jones, before continuing in a voice similar to that of a schoolteacher explaining to a particularly slow child, 'As the body ages the bone structures become weaker, density lessens and bones become brittle. We are all familiar with the elderly falling in the winter time on snow and ice and easily breaking their limbs. Arms, legs even hips on occasion. This is down to the bones weakening. The same thing happens to the numerous bones of the skull. It would appear that this is the case here. I've taken samples of the skull bone and I fully expect them to show that lack of density. To make a comparison, that rock hitting this poor man's skull would have been like hitting a boiled egg with a spoon. Any other questions?'

As both detectives shook their heads he continued, 'Thank you for attending this morning gentlemen but I can't see anything here that would lead me to believe any sort of foul play has occurred.'

Danny spoke up, 'Ok Professor Haynes, thank you. I look forward to reading your report in full.'

Both detectives then stepped out of the room followed by Stewart.

As they got out of the robes, Danny said, 'I know he's the pathologist Stewart, but something about that wound doesn't look right to me, make sure he's thorough with the rest of the exam will you and let me have his report as soon as possible. Thanks mate.'

Stewart nodded before returning to the grisly task of the remainder of the post mortem.

Danny and Rob walked slowly back to the police station, both deep in thought.

'What are you thinking Boss?' asked Rob.

'I was just wondering how easy it would be to kill somebody down the mine and make it look like an accident. I'm not happy with this, but everything points to it being just an accident. Let's see what the rest of the post mortem reveals when the full report from Professor Haynes and the photographs of the scene land on my desk.'

'I know one thing boss' said Rob seriously, pausing before continuing, 'I won't be having a boiled egg for my breakfast any time soon!'

'Idiot!' laughed Danny as both men walked through the large double doors of the police station.

CHAPTER 6

Mansfield – March 31st 1984

It had been just over two weeks since Arthur Scargill had called upon the National Union of Mineworkers to begin a national strike.

As predicted by the experts the strike hadn't been accepted right across the coalfield. The dissent was mainly in Nottinghamshire where some miners felt they had been railroaded into striking without having a ballot on exactly what they, the Notts Miners, wanted. Scargill maintained an intransigent stance that no ballot was necessary, he claimed that his mandate to call a national strike came when he was elected leader of the National Union of Mineworkers.

The moderate leaders in the Nottinghamshire Branch of the Union had tried to reason with Scargill that the timing for action was wrong. Summer was just around the corner and the stockpiles of coal at the power stations had never been so huge.

It was obvious to all parties that any strike would be a very long drawn out affair and it was also obvious, except maybe to Arthur Scargill, that the government and Margaret Thatcher in particular had shrewdly chosen her time to make a stand against the miners' union and the power she believed that union wielded.

The Prime Minister had been instrumental in the appointment of John McGregor to oversee the running of

British Coal during the strike. John McGregor had previously fought and won a long drawn out battle with United States coal miners and won. In the process decimating that country's once proud coal industry, laying waste to large once prosperous communities.

Arthur Scargill meanwhile was constant in his message that pit closures were happening now and that miners were already losing their jobs; his mantra was that the time to fight for the industry was now.

It was becoming clear that hard times were coming to the small market town of Mansfield that had always been so reliant on the coal industry to prosper.

It was now two weeks since Danny had been instructed to run his CID office on a skeleton crew for the duration of the strike. Most of his staff had been deployed on to Police Support Units to contain flying pickets that were regularly coming into the area from South Yorkshire and other coal fields in order to make the strike solid nationally.

It had taken that two weeks for him and his small team of Det Sgt Rob Buxton and Detective Constables Andy Wills and Rachel Moore to make the skeleton crew staffing levels viable.

Danny felt he was fortunate in so much as the two detectives that remained in the office were both serious grafters.

Dc Andy Wills was a smart dressed individual who wore dark suits that were cut well, he was always well groomed and was in every way an immaculate man.

He had just over eight years' service in the Police Force, the last five of which had been spent on the CID at Mansfield. He joined the Force just before his twenty second birthday after leaving Sheffield University with a first in English Language.

Andy was a very intelligent man and an extremely competent detective with a strong work ethic. He was also very ambitious, he had passed his qualifying promotion exam to Sgt just over six months ago and was already studying in preparation for the Inspectors exam.

Danny knew Andy would be a certainty for promotion to sergeant very quickly in normal times, unfortunately for Andy, these were far from normal times.

At the beginning of the strike Danny sat Andy down and spoke to him one to one, he asked him to put aside his personal ambition for the duration of the strike and to concentrate solely on the job of maintaining CID cover for the Division. Danny assured him that as soon as the strike was over he would be pushing for him to obtain the promotion he deserved.

To his credit there was no argument from Andy, he totally understood the situation they were all in, he even offered to curtail the studying he was currently doing for the Inspectors exam in order to work the longer hours that would be required. Danny appreciated this commitment greatly because he knew Andy Wills would be getting some serious grief at home because of the situation.

Andy had married just over a year ago. His wife Sally, was a very successful Crown Court Barrister and the driving force behind his ambition. Sally Wills was extremely intelligent, very forceful and very beautiful. Her ambition for the Wills family was simple, in ten years' time she would be a High Court Judge and her husband would have achieved ACPO rank within the police.

Factor into that equation, that both Andy and Sally wanted children, it was easy for Danny to appreciate the time schedule pressure Andy was under.

The other detective who remained in the office was Detective Constable Rachel Moore, she had her own different reasons to excel both in the police service generally, as well as in the CID.

Rachel was now twenty-nine years old and having joined in 1974, she now had just under ten years' service in the police force.

She had witnessed first-hand, and often been the subject of, the outrageous bigotry and sexism that was rife throughout the service at that time.

After completing her ten week initial Police Training Course at the Police Training College, RAF Dishforth in North Yorkshire, her first posting was to Hyson Green Police Station in inner city Nottingham.

From the outset the shift she was assigned to at Hyson Green made it obvious that they didn't welcome her. Rachel was the only woman on the shift and constantly put up with sexism and harassment on an almost daily basis. In spite of this pressure, she kept her head down and worked hard and easily completed her two-year probation.

On the day she completed her probation, she immediately applied for a transfer to Mansfield Police Station to continue her career.

The reason for the transfer request was simple, she knew other female officers already working at Mansfield Police Station who assured her that, although still present, the sexism and favouritism was nothing like on the scale of the police stations in Nottingham city.

Rachel was successful in her transfer request and after arriving at Mansfield she went from strength to strength, proving to everyone that she was a hardworking and competent police officer.

It came as no surprise to anyone that her subsequent application to join the CID was successful. After passing the Detective Training Course at Wakefield with ease she braced herself for another posting back to Nottingham city. She had been pleasantly surprised however, when she was offered the post of detective constable with the Mansfield CID.

That had been two years ago.

What Rachel had not been aware of at the time was the fact Danny Flint had been instrumental in getting her the posting. He had watched Rachel work and admired her drive and tenacity. He was also aware that there were no female detectives at the Police Station, a situation that needed addressing.

Rachel was a single woman who lived alone in Mansfield. Now approaching her thirtieth birthday, she was an attractive woman with long chestnut brown hair and dark brown eyes. A keep fit fanatic, Rachel was very slim and toned but curvaceous at the same time. Although admired by many of her work colleagues, she had made the decision early in her career never to date a fellow officer.

She had been in a long term relationship with a dentist from Nottingham, however this had been brought to a sudden end a year before when he began talking about marriage and settling down. Rachel felt she wasn't ready for such a commitment, the relationship ended soon after. She had remained single ever since.

Apart from going to the local gym her passion was fell walking and most of her time off was spent hiking in the nearby Derbyshire dales.

Danny was now extremely pleased he had pushed for Rachel to remain at Mansfield, since the start of the strike her work rate had been phenomenal.

Since the 12th March, the first day of the strike, Rachel had systematically gone through three quarters of the other detectives outstanding work load and through her efforts effectively cleared the decks.

She had regularly worked between twelve to fourteen hours a day to achieve this.

Andy Wills meanwhile cleared the remaining quarter of the outstanding work load and together with Det Sgt Buxton took on all the new work that came into the office.

Danny now felt encouraged that with this small but very enthusiastic team he would be able to provide a suitable CID response to most situations. He knew this would only be the case as long as a major enquiry necessitating large amounts of manpower didn't materialise.

If that happened they would be in serious trouble.

Providing the adequate cover meant working long hours but they were all committed to doing just that.

Now they were on top of the existing workload, Danny decided that every one of the team would have at least one day off a week. Obviously these days would need to be staggered and must be flexible and subject to work commitments.

The team were overjoyed to know that through their hard work they were now in line to spend some time at home with their families and, weather permitting, Rachel would get to spend a day out in the fresh air.

It was now eight o'clock at night, the detectives had all been at work since eight that morning.

Danny came out of his office carrying his coat and said, 'I reckon that's enough for today folks, what say we all adjourn to the Railway pub next door. It's my round. I just want to say thank you for the way you've grafted over the last two and a bit weeks, I know it's not been easy. I never thought as a Detective Inspector I would find myself interviewing and charging a shop lifter, but these are the times we're living in folks.'

He smiled saying, 'Now who fancies a quick beer before home?'

They all chorused, 'Just the one Boss', before laughing and heading out the door to the Railway pub.

The pub was literally fifty yards from the front door of the Police Station and had always been frequented by officers just finishing their shifts.

Recently the police had opened their own Social Club upstairs in the station, this tended to be used more by the uniform officers and since the strike began it was full most evenings with various foreign force PSU's that had just finished policing pickets for the day.

Inside the Railway pub the lounge bar was small and very cosy with a welcoming open fire burning.

It was a typical mining town pub with prints of local mine headstocks and pictures depicting old miners with ponies down the mine. There were genuine, grimy and battered Davy Lamps swinging from the ceiling. Ancient horse brasses were nailed to the dark wooden beams, a constant pall of blue smoke emanated from the tap room and there was the smell of stale beer that had been spilt.

The team all sat in one corner of the lounge bar, there were no other patrons in the bar and inevitably after taking the first few sips of their drinks the conversation turned to police work.

Danny turned to Rob and said, 'Rob now we're a bit more on top of the workload, I'd like to take a closer look at the circumstances surrounding the death of that miner over at Warsop Colliery.'

'You mean Albert Jones?'

'Yes that's the man. I know Andy's rostered for his day off tomorrow, but if you can look after the office in the morning, I'd like to take Rachel to the Mines Rescue Station at Woodhouse and do some digging. It's the Coroner's Inquest next week and from everything I've seen so far a verdict of accidental death will be the outcome. Something about the magnitude of that man's injuries just doesn't seem right to me Rob. I heard what the professor said to you and his explanation was very plausible, but If only for my own peace of mind, I want to try and dig a little deeper.'

'I can look after the office Danny, if anything major comes in I'll contact you by radio. For what it's worth, as you know I had the same gut feeling about that job, and we should always follow our gut, right?'

'Dead right, Cheers Rob.'

Raising his glass to the small team of detectives Danny said, 'Ok folks listen in, I don't know how long this bloody strike's going to last but what I do know is this, we're a team that's willing to graft and work long hours and there's nothing we can't handle if we continue to pull as a group. I just wanted to say thanks everybody, I really appreciate your efforts. Cheers!'

The glasses clinked to a chorus of cheers.

Twenty minutes later and Danny was making the short walk back up the hill to his father's house.

As he walked his head was full of thoughts.

Tomorrow heralded the start of April, a new month. With a bit of luck this strike wouldn't last long and normality could return.

It was dark, but the sky was clear with a stunning full moon. The brightness of the moon matched his mood as he walked briskly up the hill.

He felt more content and happy than he had at any time in the last few weeks.

If Danny had known of the challenges that lay ahead in the coming months, he may not have been so confident or felt so cheery.

CHAPTER 7

Cuckney Crossroads, Nottinghamshire – April 1st 1984

Sgt Mick Reynolds was totally pissed off, he had been in the Nottinghamshire coal fields on strike duty for three weeks now and he couldn't wait to get home for a week off, even if that meant going home to his nagging bitch of a wife.

The duties were onerous, long and mind numbingly boring.

It was just after four in the morning and as usual his Police Support Unit were sitting at the Cuckney crossroads ready to intercept pickets travelling down from Yorkshire.

Cuckney was a tiny village situated on the main A60 road between Mansfield and Worksop and from this particular crossroads striking miners could make their way into the small towns of Warsop, Mansfield or Ollerton to picket any one of several pits.

The intelligence at the briefing that morning was that large numbers of striking miners were expected to be travelling to Ollerton Colliery to stage a mass picket. It wasn't hard to understand why.

The only people going down Ollerton pit at the moment were Deputies carrying out essential maintenance and safety work. However, fleets of lorries were still going in and out carrying more coal to swell the already huge stockpiles of coal at the nearby power stations dotted along the River Trent.

Mick wondered how they were getting the intelligence on the pickets intended targets. However, it was gained it was usually extremely accurate.

'Come on lads, I want three volunteers to get out of the van for the first hour, I'll swap it about after that, any takers?' said the sergeant.

The ten officers sitting in the back of the unmarked Ford Transit made no effort to stir and certainly no volunteers were forthcoming. After three weeks of grinding boredom they were all just looking forward to a week off.

'Ok, Jackson, Miller and Venables out you get, you're up for the first hour.'

Loud grumblings came from within the van.

Sgt Reynolds rounded sharply and snarled towards the rear of the van, 'Look I don't want any of your shit, just grab a Maxpax coffee and get out ready to stop any motors that turn up. You know the score, any car with more than two blokes in turn 'em around. It's easy money for fucks sake. You've all earned a small fortune doing this shit, so stop fucking moaning!'

Slowly the three selected officers put on their helmets, gloves and coats, then after grabbing a hot drink they went and stood in a little group at the centre of the crossroads.

It had been a very cold night with a clear sky and from his front seat in the van, Mick could see the clouds of breath coming from the three men who were stamping their feet on the frosted tarmac and waving their arms to try and stay warm in the freezing cold air.

'Maybe I'll change it after half an hour', Mick said quietly to himself.

Nobody else in the van was listening, the rest of the lads

were already nodding off back to sleep. Only the driver of the van, sitting next to the sergeant remained alert and awake.

'What do you reckon Ken, shall I change it every half hour?'

'Nah skip, it's too much pissing about, they ain't gonna freeze to death are they.'

Just at that moment a single vehicles headlights could be seen approaching from the direction of Worksop.

Mick wound the front passenger window down, 'Heads up lads here come our first customers!'

One of the cops stepped into the road switching his torch on and raising his right arm in the air signalling for the approaching vehicle to stop.

The vehicle, a red Vauxhall Viva, came to a gentle stop in front of the officer who then stepped around to speak to the driver. The other two officers took up a position in front of the car.

Mick listened to the conversation from the front seat of the Transit.

The driver of the Vauxhall wound down the window on the car and said, 'What's up mate, why've you stopped me?'

The car contained two other occupants, both men in their thirties.

The young constable who had stopped the car, leaned forward and said robotically, 'I believe you're striking miners who have the intention of unlawfully picketing premises that aren't your usual place of employment. Please turn the vehicle around and go back where you came from.'

'No owd lad you've got it all wrong. Us lads in here, we all work at Ollerton pit, we're on the day shift', one of the men in the back seat of the car said in a broad South Yorkshire accent.

The comment was accompanied with sniggers and chuckling from the back of the car.

One of the other officers standing in front of the car, a big burly man in his forties now approached the drivers open window and said loudly, 'Listen to me you dickhead, there isn't an early shift at that mine this morning. Do yourselves a favour and fuck off back to which ever northern shithole you've just crawled out of, before we nick the lot of ya!'

The chuckling in the car stopped.

Mick heard a voice from within the Viva say, 'Come on lads it's not worth getting nicked for. You know what these Met coppers are like, bastards the lot of them. We'll try and find another way through.'

Good luck with that thought Mick, he knew there were intercepts like this on all the roads leading to Ollerton.

He shouted over to the three officers, 'Well done lads! They'll be on their little CB radio now telling the rest of the fuckers travelling down not to try and go through Cuckney as them horrible Metropolitan Police fuckers are there, miserable cockney bastards the lot of em.'

'Oi Sarge I'm from fucking Lancashire me', shouted one of the men.

'Well that's alright son, it's like the War of the Roses for you innit, you hate Yorkies more than us, don't ya!'

'What's the War of the Roses Sarge?'

'Never mind, get another hot drink down ya!'.

Mick had only been involved in similar boring duties to this ever since he had arrived with his PSU serial on the night of the 12th March. Rushing out to various intercepts early doors trying to turn around pickets as they travelled in.

At the very first briefing they had been told that their actions were perfectly legal and they were acting within the law. If any miners refused to turn around they were to be arrested for Police obstruction. Mick hadn't been convinced but briefed his men accordingly anyway.

From that first night Mick and his PSU had been billeted in an old disused army base called Proteus Camp just outside the small town of Ollerton.

They were sleeping in dormitory like Nissan huts, conditions were Spartan to say the least. Meals were provided at the camp by outside caterers. The food was basic but it was hot and there was plenty of it.

Nobody moaned about the conditions too much as they were being paid handsomely. Because they were, in effect, living away from home on a permanent basis there were all sorts of allowances they could claim on top of the huge overtime payments.

The main issue was the boredom. There was nothing to occupy the men when they weren't working. They had been instructed that under no circumstances were they to stray away from the army base when they were off duty. Anybody caught drinking in any of the pubs at nearby towns would be disciplined and sent directly back to their own force.

As well as serials from the Metropolitan Police, there were others from as far afield as Hampshire, Essex and Kent all staying at Proteus Camp.

All the Metropolitan Police officers had initially travelled to Nottinghamshire in double decker buses. After a briefing at the Police Headquarters they were deployed in hired Ford Transits as individual Police Support Units, each with its own radio call sign.

For the first week each PSU had a local Nottinghamshire officer on board as a guide. After that they'd been expected to know the area a little better for themselves.

Luckily for Mick, his driver Ken had spent quite a bit of time holidaying with his family in the area a couple of years before the strike, so he knew the area reasonably well.

Sitting bored in the van, Mick now rejoiced in the fact that at three o' clock that afternoon they would all be going home for a week.

He couldn't wait, he was excited about the prospect of visiting the red light area again.

With the hours of boredom, his mind had constantly thought about the last time he was there. How he'd taught that mouthy little whore a lesson. He had relived the moment over and over again.

The feelings he experienced when he thought about that punch landing so hard in her face was almost electric. The fact that it was his wife's face he saw every time the punch landed only intensified the feelings. Every time he thought about the assault he could feel himself getting sexually aroused.

At first he had felt a little shameful about experiencing those kinds of feelings over an assault, but over the four weeks he had come to embrace them and had often masturbated when recalling the assault.

He knew that as soon as the nagging from his bitch of a wife got too much, he would take himself off to the whores and one of them would get it big style.

Breaking through his thoughts, he heard Ken's voice at the side of him, 'Time to change over Sarge.'

'Alright three more of ya, out ya get, I ain't bothered who it is, look lively.'

As three more men clambered out the back of the Transit he looked at his watch, not long to wait now.

He would soon be back in London and would soon be with one of the whores.

His thin lips formed a cruel smile just thinking about that prospect.

CHAPTER 8

Mines Rescue Station – Mansfield Woodhouse
– April 1st 1984

'Yeah, I remember poor old Albie Jones. It was all so sad, he was into his last week of work after spending a lifetime at that pit and then goes and does something so stupid.'

The voice belonged to Ray Machin, the leader of the Mines Rescue team that had recovered the body of Albie Jones from Warsop Main Colliery.

'Do you mind if we come in and have a chat about the recovery of Albie from the mine. You know, what you found when you first got there, that sort of thing?' Rachel Moore asked.

Rachel was standing with Det Insp Danny Flint outside the large red brick building that housed the two Mines Rescue vehicles.

The imposing building stood in between the towns of Mansfield and Mansfield Woodhouse. The building was regarded almost with a reverence by the people of both towns in much the same way as the buildings that house lifeboats at fishing villages on the coast are.

The people of the towns realising that the men who work there, and the equipment housed there, could one day be saving the life of a loved one deep underground.

The Mines Rescue Team were quite rightly regarded as heroes of their community.

'Yes of course we can have a chat, both of you come in out of the cold. It's half past nine now and I've got to hold a drill at eleven. Will that be long enough to go through everything?'

Danny replied, 'Thanks, Mr Machin that should be plenty of time, we just want to go over a few things. I've read the report you provided to the Mines Inspectors and I've seen the photos they took. It's just a couple of things that are nagging at me.'

'No problem Inspector, everyone here calls me Ray so feel free to do the same.'

Ray Machin showed the detectives into a classroom that doubled as his office.

'I'll grab us all a brew and then we can get started, will tea be alright? We don't drink much coffee here, I'm afraid we're all tea monsters.'

'Perfect', said Danny

Within minutes Machin had returned carrying three large mugs of builders' tea, strong and very sweet.

'Right fire away Inspector, what do you want to know?'

'Firstly, who moved the lump of rock that killed Albie. I've noticed on the pictures taken at the scene that it was lying near to his right shoulder when he was found. Where was the rock taken after you got Albie out of there?'

'It was chucked under the belt; it will still be there as far as I know.'

'Who actually moved it?'

'I did as it happens, I'm always the last person at the scene. I like to make sure no equipment has been left lying about. I always make a final check, that sort of thing, you know how it is. Well I saw that the rock was still in the middle of the gate, so I shifted it under the belt.'

'This might sound a strange question Ray, but how heavy was it?'

'Yeah that does sound strange. It was fairly heavy, it was quite a big chunk of rock. I could manage it pretty well on my own though thinking about it.'

This time it was Rachel who spoke, 'Obviously Ray we've nowhere near as much experience as you have when it comes to witnessing various injuries down the mine. You must have seen quite a few roof falls in your time and the damage they cause?'

'I have lass, far too many for my liking I'm afraid.'

'My point is; you saw the injury to Albie. Do you think that piece of rock falling from the height of the roof at that part of the gate was big enough and heavy enough to cause that injury?'

'I couldn't say for certain detective. I've seen some awful injuries down the pit but Albie's was one of the worst I've got to say. The human head's a very fragile thing next to rock. If only he'd been wearing his helmet he'd still be alive and enjoying his retirement.'

Danny said, 'I've only one more question Ray. Could you have lifted that piece of rock right above your head?'

'It would have taken some effort but yeah I reckon I could have done. Am I missing something here? Do you people suspect some sort of foul play down there?'

'Not at this time Ray. Everything's pointing to Albie's death being a tragic accident. Like you say if only he'd been wearing his helmet. Thanks for your time Ray, and for the brew. Talk to you soon.'

'No problem Inspector, any time.'

The two detectives left the Rescue Station and walking back to the car Danny said, 'Rachel will you drop me back at the station. I'm going to pick up another car so we can split up. We need to save a bit of time in case anything else comes in. I want us to see both the Deputy in charge and the miner who was injured on the day Albie died. I'll visit the Deputy and you can nip and see the injured miner, I think his name's James Wade. The addresses for both of them are in the file on my desk, come on let's go.'

CHAPTER 9

Mansfield Woodhouse -April 1st 1984

Rachel Moore parked the CID car directly outside the smart three bedroomed semi-detached house on Marples Avenue. She glanced down at the report on the passenger seat checking the address.

"Mr James Wade, 56 Marples Avenue, lives alone", she muttered to herself. She noted there was no vehicle on the drive.

The house was typical for the street and the area. It was a fairly spacious three bedroomed house that had been built sometime in the late fifties, early sixties.

It was obviously very well looked after, it had freshly painted guttering and drainpipes and all the windows had new double glazing. The front garden was very well kept and the grass was short and well cared for.

As she got out of her car she thought she saw movement at one of the upstairs windows. Good, she thought, he's in. I can have a quick chat with him and get this enquiry put to bed.

Rachel walked up the slight incline of the driveway to the front door. Ignoring the doorbell, she knocked loudly on the door.

'Just a second!', a man's voice yelled from within.

Almost immediately the door swung open, standing in the doorway was a very good looking man, around six feet tall with quite short, well-kept blonde hair. He had the most piercing blue eyes she had ever seen and was dressed casually in Levi jeans and a blue and white check Ben Sherman shirt.

Rachel took a breath and said, 'I'm looking for Mr James Wade?'

'That's me, and you are?'

Raising her police warrant card for him to see she said, 'Sorry Mr Wade, my name's Detective Constable Rachel Moore, I need a moment of your time please. There's a few questions I need to ask about the accident at Warsop Main Colliery when Albie Jones died.'

Without a flicker of emotion Wade said, 'I thought that had all been sorted. Why do the police need to ask me questions? I've already said everything I know about the matter to the Mines Inspectorate.'

Rachel noted there was an attitude to James Wade, it wasn't quite animosity more like antipathy. It was as if it was all too much of an effort to speak to her.

She pressed on, 'Do you mind if I come in, it won't take long I promise you.'

Suddenly Wade's entire manner changed, it was like a switch had been turned on, 'Of course Detective Moore, where are my manners, my grandmother would be spinning in her grave, me leaving you on the doorstep like that, come in out of the cold, please.'

He gestured for her to follow him and showed her into the lounge.

When Rachel followed him into the room she saw that the lounge was extremely tastefully decorated with a huge colour TV at one end of the room and a brand new multi change CD player at the other. The CD player had only just come onto the market and Rachel could only guess at what they had both cost.

There was a tan coloured leather three-piece suite that dominated the rest of the room.

Pointing to the sofa, he said, 'Take a seat detective, I was just making a coffee would you like a cup?'

Rachel sat down on the large sofa, she hadn't touched the builders' tea at the Mines Rescue Station and was actually gagging for a hot drink.

'Yes please Mr Wade that would be lovely, thank you.'

'How do you take it?'

'Just milk no sugar, thanks.'

A few minutes later he returned carrying two very nice earthenware coffee mugs.

Coasters were already on the walnut coffee table in front of the sofa, he carefully placed the hot drinks on them and then sat in one of the armchairs opposite her.

Rachel said, 'I'm sorry for the intrusion Mr Wade and like I say it's just a couple of questions, it won't take long.'

'No problem. I've got nothing planned today, and please call me Jimmy.'

Rachel was aware now just how large Wade's piercing blue eyes were, he was staring hard into her eyes, it was almost too intense.

She forced herself not to look away and said, 'On the day Albie was found dead, you were one of the last people to have seen him alive. What was your overall impression when you last saw him?'

'To be perfectly honest detective, I never really thought too much about old Albie', he shrugged nonchalantly.

He finally looked away, glancing out of the window.

Rachel couldn't believe the relief she felt just because he had turned to look away. She hadn't been aware of just how uncomfortable his piercing stare had become until he looked away.

He continued, 'I often saw Albie at the pit, he was like part of the fixtures and fittings. He'd worked there for ever I think. He was a good bloke, always friendly. You know that sort of thing.'

Rachel noted there was no warmth to anything Wade said, no depth of feeling at all. It was as if he knew he was expected to say these comments, so he just said them.

Just trotting out platitudes, she thought

'Tell me about that particular day?' she said taking a sip of her coffee.

'It was exactly the same as any other day down the pit, until I got a load of crap in my left eye. It happens all the time, you get muck and dust in your eyes but you can usually shift it with water. On that day, one of the cutters flirted a bit of loose muck out that hit me straight in the face. I never even had time to shut my eyes. Well try as I might, I couldn't get the muck out of my left eye. If you can't get it out, it can become a serious problem as the grit can scratch your eyes and cause lasting problems.'

She found herself locked onto those piercing blue eyes again, she started to feel like a rabbit being circled by a predatory fox.

Glancing down towards her cup of coffee she continued, 'Then what happened Mr Wade?'

'I went to the Deputy in charge, Dave Smedley, and asked him if I could go topside to the Medical Centre to get sorted. He wasn't best pleased as we were just starting a fresh stint on the face, but he appreciated the problem I had and walked with me from the coalface to the pit bottom. We passed Albie on his button on the way to the pit bottom. Nothing was said, only a quick "Ayup", you know.'

'Was Albie wearing his helmet?'

'I reckon so. Thinking about it he must have been otherwise Dave Smedley would have bollocked him, excuse my French, sorry.'

'So that's everything is it, nothing else that comes to mind?'

'Yep that's it, the whole kit and caboodle. Sorry if you've had a wasted trip, but at least the coffee's good, right?' he grinned.

Taking a large sip of her coffee Rachel said, 'Yes the coffee's good Mr Wade, thank you for your time and the drink. Have you been notified to attend the Coroners Court for the Inquest next week?'

'No I haven't, do you think I'll have to go?'

'If you've not heard already, it's doubtful you'll be called at this late stage. Thanks again for the drink.'

Rachel stood up smoothing down the skirt of her suit as she got up from the sofa.

He stood up and showed her to the front door.

'Have a good day detective!' he called after her as she walked down the sloping drive.

As she walked to the car Rachel felt uneasy.

She couldn't fathom out why, until she sat in the car. Just as she was about to switch the ignition on she said aloud, 'That bastard was smirking at me.'

Half an hour later back in the CID office Rachel outlined the uneasy meeting she had experienced with James Wade to Danny.

'It's just a feeling boss, I know it's nothing concrete, he just gave me the creeps that's all. There you are pure and simple, it's a woman thing, he was making me feel really on edge. It was like he thought me asking him questions was all a huge joke, a game. It felt like he was laughing at me boss.'

'Did he say anything incriminating Rachel?'

'No he didn't, he answered all my questions and was extremely polite.'

'Well I couldn't verify his story with Dave Smedley. He's been seconded over to South Wales for the duration. They're short of Deputies to do the safety work at their pits while the strike is on. They've both made statements for the Coroner already so I don't think there's anywhere else we can go with this. All the evidence suggests Albie's death was nothing more than a tragic accident. At the moment there's not a shred of evidence to say it's anything other than that. No doubt the Coroner will confirm it was just a pointless tragic accident.'

Rachel shrugged her shoulders, she wasn't happy but he was right, there was nothing else to be done, there were no other enquiries to follow. The Inquest would reach a verdict of accidental death and unless something new came to light that would be that.

She wasn't easily spooked but Rachel knew it would take her a long time to shake off the unnerving feeling she experienced when staring into James Wade's piercing blue eyes.

She shuddered involuntarily.

CHAPTER 10

Mansfield Woodhouse – April 1st 1984

He had sat there motionless for over an hour.

There wasn't a sound in the room. He could still see the half empty coffee mug on the walnut table in front of the leather sofa. It was exactly where she had placed it before leaving.

Jimmy Wade had stared into the detective's dark brown eyes and realised that she was to be the next one.

Once she left the house he had returned to the living room and sat quietly trying to suppress the urges.

It was impossible, he couldn't even think about it. She was a police officer, a detective. It just wasn't worth the risk.

Try as he might he couldn't remove the nagging voices pounding in his head. Deep down he knew they wouldn't be denied.

Finally, he stood up from the leather armchair and took both his own and the detective's coffee mug into the kitchen.

In the kitchen he placed both the mugs on the draining board next to the sink ready to wash.

He picked up her mug and stared intently at the red lipstick ring on the rim. Very carefully he put his lips directly over the faint red mark until there was the slightest tinge of red on his own lips.

He closed his eyes and licked his lips, tasting her lipstick.

As he vigorously washed the two mugs in the sink he looked at his reflection against the glass of the kitchen window. In that moment he knew; it didn't matter that she was a detective, it didn't matter how long it took, he would find a way to have her.

He knew he had no choice and that it would happen. Detective Constable Rachel Moore was destined to die and he was going to kill her.

The eyes never lied. As soon as he stared into those deep, melancholy dark brown eyes they had told him.

Her fate would be her release.

CHAPTER 11

Wembley, London – April 7th 1984

It was sheer hell.

Mick Reynolds had only been back six days and Rita was being a complete cow.

It didn't matter what he did or said, she would criticise. It had been a welcome relief when his tart of a wife went out each evening to some sordid, illicit liaison.

Mick didn't give a toss anymore he just wanted the disgusting woman out of his life for good, one way or the other.

He knew she was on too much of a good thing for her to ever consider leaving him. While ever she was living in his beautiful house sponging off him, she would never go anywhere.

No, he was going to have to deal with the problem of Rita a different way.

It wasn't even as though she was attractive in any way shape or form. She was forty something, short, plump and had hit every branch of the ugly tree on the way down from the top.

The hours of boredom up in Nottinghamshire had polarised Mick's thoughts. After tomorrow he would be back up there for another four long weeks. He was going to use the time up there wisely and think of a way to be rid of Rita permanently.

He was a cop for Christ's sake, he should know better than anybody how to work this problem out without spending the rest of his life behind bars for doing it.

All he could think about tonight though, was to try and get some relief from the pent up anger and frustration she had built up in him all week.

Tonight was his last opportunity; he was travelling back to Nottinghamshire at five o'clock tomorrow morning.

It was now eight o' clock in the evening, he knew that any time now Rita would be going out to meet some sleaze ball, and after drinking vodka and tonics all night she would end up with her mini skirt hitched up around her waist as she got shagged behind some backstreet pub somewhere down the East End.

God help the poor bastard that wants to shag the ugly cow, he thought.

Another painful hour ticked by, then suddenly he heard the tell-tale noise of the front door slamming. He looked out of the front window of his lounge and saw her tottering towards a waiting black cab.

He dismissed his earlier thought, tonight she'll be getting shagged behind some poncy wine bar up West.

She disgusted him, he watched as she tottered along the path, ungainly on the five inch heels. Her fat legs bulging the black stockings in all the wrong places, the way too short skirt and finally the black shiny leather bomber jacket that looked a size too small and had ridden up over the rolls of fat at her midriff.

'Go on hurry up and fuck off!' he said out loud.

As soon as the taxi pulled away from the kerb he raced downstairs and picked up a small grip bag from the hallway.

He quickly opened the black holdall to make sure everything he needed was there.

Inside the bag there was a set of blue forensic overalls, a few pairs of forensic gloves and overshoes. He had taken these items from the exhibits store at work. Also in the grip bag was a roll of sticky brown Gaffer tape, a plastic bag containing black plastic cable ties, a small pair of gardening shears, a Stanley knife and a claw hammer.

All the hand tools had been purchased earlier in the week from the local DIY store on Wembley High Street.

Picking the bag up, he walked into the garage to his midnight blue Ford Sierra.

Bending down at the front of the car, he used some black electricians tape to change the number 3 to an 8 and the letter F to an E on the front registration plate. He then walked to the rear of the car and did the same to the rear plate.

It wasn't perfect but unless somebody got a really close look it would effectively change the registration number of the car.

Mick had been worried that the first tart he punched may have somehow clocked his car number, tonight he was taking no chances.

If, as expected, he felt the same urges tonight he wanted to be prepared and not run any unnecessary risks.

Mick felt ready and strangely excited about what he was setting off to do.

Tonight, in his mind at least, was the night he was going to rid himself of that disgusting bitch of a wife.

In reality his intention was to pick up and badly assault, or worse, a prostitute off the street.

He drove for the fifteen or so minutes it took to reach the

red light area he preferred. Mick cruised up and down the roads slowly looking for two things. Firstly, any sign of the Vice Squad. He knew a couple of the guys that worked on the squad and he had made it his business to know exactly what vehicles they were currently using.

Secondly he started searching the empty, desolate and dark streets for his prey.

The prostitute needed to be carefully chosen. She had to be small enough to be easily overpowered, he didn't want a big fat thing that would fight back and struggle.

She would also need to be young enough to still have that slight naivety that he needed to achieve his objective.

Mick had driven around the red light area for a good ten minutes before he spotted her. She looked to be the perfect target.

Even better, she was standing alone on a stretch of the road where none of the other working girls were plying their trade.

There wasn't another person within two hundred yards of her. The stretch of road where she was standing was also particularly dark. The one working street light was very weak, the light it gave out was more of an ethereal glow.

Making one last check all around, he pulled his car slowly to the side of the road and stopped opposite the young girl.

He wound down the front passenger window and beckoned for the girl to come over to the car.

Slowly, almost hesitantly, the girl walked over.

Mick could see her better now as the glow from the weak street light illuminated her face. The white light reflecting off her pale drawn face gave her an almost ghostly appearance.

Her pale features were framed by long dark hair.

She looked to be young, in her late teens at most. She was wearing a short denim skirt, black patent leather knee length boots that looked scuffed and worn. A short sleeved black cotton blouse that was undone to her navel, exposing a black lacy bra that covered very small breasts.

It was a bitterly cold night and the girl was shivering so badly her lank, dark hair was wriggling at the bottom of her jaw line like worms on a fishing line.

As she got closer Mick saw the tell-tale signs of drug addiction, her brown eyes were deep set and surrounded by dark rings, there were fresh sores on her face and looking at her skinny white arms he could see where she had recently injected.

'You looking for business love?' she stuttered, her voice reflecting her shivering body.

Mick noticed the accent wasn't a London one.

'I might be darling, how much for full sex?' he said.

Her eyes suddenly got bigger at the prospect of all the smack she was going to be able to buy with fifty large ones.

'Full sex is fifty quid and I'll need the cash first.'

'No problem, get in.'

Mick reached over and opened the passenger door.

He gave her five ten pound notes as soon as she got in, he watched as she stuffed the banknotes into the top of her right boot. He had no intention of having any kind of sex with this drugged up slag and he knew he would get the money back off her, all in good time.

He turned to her and said, 'Do you have anywhere you normally go?'

'No I don't really know this area. I've only just come up to London. Go where you like darling, so long as there aren't any Vice coppers knocking about. I can't afford to get pinched again already.'

Mick started to drive off, this was perfect he thought to himself.

Only just in town. No fucker will know who she is or where she's from, the silly cow won't have a clue where I'm taking her.

Furtively he glanced over at the girl now sitting in the passenger seat.

She looked as though a breath of wind would knock her over. Looking closer he could see that the girl had scored some smack quite recently, she kept licking her lips and her head was lolling from side to side.

She looked totally out of it.

Only one thing worried him, her comment about being pinched again. If this girl had come to the notice of the police before, that might cause him a problem. He let an evil smile play over his lips as he thought about the contents of the grip bag. He knew exactly how to overcome that little problem.

His excitement was mounting and already he could feel familiar stirrings down below. He was glad he had prepared well and brought his grip bag along.

He picked up speed and drove quickly away from the red light area.

In his mounting excitement Mick had failed to spot the skinny red haired youth with his ferret like eyes and thick glasses watching as he drove the girl away.

What the girl hadn't said was that she had only just arrived in London from Norwich with her junkie boyfriend. The only reason she was out on the street tonight was because he needed to score. She'd taken the last of their gear just before she came out onto the streets.

The skinny boyfriend got the broken pencil out of his pocket and scribbled down the car registration number on the scrap of paper she had given him.

He had done what she asked.

The girl always told him to write down the registration numbers of any cars she got into, just to be on the safe side.

He stepped back into the shadows and clutched his skinny arms tightly around himself.

He hoped she wouldn't be too long, he was already hanging, desperate for a fix.

With a low moan the cold wind blew along the dark street and he started to shiver again.

CHAPTER 12

River Thames, London – April 8th 1984

The weak early morning sun shimmered softly on the chocolate brown waters of the River Thames as it flowed swiftly by. The river here was tidal and at certain times of the day the currents were fast.

The body of the naked woman was no more than ten feet from the water's edge and was lying on the top of the thick black mud. She had been left lying face up with her arms splayed out at odd angles, her legs were crossed at the ankles, the right leg on top of the left.

It had been the police launch that first spotted the body lying on the mud at the side of the river. It was a lonely and desolate spot here and river traffic was light.

None of the tourist pleasure boats came to this part of the river.

At first glance the sergeant on the police launch thought he was seeing a shop mannequin, but something about the position it was lying in made him squint through his binoculars to get a better look.

Only then did he realise it was the body of a young woman and that the dark area around the head was actually congealed blood.

The sergeant had spent a lot of years on the launch and had seen countless victims of drowning in the fast flowing river, he knew that the tide was still on the way out and would be for another hour, only then would the water start creeping back over the mud towards the body.

He estimated it would be around four and a half hours before the muddy river would claim the body.

He had immediately swung the launch over towards the bank to get a closer look. Once the boat was manoeuvred as close to the bank as possible, he could see the horrific injuries to the woman's head.

The sergeant could also see that the woman had not yet been in the river and had just been placed on the muddy bank, there was a scaffold board left lying across the mud down to the side of the body.

He immediately radioed in the sighting to the control room, then remained as close to the bank as possible to ensure nobody approached the body.

Following his radio message, the police quickly arrived in numbers to the scene. As he looked over towards the bank the sergeant could now see two detectives as they squatted down next to the body.

Detective Inspector Glyn Johnson had arrived about five minutes ago.

He was the only black Detective Inspector in the Metropolitan Police and this deprived area of London, south of the river, was his patch.

There were no upmarket penthouse flats or trendy wine bars near this part of the river.

This area was inhabited solely by criminals, whores and junkies. It was the type of area decent, ordinary people went out of their way to avoid.

All large cities have them, sinkholes of desperation and criminality where the occupiers all have the same law of the jungle mentality.

Glyn Johnson was now fast approaching forty-three years of age and his short hair and goatee beard were starting to show flecks of grey. He was a tall, thin athletic looking man who would not have looked out of place on a basketball court.

He was a career detective whose only interest in life was his work. It had not always been that way. In his younger days he was very happily married with many friends away from the police force.

All that changed on the day, ten years ago, his wife sat him down and dispassionately gave him the news that would change his life forever.

The love of his life, his soulmate quietly told him she had been having tests at the doctors and they had diagnosed that she was in the advanced stages of Pancreatic cancer.

She had given him this devastating news with a dignity and courage that amazed him. There was nothing to be done and the doctors advised that it was likely to be weeks rather than months, before she succumbed to the dreadful illness.

Only four short weeks came and went before his beautiful wife lost her fight. A stunned and shocked Glyn had been unable to grieve due to the speed everything had happened.

Just two days after he buried his wife, he had returned back to his job and thrown himself hard into his work. While ever he was totally engrossed in his work he could ignore the feeling of despair and loneliness. He soon abandoned any hope of finding the answer as to why this fate had befallen both himself and his wife.

Unable to rationalise what had happened Glyn quickly retreated back into himself. His abrupt, stand offish behaviour rapidly distanced him from his friends and what little family he had in the UK. Only a very few select colleagues remained close to him as he tried to work his way through his personal anguish and torment.

Eventually he achieved an existence that was manageable, where he went to work did his job and then returned home to his quiet house, to his memories and his thoughts about what may have been.

Now on the riverbank squatting over the body of another victim he pondered over the way life was so indiscriminately unfair and brutal.

Glyn stood up and stretched, the sleeves of his suit had ridden up his long arms. He quickly smoothed them back down again.

As he glanced back up towards the bank he could see that most of the buildings were falling down and as he looked around he saw there were no houses that appeared occupied within view.

He might get lucky and find that one of the derelict houses or disused warehouses was a squat where the occupiers didn't all have selective deaf, dumb and blindness.

Glyn Johnson had over twenty years' service and had dealt with more than his fair share of violent and suspicious deaths.

'What's the word Craig?' he said in his soft voice that still carried more than a hint of a Jamaican accent.

The other man squatting at the side of the dead woman stood up and spoke, 'She was discovered on the mud flats at around six o' clock this morning by the River Police, Sgt Davies on the launch spotted her on the mud flats as he was patrolling up river. He's still standing to off the bank.'

Glyn turned back towards the river and saw the sergeant standing on the deck of the launch.

'Make sure we get his statement as soon as possible Craig, advise control there's no longer any need for him to remain standing to in the boat, everything's under control now.'

'Will do Guvnor'.

Detective Sergeant Craig Fraser immediately got on the radio and relayed the order for the Launch to stand down and also to request the statement from Sgt Davies.

'Do we have any other witnesses Craig?'

'No, nothing so far but it's early days.'

'Ok, soon as we can I want search teams going through all the buildings up on the embankment, it's obvious she wasn't killed here, we might just get lucky and find where she was actually killed. God knows, we may even hit gold dust and find a witness.'

'I'm on it Guv', the Detective Sergeant said in his broad Scottish accent.

Craig Fraser had been a Detective Sergeant for four years and had been promoted onto Glyn Johnson's team in South London.

He knew how the Detective Inspector ran his operations and prided himself on taking steps under his own initiative that he knew the Det Insp would be asking for.

Craig had been born and raised in the Gorbals area of Glasgow and was hard as teak. He was a short, powerful man with a face that looked as if it had been carved from granite.

He was a similar age to Glyn Johnson and the two men were close friends as well as colleagues.

'I've got two full search teams on the way to start going through the derelict properties and I've also blagged the uniform Inspector to send me whatever uniform staff he can spare. They can start talking to anyone who turns up.'

'Thanks Craig, good work.'

Looking down at the scene once more Glyn could see the long plank of wood, a disused scaffold board, that had been placed out over the mud down to the body.

'Looks like our killer used that to bring the body down onto the mud.'

'Yes guv, when I first got here there were no footprints in the mud. The ones you see now around the body are ours and the Scenes of Crime officers. I've taped off the board. Scenes of Crime are going to drag the board up onto the flat in a couple of minutes and will be having a close look at it. They've already photographed everything here in situ, and they've taken photographs of the girl as well, including the wrists and what's left of the face. It looks like she's been bound and gagged at some stage. You see the cuts into her wrists, they reckon something like plastic cable ties or similar. There's a residue around the damaged mouth that looks like glue of some description. They've taken swabs but their educated guess is Gaffer tape.'

'Ok Craig, make sure that information's passed on to the search teams, the killer's obviously removed the ties and the tape before dumping her here, he may have got careless and left them behind where he killed her.'

Glyn looked down at the mangled remains of the young woman and said, 'You know the score Craig, it's imperative that we identify who this woman was as soon as possible. Once you've finished up here I want you to concentrate solely on that. I want three detectives working specifically on her identification. Fingerprints may help us out, but in the meantime get them trawling through any missing persons reports that come in. I'll deal with the Post Mortem side of things, I'll take Dc Briggs with me, he's had plenty of experience doing the exhibits job.'

He paused and looked down at the pitiful sight of the naked woman.

There really was no dignity in death he thought to himself.

'How long before the river becomes an issue here Craig?'

'Sgt Davies on the Launch reckons we've got until ten thirty at the latest to have either finished here or get swept into the river.'

Glyn glanced at his wrist watch. The time was fast approaching seven fifty.

Plenty of time left to do what needed to be done.

'Can we expect the arrival of the Home Office pathologist any time soon? Or am I going to have to organise a fucking tent to cover this poor woman up? Before all the gawkers come out to have a stare!'

The Jamaican accent becoming more pronounced as his temper frayed a little.

'Speak of the Devil guv, she's here now'.

Walking down the boating ramp towards the stinking mud Glyn saw a slim attractive woman in her mid to late thirties wearing a white forensic suit and carrying a holdall that held the equipment she would need.

'Who the fuck's this Craig? Where's Jock McArdle?'

'Retired a month ago guv. Don't you ever read memos?'

'Not if I can help it', he growled.

Craig indicated for the woman approaching to follow the footmarks they had made previously through the thick mud. The mud was black and had the same consistency as molasses, the smell was a cross between rotten fish and vegetables. Eventually the slim woman reached where the two detectives were standing ankle deep in the glutinous mud.

Craig said, 'Guvnor this is Emily Cook, our new Home Office pathologist. Ms Cook this is....'

Before he could finish speaking, she finished the sentence for him, 'This is Det Insp Glyn Johnson, we haven't met but I've heard a lot about you.'

She held out a small gloved hand.

Her accent was like cut glass, it was obvious she hailed from the Home Counties. Surrey guessed Glyn, probably around Virginia Water.

'All bad I expect?' he said reaching over and gently shaking the proffered hand.

'Quite the contrary actually, now what do we have here? Any idea who she is?'

'Other than a young woman who probably sold her body, abused Class A controlled drugs and ended up getting her face smashed to a pulp and being dumped at the side of the river in the largest City in the country, without anyone seeing or hearing a thing. No, not a clue.'

Smiling she said, 'It seems that everything I've heard about your succinct manner sounds about right. Ok, Detective Inspector you're obviously looking at a murder enquiry. I'll do the necessary here, quick as I can before the tide becomes an issue, and then arrange to get the poor woman back to my office for the post mortem. It's still the same place as Jock McArdle used. See you at St Barnabus hospital mortuary in a couple of hours, shall we say ten o'clock?'

Glyn nodded curtly, 'Ok Ms Cook, I'll see you up at St Barny's at ten.'

With that she turned and started the procedures to gather any evidence possible from the scene.

Leaving Craig with the pathologist, Glyn walked slowly through the mud and up the slope to his waiting car.

This was all he needed on a Monday morning.

As he quickly removed the mud covered Wellington boots, he glanced over his shoulder at the new pathologist now going busily about her business. All he could see was the blonde hair tied back in a ponytail above the white suit.

'Emily Cook eh? I like her already', he said softly to himself.

CHAPTER 13

St Barnabus Hospital Mortuary, London – April 8th 1984

'Hello again Inspector', said Emily Cook as Glyn walked into the mortuary examination room. Lagging behind was Dc Briggs who was weighed down with a large bag full of various size exhibit bags and labels.

He would use these to bag up various items for evidence as the examination progressed.

The examination room was large and had four stainless steel bench tables in the centre of the room, each bench was fitted with an independent sluice system. One wall was made up of floor to ceiling refrigerated drawers that were the temporary home of the recently deceased.

The walls were all covered by large white porcelain tiles and the floor was a lime green linoleum. There was an almost overpowering smell that was a mixture of disinfectant and formaldehyde. It was one of those smells that once experienced stays with you for the rest of your life.

In front of them, lying on one of the stainless steel examination tables was the naked body of the white female, she was still covered in the stinking mud and debris of the riverbank.

Emily Cook was standing the other side of the bench already wearing a white protective suit and mask.

'Good morning again Ms Cook, shall we make a start', replied Glyn curtly.

She began the post mortem examination by taking samples of the mud and debris that covered various parts of the woman's body, these samples were carefully bagged and labelled by Dc Briggs.

After this was done, a preliminary visual examination was carried out with photographs being taken every step of the way.

Once this had been completed and notes made, the post mortem proper began.

Fifty-five minutes later Emily Cook stepped away from the cadaver and pulling her mask away from her face she spoke directly to Glyn, 'I've examined every orifice and it would appear that there was no sexual activity immediately prior to her death. There's no semen present anywhere. The woman was obviously a drug abuser, there are numerous injection sites on both arms and even on the lower legs and feet. I've taken bloods so this may give us some idea of her drug of choice but from her general physical appearance I would say most likely it'll be Heroin.'

She continued, 'As far as identification of this woman goes, you may be in some difficulty. Dental records are going to be useless as the damage to her face and in particular her mouth is devastating. Her lower jaw's been completely smashed and all of the upper teeth have been smashed. I don't know if you noticed this at the river bank Inspector but whoever did this paid particular attention to the woman's hands. Because her hands were bunched into fists, it was only when I got her back here that I noticed that every finger and both her thumbs have been severed with a sharp instrument. Probably a small set of pruning shears or such like. The palms of both hands have also been damaged beyond all recognition with numerous slash marks across each one until the inside of the hand has been reduced to a lattice work of destroyed flapping skin. What I can tell you is that interestingly all the damage to the face, jaws and hands has been carried out after she died. She wasn't tortured and it looks to me like her killer's somebody who's very aware of how the identification process works.'

Glyn nodded taking in everything the pathologist had told him, he stroked his goatee beard thoughtfully before saying, 'I read recently about a case where they'd recreated a blokes face from a skull, is there anyway of carrying out some sort of facial recognition from the bones of this skull?'

He continued, 'It's vital for the enquiry that we have something to work with to try and identify this girl.'

'My old professor at Bristol University is a leading expert on facial recognition and mapping. The best he could do, would be to give you a visual likeness of how this woman looked in life, but it's only ever an approximate likeness. It would be especially so in this case because of the massive damage to the facial bones around the eye sockets and the extensive damage to the lower jaw.'

'That would at least be something. How soon could you speak to your professor? I need to know from him if it's feasible to do, and more importantly, if it is, how soon could he get a likeness to us?'

'You're in luck Inspector, I've arranged for him to come up to London tomorrow to have lunch and take in a show with me. I can ask him to examine her for you, I'm sure he'll oblige. It's not something he has the opportunity of doing very often.'

'Thank you Ms Cook, that would be very helpful', he said smiling broadly.

Old Jock would never have sorted that out so fast, he thought. Chalk up one for the new girl.

Emily Cook smiled back before saying, 'The only other identifying feature I can find is a very small tattoo on the heel of her right foot. The killer probably missed it, because it's so small and in such an unusual place. It's a picture of a small blue cartoon rabbit with what looks like a date below.

The date is 12/07/83. I can also tell you this woman has recently gone full term with a pregnancy and this date may have something to do with that. I've got plenty of photographs of the tattoo.'

Glyn leaned forward to look closely at the small blue mark on the woman's heel, 'That's fantastic news. This date's going to be personal to someone. Somebody out there will know someone who has that tattoo and if we can match it to a facial likeness we might be in business.'

Emily now continued her summation, 'The cause of death was a massive brain haemorrhage caused by the severe trauma of several major blows to the head with a blunt object. My guess is a hammer, of some description, with a rounded head, some of the fractures, as you've seen for yourself have a pronounced round depression at the centre that are consistent with that type of implement.'

With a worried expression she continued, 'I know I've only been here just over a month Inspector, but I think this case has some very strange implications.'

'In what way, strange Ms Cook?'

'Well the injuries are consistent with an attack carried out in a rage, too much force used etc. But then after the frenzied attack the killer displays a large element of control, an ordered mind. This is shown by the damage that was all caused post mortem to try and avoid identification. All the research that's been done on offender profiling points to either one or the other, rage or order, it's strange to find the two together. The worrying thing for me Inspector is that the ordered side of the individual responsible, displays all the traits of somebody who will definitely kill again.'

'Bloody marvellous! What you're telling me is that we have a potential serial killer on our hands.'

'I'm afraid so Inspector.'

'Great, that's all we need!'

'I'll get my full report to you as soon as I can Inspector, and I'll call you after I've seen the professor about the facial recognition.'

'Thank you Ms Cook, after what you've just told me the sooner the better please.'

Glyn walked out of the mortuary and made his way through the maze of hospital corridors back to the car park. He walked briskly, his long legs striding out. His face was set in a mask of concentration. It was only a couple of years ago when Peter Sutcliffe, a lorry driver from Bradford, had led the West Yorkshire Police a merry dance all over Leeds and other northern cities, killing thirteen women and being dubbed 'The Yorkshire Ripper' by the press, before he was eventually caught.

It was every detective's worst nightmare, a killer on the loose targeting total strangers for no other reason than the uncontrollable urge to kill.

Glyn walked to the large hospital car park and found his car.

He jumped in and gunning the motor he raced away from the car park. He realised he didn't have much time, this monster needed to be caught before he murdered another young woman and the press were thinking of a new name for the latest serial killer.

CHAPTER 14

Mansfield Town Centre, Nottinghamshire – April 10th 1984

Jimmy Wade had been waiting patiently for over an hour. He had now parked his car towards the back of the large car park normally used by the clients and staff of a large solicitor's firm.

The car park was poorly lit and there were large trees around the edges. More importantly it was located directly opposite the entrance to the police station car park.

It was well after ten o' clock at night and he had expected her to be finished over an hour ago.

Earlier that day he was on the same street waiting for her to arrive at work. He'd been standing outside an estate agents pretending to look at properties for sale. The agents window was just down the road from the police station. Jimmy watched as she arrived at the police station just before nine o'clock that morning. He kept the hood of his Parka coat up and thrust his hands deep into the coat pockets.

Rachel Moore had driven straight past him in a small red Mini Cooper. He walked slowly up the road and watched her as she parked her car in the police station car park.

He had spent the rest of the day either driving slowly past the station in his car or walking past to see if the red Mini was still there.

Once it reached nine o'clock at night he knew she had been at work for over twelve hours and he took the decision to park up and wait for her to drive her red Mini out of the car park.

Jimmy chose the darkest area of the car park where he knew there was very little chance of anyone seeing him waiting in his car.

His Ford Cortina was a dark green colour and was almost invisible in this poor light.

As he was out on strike at the moment, he had plenty of time on his hands.

He was seriously pissed off about his situation, he felt as though he had been forced into joining the strike. He was worried as he had large bills to pay.

Most of the nice things in his house were being paid for on hire purchase and there was a small mortgage to find every month, not to mention the usual utility bills like, gas, water and electricity.

He was sitting pretty before the strike, he had money in the bank and everything he wanted.

The bills weren't a struggle for him while ever he was earning.

Jimmy knew that by the beginning of July his savings would run out, by then he either went back to work as a scab or he lost his house.

The choice really was that simple.

The strike didn't look like it would be over by then, not a chance.

Jimmy knew a lot of other miners that were in the same position as himself. He heard them moaning on about having no money, usually as they downed another pint and smoked another cigarette in the local Miners Welfare.

Jimmy had cut down his smoking to just five cigarettes a day and had stopped drinking alcohol altogether in an attempt to save money.

On one occasion when he'd ordered an orange squash to drink in the Welfare the other blokes had taken the piss out of him mercilessly.

Well they could all fuck off, and Scargill could fuck right off too.

There was no way he was going to lose his house because of that Yorkshire twat.

Suddenly car headlights being switched on in the police car park snapped him away from his thoughts. Instinctively he slunk lower down in his car seat. Two cars were coming out at the same time. The first car was a white Datsun and was being driven by a stocky looking bloke with a bald head. This car turned right out of the car park and was quickly followed by the red Mini Cooper, Rachel's car.

The red Mini was driven left out of the car park.

Jimmy was surprised to see there was somebody in the front passenger seat, and that person was obviously a man.

As the Mini pulled away from the car park he followed, at first with his cars headlights off.

Once on the road he switched the vehicles lights on and maintained a discreet distance from the car in front.

Jimmy followed the Mini out of the town centre until it turned right onto Garth Road.

He watched as the brake lights on the Mini lit up, and the vehicle slowed to a stop.

He drove straight by and parked up further along the road. In the rear view mirror, he saw the front seat passenger get out and wave before walking up a driveway.

She must have been dropping him off he thought, he made a mental note to watch that address and find out who the mystery man was who lived there.

He let the Mini drive past him quite a way before again pulling out from the kerb and following the vehicle.

This time he followed the Mini through High Oakham and up onto Berry Hill Lane. From there the vehicle was driven behind Bateman Court, a block of flats near to the Bellamy Road Estate.

Again he stopped his vehicle some distance away and watched as Rachel Moore parked up and then walked to the block of flats.

Bateman Court was only a small block that held four separate flats. Two on the ground floor and two on the first floor.

It was quite late and the entire block was in darkness.

All he had to do was wait to see which lights came on. A minute later and the lights in the left hand flat on the first floor came on.

'Bollocks!' he said aloud. He had been hoping she lived in one of the ground floor flats.

At least he knew where she lived now.

All he had to do now was carry on watching both her and the flat. He'd soon ascertain everything he needed to know about her life and who else, if anybody, featured in it.

He needed to gather as much information as he could about her. Only then would he be in a position to formulate a successful plan that would ultimately result in the death of Rachel Moore.

CHAPTER 15

Peckham, London – April 10th 1984

Two days had gone quickly by since the young woman's body had been discovered on the riverbank and Glyn Johnson was no closer to identifying her. The three detectives guided by Det Sgt Fraser had certainly put the hours in trying to find out who she was, but to no avail.

They had trawled through hundreds of missing persons' reports looking for anyone who came close to the description of the dead girl. After hours of painstaking work, they had drawn a blank.

Every different enquiry they tried resulted in nothing, the frustration was mounting.

Acting on Glyn's orders the detectives visited each hospital in the Greater London area and researched the records for every infant born on the 12th September 1983. After completing that mammoth task, they then set about the painstaking task of tracing every mother.

This enquiry alone required a further two detectives being added to the team dedicated to identifying the woman.

Glyn knew it was a long shot, the woman could have given birth at home or more likely outside of the London area.

He had to try something though, without an early identification of the victim he knew the trail to the killer would rapidly go cold.

The only piece of good news was that Professor Mason from Bristol University, at the request of Emily Cook, had spent the last two days carefully and skilfully recreating a facial mould from the reconstructed bones of the dead girl's face. Professor Mason had worked long into the night without rest and promised Glyn that a preliminary image of the dead girl's face would be ready before the end of the day.

Glyn didn't care how preliminary it was, he wanted to get the face and the tattoo out there, the sooner the better.

He was confident that someone out there would know who she was.

Suddenly he was disturbed in his thinking by an urgent knocking on his office door, 'Come in!' he bellowed.

A very young and very nervous police woman timidly opened the door.

'Sir, control room thought you'd want to know, one of the search teams just radioed in, they've found cable ties and blood on the floor of a derelict property on Wharf Road. It's about a hundred yards from the riverbank where the woman was found.'

'I bloody knew it!' he yelled, as he jumped from behind his desk.

Grabbing his coat he shouted, 'Craig have you got a motor?'

Craig Fraser appeared immediately from the general office, 'Yes guvnor.'

'Come on then, Wharf Road sharpish. I reckon there's a good chance they've found our fucking murder scene!'

'That's great guv, I'll make sure Scenes of Crime are travelling too.'

Twenty frustrating minutes later, after ploughing through the beginning of the rush hour traffic, they were finally approaching the derelict building on Wharf Road.

The building was a disused warehouse with a row of small offices on the ground floor and large open plan storage areas on the other three floors. It had fallen into disrepair after the company that owned it went bust in the late seventies. It was now a haven for junkies to shoot up in, and a place for prostitutes to bring their punters.

There was one of the distinctive plain white Ford Transit vans that were used by the Tactical Support Group, parked outside the main entrance to the disused building.

Standing by the side of the van, was a sergeant and eight officers, drinking coffee from paper cups.

Seeing the CID car approaching the young sergeant threw his hot drink onto the floor and walked towards the car.

As the two detectives got out of the CID car, the TSG sergeant spoke, 'DI Johnson?'

'Yeah Skip, that's me. What've you got?' said Glyn evenly.

'We'd only just started on this building guvnor, when one of my lads shouted up on the radio and told me he'd found something in one of the front ground floor rooms. It's a proper shit hole in there guvnor, the light ain't the best, but he's adamant there are plastic cable ties and brown tape on the floor and what looks like plenty of blood. As soon as he told me what he'd found I pulled the rest of the lads out of the building. I've left him in there guarding the interior door leading to the small room where he's made the discovery. I've also instructed him to start and maintain a log of the scene. He's a good lad who knows the crack, he hasn't touched a thing. I hope you don't mind guvnor, but I've already set things in motion and there's a Scenes of Crime team already en route.'

'That's great work skipper, tell your lads I appreciate it. It's no fun crawling around in these shitholes, with all the dirty needles and crap everywhere. You've done a professional job and I'll be having a word with your guvnor. What's the lad's name inside?'

'It's Tom Kane, guv.'

With that, Glyn and Craig grabbed overshoes and an overall each from the boot of the car. As they quickly donned the protective clothing Glyn looked over his shoulder back towards the fast flowing river. Less than a hundred yards away he could see the part of the riverbank where the young woman had been dumped.

Finally, after putting gloves on both men made their way into the decrepit building.

The stench of stale urine and faeces hit them as soon as they walked into the filthy building.

The door led onto a dark corridor, Glyn took a small Mini Maglite torch from his pocket and shone it along the corridor. The beam from the torch picked out the young constable standing about five yards down the corridor. He was outside one of the rooms that must have previously been used as an admin office when the building was part of a thriving business.

Picking their way carefully through the excrement, condoms and used needles that littered the floor the detectives made their way to the officer, 'You must be Tom Kane' said Glyn.

'Pc Tom Kane, yes sir. Can I have your names and ranks for the log?'

He opened his pocket book, to note the names and the time.

Craig spoke quietly in his guttural Scottish accent, 'Aye lad you can, I'm Detective Sergeant Fraser and this man here is Detective Inspector Johnson, the time is now fourteen minutes past four.'

Glyn put a reassuring hand on Tom Kane's shoulder and said, 'Well done son, you've followed the book to the letter. I want you to point out to me exactly where you've been and what you've touched.'

Pc Kane stepped sideways to allow Glyn line of sight into the dirty room littered with rubbish and a small pile of broken up furniture.

He said, 'I took one step inside the room, then I stopped to let my eyes get adjusted to the gloom before going any further. Once I could see properly I moved that piece of newspaper there.'

He indicated a screwed up sheet of old newspaper before continuing, 'Directly underneath the sheet of old newspaper were two black plastic cable ties like we'd been briefed about. They'd both been used and had been snipped in half. I straight away stepped back out of the room and radioed up my skipper to tell him what I'd found. While I waited for him to come in, I stayed here at the door looking around the room. Over there in the corner is what looks like screwed up brown Gaffer tape and that stain on the floor, just there, looks like old dried blood to me guv.'

'Well done son, good stuff. I want you to tell the Scenes of Crime people exactly what you've told me when they get here', said Glyn with a smile.

The two detectives retraced their steps and made their way back out of the building.

Only once they were back outside in the daylight did they realise just how dark and gloomy it was inside the building.

Both men breathed in deeply trying to get the stench of the building out of their noses.

'Finally a break!' exclaimed Glyn.

He continued, 'Any other day and that young lad would've trampled over everything before he even saw it.

He's got the makings of being a bloody good copper. Craig make sure he gets commended to his guvnor for today, the professionalism he's shown today could prove vital.'

'Will do guvnor. Scenes of Crime are here now; I'll go back in with them.'

The TSG sergeant approached Glyn saying, 'Guvnor, your office has been on the radio looking for you. Apparently the item you've been waiting for is now ready at St Barnabus Hospital Mortuary.'

'Thanks skip, well done today. Your team are a credit to you, good work.'

'Thanks guvnor, we do try', grinned the sergeant.

As soon as Craig had finished pointing out the room and the items on the floor to the Scenes of Crime officers he re-joined Glyn who was standing at the side of the CID car.

As both men removed the protective overalls and overshoes Glyn grinned at Craig saying, 'Finally we're getting somewhere Craig. I've just had notification that Professor Mason has finished his work and the image of the dead girl's face is ready at the mortuary. Let's get over there and see what she looked like in life shall we?'

As the two men left the riverside once more Glyn said evenly, 'Craig, I want this woman's face in every newspaper, on every TV channel and on every cell block wall in every

London nick. Someone somewhere will know who she is. I still want your team to keep working on the hospital enquiries. You never know that might just turn something up. All we need now is to get lucky and for that bastard to have left us some little scrap of forensic evidence in that shit hole back there. We're getting closer Craig, we're getting closer.'

'Aye guvnor, I reckon we just might be at that.'

CHAPTER 16

Proteus Army Camp, Ollerton, Nottinghamshire – April 28th 1984

Mick Reynolds was in a foul mood, he'd already bollocked two of his men for next to nothing and was now sitting in the front of the Transit van seething. He glanced at his watch, it was still only seven thirty in the morning. He let out an audible groan and sat back in the seat.

His PSU had started their shift at three thirty that morning, and travelled to Cuckney crossroads again for more intercept duty. They had been relieved at seven o'clock and were now back at Proteus Camp for food. Mick couldn't be arsed to eat yet another greasy fry up, so he stayed in the van while his men went to eat.

He now sat quietly in the van, alone in the darkness with his thoughts.

It was the last week in April and Mick knew he still had two more weeks of picket line duty before he could get another week back home, away from this God forsaken shithole.

It was also three weeks since he had picked up and killed the young prostitute in London.

Some days he still couldn't quite believe what he'd been capable of that night. He was confident that he'd committed the perfect murder, surely they would've come for him by now if he'd slipped up.

The days he'd spent since with his PSU on intercept duty were just a blur, he knew he was just going through the motions. Every shift, every day, every week was the same mixture of mind blowing boredom.

A couple of times earlier in the day, Ken, the driver of the PSU van had asked him if he was alright, 'You seemed a million miles away there Sarge' he had commented.

Now, as he sat alone in the quiet of the van, his mind drifted off replaying the moment he had killed the girl over and over again.

That joyous moment when she first got into his car and he knew that once and for all he was going to shut her up.

Whenever he replayed the killing in his mind it was always the face of his wife Rita he saw, not the dishevelled junkie prostitute that he had actually killed.

At the precise moment of the killing he found himself in the grip of the deepest rage he had ever experienced.

It had been the single most intense moment of his life.

He had driven her off in his car and parked up in a dark unlit corner of the red light area, before she could do or say anything he punched her once hard in the face knocking her unconscious.

It was then an easy task to wrap the plastic cable ties around her puny wrists so tight that her wrists had bled a little.

He wrapped the Gaffer tape three times around her head covering only her mouth, leaving her nostrils clear so she didn't suffocate.

He forced her down into the foot well of the front passenger seat so nobody could see her while he made the short drive over to the derelict buildings next to the Thames embankment, not far from Peckham, south of the river.

She started to come around again when he was nearly at the derelict buildings and began to snuffle under the gagging brown tape.

Mick ignored her pitiful muffled pleadings and parked up close to the side of one of the buildings. He then got out of the car and stepped into the shadows where he quickly donned the full forensic suit, overshoes and gloves. He picked up his small grip bag and placed it in a room a little way along the dark corridor inside the disgusting building.

He quickly checked the other rooms in the building, he didn't want to risk being disturbed by some addict looking to score their next fix, or by another prostitute with a punter.

Satisfied the building was empty he returned to his car and dragged the young girl from the foot well. She weighed nothing and he carried her quickly into the building before dropping her roughly onto the floor of the same room he had left his grip bag.

Once inside the room he quickly ripped off her clothes and stuffed them into a bin liner that he took out of the grip bag.

He closed his eyes as he sat in the van replaying the actual murder. A cruel smile crept across his face as he recalled how he had made the girl sit naked on the filthy disgusting floor in the pitch dark. He shuddered involuntarily as he remembered her making the whining noise beneath the suffocating Gaffer tape.

He recalled everything in vivid detail.

The noise she was making eventually got on his nerves and once again he reached into the grip bag, this time grabbing the heavy ballpein hammer. He then walked behind the woman and half closed his eyes.

His head had been filled with the sound of Rita's voice nagging him again, taking the piss out of his manhood again, ridiculing him again.

Suddenly something inside him snapped and he started to rain down blow after blow on the prostitute's head.

Mercifully she was probably dead or at least unconscious after the first blow. He continued to rain down blow after blow until he felt physically exhausted and was gasping for breath.

Finally, he stopped and surveyed the scene of carnage.

There was blood everywhere. The forensic suit was covered in the prostitute's blood and his gloved hands were glistening.

Quickly, he regained his composure and began to think rationally again.

He could not allow the police to identify the girl, so he put on a further pair of gloves over the blood soaked ones and grabbed the shears from the bag. Painstakingly he cut off each of the fingers and thumbs from the dead girl's hands, placing the severed digits into a plastic bag.

He then used the Stanley knife to slice up the palms of her hands before snipping off the cable ties.

Carefully he then removed the brown Gaffer tape from around her mouth and placed it in the corner near the cable ties. He then began systematically smashing her lower jaw and teeth with the hammer. Finally, he stuffed all the tools back into the grip bag and after checking the coast was clear he furtively walked out of the building.

He walked down to the path at the side of the river.

The moonlight was dancing on the dark water as it raced by. He saw in the moonlight the blood on his forensic suit, it was glistening and black, like molasses.

From the path he surveyed the bank down to the water's edge, it was thick glutinous mud.

Mick needed to get the body down to the water's edge so the tide would wash it away before anybody discovered it in the morning.

At the side of the building he saw a long abandoned scaffold board propped against the outside wall.

He placed the scaffold board out over the cloying mud down to the water's edge.

The board fell about ten feet short of the flowing river.

He cursed silently for not researching the times of the tide, he could only hope the tide would rise enough to dispose of the body downstream before it was seen.

Ensuring there was still nobody about he returned to the building and picked the woman's body up, carrying her out of the building and down to the river.

He carried her along the board, and had dumped her on her back on top of the stinking mud.

Carefully he tiptoed back along the board to the bank making sure he left no marks on the soft mud.

Standing at the side of his car he then removed the overshoes, forensic suit and gloves before dumping them all in a bin liner. The bin liner then went in the grip bag.

He had then driven back over the river, back to his house at Wembley.

Rita had still not returned home from her sordid night out, so he took out the bin liner containing the prostitute's clothes and the forensic clothing that was heavily bloodstained from the grip bag.

He left the blood stained tools, the unused cable ties and the roll of Gaffer tape in the bag in the boot of his car.

Mick then quickly showered before getting changed into his police uniform.

It had been nearly two o'clock in the morning when he had packed all the kit he would need for the deployment to Nottinghamshire into his large black PSU bag.

At the bottom of the PSU bag he stuffed the plastic bin liner full of the bloodstained clothes. He knew he would be able to dispose of all the items in the incinerator at Proteus Army Camp when he got there.

Finally, he'd put the kettle on and made himself a cup of tea. He sat in his lounge sipping tea, while he waited patiently for the police transport to pick him up ready to go back to the coal fields of Nottinghamshire.

Now alone in the van he was smiling broadly at the memories of that night.

Suddenly his recollection of those momentous events was brought to an end as the silence was shattered by his men returning to the PSU van.

'Bloody hell Mick, you've missed a belting fry up there!'

He just grunted a reply to the comment.

Mick couldn't wait to get back down to London. Another fourteen days of this shit was really going to drag. He was desperate to get back home because he'd finally come to a decision. The next time he killed, it really would be Rita who would die. He had proved to himself now that he could kill, and also more importantly that he could get away with it.

The only thing he needed to concentrate on now was how to dispose of Rita's dead body.

He smiled as a number of options instantly flashed through his brain.

CHAPTER 17

Peckham, London – May 3rd 1984

The skinny red haired junkie was literally starving. His jaundiced skin was stretched taut across his skeletal face. The blue eyes were sunk deep into dark rimmed sockets. Only that morning one of his back teeth had fallen out for no apparent reason.

It was now almost four weeks since he had watched his girlfriend drive off in that posh motor. He was now very weak and felt slightly dizzy, he'd been existing on meagre scraps of food that he managed to scavenge while wandering the streets.

The rich geezer who owned the car she got into must have set her up very nicely for her not to come back to him.

He was angry but not surprised, deep down he knew that she would do anything for money or another hit of heroin.

He allowed his mind to drift, and saw an image of his girlfriend in some posh pad living the highlife, eating, drinking, getting as much smack as she wanted and all the time getting fucked by the bastard in the posh motor.

He grew angry at the thought of her living the dream, while he'd been reduced to robbing bins at the back of shitty restaurants just to survive, nicking anything he could get his hands on, just to get his next bag of heroin.

Lee Skipton had just turned nineteen, he first became addicted to heroin when he was seventeen.

It had been easy to drift into drugs back home in Norwich, there was fuck all else to do in the town. There were no jobs anywhere, it was a simple choice for everyone, the dole or the dole.

It was a proper dump.

He first met the girl in Norwich town centre just before Christmas last year, he watched her spellbound as she went round the various shops in the precinct. He could tell she had no money and it was obvious she was out on the rob, but she looked fantastic, there was an air of confidence about her.

He watched her go into Miss Selfridge and stick two tops up her baggy jumper before sauntering out of the shop.

She had made it look so fucking easy, it was like she was daring the security guards in the shop to stop her. He was totally captivated and continued to follow her around the shopping precinct like a lost puppy.

He had followed her, watching her every move for over half an hour until suddenly she turned around and walked straight up to him, 'What's your fucking game! Are you a perv or something?' she yelled.

'I'm sorry, but you make this robbing shit look so easy.'

They had both laughed, before she said, 'Come on then copper knob, I'll show you how it's done, we can both go shopping!'

He had then spent the next two hours with her being taught the finer points of shoplifting, most importantly how to get away with shoplifting.

They had been together ever since, moving from one squat to the next, scraping enough money together to feed each other's drug habit and get enough food to live on.

Since they had been together, there were two occasions when times had been so rough, when neither of them had any money that she'd taken the decision to sell her body to get enough cash to score.

Lee knew she hated doing it, and he never asked her or tried to force her into prostitution.

The second time she went on the streets soliciting in the red light area of Norwich, she was arrested by the Vice Squad. As it was her first arrest she was given a caution.

The Vice Squad cops made it clear to her that if they caught her again she'd be charged and taken to court. The cops set up a meeting between the girl and her social worker, but she skipped the meeting.

It was her idea to get a fresh start and to travel up to London, it had taken them from January to the middle of March to scrape enough money together, for the two National Coach fares.

From the minute they arrived in London everything went to ratshit. Far from being the fresh start they hoped for, very quickly they found themselves in a shithole of a squat not far from the coach station, with no money.

There were no jobs going, they had nowhere to live and everything was twice as expensive. The area they were in was full of prostitutes and pimps. In no time at all the little money they managed to bring with them from Norwich had been spent on their habit. The night she went missing she had taken their last deal bag of heroin. He was left hanging and desperate to score. As he rattled around the squat, suffering, she made the decision to go out on the street to try and make some money.

In their desperation they had left the filthy squat together. They didn't want any trouble so they picked a stretch of the road where none of the other prostitutes were out plying their trade. She had only been on the street for half an hour when he saw the dark blue car pull up, it was an almost brand new Ford Sierra.

The one thing Lee Skipton knew about was cars. He had stolen enough in his joyriding days. Squinting through his glasses, he scribbled the registration number of the Sierra onto the scrap of paper he carried in his pocket. He always did this in case there was a problem and the punter got nasty.

It never occurred to him now, that the punter had got nasty, he just assumed his girl had not returned because she had got a better offer.

Now, as he slouched listlessly along Peckham High Road he caught a glimpse of his reflection in a shop window.

He barely recognised himself, he looked as white as a ghost, his mop of red hair was unkempt and unwashed, his blue Adidas track suit bottoms and his maroon hooded fleece top were hanging off his skinny frame and both were filthy dirty. His training shoes were worn down and dirty and one of the laces was missing.

He looked like a tramp.

Suddenly the hunger pangs hit home again, he desperately needed something to eat.

Lee slipped off the busy street and into a small convenience store. As he walked in he saw the burly Asian shopkeeper glaring in his direction from the far end of the shop. He quickly ducked behind the shelving so he was out of his sight. In front of him was a chiller cabinet full of food. There were pies, cakes, sandwiches and cartons of milk.

Quickly he grabbed a carton of milk, a couple of pies and a couple of packs of sandwiches, stuffing them beneath his baggy fleece top. With the food stashed he immediately turned and made for the door.

Suddenly he could see the shop keeper bearing down on him. Panicking he ran outside the shop, but as soon as he went through the door, he stumbled over the unlaced training shoe going down hard on the pavement. The carton of milk and the food scattered noisily all over the floor.

He was grabbed roughly from behind and pulled to his feet, 'You filthy bloody bastard. I'm sick of you tramps trying to rob me I'm calling the Police right now!'

Desperately he tried to plead with the shopkeeper not to involve the police and that he had only taken it because he was starving.

'Shut your bloody mouth before I shut it for you, you're not getting away with it this time!' the shopkeeper raged.

He felt himself being manhandled back into the shop, he was dragged behind the counter and locked in a stock cupboard, full of empty boxes and old magazines.

From inside the cupboard he could hear the muffled angry tones of the shopkeeper as he spoke to the police on the telephone, 'Please send someone straight away, I've caught a thief and I want him arresting.'

In the dark of the cupboard Lee Skipton started to sob, he knew he was a petty criminal but until now he had never been caught. When he went joyriding with his mates and drove stolen cars he always dumped the cars without a drama. Even though he regularly stole whatever he could to pay for his drugs, up until now he'd never been caught. If it wasn't for that poxy training shoe he wouldn't have been caught today.

Finally, after what seemed an eternity the cupboard door was yanked open and in the bright shop lights he could see two police officers standing there.

One of them grabbed his arm and pulled him roughly out of the cupboard, while the other one pinched his own nostrils between his index finger and thumb.

'Fucking hell, what's that smell?' the cop said.

'When was the last time you had a wash son?' the other one asked.

It was said more out of disgust than pity.

The officer turned to the shopkeeper who was holding open a carrier bag that contained the milk, pies and sandwiches that Skipton had tried to steal, 'Not exactly the great train robbery is it Mr Patel?' he said quietly.

'I don't care officer, I'm sick of these bastards coming in here every day robbing me, I want him arresting.'

Lee Skipton finally found his voice, 'I've never been in this shithole of a shop before you lying Pakki cunt!'

It was the worst thing he could have said. Suddenly he felt his skinny arms being twisted behind his back by the nearest policeman, he felt the cold steel handcuffs going on his wrists, and heard the noise of the ratchet on the cuffs as they secured his wrists together.

'Come on mouth, you're coming down the nick you gobby piece of shit!' said the cop.

The officer turned to the shopkeeper, 'I'll be back to get your statement later Mr Patel, once we've got this little tow rag banged up down the station, ok?'

'Yes Constable, thank you very much. See you later.'

Once in the police car the officer said, 'You had to open your big mouth didn't you ginge. If you hadn't started with the abuse, we could have talked old Manny around and just given you a bollocking!'

'I'm sorry', Lee Skipton stammered before saying quietly, 'What time is it please?'

'Just coming up to seven o'clock at night. Why have you got somewhere to go?'

Both the officers laughed.

In the back of the car Lee could feel the metal of the handcuffs biting into his bony wrists, he looked out of the car window and said quietly to himself, 'I wish I'd never come to this fucking shithole.'

Ten minutes later, Lee and the two cops were all standing in the cell block at Peckham Police Station.

'What have we got then lads?' asked the desk sergeant.

'This ginger ninja was caught nicking food from Manny Patel's off licence on the High Road. He's got no money on him and started getting abusive towards Manny when we were there, so he's been arrested for the theft of one carton of milk, two Ginsters steak pies and two packs of readymade egg and cress sandwiches. Total value £1.75.'

'You've heard all that son, what have you got to say for yourself?' the sergeant asked Skipton.

Skipton stared past the sergeant transfixed by the poster on the wall behind the desk.

'I know that girl on the poster, she's my girlfriend.'

'Yeah course she is, stop messing me about old son.'

'I'm not messing you about, seriously that's my girlfriend, but something's wrong with her face.'

'Alright son, I'll talk to you about that in a minute. For now, do you want a cup of tea and something to eat?'

'Yes please.'

'That's it son, you just keep remembering your manners while you're here and we'll get along fine. I'll get you sorted out and then we can think about getting you out of here. Now where do you call home son?' said the sergeant.

'I'm from Norwich.'

Patiently the sergeant obtained Lee Skipton's personal details before putting him in a holding cell with a cup of tea and a sandwich.

The two officers went back to the shop to get a quick statement from Manny Patel.

As far as they were concerned this job had police caution written all over it and they didn't want to waste all night on it.

The sergeant glanced at the clock on the cell block wall it was now almost a quarter to eight in the evening. He reached for the phone and dialled the control room, 'Would you page Detective Inspector Johnson for me and tell him we may have struck lucky about the dead girl on the poster. I've got a scruffy little shit from Norwich in the cells who's been nicked for shoplifting. He's telling me that he only came to London recently with his girlfriend and that the woman on the poster is her.'

CHAPTER 18

Masonic Lodge, Peckham – May 3rd 1984

Glyn Johnson had to admit, he was mightily impressed by the building. The carved stone columns that framed the heavy oak door of the Masonic Lodge in Peckham were built on a very grand scale. The building was made entirely from dressed stone and unlike most stone buildings in London, this one was immaculately clean and pristine.

It was illuminated by floodlights set in the ground that shone upwards bathing the entire building in a ghostly white light. From the driveway it almost appeared as though the building was floating.

As he walked towards the oak doors they opened as if the building itself were expecting him.

A tall man stood in the doorway dressed in dark trousers, a cream tuxedo jacket with a matching cream bow tie.

'May I see your invitation please sir?' the man asked.

Glyn fished into his coat pocket and found the envelope with his name in gold handwriting on the front.

He opened the envelope and passed the invitation to the man at the door.

'Detective Inspector Johnson, thank you for coming. Your host is pleased you could attend, his party is in the main hall. Please allow me to take your coat and follow me.'

Glyn removed his black Crombie coat and gave it to the doorman. The man turned and walked briskly down a corridor that led to a further set of large imposing oak doors. The walls either side of the corridor were adorned with portraits of men wearing the full regalia of the Freemasonry.

He hated wearing a formal dinner jacket, he hated the Masons and everything the Masonic Lodge stood for but most of all he hated police retirement party's.

Glyn had readily made an exception in this case, as the retirement party tonight was for the man who had been his first Detective Sergeant when he joined the CID as a wet behind the ears, know nothing temporary Detective Constable all those years ago.

Jack Swift had ultimately reached the rank of Detective Chief Superintendent but when Glyn first met him he was a newly promoted Detective Sergeant.

Swift had been both mentor and teacher to Glyn. But far more importantly than that he was a beacon of decency towards a young black officer in a totally white dominated world at that time.

Jack Swift had stood by his side and consistently challenged the overt racism whenever he heard it and spent hours encouraging Glyn to stay on the CID to prove all the bigots wrong.

Glyn would be forever grateful to Jack Swift for that and had the utmost respect for him as a detective and more importantly as a man.

As the double oak doors were opened, Glyn was once again impressed by the splendour and the architecture of the main hall.

The floor was a black and white checkerboard of marble tiles, the walls at either side of the hall were supported by large stone columns that looked like they had been copied from the Greek acropolis.

The large spacious room was full of men in black dinner jackets and bow ties, they held cut glass tumblers of whiskey, or brandy glasses full of cognac.

The air was thick with the smell of cigar smoke, and there was the low hum of conversation, punctuated by the odd raucous laugh.

Glyn looked around at the sea of faces, some he recognised as fellow detectives from the Met.

A passing waiter carrying a tray of drinks paused at the side of him after noticing he wasn't holding a drink.

Glyn surveyed the collection of drinks on the large silver tray and selected a malt whisky in a cut glass tumbler. He took a sip of the whisky and felt the warmth of the amber liquid course through him as he looked across the room.

Jack Swift was approaching him now with his hand outstretched, 'Glyn my old friend, really pleased you could make it tonight. How are things?'

'I'm really well, thanks Jack. How's retirement suiting you?'

'I think I could get used to it, my roses have never looked better.' he chuckled.

'Have you got anything lined up to keep you occupied?' asked Glyn.

'I've made a start on the obligatory memoirs of a retired detective, but apart from that, no I haven't. I intend to take life a bit easier. I think it's time for me and Mabel to see a bit of the world before we're both too old to enjoy it.'

Again Jack smiled and said, 'How's things at work Glyn? Are you any closer to finding out who that young woman found on the embankment was?'

That was typical Jack Swift, thought Glyn, he'd been away

from the job for at least three months and he still had his finger on the pulse of every outstanding case.

'Still working on it guv, no further forward I'm afraid.'

'Keep at it Glyn, from what I've heard we need to catch the maniac that killed her, he sounds a right evil bastard.'

'You're not wrong there Jack, I must admit it's been giving me a lot of sleepless nights. I keep expecting to arrive at work and be told there's another dead girl.'

'A proper Jack the Ripper eh?'

'I bloody hope not guv!'

'Glyn, did you know there's a theory that the original Jack the Ripper may have been a member of this very Masonic Lodge?'

'That's probably why he was never caught Jack, this whole organisation's as bent as fuck!'

Both men laughed.

'You're spot on Glyn; this is the first time I've ever set foot in here. My good friend the Assistant Commissioner, who by the way, may or may not be the Grand Master of this Masonic Lodge, offered me the hall as the venue for my retirement party. It would have been rude not to accept, it's a great place isn't it?'

Glyn nodded, smiling 'It's certainly very impressive Jack.'

'You keep at it Detective Inspector, like I always said to you, if you put the hours in eventually you catch the bastards. This one's no different, I know you'll put the effort and dedication in and I'm sure you'll catch this bastard before he does become the next Ripper.'

Swift took a sip of whisky before continuing, 'How good does that sound? Detective Inspector Glyn Johnson. I always knew you were destined for great things, I reckon you could go all the way and have my job now that I don't need it anymore. The sky's the limit for you old son.'

'Thanks guv, it's nice of you to say that, but I'm a detective, I like the streets, that's where police work is for me.'

'You've got a good point there Glyn, I was never happier than when I was feeling the collar of some low life, you stick at it Glyn. Keep doing what you do best. I've got to go and mingle with some of these Command wankers now, enjoy the night Glyn. Get that drink down you and get another.'

'I can't Jack. I'll just take my time with this one, I'm on call tonight.'

He waved his pager in his hand.

Right on cue the alarm on the pager went off.

'Sorry Jack, I've got to find a phone.'

'Over there Glyn, go through the door and ask the attendant he'll direct you to a telephone. Glad you could make it tonight my friend. Come and visit me and Mabel at home won't you?'

'Of course I will Jack, it'll be a pleasure. Give my regards to Mabel please'

Jack nodded and then he was off mingling with his other guests.

Glyn found the attendant who directed him to a telephone in a small office off the corridor.

He called the number on the pager.

The voice at the other end said, 'Hello guv, it's the control room. We've had a call from Peckham nick, they've got a young lad in their cells who's claiming to be the boyfriend of your unknown dead female from the embankment.'

Glyn's eyes lit up and his mind raced, quickly he said, 'Under no circumstances is he to be released. I'm on my way. Contact Craig Fraser for me and have him meet me at Peckham nick as soon as possible.'

Glyn put the phone down and walked out of the office, he found the attendant standing directly outside the door.

'Would you get my coat please and could you arrange for a cab to pick me up here?'

'Of course Sir, I'll get your coat straight away. There are four black cabs already outside, just take one of those Sir.'

'Thank you.'

Glyn quickly donned his coat and raced out of the building to one of the waiting cabs.

'Peckham Police Station, quick as you can please', he instructed the cabbie.

'Right you are guvnor.'

Immediately the black cab sped off away from the Masonic Lodge.

Sitting in the back of the cab Glyn removed his bow tie and undid the top button of his shirt. Looking out of the window as the city streets swept by, he wondered if this was the breakthrough that would help him catch the bastard that had butchered the young girl.

CHAPTER 19

Peckham Police Station Cells – May 3rd 1984

'Bloody hell guvnor, you're a wee bit overdressed for this gaffe', chuckled Craig.

'Yeah, yeah, very good Craig. I was at Jack Swift's retirement bash. It was a bleeding black tie job.'

'You look very dapper guvnor.'

'Thanks for getting here so quick Craig, were you at home?'

'Yeah I was just watching a bit of telly with the wife.'

Both men walked into the cell block just as the sergeant was administering a caution to Lee Skipton for the theft from shop.

The sergeant finished and said, 'Lee these are the detectives I was telling you about, they want to talk to you about the woman on the poster.'

'No problem, thanks for the tea and the food Sarge.'

The two detectives now approached Lee Skipton, 'I'm Detective Inspector Johnson and this is Detective Sergeant Fraser. Lee how sure are you that you know the woman in this poster?' Glyn indicated the poster on the wall behind the custody desk.

'I'm pretty sure it's Jenny, there's something about her mouth that looks a bit different though.'

'Can you see the photo of the tattoo at the bottom of the poster?' asked Craig

'Jenny definitely has a tattoo on her heel, can you get the poster off the wall so I can see it properly. I should wear glasses but I've smashed them, the poster looks a bit fuzzy from here.'

The sergeant leaned over and said, 'Here Lee have a look through these', he passed over his own spectacles.

'Oh my God! That's Jenny's tattoo, that's the date her baby daughter was born, the 12th July 1983. Why is her picture on a poster here? What's happened to her face?'

'You'd better come in here where we can talk properly son', said Craig.

The two detectives led Lee Skipton into an adjacent interview room.

Craig spoke first, 'Sit down son, I want you to tell us everything you can about Jenny.'

'I want to know what's happened to her first, I haven't seen her for about four weeks. Ever since she went off in that bloody posh motor.'

Glyn leaned forward and spoke softly, 'Listen to me Lee. What I've got to tell you isn't good news. Around four weeks ago we found the woman in the poster. I'm sorry Lee, but when we found her she was dead. She had been murdered.

I'm sorry to have to tell you like this Lee, but we're going to really need your help to find out what happened to her.'

Lee Skipton visibly disintegrated before their eyes, he held his face in his hands and his whole body trembled and when the reality of what he was being told registered he let out a long anguished cry, 'No!'

He stammered, 'Why would anybody want to hurt my Jenny?'

Glyn looked into Skipton's eyes and said, 'Tell us about the last time you saw her Lee, what happened?'

Lee took a breath between sobs and said, 'We were strapped for cash, we both have a habit see. She'd just scored but I was on my arse, desperate for gear. I was hanging. Jenny said she'd go out and earn a few quid. I knew she meant she'd get a punter and sell herself. I told her not to and that I would be ok until the morning. I knew we could get some cash from somewhere even if it meant going on the rob in a few shops. Jenny wouldn't listen, she said I needed the gear straight away or I'd be really bad. We didn't really know the area but had seen girls working the streets over at the railway station not far from Wembley Stadium.'

He started to sob again, Glyn coaxed him gently, 'What happened Lee?'

'Jenny stood on the street away from the other girls and I stood in a dark doorway just looking out for her. We'd only been there about half an hour when this car cruises by and stopped. He only saw Jenny he didn't see me.'

'What sort of car was it Lee?'

'It was definitely a dark blue Ford Sierra; I know my cars.'

'Did you get a look at the driver?'

'No it was too far away, I couldn't see him properly. I could tell it was a bloke though and he had dark hair.'

'What about the car can you tell us anything about that?'

Suddenly Lee sat upright in his chair, 'I wrote the reg number down, I think I've still got it.'

Lee stood up and frantically started to go through the pockets of his scruffy jogging bottoms finally pulling out a scrap of screwed up paper.

He quickly flattened the paper out on the table.

He handed the scrap of paper to Glyn, 'B 628 EJH, is that the car?' asked Glyn.

Skipton nodded.

Glyn handed the piece of paper to Craig.

Craig said, 'Lee, are you sure this number's right?'

'Yeah pretty sure. We always did it, whenever she went with a punter in a car I'd write the car number down, in case anything got nasty, you know.'

'Yeah, we know', said Glyn.

Glyn nodded towards Craig who immediately stood up and left the room to go and check the vehicle registration number on the Police National Computer.

Glyn turned to Lee and said, 'Thanks Lee, I know this isn't easy for you, but I need you to tell me everything you can about Jenny. I want to know her full name, where she's from, her family. Anything you can think of about Jenny I want to know. Can you do that for me Lee?'

Lee Skipton nodded and slowly told Glyn everything he knew about Jenny.

Her name was Jenny Taylor, she was nineteen years old and was from Norwich. There was no immediate family and she lived in care until her seventeenth birthday. She had either lived rough or slept in squats ever since. She was an addict and had been on heroin from around the age of sixteen. He met her just before Christmas last year and had been with her ever since. The tattoo on her heel was to remind her of her daughter.

She had called her daughter Bunny.

He had no idea what the baby daughter's real name was or who the father was.

Jenny's daughter was born on the 12th July 1983 but because of her habit the baby was born addicted to heroin.

The Social Services had taken the baby girl into care straight away. Jenny knew that Bunny was put up for adoption but she did not know who adopted her or even where the adoptive parents lived.

Jenny still had a social worker back in Norwich.

Craig came back into the interview room, 'Are you sure you've got this car number right Lee?' he asked.

'Yeah, a hundred per cent, I know I was rattling but I'm sure it's right.'

'What about your eyesight lad, you couldn't read the poster on the wall could you?'

'I know that, but I still had my glasses when I wrote the number down. I only smashed them last week. I definitely wrote the number down right', he started to sob again.

Glyn said softly 'Ok Lee, don't worry about the number. I'm going to get somebody to come and write down everything you've told me, ok? Before you leave tonight I want you to show the detective exactly where you were when Jenny got picked up in the car, ok? I'll arrange a bed for you at the local YMCA. Don't leave London without me telling you its ok. Do you understand Lee?'

'I'm not going anywhere; I've got no money to go anywhere.'

'I'll make sure you get fed at the YMCA, but don't go taking any smack in there or you won't be able to stay. Do you understand?'

'Yeah, I know. One thing detective, when can I see Jenny?'

'We'll talk about that in the morning Lee, I'll see you tomorrow.'

A detective police woman came into the interview room to take the written statement from Lee.

Glyn and Craig walked out of the room.

'Ok Craig, what's the problem with the car reg?' said Glyn.

'It comes back to a red Opal Kadett Glyn, that's what's wrong with the fucking number!'

'Bollocks!' said Glyn under his breath.

'Look, first thing tomorrow Craig I want somebody at the PNC to be checking similar reg numbers to see if we can get a hit on a blue Ford Sierra. I want someone to track down this social worker in Norwich and get chapter and verse on Jenny Taylor. I also want full background checks doing on Lee Skipton, I don't think for one second that he's our killer but stranger things have happened.'

'Ok boss, I'm on it. Are you ready for some more bad news?'

'Go on, what now?'

'I was speaking to Scenes of Crime before I left work earlier today, they've found absolutely nothing from the murder scene at the warehouse.'

'Nothing?'

'Not a fingerprint, not a fibre, the only thing they did find was a partial footprint in the blood on the floor of the disused building.'

'Well at least that's something', said Glyn.

'It is something, but this is where it gets weird guv, we didn't go in the room did we? The footprint they've found is identical to somebody who's wearing forensic overshoes. Scenes of Crime have done some comparisons and they think it's the same overshoes as issued to the Metropolitan Police.'

'For fucks sake!' muttered Glyn.

Glyn could hear the conversation he had earlier with Jack Swift replaying in his head.

He could hear Jack saying, 'The original Jack the Ripper was thought to be a member of this Masonic Lodge'

With that thought racing through his mind Glyn walked off.

'Be back here at eight in the morning Craig, we've got a lot to do tomorrow.'

'Ok guvnor, no problem', said Craig glancing at his watch.

It was just after two in the morning.

'I think you mean we've got a lot to do today Guv', he muttered to himself.

CHAPTER 20

Peckham, London – May 5th 1984

It had been two days since the dead woman found on the embankment was finally identified as being Jenny Taylor, a young runaway from Norwich.

Glyn Johnson and Craig Fraser now sat in the Black Prince pub just off Peckham High Road having a brainstorming session over a couple of pints.

It was something Glyn had adopted after working for so long with Jack Swift.

Jack always maintained that it was good practice to talk things through and get ideas from everyone working on a case rather than to try and think of everything himself.

When a case became bogged down or an enquiry was stalling through lack of evidence or witnesses, these discussions very often revealed new lines of enquiry.

Both Glyn and Craig sat nursing their almost empty beer glasses, it was amazing what a change of venue and the relaxation of a couple of beers could do. Many a tough case had been solved inside the smoky rooms of the small cosy pub.

The Black Prince pub had the reputation of being a coppers watering hole. There were several such establishments across London where ex coppers were the licensees and police officers were the main or only customers. Just as villains had their favourite pubs, where past and future crimes were discussed and planned openly, so the police had their licensed haunts as well.

The Black Prince was a very small pub that comprised of a lounge bar and a smoke room or snug.

The landlord, Geoff Greer, was a large man standing well over 6feet 4inches tall, he had been a Grenadier Guardsman before spending twenty years in the City of London Police. He had taken on the Black Prince public house upon retirement from the Force. With Greer installed as landlord the establishment quickly became known as a police pub

Greer was now completely bald and as a result was known by the nickname of Curly, which secretly he rather liked. His only customers in the snug that afternoon were the two detectives, 'Same again Gents', he asked from behind the bar.

'Yes please Curly, a pint of Guinness for me and a pale ale for Craig', said Glyn.

The landlord pulled the two beers and brought them over to where they were sitting. Placing the beers on the table he said, 'I won't disturb you gents, just give me a shout through to the lounge if you need anything else.'

'Thanks Curly.'

He waited for the landlord to move out of earshot before continuing, 'Right Craig, these are the facts we've established. Jenny Taylor, a heroin addict, left Norwich in company with her boyfriend Lee Skipton, also a heroin addict for a better life. She had no ties in Norwich, her family's all dead. She gave birth to a baby daughter who was born an addict and was immediately taken into the care of the Social Services. That child has subsequently been adopted. What's the news from the Norwich Social Services?'

Craig replied, 'We've identified her social worker as being a Ms Tracy Price. I sent two detectives over to Norwich to get chapter and verse. It would appear that Ms Price was saddened but not overly surprised when she was told of Jenny's death and the nature of it. She confirmed the story about the baby girl and told us that the child was now living with its adoptive parents up in Lanarkshire, Scotland. The couple have no knowledge of the child's birth mother other than the fact that she was a heroin addict who was forced to give the child up for adoption. As far as Ms Price was aware there's been absolutely no contact between Jenny Taylor or Lee Skipton with the adoptive parents from Scotland. Ms Price said that although Jenny had been saddened to give up her daughter she soon got over it and moved on. Ms Price was also aware that Jenny was spending a lot of time with Lee Skipton. She saw Lee as a damaging influence in Jenny's life purely down to the fact that they fuelled each other's addiction, apart from that he was harmless. It was Jenny who was the dominant one in their relationship.'

'Ok Craig. I don't think we need to bring the adoptive parents in Scotland into the enquiry at this stage. Any more on Lee Skipton?'

'We've done all the background checks on Skipton, he's definitely not in the frame for her murder guv. He's soft as a brush and harmless. I've let him return to Norwich, back to his parents' address. I asked the local police to check that it was a suitable address and I've asked Lee to attend Norwich police station every day to sign on, he's not on bail for anything but he agreed to do it anyway. I reckon we can rule him out other than as a witness, what do you think?'

'Ok Craig I'm happy with that. What about the car he claims he saw Jenny getting into?'

'Right guv, we've no progress there I'm afraid. A dark blue Ford Sierra registered number B 628 EJH does not exist. That registered number was issued to a red Opal Kadett, the owner of the car has been traced to an address in Kent. It's a Mrs Brenda Owthorpe who lives in Deal. I've already sent two detectives down there and they've seen the Opal Kadett with that plate on. Because Lee is so adamant that it was a Ford Sierra it leads me to believe that he got the make of the car right, but it's being driven around on false plates.'

'It looks that way Craig, how about the PNC checks on similar registration numbers?'

'They've tried over two hundred different permeations of the number and not pulled one Ford Sierra, it literally is like looking for a needle in a haystack and is extremely time consuming. The PNC have asked us to consider it a last resort as an enquiry.'

'Ok Craig, until we can firm up any more on this registration number we are going to have to leave that in abeyance for the time being. What about our second scene, the room in the warehouse where the murder was committed?'

'Right, Scenes of Crime have confirmed that nothing of any evidential use was found at the murder scene apart from the footprint of the police issue forensic overshoes. The cheeky mare in the Scenes of Crime department asked me again the other day if either of us two had walked into the room. I told her exactly what I thought of that comment. What's more interesting to me guv, is what we didn't find at the scene.'

'What do you mean Craig?'

'Well our killer went to a lot of effort painstakingly snipping off all the fingers and thumbs from our dead girl's hands and has then taken the time and trouble to carefully remove all the body parts from the scene.'

'I think I know what you're driving at Craig. Our killer's very forensically aware and is desperately trying to stall this enquiry by making it nigh on impossible for us to identify the dead girl. If we hadn't had a lucky break when Skipton saw the poster after his arrest, we would still be no further on. This business with the forensic suit really worries me though Craig. I'm going to throw this out to you for a reaction. Do you think our killer could be a cop?'

'You know me guvnor, I never rule anything out. The lack of forensic evidence is certainly pointing us that way, but this bastard has a cold calculating mind. Is this what he wants us to think? Or is it his first genuine mistake and we're on the right track?'

'Right Craig, as I see it, these are the things we need to do right now to try and move the enquiry on. Firstly, I want you to arrange a full briefing for all the Vice Squads working anywhere in the City. I want them all to be looking for a dark blue Ford Sierra cruising their red light areas. I want all the numbers of such vehicles, logged and the details passed to our incident room for tracing and follow up enquiries. I don't want the drivers being stopped or spoken to by Vice officers. I don't want this bastard being given a heads up.'

He took a sip of his Guinness and continued, 'Secondly, I want you to find out if the forensic suits we use can be obtained by the general public, or if any other organisations use them. Prison service, hospitals etc. Lastly, I want you to draw up a list of all professions that may have some knowledge of the forensic procedures used by the police. Just off the top of my head there's a couple I can think of, pathologists, criminology students and I'm sure there's many more.'

'Ok guv, no problem.'

'We can catch this nutter Craig, we've just got to get right back to basics and do the painstaking, time consuming enquiries. I don't think he's going to make many mistakes and I want him locked up before he has the chance to kill again.'

Glyn drained the last of the Guinness from his glass and stood up.

'See you at work in the morning Craig, I need to call in somewhere before I go home.'

'No problem guv. You do realise it's our scheduled rest day tomorrow, don't you?'

'We need to get these enquiries moving Craig. I'll be in tomorrow, are you ok to get in as well or have you got stuff planned?'

'I'll be in at eight o'clock guv, I've nothing planned for tomorrow.'

'Thanks Craig, I appreciate that. See you in the morning.'

Glyn stepped out of the gloomy pub into the bright light of a pleasant May afternoon. He glanced at his watch, it was now two fifteen in the afternoon. If he set off now, he could be there in just under an hour.

Getting into his black BMW he started up the powerful three litre engine, and immediately turned on the car stereo. He drove away from the pub just as the Bob Marley reggae classic 'One Love' boomed out of the car stereo cassette player.

Just under an hour later and he drove his car onto a leafy lane in the beautiful village of Theydon Bois that lay in the middle of Epping Forest in Essex. The houses here were large and set back from the road.

Finally, Glyn found the house he was looking for and parked the car on the road outside.

The house was beautiful, set in large well-kept gardens.

It was red brick with a red tiled roof. The windows all had leaded lights in a harlequin pattern. There was a large wrought iron gate that was already open and a gravel driveway leading up to the house. Glyn locked his car and walked up the driveway to the house.

Parked directly outside the house was a British racing green Jaguar and a small red MGB roadster. He walked up to the large oak door of the house and rang the ornate door bell. The chime of the doorbell sent out a loud rendition of Land of Hope and Glory.

Glyn grinned at the tune.

There was movement inside the house and suddenly the door was flung open. Standing in the doorway was a tall, slim woman with greying hair tied back in a bun. She was dressed for gardening in brown trousers and an old sweater.

'Hello Mabel, it's good to see you. Is Jack about?'

The woman's face lit up, 'Hello Glyn, it's lovely to see you too, come in come in', she said.

Mabel ushered Glyn into the house, 'Jack's out in the back garden, it's been such a lovely day. He'll be so pleased to see you, you were always his favourite', she winked.

She waved for Glyn to follow her as she walked through the large house.

'What do you think to our bloody doorbell Glyn? Isn't it atrocious?'

'Typical Jack, I thought', he said grinning.

Finally, they reached a pair of open French doors that led out onto the rear garden of the house.

The garden was beautiful. There was a large manicured lawn that had recently been cut and still showed the mower lines. The grass was surrounded by borders filled with flowers that were just starting to bloom.

'This is beautiful Mabel. Do you maintain all this yourselves?'

'We potter Glyn, the hard graft's done by our gardener, he comes in twice a week. Jack's over there on the patio reading a golf magazine. Go over and say hello while I put the kettle on. Would you like tea or coffee?'

'A cup of tea would be lovely, thanks.'

Glyn walked along the garden path up the gentle slope towards the patio. Jack Swift was sitting on a garden chair reading a copy of Golf Weekly. There were three other chairs all with thick green cushions and a cast iron table. There was already a tray of empty cups and saucers on the table.

Jack looked up from the magazine and his face creased into a wide grin. He immediately put the magazine down, stood up and approached Glyn.

'Glyn, what a lovely surprise.'

'Hello guvnor, your good lady let me in, she said I should surprise you while she went to make the tea. I didn't know you were a golfer Jack?'

'I'm not Glyn, I've never swung a golf club in my life. One of my friends from the Rotary Club dropped the magazine off this morning to see if I fancied taking it up. What a lovely surprise, it's great to see you. It was a pity you had to shoot off quick from my party. I was glad you came though; I reckon you hate them backslapping events more than I do myself.'

'If it had been for anybody else Jack, I wouldn't have even been there.'

'Grab a seat Glyn, what brings you all the way out to Theydon Bois? Is it purely a social call, or something else?'

Still razor sharp, thought Glyn.

He was just about to reply when Mabel arrived with a new tray containing a pot of tea, two cups, two saucers, a small milk jug, a sugar pot and a plate of biscuits.

She carefully placed the tray down onto the cast iron table, before picking up the tray that had been used earlier.

'I'll leave you boys alone to have a catch up, no doubt you'll be swinging the blue lamp and talking about nothing but police work. I've a stack of housework still to do this afternoon.'

With that she walked away back to the house.

Jack picked up the tea pot and poured two cups of tea.

'Help yourself to milk and sugar Glyn'.

Both men sipped their tea before Jack broke the silence.

'Ok Glyn, you didn't come all the way out here to sip Earl Grey tea, what's up?'

'Is it that obvious Jack?'

'Let's put it this way Glyn, you look like you've got the weight of the world on your shoulders.'

'Sorry Jack, I promise I'll come over again soon when it will be a purely social call, but right now I need to run some things by you.'

'If I can be of any help Glyn, you know that I'll do what I can.'

'It's this dead girl from the river.'

'I heard you've identified her now, has that taken you forward?'

'Ordinarily you'd expect it to, but this is not an ordinary case. The killer went to great lengths to try and prevent us identifying the girl.'

'Yes I heard about that Glyn, usually that can mean one of two things. That the killer's somebody close to the victim, or the killer's well aware that a crucial part of any murder investigation is identifying the victim.'

'Jack I'm pretty satisfied that our victim wasn't known by the killer, which points to the second reason. The worrying thing for me is that there's absolutely no forensic evidence left either at the murder scene or the deposition site.'

Jack Swift looked deep in thought, 'Mmmmm, I see where you're going with this. Steps taken to hinder identification, along with great efforts to avoid leaving forensic evidence. You're starting to think your killer's a cop aren't you?'

'Yes I am Jack, there's one last thing you should know. Our killer was wearing a police issue forensic suit and overshoes both at the murder scene and the deposition site.'

'Bloody hell!' Jack took a deep breath before continuing, 'Glyn that's a first even for me.'

Both men sat in silence drinking tea for five minutes before Jack spoke again, 'Don't put all your eggs in one basket Glyn. I know everything's pointing you towards the killer being one of our own, but just sitting here I can think of any number of people who in their professional lives would have that knowledge of forensics. When you said a police issue forensic suit, do you mean it's the same type as we use? Check the suppliers of the forensic suits for any single orders. Your worst case scenario is going to be some lone wolf nutter who's taken the time to read all the literature on police techniques.'

Glyn nodded his head and sighed deeply before saying, 'How do I go about catching one of our own Jack?'

'There's no easy answer to that question Glyn, the same way we catch everyone else. Do the hard yards, the leg work, the painstaking, time consuming enquiries, sift through all the crap and then hope for that one little mistake, that single careless moment from them.'

'Thanks for listening Jack, I just needed to know I was doing the right things.'

'Be confident Glyn, you never did miss much. I bet these enquiries I've just mentioned are already being implemented, am I right?'

Again Glyn nodded, 'They are Jack. Do you mind if I keep you informed I still value your opinion very highly?'

'Of course not Glyn, you know me, I'm a detective through and through and will be until the day I die. Anytime you want to use me as a sounding board you know where I am.'

'Thanks Jack.'

Both men stood and shook hands.

'Come and say goodbye to Mabel before you go, you always were her favourite you know.'

Glyn smiled, 'Of course Jack, let me grab this tray.'

Both men walked towards the house, Glyn carrying the tray and following his old mentor.

CHAPTER 21

Proteus Army Camp, Nottinghamshire – May 31st 1984

It was the last day of May and more importantly it was Mick Reynolds last day in Nottinghamshire for two weeks.

The current tour of duty had really dragged by.

The shifts worked were long and unsociable. The off duty time was mind numbingly boring with absolutely nothing to do.

All the officers on deployment were getting listless and irritable. Cases of assaults by the police on pickets were getting higher as tempers started to fray quicker.

The Metropolitan Police officers had all been informed earlier that morning that their next deployment would start on June 14th. They were then instructed by their senior officers in the Met to take the next two weeks off work.

Mick Reynolds was overjoyed at the news. Like everyone else he had become totally bored and disillusioned with the role they were performing. It was getting harder and harder to maintain the morale of the constables in his Police Support Unit.

He was also excited because the two weeks off work would give him plenty of time to plan getting rid of his loathsome wife Rita. As he boarded the coach that would transport him and his officers back down to London he mulled over what he needed to do when he eventually arrived back home in Wembley.

The first thing on his agenda was to meet up with an old friend. Mick had arranged to meet Sergeant Ted Smith over a pint at the local pub, this had been done under the guise of simply having a catch up after being away up in Nottinghamshire for so long. The real reason for the meeting was that Ted Smith was a sergeant on the Vice Squad and Mick needed to know if there had been any updates on the prostitute he had killed.

The second thing he needed to do was finally put into practice what he'd spent weeks thinking about while he was bored shitless in Nottingham. It was finally time to get rid of the bitch he was married to. It had been a long time coming but things were starting to form in his mind, he had finally worked out how he could be rid of her. There were a few things to sort out first but that would only take a couple of days.

He continued making plans and refining ideas during the long journey back down the motorway.

CHAPTER 22

Wembley, North London – May 31st 1984

Mick Reynolds was the last of his serial to be dropped off.

Finally, the coach had pulled up outside his home in Wembley. The journey back to London had been horrendous, the motorway was like a car park with tail back after tail back of unmoving stationary cars. The North Circular had been no better.

He got off the coach carrying his large black PSU bag and a holdall containing his personal belongings. He yawned and stretched before he walked down his short sloping driveway. Dropping the two bags on the floor he fumbled in his pockets for the keys to his house.

He opened the front door and shouted, 'Rita, I'm home!'

The house was silent, that was unusual. Normally there would at least be a snarling acknowledgement of his presence, something like, "so fucking what!"

Today there was nothing, just a stony silence.

Leaving the bags in the hallway Mick walked into the lounge, nothing. From there he went upstairs checking each bedroom and the bathroom. Realising that the house was empty, he checked his watch it was still only four o'clock in the afternoon.

'Christ, she's started early', he muttered to himself.

Finally, he walked into the kitchen to put the kettle on.

There leaning against the kettle was a white envelope. It had a single word written in black felt tip pen on it, "Mick".

It had been deliberately left in a place where he was sure to find it almost as soon as he walked in. Normally the first thing he'd do when he walked in was to put the kettle on and make himself a cup of tea.

He picked up the envelope, tearing it open quickly. He scanned the content of the short note that had been left inside the envelope,

Mick,

I got the chance to go to Benidorm for three weeks with the girls.

Back on 20th June.

Rita

Angrily he screwed up the note and hurled it across the room. On any other day her prolonged absence would have been met with joy and a feeling of relief.

Today was different. He'd made plans, and now she had scuppered them again. He paced angrily around the kitchen. Back on the 20th he'd be back in Nottingham by then.

'For fucks sake!' he shouted out loud.

Mick started to calm down, he filled the kettle and made himself a cup of tea with milk and two sugars. Sipping his tea at the kitchen table, slowly he calmed right down.

This wouldn't change anything. It was merely a stay of her execution. He smiled to himself at that thought, he liked the sound of the words 'her execution'.

He did feel a tad frustrated though, he needed a release.

He felt a strong urge to drive straight to the red light area, where he could pick up a whore, and buy some relief.

Suddenly he remembered he'd arranged to meet Ted Smith that evening at the Eight Bells pub. He was in two minds whether to call Ted and put their meeting off until tomorrow night.

Finally, he decided his relief and the tart would have to wait. He would have a catch up with Ted tonight, in fact he would order a cab. He felt like getting pissed. Mick finished his tea and suddenly felt drained. He lay down on the settee in the lounge to have a nap and quickly drifted off to sleep.

He woke with a start and looked at his watch, it was just coming up to seven o'clock. He'd arranged to meet Ted at seven thirty. He grabbed the phone and ordered a minicab to pick him up at twenty past seven. He ran upstairs and quickly changed into jeans and a t shirt before cleaning his teeth and combing his hair.

He grabbed his wallet and checked there was enough cash in it. The doorbell rang. Mick looked out of his bedroom window and could see the black cab waiting outside.

Ten minutes later and he was walking into the Eight Bells pub on Wembley High Road. Already standing at the bar was a forty something, tall, skinny man with a comb over hair style Bobby Charlton would have been proud of. He was wearing wire framed glasses and a camel coloured Crombie style coat over blue denims and ox blood Dr Marten boots.

Mick walked straight over, 'Hello Ted, sorry I'm a bit late. What you having?'

He could see that Ted Smith was only about a quarter of the way down his pint but he knew exactly what would happen next.

Mick watched as Ted picked up his glass and drained the rest of his pint before belching loudly and saying, 'I'll have a pint of Harp mate, cheers!'

Ted might be a skinny fucker, but he drank like a fish. Glad I booked a cab, Mick thought, this could get messy.

Both men stood drinking at the bar for the next hour or so, talking over general things, like how Spurs were faring as opposed to Arsenal. Eventually after four more pints the talk started to veer towards police work.

Moving from the bar with two more pints of lager they went and sat in a booth. Ted was moaning, 'We've just been given a shit load of more work to do.'

'What on Vice? You lazy fuckers don't do any work', laughed Mick.

'For your information Mick, we do plenty and on top of all that we've now got to clock and write down a shitload of car numbers we see driving around the red light areas. As if we haven't got enough to do already pulling tarts and punters', he moaned.

'Car numbers? What's that all about then Ted?' asked Mick.

'It's all to do with that young prossie who was murdered and dumped on the embankment over Peckham way. That fucking black D.I. over there wants us to note down the registration plate of every dark blue Ford Sierra we see driving through the red light areas. Does he give a toss how many of them fucking motors there are? No he doesn't. Waste of fucking time if you ask me.'

Mick felt sick, he felt bile rising up his throat, 'Just nipping to the bog mate.'

He stood up and rushed into the gents. Pushing open a vacant cubicle door he vomited into the toilet. The regurgitated lager burnt the back of his throat, he continued to dry retch. His stomach hurt and his eyes were streaming, tears rolled down his face caused by the strain of vomiting.

Finally, the retching stopped and slowly he stood up.

He walked out of the cubicle to the sink and splashed cold water on his face. By the time he had dried his face on a paper towel and rinsed his mouth with a mouthful of cold water from the tap he had composed himself.

He walked back out to join Ted who by now had two more pints of lager sat on the table.

'Sorry about that Ted, I needed a shit!'

Mick very gingerly took a sip of his lager and felt it burn down his throat as he swallowed it.

'Who's this dickhead that's got you running around then Ted?'

'It's that black D.I. you know the one, he's always trying to make a name for himself. It's fucking Johnston or Johnson, something like that. Whatever his name is, he's a proper pain in the arse.'

'But what's the point of it Ted? I don't get it.'

'Are you thick or just pissed? It's bleeding obvious innit. They've obviously linked a blue Ford Sierra to this murder but they ain't got the number have they, and now they want us to find it for them. Bloody wankers!' he said angrily.

For the second time that night Mick was glad he had called a cab and not driven over in his Sierra. He was also extremely glad he had disguised his car number plate with the black electricians' tape.

'One for the road then Ted? I'm off on my holidays tomorrow and don't want to be too late in bed tonight.'

'Fucking lightweight, it's only just gone ten o'clock. Go on then mate, I'll have a Bells whiskey seeing as how you're paying', he laughed before saying, 'Going anywhere nice on your jollies pal?'

'Just down to Cornwall with the wife for a couple of weeks. It's all been paid for by good old Arthur Scargill, the wanker!' he laughed and went to the bar to order the whiskies.

He'd decided there and then that his car would stay in the garage at home for the foreseeable future.

He would at some stage have to get rid of it, but for now he needed a bit of time to himself away from London.

A quick break seemed the perfect solution.

He would get the train down to Cornwall in the morning, then find a cosy little Bed and Breakfast down near the sea somewhere.

Thank fuck he'd decided to meet Ted first and not gone driving straight down to the red light area in his motor, he thought to himself.

He felt bile rise again in his throat, but this time he controlled the fear.

He turned to the busty barmaid, 'Two large Bells, love', he said.

She winked at him and laughed before saying, 'Good of you to notice sweetheart, now what do you want to drink?'

'Bells whiskies, darling', he growled.

The smile disappeared from her face, 'Alright, keep your hair on you miserable sod.'

Fucking women, tarts all of them, he thought.

CHAPTER 23

Mansfield, Nottinghamshire – June 3rd 1984

Danny Flint had been in the office of Supt Ken Jackson for twenty minutes now and the conversation was starting to get heated.

'Look sir, I'm just about holding the lid on things here', said an exasperated Danny, before continuing, 'Unless you give me back some staff soon the shit's really going to hit the fan. The team I've got have been working non-stop for three months solid now. They're working their arses off every shift, while hundreds of coppers, including the CID staff you took from me, are sitting around in vans drinking Maxpax coffee doing next to nothing, it just can't continue!'

'They're not sitting around in vans doing nothing Danny. Every PSU is tasked separately each morning from the command centre in London. They take into account current intelligence and deploy the PSU's accordingly. You've seen for yourself in the last two weeks alone, we've had three occasions around Mansfield where mass pickets have got through and caused mayhem. There's been hundreds of arrests already Danny. The bottom line is you're going to have to suck it up, that's all there is to it.'

'I'm sorry sir, but that's not good enough. All it will take is for one major incident to come in and we'll be well and truly screwed. All I'm asking for is a few more detectives to spread the load, can't you get some from the City temporarily?'

'It's not my decision Danny, I'm sorry.'

Jackson paused before continuing, 'Look Danny, I'll make representation with the Chief Constable tomorrow. All the Superintendents have been called to a meeting about the state of general policing across the County. I'll see what I can do but my guess is, every one attending that meeting will be saying the same thing. We all need more men back on the Divisions. We're reliant on the good will of the Special Constables on the uniform side Danny, its dire everywhere.'

Danny was about to protest further when suddenly there was a loud urgent knocking on the door.

'Come in!' shouted Jackson.

The door opened and Dc Rachel Moore stuck her head around the door, 'Sorry to interrupt your meeting sir, but there's an urgent telephone call for D.I. Flint.'

'The meeting's over anyway. I'll see what I can do Danny. Go get your phone call.'

'Ok Sir, you know I wouldn't ask unless it was absolutely necessary.'

'I know Danny.'

Danny then stepped out of the office, 'What's so flaming urgent Rachel? I think I was finally getting somewhere then. You know how desperate we are for more staff!'

'Sorry boss, but the phone call is from your next door neighbour, Rosemary. She told me she's called an ambulance for your Dad.'

'What?' said a shocked Danny.

Danny was striding very quickly now and Rachel was all but jogging alongside him just to keep up as he powered down the corridor back to the CID office.

'The neighbour said she'd popped round after hearing a

thump and found your dad lying on the floor. She called an ambulance first and then our office for you boss.'

Bursting into the CID office he shouted, 'Which phone?'

'My desk', said Rachel.

He picked up the receiver, 'Hello Rosemary, its Danny. What's happened?'

'Thank God you're there Danny, I heard a loud thump, so I went around to yours and banged on the door. When there was no reply I looked in through the front room window.

I could see your dad lying on the floor of the lounge. I rushed back home and got the key you gave me. I went straight in Danny but I couldn't rouse your dad so I called an ambulance and then the police station.'

'Has the ambulance arrived yet Rosemary?'

'It's just left Danny, they're taking your dad up to Kings Mill Hospital, the ambulance man told me he thought that he'd suffered a stroke, but they couldn't tell how bad yet. I'm so sorry Danny.'

He could hear the old lady sobbing as she breathed out, desperately fighting to hold back tears. Rosemary had lived in the house next door ever since Danny was five years old.

She had been great friends with his mother right up until she passed away. Danny had given her a key to his dad's house so if ever there was an emergency while he was at work, she would be able to get in. He counted his blessings now, that he'd made that decision. His voice was softer now, less urgent, 'Don't worry Rosemary none of this is your fault, you've been brilliant. You did exactly the right thing. Thank you so much, bless you. I'm going straight up to the hospital now to be with my dad, I'll call you when I know what's happening. Are you ok Rosemary? Do you want me to send someone up there to be with you? You sound a bit shaky.'

'Could you do that Danny? I'm trembling here. It was such a shock seeing your dad like that.'

Suddenly the flood gates opened and the muffled sobs turned to full blown crying.

'Someone's on their way now Rosemary, I'll send the police woman you spoke to on the phone, her name's Rachel. She'll look after you. I've got to go now Rosemary.'

'Thank you Danny', the old lady said between sobs.

Danny put the phone down and turned to Rachel, 'Did you hear all that Rachel?'

'Yes boss. You get going up to the hospital, I'll take my car up to your house. I've nearly done for the day anyway. I'll go and make Rosemary a nice cup of tea, she sounds like a lovely lady.'

'Rosemary's one of the best Rachel.'

'Don't forget to call from the hospital as soon as you know anything boss.'

Danny was already out of the door.

Rachel grabbed her keys and went to the car park. She threw her bag and coat onto the back seat of the Mini and drove out of the police station car park.

Five minutes later and she was parking her car outside the family home of Danny Flint. Rosemary was standing in the doorway with tears flooding down her face.

'Hi Rosemary, I'm Rachel we spoke earlier on the phone. Shall we go inside and I'll make us both a nice cup of tea.'

She gently put her arm around the old lady's shoulders and guided her back inside Danny's house.

Rachel didn't notice the dark green Ford Cortina parked up just along the street in the shade of a large tree. The car contained one person sitting in the driver's seat, Jimmy Wade.

He was sitting in his car watching the house where he had previously seen Rachel drop off a male passenger.

Having seen her arrive he was now even more intrigued to find out exactly who lived at the house.

About half an hour before, he'd watched the neighbour go to the front window and then race back home before returning and letting herself in. A few minutes later an ambulance arrived with its blue lights on.

The two ambulance men raced into the house emerging ten minutes later with an old man strapped to a stretcher. He could see it wasn't the man Rachel had dropped off, way too old.

Then this, a real bonus. The lovely Rachel Moore herself had turned up in her little red Mini.

He was really intrigued, and desperate to find out who lived at this house.

CHAPTER 24

Kings Mill Hospital, Mansfield – June 3rd 1984

Danny had driven like a man possessed to Kings Mill Hospital.

It was only a five-minute drive from the police station to the hospital, that was located between the towns of Mansfield and Sutton in Ashfield.

He parked the CID car in the bays reserved for police vehicles directly outside the Casualty Department of the hospital and raced through the doors.

He ran straight up to the desk and shouted breathlessly, 'My father's Frank Flint, he's just been brought here by ambulance suffering from a suspected stroke, can you tell me where he is please?'

The young woman on reception was calmness personified, 'Your father's being assessed by the doctor now, take a seat and she'll be out to see you shortly. I'll get a message to her that you're here, ok?'

'Thank you, I need to know what's happening as soon as you can please.'

Danny was not normally this good at controlling the panic he felt whenever he was in a hospital, but he had seen first-hand the way that panic and fear over a sick relative can turn normally mild mannered people into rude, aggressive morons.

He was determined he wasn't going to behave that way and would wait patiently for news. After five minutes of pacing up and down, he was losing his personal battle to remain calm and he returned to the reception desk. He stared hard at the young woman behind the counter and his voice raised a little when he said, 'I need to know what's happening with my father. Right now!'

The receptionist was about to respond to his raised voice when Danny heard a door open behind him, 'Daniel Flint?'

He immediately spun around and saw the doctor who had called his name. She was about thirty-five years of age, very slim and petite with long dark hair tied back in a ponytail. She was wearing the usual white coat and had a stethoscope hanging around her neck.

'I'm Danny Flint, how's my father?' he demanded urgently.

'Please follow me Mr Flint', she said and he noticed a London accent.

He followed her back through the door she had emerged from into a small private room.

Danny recognised the room, it was known as the relatives' room. It was where doctors and sometimes the police had to break the worse news imaginable to relatives of the badly injured or the deceased.

Danny suddenly felt dizzy, 'My dad, he's not dead is he?' he stammered.

'No Mr Flint your father's not dead, but he's a very poorly man.'

He felt the waves of initial relief rush over him, then suddenly he felt very cold and could feel his legs weakening.

Quickly he sat down on one of the chairs in the room.

'What's wrong with him?' he asked in a whisper.

The doctor sat down in the chair opposite him and looked him directly in the eyes before saying gently, 'My name's Dr Rhodes. I've been tending to your father since he was brought in about half an hour ago. Your father's had quite a serious stroke, a bleed on the brain. He's being prepped for theatre as we speak. We need to stop the bleeding and then we can assess how much damage has been done. I'm not going to sit here and lie to you Danny, at the moment your father's critically ill. Once we've done the operation we'll quickly be able to give you a better prognosis. First we've got to get your father through the operation. Are there any questions you have for me Danny?'

Danny felt like he'd been hit with a hammer. He could feel his heart pounding and the blood pulsating through his temples. He felt breathless and his mouth was suddenly very dry. He heard himself saying, 'Are you doing the operation Dr Rhodes?'

'No Danny, I'm not a neurosurgeon. The on call neurosurgeon, Mr McCaffery, is already prepping in the operating theatre. I'll be here all night though, so if you need anything just ask on reception for me. I'll keep coming back and inform you of any updates I hear. Stay in this room, nobody will disturb you here. There's a drinks machine outside the door and the toilets are across the hall from the reception desk. I'm sorry the news isn't better Danny.'

Danny stammered, 'Me too Dr Rhodes, but thank you for everything you're doing.'

'I'll be back soon, Danny. Call me Sue ok?'

'Ok, thanks Sue.'

They were undoubtedly the longest hours of his life,

he just sat there running through all the different possible outcomes in his head.

Two hours had passed by before he suddenly remembered to call home and let Rosemary know what was happening. When he finally made the call home he wasn't surprised when Rachel Moore answered the phone. 'I'm so sorry Rachel, thank you so much for staying with her, how is she?'

'She's ok boss, just a bit on tenterhooks not knowing what's happening.'

'The news isn't great Rachel. My dad's currently having an operation to stop a bleed on his brain. He's had a massive stroke. They won't know how bad the damage is until after the operation. Rachel could you do me a huge favour please, take Rosemary home and make sure she's settled, then lock my place up for the night using her key. I think It's going to be a long night for me here. Rachel, thank you so much for staying with her today. I really appreciate it I know you should've been home hours ago.'

'No problem boss, we're a team it's what we do.'

From his car parked up the street Jimmy Wade watched with interest as Rachel took the neighbour back to her own house before returning and locking the house where the old man lived, leaving it in darkness. He slunk down in his car as Rachel Moore drove by in her Mini.

It was time to find out who lived at that house once and for all. Now was his chance to get in and have a good look around. He knew already that there was no burglar alarm fitted to the house. A quick in and out would tell him all he wanted to know about the man who lived there. Who he was, and why he played such a big part in Rachel Moore's life.

Four hours after he made the call to Rachel asking her to settle Rosemary down, Danny again spoke with Dr Rhodes.

He was sitting in the relatives' room sipping a strong coffee from the vending machine when she came into the room with a beaming smile, 'Danny its good news, the surgeon's completely stopped the bleed on your father's brain. He's come through the operation well and is doing fine. He's currently in the recovery room and we've just taken him off the critical list. We're not going to be in a position to do any tests, to see how much damage has been done, for at least forty-eight hours. Danny you look dreadful, my advice is go home and get some rest. I'll be monitoring your father's progress throughout the night, if there's any change I'll let you know immediately. Where can I reach you if there's any change?'

Danny gave her his home phone number and then the number for the police station saying, 'Here's my home number and this is the direct line to the police station. I'm the Detective Inspector at Mansfield and just lately, because of this bloody strike, I've been living at work so you'll probably find me there.'

'Ah yes, the miners' strike. We've had so many injuries to striking miners and officers coming through here lately. It's been madness.'

For the first time since he had met her Danny found himself looking closely at the doctor. She had the most beautiful dark brown eyes and the most perfect white teeth. He now looked past the white coat and saw the woman not the doctor and Sue Rhodes was a very beautiful woman.

'Thank you so much Sue, for taking care of my dad. I would've gone out of my mind in this room without your updates and moral support. So thank you.'

She smiled and said, 'Well I'm sure I'll be seeing much more of you Inspector, I'm still going to be looking after your dad.'

'That's good to know Sue, thanks. I think I prefer Danny to Inspector.'

'Ok Danny, see you soon.'

A near exhausted Danny then made the short drive home, his head was spinning. He was very worried about his father but also excited about meeting Sue Rhodes. There was a strange mixture of emotions racing through him as he stopped the car outside his house. As soon as he got out of the car he saw that the front door of his house was slightly open.

Suddenly his fatigue was forgotten and all his senses instantly kicked in.

Somebody was in his house.

Silently he crept into the house, his fists bunched and his muscles taught ready to launch himself at any intruder. He locked the front door behind him, then quietly and methodically stalked through every room.

Whoever had been in the house was now long gone.

Danny switched on the lights and found that a window at the rear of the house was open after being forced from the outside. Whoever climbed in through the window had then let themselves out the front door. The perfect end to the perfect day, he thought to himself.

There were letters strewn over the lounge floor and a photo of him receiving a commendation from the Chief Constable had been moved from the sideboard where it normally sat and was now placed flat on top of the TV.

He quickly checked the house but his cursory search revealed nothing of any value obviously missing. He wondered if the burglar had been disturbed, there were a lot of valuable items on show that would normally have been taken by a thief.

It was all very strange.

Danny was too tired to think about any of it now, and way too tired to really check thoroughly to see if anything had been stolen. He would make out the burglary report in the morning after he had spoken to Rachel.

All he could think about now was sleep.

CHAPTER 25

Proteus Army Camp, Nottinghamshire – June 20th 1984

It was a beautiful June morning.

The sun was out and the temperature had risen steadily as the day wore on.

Sgt Mick Reynolds was lying on his back staring at the blue sky, there wasn't a cloud to be seen anywhere.

He was shirtless on the grass, outside the dormitory hut he shared with the rest of his PSU serial. There had been no deployment that morning and they had been instructed to remain at the disused Army camp where they were based.

This order had initially been met with groans at three thirty that morning as the men all anticipated another boring day. As the day had gone on though and the sun had got hotter and hotter, the men were all glad of the day off now and were busy topping up their tans on yet another glorious June day.

A young constable from his PSU approached Mick and asked, 'Skipper any objections if a couple of us nip into the town to get a few cold cans?'

'That'll be fine once your shift finishes at three o'clock, just make sure you're wearing civvies, you know the rules.'

It was now two thirty in the afternoon.

'Ok Skip, do you want anything from the shop?'

'I could do with a tube of toothpaste. I've run out this morning, I'm not bothered which brand. I'll give you the dosh when you get back. Don't go upsetting the locals and getting yourself in the shit. I won't back you up if there's any trouble, understand?'

'Yes Skip, straight there and straight back, we'll keep our heads down. Are you sure you don't want a few cold beers bringing back?'

'Yeah go on then, I could murder a cold beer, cheers.'

Mick was cautious about allowing his staff into the town, there had been a couple of occasions recently when officers from PSU's billeted at Proteus Camp had been involved, while off duty, in scuffles and altercations with striking miners in both Ollerton and Edwinstowe.

The officers involved had been dealt with swiftly and were immediately sent back to their own force where they had been subsequently charged under the discipline code.

Although strike duty was onerous, boring and sometimes dangerous, nobody wanted to get sent back to their own force. All officers deployed as mutual aid from foreign forces were earning a small fortune during the strike in overtime and allowances.

After his last period of leave back in London and his meeting with Ted Smith, Mick had been fretting about how he would be able to afford to get rid of his Sierra.

Thanks to Arthur Scargill and the strike, all the overtime he was earning now meant that problem had solved itself. He could now easily afford to scrap the Sierra and buy a brand new one.

Scrapping the car was definitely the best option with the least chance of the car ever being traced back to him. It was something he planned to do at the end of the strike. For now, the car was safely tucked up in his garage at home in Wembley.

Just after being given the news that there would be no deployment for his PSU that day, Mick was taken to one side by the Operations Commander at Proteus who informed him that his serial was earmarked for a different role. This new duty would be to provide the daily escort for working miners, wanting to break the strike going into Warsop Main Colliery.

The new role would start next week, at the moment there were only two miners willing to go into work at that particular colliery. They had been going into the mine in secret for over a week with no problems but now the government were keen to make a big show of the fact that miners were starting to drift back into work.

There had been ugly scenes at one of the other collieries nearby when miners started to drift back to work. Pickets from South Yorkshire descended in droves and the risk of violent confrontation was very high.

Mick relished the prospect of this new duty as although it would still mean a very early start, there was the promise of plenty of action instead of the mind blowing boredom of intercept duties standing around at crossroads out in the countryside. The real bonus was that he and his PSU would have an early finish every day. Another Police Support Unit would be used to escort the working miners out of the mine. The only downside being they were now expected to be on it for a minimum six-week period. This meant it would be very nearly the end of July before they got any time off back in London.

When Mick later briefed his PSU about the new duty, the fact they wouldn't be stood down until almost the end of July was met by a loud chorus of cheers by the men, it would mean yet another bumper pay day heading their way.

Mick had been a bit more reluctant to celebrate.

All it meant to him was that Rita had achieved one more stay of execution. He had used the time spent in Cornwall well and had identified a number of locations where he could easily dispose of her body, safe in the knowledge that it would never be discovered. His favourite option was an old abandoned tin mine he'd found near to an isolated stretch of rugged coastline, not far from Penzance.

The mine was boarded up with wriggly tin that could easily be moved. He'd ventured inside and was excited to find an abandoned shaft that was at least fifty feet deep.

He had thrown a couple of rocks in and could hear that fifty feet down the shaft was full of water. A correctly weighted body would sink to the bottom of the shaft and would never be found.

Mick found himself smiling at the prospect of rolling his wife into that disused tin mine in the very near future.

The next time he was home he planned to buy a cheap Ford Escort van. He intended to scrap his Sierra, and then use the van to dump his dead wife. He would then sell the Escort van and buy a brand new Ford Sierra Cosworth.

Happy days.

CHAPTER 26

Warsop Miners Welfare, Warsop, Notts – June 21st 1984

The main hall of Warsop Miners Welfare was used to hosting fun filled, joyous activities. It was the heart and soul of the small mining community. In normal times, every Friday and Saturday evening, the hall would be filled with men and women spending their hard earned cash on beer and cigarettes, while watching the entertainment or playing Bingo. During the week the hall would be used for all manner of community based activities such as Keep Fit classes and Mother and Toddler groups, it was even the venue for the annual vegetable and flower show.

These were not normal times though and ever since the start of the industrial dispute, the main hall had been taken over by the local strike committee and was now being used on a daily basis to provide hot meals for families that were struggling to make ends meet.

It was the place where strategies were discussed about how to move the strike forward and where various fund raising ideas were put forward. Even during these troubled times, the main hall was still usually a positive and upbeat place. The women who provided the hot food saw to that. Although the strike was hitting them hard, they were fiercely loyal to their men and to the cause.

Today was very different.

The mood in the hall was dark and sombre, it resembled a wake and there was a totally despondent air in the room. The large room was full of tough men cradling pints of beer in their big hands, taking small sips. Their heads were bowed and there was a low rumble of murmurings as they talked quietly amongst themselves. A thick pall of acrid blue smoke from their cigarettes hung in the air.

The strike committee had called a general meeting and asked as many of the striking miners to attend as possible. The committee had then informed the gathered miners that the strike at their mine was about to be broken. Rumours were rife that a few individuals had decided to provide scab labour and go back to work.

The news was a devastating blow to the strikers and was met with anger and incredulity. The men gathered in the hall knew that once the drift back to work started it would only grow. In that tense, angry atmosphere the men were slowly coming to terms with the fact their months of sacrifice was going to count for nothing.

They would try and turn it around and get the strike solid again but deep down they all knew defeat was on the horizon. The mood in the hall had now turned from anger to an almost resigned despondency.

Jimmy Wade was sitting with two other men at a table next to the door that led into the reception area of the Welfare.

'Can you believe it Jimmy; we've got fucking scabs at our pit?' said one of the men at the table.

Jimmy replied, 'I think it's all bullshit Stan, nobody's seen anyone go in yet?'

'I'm telling you, it's the thin end of the wedge Jimmy, once one scab sets foot through the gate we're all fucked. All this shit will have been for nothing.'

Stan slowly shook his head, before taking another sip of his beer.

What Stan didn't know was that Jimmy Wade had contacted British Coal the day before to make arrangements about going back to work. He'd stayed out for as long as he could, but his savings were now gone.

He had bills and a mortgage to pay if he wanted to keep his house, he was not about to let Arthur Scargill or any of his Yorkshire bully boys make him lose it.

As he looked around the Welfare now at the despondent, broken faces of his colleagues he was starting to harbour a few doubts. He knew that every man in the room was going through the same shit, not just him.

His thoughts were troubling.

Margaret Thatcher was a fucking cow and no mistake, she had deliberately orchestrated the strike to start in March, knowing it would continue through the Spring, Summer and Autumn when demand for electricity was less.

She knew that the stockpiles of coal at the power stations were mountainous and that she could count on a well-trained, almost para military style police force, the likes of which had never been seen before in the UK. The woman was an unfeeling cow, all this grief and hardship caused to entire communities just so she could achieve her own political ambitions.

Suddenly the door to the welfare burst open, shaking Wade from his personal thoughts. A group of a dozen or so very large burly men strode purposefully into the Welfare.

'Is this where t' scabs are drinking then?' shouted the leader of the group in an accent that was obviously from South Yorkshire.

Not getting any response he continued, 'We've come down here today, dodging t' filth on t' way, to impress on you men to stay strong and support t' fight. We've heard there are some here thinking of scabbing. I'm here to tell you, don't even think about it.'

A voice at the very front of the hall shouted back, 'Who do you think you are? There's no scabs here. It's bullies like you that's caused all this shit, you and that lunatic Scargill. The little ginger twat has danced to every note of that witch Thatcher's tune! So why don't you fuck off back to whatever part of Yorkshire you've come from. Don't come in here like you own the place giving these good men shit!'

A loud cheer went up from the gathering of Warsop Miners.

The Yorkshireman who had spoken out, now held his massive tattooed arms up with his palms outspread in a sign of appeasement and shouted, 'I can't agree with you about brother Scargill, but it's good to hear you men are still up for t' fight and there's still fire and passion in your bellies.'

Another cheer went up.

'We've travelled down today from Grimethorpe, just to let you know, you're not in this fight alone. If there are backsliders here who want to scab and shit on us all, we'll be down every day to stop them getting through t' gates of t' pit. We'll hunt the scabs down to their homes and burn them out, like rats out of a nest. Are we solid brothers?'

More loud cheers.

Jimmy Wade had heard enough, any feelings of pity he felt for his fellow Notts miners had just evaporated listening to them cheering the big Yorkshire bastard. Who did he think he was coming down here preaching that he was going to burn people out of their homes.

Jimmy Wade despised being told what he could and couldn't do, he hated being a follower, a sheep. He had always considered himself to be the wolf that selected and killed the weak in society. The loud mouthed Yorkshireman had made his mind up for him. He was definitely going back to work on Monday. Fuck Scargill, fuck Thatcher and fuck being a scab, he would never be a scab.

He was Jimmy Wade.

He finished the rest of his pint and slipped out of the Welfare, he walked to his car still seething at the loud mouthed moron from Yorkshire. As he drove slowly home he began to calm down and his mind turned to other matters and to a certain project he had been busy with while he had time on his hands.

What to do about Detective Rachel Moore?

He knew everything about her now, she lived alone in a first floor flat in Mansfield, she drove a red Mini Cooper. The only significant man in her life was her boss, Detective Inspector Danny Flint. She worked at Mansfield Police Station and it appeared that she was a workaholic the hours she spent at that place. He knew it would be difficult to get close enough to do what he intended to do and now the project would have to go on the back burner for a little while. Now he intended going back to work, he would have less time to plan.

He knew the outcome for her was inevitable.

Once he had selected the target it was only a matter of time and careful planning.

CHAPTER 27

Peckham Police Station, London – June 21st 1984

Time had passed by in a blur since the meeting between Glyn Johnson and Craig Fraser at the Black Prince pub.

Glyn had used that meeting followed by another with Jack Swift at his home, to try and hammer out a strategy to move the investigation into the brutal murder of Jenny Taylor forward.

His team of detectives had methodically carried out all enquiries into the purchasers of forensic suits.

On one occasion the hopes of the enquiry team were significantly raised when they discovered a single order for just two forensic suits. The detectives quickly traced the recipient of the order to a private address in Hackney.

Glyn immediately deployed an arrest team to the address. The team were making entry to the property within twenty minutes, only to find it occupied by a transgender dominatrix who answered to the name of Trixie, but whose real name was Peter Geddes.

Geddes was detained and his address searched.

Detectives searching the property following the arrest of Geddes, found that the basement of the house had been converted into a makeshift dungeon ready for use by his clients.

Geddes was interviewed at length and described in graphic detail to the interviewing officers how part of the experience for some clients was for him to dress up as a surgeon who then prescribed and carried out all kinds of sado- masochistic treatments.

The two forensic suits had been ordered from the suppliers so that Geddes could realistically play the part of the surgeon.

Both suits were seized and submitted for forensic examination. Although several traces of blood were found on the suits, none of the traces matched the blood group of Jenny Taylor.

Geddes was subsequently released on bail and the Vice Squad informed to keep an eye on his address as a potential brothel.

The team were getting hit with dead end after dead end and the frustration was starting to show.

Glyn had pinned his hopes on finding the dark blue Ford Sierra described by Lee Skipton. He felt sure the killer would at some time revisit the red light areas.

Some of the Vice Squad were reluctant at first to log sightings of vehicles matching the description provided by Skipton. Glyn and Craig had personally visited each Vice Office in the Metropolitan Police area to impress on them the importance of finding this car and hopefully their killer, before he struck again.

Glyn's greatest fear was another murder happening soon after the first, which would mean the press whipping up a frenzy of sensationalist reporting about the emergence of another serial killer on the loose in London.

The last thing he wanted was another Yorkshire Ripper scenario here in the capital. His hopes of a new lead had been boosted again when Vice Squad officers found a further potential witness.

A well-known prostitute, Selena James, had approached Vice Squad officers near Wembley and told them how she was picked up by a punter in his own car from the same area Jenny Taylor had been abducted.

The punter had suddenly turned nasty and punched her in the face before he kicked her out of his car.

She complained her nose had been smashed.

The Vice Squad Officers, at first thought it was just a punter trying to get his jollies for nothing but then the prostitute told them that he'd already paid her, before the assault happened. Their interest picked up even more when she told them the car was a dark coloured Ford Sierra, either black or dark blue. The Vice Squad officers had taken the woman straight to the incident room where she was interviewed for over two hours by Craig Fraser and a female detective from the enquiry team. Again it turned out to be a major disappointment, the woman could remember next to nothing about the man who assaulted her. The description she gave the detectives was that he was a white man, late thirties to early forties with short dark hair.

He was generally smart and she remembered that he was wearing dark trousers and boots that were well polished.

The description, for what it was worth, was circulated out to all stations of the Metropolitan Police, the City of London Police and the British Transport Police.

Craig in his Scottish brogue had commented, "That description could fit two thirds of the Met"

Glyn Johnson could feel the enquiry stalling again.

The only positive was that the killer hadn't struck again. Yet.

CHAPTER 28

Kings Mill Hospital, Mansfield – June 24th 1984

Thoughts were racing through Danny Flint's head as he sat in the car park outside Kings Mill Hospital.

It had been three weeks since his father had suffered a massive stroke and three weeks since he first encountered Dr Sue Rhodes. That was also the same day his father's house had been burgled. All of these things were rushing in and out of his mind as he tried to clear his head before visiting his ailing father in the hospital.

The year was flying by.

He still had no extra staff at work and even with the best efforts of his small team a backlog of outstanding cases was beginning to form. Danny made a mental note to again challenge Superintendent Jackson over the current staffing levels as soon as he got into work that morning.

First things first.

Every morning since his father had suffered the stroke, Danny had made the short drive to the hospital to check on his condition before going into work. His father, Frank, was still on one of the high dependency wards.

The stroke had been far more catastrophic than they had first hoped, as a result Frank had completely lost the use of the right side of his body. His speech had disappeared completely, although there had been a very slight improvement of late. Any words he attempted were barely comprehensible.

There was also incontinence, since the stroke his father had lost control of his bladder and bowel movements.

Danny visited him twice every day. Once early in the morning, and then again last thing at night, work permitting.

Each morning he went into the ward filled with hope and determination to get his father well enough to return home so he could look after him. Every evening he left the hospital feeling desolate and desperately sad.

Danny was only too aware that the prognosis for any kind of full recovery wasn't good. He had a meeting scheduled with Dr Rhodes this morning to discuss what would be the best thing for his father, now that he was well enough to be moved from the hospital.

He made his way up to the ward and was surprised to see Sue Rhodes already standing at his father's bedside.

His father was fast asleep and Sue put her index finger over her lips signalling for Danny to approach quietly so as not to wake him.

She then stepped across to meet Danny and took his arm, 'Your father's had a very bad night Danny. He's only just dropped off to sleep. Unfortunately, there'll be a lot of nights like this in the future. He's going to need twenty-four-hour care and with the job you do there's no way you're going to be able to provide that for him, even with the help of your lovely neighbour.'

'What are you saying Sue?'

'I'm saying, in the kindest way I know how, to consider looking at the Nursing Home option. I know you're resistant to the idea Danny, he's your father and you want to care for him, I do understand that, but this is about what's best for him and also what you can achieve as a son.'

She tenderly gripped his forearm before continuing, 'Danny I've got a day off tomorrow, why don't you let me show you around some of the nursing homes in the area. There are some very good ones that are run in an extremely professional manner with competent and friendly staff.'

Tears welled in Danny's eyes and he felt a huge lump forming in his throat. He rubbed his eyes and swallowed hard before nodding slowly.

'Ok Sue, my head's telling me that every word you're saying makes sense, but in my heart it's so hard to even think about my dad being in a home. There's a chance I can get away from work for a few hours after ten o'clock tomorrow morning, so we can go and have a look by all means. I can't promise it will change my mind though', he said shakily.

'That's ok Danny I'm not trying to force you into anything. I'll drive over in my car and pick you up from the front of the police station tomorrow morning at ten o'clock. Just come with me and have a look, I think you'll be surprised what's out there.'

'Thanks Sue. Won't your husband mind you spending your day off with a strange man?'

'What made you think I have a husband Danny?'

'I didn't see how you couldn't have a husband, you're a beautiful intelligent woman.'

'Be careful detective, you'll have me blushing, I'll see you tomorrow.'

'Thanks Sue, I really do appreciate all you're doing for us, see you tomorrow.'

Danny smiled at her before sitting at his father's bedside

and gently holding his hand. There was still half an hour before he had to be at work.

At the door to the ward Sue paused, she turned and looked at Danny. She couldn't help but notice the thrill of excitement she felt about her appointment tomorrow morning with the dark, handsome detective. She noticed how quickly he had coloured up when she commented that she wasn't married.

Sue Rhodes was a very private person and nobody who worked at Kings Mill Hospital knew her story. When she was in her final year studying medicine at Oxford University she had met and married an American who was also in the final year of a medical degree at Oxford.

Peter Rhodes was a tall, muscular, sun tanned Texan from Austin.

It had been love at first sight for both of them. They both graduated with first class degrees, and were married a fortnight later. Sue achieved her ambition and started work at Great Ormond Street as a junior doctor to follow her dream of becoming a paediatrician. Peter had followed his own path and became a volunteer doctor working for Medicine Sans Frontiers.

His first assignment was to provide emergency medical care in Angola, Central Africa during the bloody Civil War.

They had only been married nine months when Sue received a telegram informing her that Peter had been captured and subsequently killed by rebel forces who believed he was an American Special Forces soldier advising the Government troops.

Sue was devastated, initially turning her back on medicine. She believed that it was Peter's career and love of medicine that was responsible for taking him away from her. Eventually she realised that his death was nothing to do with medicine. It had taken six months for Sue to return to her passion, caring for the sick.

Initially she returned to work at Great Ormond Street but after a few years of just going through the motions she realised what she needed was to make a fresh start in her life, she wanted a complete change of scenery.

Three years ago she had applied for and subsequently accepted a role in the Casualty Department at Kings Mill Hospital, she had remained in that post ever since.

When she first started doing emergency work, she somehow felt close to Peter, it had been his passion to help the sick and injured when they needed it most.

Sue still wore her wedding band, but on a gold necklace around her neck.

It was the first time since the death of her husband that she had even considered feelings for another man, it felt strange but also very natural.

In the tenderness the detective showed towards his sick father, Sue could see the same care and compassion that had first attracted her to her late husband.

She hoped the detective felt the same way about her.

Tomorrow couldn't come soon enough.

CHAPTER 29

Mansfield Police Station, Notts – June 25th 1984

It was nearing eight o'clock in the morning when Danny drove his grey BMW saloon into the car park at Mansfield Police Station. He'd spent nearly an hour at the hospital, as usual, visiting his father.

He knew the rest of his small team would be arriving at work around fifteen minutes later and he wanted to give himself a little time to sort out anything that may have come in overnight. He found a bay towards the rear of the car park and parked up, grabbing his jacket from the front passenger seat he walked briskly into the building.

Sleep had not come easily the previous night. His mind had been racing. Even now his head was filled with a strange sense of guilt, over today's trip with Sue Rhodes to look at nursing homes for his father. The guilt was not because he was looking for a nursing home, he'd already decided that was the right course of action and the best thing to do for his father. Danny felt uneasy because he realised that he was actually looking forward to spending some of the day with Dr Sue Rhodes.

He hadn't experienced these feelings about a woman since his divorce a few years back.

He'd been out for drinks or meals on a couple of occasions with different women, but had always known deep down that they were just one off dates and that nothing would ever come of them.

This felt completely different though, he just hoped that the doctor felt the same way, or all these feelings would come crashing down.

He walked into the main CID office and sat at one of the desks. Danny had long since abandoned his own small office. With only four in the team, it felt aloof and somehow wrong to be sitting away from the staff that had worked so hard over the last four months.

He checked the tele-printer messages and was relieved to find there was nothing urgent that would need their attention immediately. Next he made a telephone call to the cells and asked the sergeant in charge if there were any prisoners detained overnight that would require CID officers to interview and process.

Again he felt an unexplained wave of relief wash over him when the sergeant said, 'No boss, nobody's been locked up overnight that the CID need to look at. There's only one daft lad who broke into a shed and tried to nick some tools, but it's a job that one of the uniform lads can deal with easy enough'.

'Thanks Mike, I appreciate that. If anything comes in later, all four of us are working today so ring the office if we're needed, ok?'

'Will do boss.'

As he put the phone down he made a mental note to ask Andy how he was getting on with enquiries into the mysterious burglary at his own home on the night his father had suffered the stroke. Gradually the team drifted in, first in was Rob quickly followed by Andy and Rachel.

'Aye aye! coming in together like that, people will start to talk', said Rob laughing.

Rachel quickly retorted, 'Only if they're small minded, jealous individuals with a particularly brutalised nose, Sarge!'

Rob laughed out loud now, 'Harsh Miss Moore, very harsh!'

Danny said good morning to both detectives before turning to Andy and saying, 'How are things progressing with the break in at my house Andy? You're aware that I consider you to be the best man to investigate this matter and that I'm expecting an arrest imminently', he said tongue firmly in cheek.

'I've finished all the house to house enquiries on your street boss. The only thing of any note was a young woman about twelve houses along from yours, who remembers seeing a dark coloured car parked up for a few hours, she thinks it was the day of your break in but can't be sure. She's seen the car a few times and remembers on one occasion seeing a blonde guy sitting in it. It was a nice smart car so she didn't pay it too much attention. She can't give any sort of description of the man in the car apart from the fact he's blonde.'

'Ok Andy, thanks. Don't spend any more time on it. I'm sure you've got plenty of other work to do. Let me know if there are any other burglaries reported around that area though.'

'Will do boss.'

At a quarter to ten the office phone rang.

Danny picked it up quickly, 'Hello, Detective Inspector Flint'.

It was the front desk sergeant, 'Sir, there's a woman by the name of Susan Rhodes at the counter, says she's got an appointment to see you this morning.'

'Thanks Jack I'm on my way.'

Danny put the phone down, turned to Rob and said, 'Rob I'm going out for a few hours, it's to do with my father. I'm trying to find a nursing home that will be able to look after him when he gets out of hospital. I've got my pager if you need me urgently, ok.'

'No problem boss, everything's under control here, I'll see you later. Good luck, I hope you find somewhere nice for your dad.'

When Danny arrived at the front desk he was surprised how different Sue looked. He'd only ever seen her in a work environment at the hospital, dressed in the baggy white doctors' coat and with her hair tied back off her face.

He always thought she looked good at the hospital dressed like that, but today she was simply stunning.

Her dark brown hair was untied and fell loosely over her shoulders, framing her face. She was wearing a clinging mustard yellow T shirt, tucked into a pair of tight fitting blue denim jeans. Danny could now see that under that baggy white doctors' coat, Sue had an absolutely stunning figure.

Danny realised he was staring and quickly said, 'Sorry Sue, but you look so different.'

She smiled and said, 'No problem Danny, are you still ok to go?'

'I'll need to be back around two o'clock this afternoon but I've left my sergeant in charge and I've got my pager, so yeah I guess I'm good to go.'

As they walked out of the police station to her midnight blue Triumph Stag she said, 'I hope you don't think I'm pushing you too hard Danny, but this will be the best thing for your father, and for you in the long run. Trust me.'

He smiled, 'Trust me I'm a doctor, where have I heard that before?'

She smiled back, 'Very funny, Inspector.'

As she drove her car away from the police station she said, 'The first place I want to show you is over at Pleasley, not far from here. It's probably the best in this area for specialist 24-hour care. It's a wonderful nursing home but it's not cheap. I think you'll see what I mean when we get there.'

'It's not about the money Sue. I want my father to be looked after but I want him to be happy as well. Pleasley sounds good, I was worried they'd all be miles away. What's the name of this place?'

'It's imaginatively called the Pleasley Vale Specialist Care Centre.'

Again she smiled.

He watched her closely as she drove the car. As they spoke on the journey she would often smile revealing those perfect white teeth, and causing the faintest of lines to crease around her dark brown eyes.

Danny felt almost mesmerised by that beautiful smile.

CHAPTER 30

Secret location near Warsop, Notts –
June 25th 1984

The disused quarry had been well chosen for its clandestine purpose.

It was set well back from the access road and both the rundown office buildings and the deep overgrown quarry itself were not visible from the road. It was also surrounded by high, well-maintained fences that had originally been put in place to keep inquisitive children and teenagers out.

Danvers & Son Stone Quarry had not been a working quarry for over five years and the office buildings at the heart of it were all dilapidated and had fallen into a bad state of disrepair.

However, the large iron gates at the only entrance to the quarry had recently been fitted with a very large, brand new padlock. The location of the quarry was a fifteen-minute car journey from Warsop town centre. Most of the inhabitants of that town had forgotten the quarry's very existence.

It was now nearing four thirty in the morning and two unmarked Ford Transit vans were being driven at speed along the quiet country lane towards the quarry entrance.

In between the two navy blue Transit vans was a private taxi.

The taxi contained the driver and three passengers. The driver and two of the passengers had made this journey every day, Monday to Friday, for the last two weeks. For the third passenger in the taxi, this morning was the first time.

Jimmy Wade sat quietly in the front passenger seat of the taxi, fiddling with the small haversack that contained his lunch.

It had been four o'clock that morning, just as the early dawn light was pushing back the dark of night and nobody was about, that he'd been picked up by the taxi at the bottom of Peafield Lane, just a short walk from his home on Marples Avenue.

The two other passengers were already in the taxi having been picked up at the other end of Mansfield Woodhouse. He didn't know either of the two men but assumed they worked on a different shift at the mine. They were laughing and joking in the back of the taxi, but Jimmy knew instinctively that the humour and brevity was masking anxiety and fear.

Jimmy remained quiet throughout the journey, there was no reason for him to speak to anybody in the taxi. From the moment he got into the taxi he had spent his time looking out of the front passenger window.

Everywhere the streets were so still and quiet.

The taxi driver had deliberately taken a route that avoided the town centre of Warsop and Jimmy stared straight ahead at the cats' eyes glistening in the centre of the road, illuminated by the taxis headlights.

It was almost hypnotic as they hurtled along the country lanes. After ten minutes of fast driving the driver suddenly pulled into a layby at the side of the lane. Waiting in the layby were the two unmarked Transit vans.

They were dark blue in colour and had been modified by having large metal grilles fitted to all the side windows as well as the front windscreen. The side windows of the vans were made from a strong Perspex like material and not glass. This Perspex was slightly tinted but Jimmy could still make out that the vans were full of uniformed police officers.

Without pausing in the layby all three vehicles quickly pulled away and continued down the country lanes to the quarry. The taxi in the centre with a Transit van front and rear of the small convoy.

At the metal gates that formed the entrance to Danvers & Son Stone Quarry the vehicles stopped just long enough for two officers to jump out of the first Transit van.

They unlocked the large padlock and swung the gates open. Once the convoy had driven through the gates the two officers closed them immediately. They remained there, while the vehicles were driven along the road towards the disused office buildings at the centre of the quarry itself.

The convoy finally came to a halt in the large car park near to the falling down offices, well away from any prying eyes.

Jimmy hadn't been aware that this place even existed.

He and the two other passengers got out of the taxi and walked over to the buildings. Immediately the driver of the taxi gunned the engine and sped off back towards the gates.

The two other miners that had been in the taxi walked off a short distance and stood together in the doorway of one of the buildings, leaving Jimmy standing on his own.

That suited him, he thought the two men were morons anyway. Jimmy waited quietly, sitting on the window sill of one of the other disused buildings.

He watched fascinated as the policemen got out of the two vans and started donning their individual riot gear. They started to resemble medieval knights clad in ancient armour.

This armour, however, was made from a hard plastic based material and was being put on over flame retardant overalls. They had plates for their chests, their knees and lower legs and also their arms and shoulders.

Finally, they put on navy blue helmets with a hard plastic visor, these were similar in appearance to a motor cycle crash helmet. Jimmy sat watching closely, he wasn't feeling nervous, just fascinated.

He knew it would be like this. There had been plenty of coverage on the news every day from other pits where miners had made the decision to return to work. They were forced to run a gauntlet of hate every morning just to get into work to feed their families. Watching those news reports had made him feel angry not afraid.

Jimmy saw that one of the police officers had broken away from the group and was now walking towards him, he was carrying his blue crash helmet by its strap.

'Good morning son, you feeling alright?' he asked in a broad cockney accent.

'I'm all good, ta', said Jimmy

'I'm Sgt Mick Reynolds, I'm in charge of the two vans that are going to escort you in to the colliery. Do you want a smoke?'

Jimmy had only really registered the last part of the sentence and right now he could really do with a cigarette.

'A fag would be great thanks. I'm sorry I didn't catch your name.'

The sergeant offered the open packet of John Player Specials to Jimmy who took one. He then struck a match and lit Jimmy's cigarette before lighting his own with the same match.

Taking a large pull on the cigarette before exhaling a cloud of blue smoke, the policeman said, 'I'm Sgt Reynolds.

Call me Mick. You must be Jimmy Wade, the third man in our intrepid group.'

'Sergeant, I've never considered myself part of any group, thanks for the fag by the way.'

'You're welcome Jimmy, and drop the sergeant bit, my name's Mick. I've always felt like that too. Its weird innit, I mean I work for a massive organisation and yet I've never really felt part of the group as a whole. Does that make sense?'

'You can be part of an organisation but still retain your own personality and have your own mind. Yeah, that makes massive sense to me Mick.'

'I can see we're gonna get on ok, I hope you're ready for what's coming Jimmy. It's a bloody nightmare from start to finish getting into the pit. Once we're through the gates its fine, it's just getting through the fucking gates.'

'How do we get in, are we all going in your vans?'

'No Jimmy old son, this is where the lies, lies and damned lies come into it. If we all went into the pit travelling in two small vans it'd appear as if no one's back at work. Mrs Thatcher and the government want people to think the strike's collapsing so we travel in the vans, but you and Pinky and Perky over there will be travelling into the pit between our vans in a great big fuck off coach', he laughed.

'If your vans are all geared up for what's coming, how's a fucking coach going to be safe?'

Jimmy cast his mind back to the images on the TV and he remembered what sort of coach it would be. He'd seen these coaches driving at speed into other pits, they were kitted out with mesh all over the windows and metal skirts protecting the tyres.

He took a last long drag from the cigarette and exhaled the smoke saying, 'I know, we're going in on one of them so called battle buses aren't we!'

Mick laughed out loud, 'You've got it Jimmy, the battle bus! Ours will be along in about ten minutes. Make sure you don't get crushed in the crowd trying to get on board. Just between you and me Jimmy, we're expecting this to be the norm for the next month or so. We may get one or two more who drift back to work, but that's all. I think you'd better get used to this routine for the foreseeable future old son.'

'Thanks Mick, I'll be fine. Been good talking to you, and thanks for the cigarette.'

Jimmy took a last quick pull of the exhausted cigarette before throwing it on the floor and grinding it out with the heel of his boot.

Mick Reynolds was deep in thought as he walked slowly back to his men waiting by the vans. This new guy had got something about him, Mick hoped he'd keep coming into work after he saw for himself what it was like trying to get in the pit later.

As Jimmy watched the sergeant walk back to his men he felt intrigued. He had studied the man as he was speaking. There was something about Sgt Mick Reynolds that he was fascinated by. He had a feeling they were similar in a lot of ways.

Then it came to him, he knew in that instant what was intriguing him. He knew that they were the same in one particular special way. Jimmy always trusted his intuition, it had never been wrong before. Already he was looking forward to talking to the man again tomorrow, he couldn't wait to find out more about Police Sergeant Mick Reynolds.

He found himself smiling, he would have to be careful, the man was a police sergeant after all, but he was excited about exploring this further. His thoughts were interrupted by the rumble of a diesel engine and looking up he saw a battered, cream and brown coloured coach being driven up the lane towards the quarry buildings. The old coach was in such a dilapidated state Jimmy wondered how it was even allowed to be on a road.

He heard Sgt Reynolds shouting, 'Come on lads, look lively, the battle bus is here. The sooner we get these blokes into the pit, the quicker we get our breakfast.'

Jimmy watched fascinated as instantly all the cops threw away half-drunk coffees and stood on half smoked cigarettes before obediently jumping into their vans.

The coach came to a stop outside the buildings, Jimmy could now clearly see that it had been modified a lot, and was worthy of its nickname, "Battle Bus"

All the windows on the coach had been replaced with the same hard Perspex material that was on the police vans and the front windscreen was covered in a steel grille while the side Perspex windows were covered with chicken wire. There was a metal plate covering the radiator grill and metal skirts covered the wheel arches to protect the tyres.

The driver of the coach opened the door from the inside, there was no outer handle. He was a man in his late fifties, wearing a dirty, check flat cap and a scruffy ripped donkey jacket over a pair of greasy, oily overalls. He had a half smoked roll up cigarette hanging from his mouth, 'In you get, hurry up, we haven't got all day.'

The remnants of the roll up fag moved as he spoke.

Jimmy and the other two men climbed into the battle bus and the driver secured the door behind them. There was a large metal bar attached to the door that would prevent it from being yanked open.

The other two remained at the front of the bus next to each other just behind the driver. It was like they were Siamese twins, joined at the hip, thought Jimmy.

He made his way down the bus until he got about half way along. He sat on the near side of the coach, next to the window. As the coach started moving he saw the other men pulling scarves around their faces to hide their identity.

'Fuck that for a game of soldiers!' he said aloud.

Jimmy was wearing a black coat and a black woollen hat which he immediately took off revealing his blonde hair, he was fucked if he was going to hide from anybody.

The small convoy paused outside the quarry gates until the padlock had been replaced and the two cops had jumped back into their vans. They literally flew down the country lanes until finally Jimmy started to recognise the streets that led to Warsop Main Colliery. He could now clearly hear raised voices and shouting above the noise of the diesel engine of the coach as the convoy approached the gates to the colliery.

Suddenly everything slowed down as the first police Transit van battled its way through a sea of bodies on the road. There were well over a hundred pickets and a similar number of policemen all in the road leading to the pit entrance.

Jimmy looked out of the window and saw that many of the policemen were using large wooden batons to force the pickets back. The coach itself was being hit with a barrage of various objects, large rocks hammered into the Perspex, a piece of metal girder was hurled at the window near to where

Jimmy sat. There was a huge bang as the piece of metal struck the Perspex and bounced off. Jimmy didn't flinch. The coach inched its way inexorably forward as the cops on the ground outside battled to clear the way for the convoy.

Suddenly there was a commotion from the back of the coach. Jimmy quickly spun around in his seat and could see three miners were hanging off the back of the coach trying to force open the emergency exit. Almost instantly the three men were battered to the floor by the police and dragged away. Progress began to get a little easier, but still the missiles rained down heavily onto the coach and the two Police vans that were crawling along one at the front and one at the rear.

Then, as it became clear to the gathered pickets that the convoy was going to get through the picket line, a chant from the mob started and grew steadily to a deafening crescendo.

'Scab! Scab! Scab!'

That single word was repeated over and over again with increasing levels of venom and hatred.

Jimmy could now see the faces and the features of the striking miners, his former work colleagues. Their faces were contorted with rage and anger, as they shouted that single word at the coach and its occupants. Several miners Jimmy knew personally, pointed an accusing finger at him as they screamed the word, 'SCAB!' in his direction. He could almost see the veins in their heads throbbing, as their faces turned red with an incandescent anger.

Jimmy started to roar with laughter at the sight of their mind numbing stupidity. In his eyes they were sheep, very loud and very angry sheep.

Jimmy didn't stop laughing until they were through the gates and being driven at speed to the pit head buildings away from all the mayhem. The driver stopped the battle bus. After removing the steel bar, he stretched and opened the door.

'There you are gents, safe and sound. I'll see you this afternoon for the return journey, it's alright don't feel you need to have a whip-round for the driver', he cackled.

The roll up cigarette was still dancing on his bottom lip as he spoke.

As he got off the coach Jimmy saw Mick Reynolds standing outside his police van.

'How was that then Jimmy? Has it put you off coming back for more tomorrow?'

'No way Mick. They're just morons who think they can bully people into thinking the same way as them. I'm a wolf not a sheep. I'll be in again tomorrow; you can count on that. I'm looking forward to chatting to you some more in the morning Mick.'

Jimmy looked directly into the eyes of the policeman who smiled and said, 'Alright Jimmy, see you tomorrow. Have a good shift.'

CHAPTER 31

Mansfield, Notts – July 16th 1984

The days were long and hot now. Summer had arrived with a vengeance. It was already the middle of July and there was still no sign of the strike coming to an end.

The dispute between the National Union of Mineworkers and British Coal had turned into an acrimonious and bitter en passé. Neither Mrs Thatcher and the government or Arthur Scargill and the Union seemed prepared to start any kind of dialogue that could lead to an end of the strike.

As the days had turned into weeks and then months the two sides had become more and more entrenched in their views.

There looked to be no end in sight.

With the staffing levels at work being so sparse Danny and his small team of detectives were regularly working twelve hours or more every day, with only one day off a week.

Danny knew that Rob hadn't taken a day off for three weeks. The tough sergeant had willingly taken on the responsibility of leading the small CID team while Danny was preoccupied with the sudden and devastating illness of his father.

Danny really appreciated the effort Rob had made on his behalf but when he mentioned his gratitude to him over a pint Rob had replied matter of factly, 'Boss it's nothing, I know for a fact if the situation was turned on its head you'd definitely be there for me.'

Danny had made a mental note of the friendship, loyalty and hard work shown by his colleague.

Three weeks had flown by since he had gone with Sue Rhodes to have a look at the specialist nursing home at Pleasley. They had visited the home together to see if it would be suitable for his father after his stroke. The nursing home turned out to be everything Sue had promised it would be.

The building itself was old but extremely well maintained. It had once been the very grand Pleasley Manor House and was set in an acre of beautiful gardens that were all easily accessible to wheelchair users. There were several beautiful, secluded corners of the grounds, where seats and benches had been placed for both patients and visitors to enjoy.

The interior of the home was beautifully appointed, each patient had a private suite of rooms and their own personal nurse who also acted as their individual carer. The furniture was modern and the rooms spacious.

The owner and manager of the home was a formidable woman named Shirley Rice.

Shirley had been a Theatre Sister at the Mansfield General Hospital but on retirement had set up the nursing home with her son, Ian Rice.

Ian was the business brain behind the home, but it was his mother who oversaw the nursing and care side of the operation. It was Shirley who ensured that only the best staff were employed, that staff included nurses, cooks, physiotherapists, secretaries, gardeners and cleaners.

The result of her efforts was a very caring and very well run establishment. On his tour of the home Danny had been shown the state of the art Physiotherapy Suite, together with the indoor exercise pool. He knew these facilities would be vitally important if his father Frank, was going to be able to make any kind of recovery after his stroke.

Danny was also shown around the kitchens where the meals were prepared. They were incredibly clean and well equipped.

Shirley Rice had explained to Danny how the meals were prepared daily by her team of cooks and that only fresh ingredients were used. All the patients were individually assessed by a dietician to establish the calorific intake they needed before the patients were themselves interviewed to establish the food groups they individually liked or disliked.

It was this attention to detail, the care shown towards other patients he and Sue had witnessed first-hand as they walked around the home, that had made up his mind.

Danny had agreed straight away that if his father had to be cared for in a residential home then this would be the one, whatever the financial cost. The only person he had to convince of the merits of the home now was his father.

Sue had been an amazing help, she sat with Danny and his father when he broke the news to him that he would be moving to the home at Pleasley so he could be cared for properly. It had nearly broken Danny in two when he saw the tears roll from his father's eyes and slide slowly down his cheeks. Tenderly Danny wiped his father's tears away with a tissue and held him close for a full minute.

Patiently and with the gentle help of Sue at his side he then carefully explained that he would only be going to the home temporarily to help him achieve a good enough recovery for him to come home.

The day had now arrived when his father was well enough to travel to the home and take up residence permanently. Sue had again taken time off work to help Danny through what was going to be a difficult day. He acknowledged to himself, that he would not have been able to do it without her. It wasn't lost on either of them how close they were becoming. They had arrived together to collect Frank from the hospital and then driven the short journey to the nursing home at Pleasley.

As they drove through the large ornamental wrought iron gates into the beautiful grounds, that looked resplendent in the July sun, Danny saw the beginnings of a lopsided grin forming on his father's face.

With his good hand the old man squeezed his sons hand and mumbled the word, 'Beautiful'.

It was now Danny's turn to feel emotional and he quickly turned away so his father didn't see the tears starting to well up in his eyes.

Danny and Sue had spent hours painstakingly deciding which of his father's personal effects he would want and need in his new rooms. Danny wanted it to be a home from home for his father and he'd tried hard to make the move as small a wrench as possible.

Witnessing his father's positive mood, after seeing the grounds for the first time, Danny was hopeful that he would accept the nursing home readily, for in truth he knew there was no realistic hope of his father ever being well enough to again enjoy an independent life at his old house.

Danny knew that this was undoubtedly going to be one of the hardest things his father would ever have to accept and come to terms with.

Frank Flint had lived in the house at Mansfield all his married life and Danny could only guess at the number of treasured memories the house held for his father. All those years with his wife, raising his family, decorating the house making it a home.

The memories held by his father would be boundless.

As Danny stopped the car outside the front doors of the home, he could see Shirley Rice waiting outside. As the car came to a stop she opened the car door and immediately spoke to Danny's father.

'A very warm welcome Mr Flint, I hope your stay here will be very comfortable.'

A wheelchair was already waiting and two nurses assisted Frank to get out of Danny's car and into the wheelchair. He was then wheeled into the building by one of the nurses led by Mrs Rice and followed by Danny and Sue.

Franks eyes widened as he was pushed through the spacious comfortable lounge areas and along the well-appointed bright corridors until they arrived at his own suite of rooms.

Opening the door to his rooms, Shirley said, 'Here you are Mr Flint, these are your own private rooms.'

Again Danny saw the smile appear on his father's face as he surveyed the room and saw for the first time the old photographs and personal items, from the house in Mansfield, already in place.

'Very nice son', he mumbled.

The nurse, assisted by Shirley, helped Frank get out of the wheelchair. They then made him comfortable on one of the armchairs in his room. The chair faced out of the large window overlooking the beautiful gardens, that now looked amazing in the afternoon sun.

To the left of the arm chair where Frank now sat was a coffee table. On the table were two cherished photographs of his late wife. With his good hand Frank reached over and picked up the first of the silver framed photographs kissing the picture of his wife tenderly before replacing it on the table.

Shirley knelt down beside him at the side of the chair and said, 'Mr Flint, this young lady is Rosie', she indicated the nurse who had pushed the wheelchair from the front of the building.

'Rosie will be your personal nurse and carer, if there's anything you need Mr Flint, you just let her know.'

'Frank', he mumbled, 'Please call me Frank.'

Both Shirley and Rosie smiled genuine smiles before Shirley said, 'Very well, Frank it is. I'll leave you with your son and Dr Rhodes to settle in and I'll pop back later to discuss your preferred option for dinner this evening.'

Shirley and Rosie then left the room leaving Danny and Sue alone with Frank.

Sue squeezed Danny's arm and said, 'Danny have some time with your dad, I'll go and get a coffee. Take as long as you need.'

She smiled that beautiful enigmatic smile that always took Danny's breath away.

Returning her warm smile, he said, 'Thanks Sue'.

As she closed the door behind her, Danny knelt in front of his father and held his hand, 'Is it ok Dad?'

He looked directly into his father eyes, before continuing, 'If you don't like it we can leave right now.'

Franks face twisted into the lop sided smile once again and he mumbled three words, 'Lovely, very happy.'

'That's great dad. I'll go and bring Sue back, we can all sit and have a coffee together. Dad, you know I love you, don't you?'

'Love you too, big softie', Frank mumbled.

Danny and Sue spent a couple of hours with Frank getting him settled and used to his new surroundings.

Rosie and Shirley returned later to discuss the choices for the evening meal and to go over how things were generally run. Once again Danny was impressed with the easy patience and understanding displayed by both Shirley and the nurse Rosie. Saying their goodbyes Danny and Sue left, with Danny promising to visit in the morning.

As they walked to the car park Danny turned to Sue with the faintest of tears in his eyes and said, 'I can't ever thank you enough Sue, I could never have done this without your kindness and support. I think you know how I feel about you and I'd very much like to continue seeing you. Now I won't be seeing you most days at the hospital that is.'

He knew his little speech had been faltering and clumsy, he could feel his face reddening.

'Detective Inspector Flint are you asking me out on a date?' she asked playfully, again hitting him with that laser beam smile.

'Well I was hoping for several actually', he quipped back.

She stepped forward and placed both her arms over Danny's shoulders interlocking her fingers behind his neck.

Looking up into his eyes she said, 'The more the merrier as far as I'm concerned Danny.'

She then tilted her head slightly so she was looking up into Danny's eyes. Taking her cue, he kissed her gently on the mouth, she returned his kiss and they remained like that for what seemed a long time. Finally, they broke off and she said, 'Shall we find a nice country pub for a drink and a bite to eat?'

'That definitely sounds like a plan Sue.'

They made the short walk across the car park to his BMW. They held hands as they walked, it seemed like the natural thing to do.

CHAPTER 32

Peckham, London – July 17th 1984

'I know there's no new leads coming in sir, but it's only been four months. We've still got a vicious killer out there. You saw the pathologists report, this attack was both frenzied and calculating, making this person an extremely dangerous individual. All the indications are, that if he's not caught, this person will kill again and again.'

Glyn Johnson was quickly reaching the end of his tether, he had patiently been saying the same thing to Chief Superintendent McCartney for the best part of twenty minutes and the senior officer was having none of it.

McCartney had arranged the meeting with Glyn to tell him that his enquiry team was to be drastically reduced and that the majority of the detectives on his team would be transferred onto more recent, hotter, murder investigations.

The Chief Superintendent leaned back into his chair and put his hands behind his head.

'I've heard that argument from you twice already Glyn. The fact of the matter is, your killer hasn't struck again has he! Without any fresh leads or new lines of enquiries I can't justify allowing you to keep all this staff. Your detectives are twiddling their thumbs Glyn. It's just not cost effective. There are two very recent murder enquiries, one in Fulham and one in Tottenham, where the Senior Investigating Officers are crying out for manpower to carry out urgent enquiries.

I'm sorry Glyn, there's nothing you can say to me that will persuade me to change my mind.'

Time for one last roll of the dice, thought Glyn.

'Peter Sutcliffe, sir. Do you really want to be responsible for the media sensation and the damage to the force when this maniac does kill again? Just because he hasn't done so yet, there's no doubt in my mind that he will kill again sir, I'm convinced of it. Are you prepared to take the heat from the press when we have a Yorkshire Ripper scenario here in the capital?'

Slowly Ch. Supt McCartney shook his head and let out an audible sigh, placing both hands flat on the top of his desk. It was obvious he was trying hard to control his own temper.

'I'm going to do you a favour Inspector, I'm not going to read any insubordination into your last comment. If I did, I'd be left with no choice but to put you on a disciplinary. Your insightful comments have been duly noted. As from today you'll run the Jenny Taylor enquiry with a Detective Sergeant and three Detective Constables. This meeting's over Inspector, close the door on your way out!'

McCartney's voice was raised to a shout by the end of the sentence.

Glyn stood up quickly, pushing the chair back hard, scraping the legs loudly over the wooden floor. He pointed an accusing finger at McCartney and said through gritted teeth, 'When this lunatic strikes again, and he will, don't say I didn't warn you.'

'Inspector, get out of my office now!' shouted a clearly livid McCartney.

Glyn shook his head, staring hard at the Chief Superintendent, before turning and striding out of the office. He slammed the door behind him.

Craig was waiting outside the office for Glyn. He stood up and said, 'It was all getting a wee bit heated in there wasn't it guvnor?'

'The stupid old bastard has cut the team! It's just you, me and three suits now, God help us when this maniac slaughters some other poor kid. Come on Craig, I need to get out of this penny pinching, cost effective, rats nest before I throw up!'

CHAPTER 33

Warsop, Nottinghamshire – August 3rd 1984

For Jimmy Wade and the other miners going into work at Warsop Main Colliery, every morning was the same routine.

Their day began with the taxi ride to the layby where they were met by two Transit vans full of police officers. From the layby it was a high speed drive to the disused quarry where they would wait thirty or so minutes for the increasingly battered battle bus. Then came the drive into the colliery itself and the daily run through the gauntlet of hate from the striking miners.

Since joining the ranks of the working miners, Jimmy Wade had been well and truly ostracised by his own community. People he'd considered as workmates before, now either abused him verbally or just totally ignored him.

Jimmy never really made any close friends and hadn't been in his current house long enough to have made a lasting impression on his neighbours. He was just amazed at how fast the word had travelled around the small town, that Jimmy Wade was now back at work. In his own community's eyes, he was now the lowest of the low, nothing more than a scab. He would hear old men and women muttering the word under their breath as he passed them in the street. The younger members of the community were far more vociferous in their displeasure. Wherever he went the cry of "Scab!" would follow him.

It had bothered him at first, but now he let it wash over him, the idiots would tire of saying it before he tired of listening to it, he told himself. He was unconcerned for his own safety. He was well aware that not many people would ever threaten him with violence or be prepared to have a go at him physically. It was common knowledge among the other pitmen how physically strong Jimmy Wade was.

He was worried about damage being caused to his house when he wasn't there, but so far nothing had happened. At least now the bills were getting paid and he was no longer in danger of losing his home. Jimmy knew that as more miners returned to work his part in breaking the strike would eventually be forgotten. He had also been carefully making plans for his future and he knew that the venomous shouts of the word "SCAB!" would soon become a long forgotten memory.

The only change in the daily routine for the miners working at Warsop Main Colliery was that there were now two cabs required. Two more men were now making the journey into the pit every day, making five in total.

It was obvious these numbers would steadily grow.

The strike was slowly crumbling, Arthur Scargill and his idiot henchmen refused to accept this was the case and continued, at every opportunity, to rant about this famous victory over Thatcherism. The one beacon of light in this depressing scenario had been the association he had struck up with the police sergeant from London. He would never have described it as a friendship, Jimmy Wade didn't do friendship. Every morning he and the sergeant, had around half an hour of stimulating conversation before the battle bus arrived. At first they had spoken about general everyday subjects, sport, politics and the like but for weeks now their talks had become more personal. Mick opened up to Jimmy about the bitch he was married to. During these deep conversations the sergeant had said on more than one occasion that he wished his wife was dead.

When during one such conversation Jimmy suggested to him that he should stop wishing it and just do it, he hadn't been surprised when Mick replied, 'I might just do that Jimmy.'

That conversation had been over two weeks ago. Every day since, Mick had steered their little talks back to the subject of murder. Jimmy had let him ramble on about the various ways he intended to kill his wife Rita. Today was no different, as soon as they arrived at the quarry he and Mick moved away from the other miners and police officers and stood out of earshot.

Once again it was Mick who started the conversation, 'I've thought long and hard about this Jimmy, I'm going to do it. I can't stand being with her any longer, she's driving me insane. It's totally unfair for her to get half of everything I've worked my bollocks off for. As far as I'm concerned I've got no option Jimmy. I've made my mind up.'

'I reckon you need to think about this Mick. If you're caught, because you're a copper they'd lock you up forever. Anyway it's all talk with you, I don't reckon you've got the balls to kill her, you're all wind and piss.'

He then fixed the sergeant with his cold blue eyes and said evenly, 'Have you Mick. Have you got the balls to take a life, to snuff out someone's very existence?'

'I've done it already', was the cold reply.

Jimmy sneered.

'Yeah, of course you have! What the fuck are you talking about Mick?'

The sergeant paused and looked around before leaning in towards Jimmy, whispering conspiratorially, 'I'm telling you I've already killed somebody. So yes I've got the fucking balls.'

It was the sergeants turn now to stare stony faced into the eyes of the miner.

'Yeah, of course you have Mick', goaded Jimmy.

'Jimmy, I've never been more serious in my life.'

'Is that right. So who've you killed already?'

'Back home in London, some silly little tart who was in the wrong place at the wrong time. Never mind who she was. The fact is I did it, so yes I can take a life. I'll tell you this, I fucking enjoyed it too. The question I need answering is this Jimmy old son. Never mind me, what about you? Could you take a life?'

'I think we need to continue this talk, in private over a couple of beers when we've got more time, don't you Mick?'

Staring at the policeman he continued 'I think you already know the answer to that question Mick. I've always thought that deep down you and I were kindred spirits.'

He grinned, 'What do you say Mick, do you want to go for that talk over a beer tonight?'

'Dead right I fucking do Jimmy. I'll go for that pint; I've been wanting to talk to somebody about this ever since it happened. I can't stop thinking about it.'

'Thinking about how exhilarated it made you feel, am I right? You end up craving that feeling of power, don't you Mick?'

'That's it exactly, I want to feel more of that amazing adrenalin rush, the buzz or whatever other way you want to describe it, I want to feel it again. If it's not that bitch Rita, then it'll have to be some other useless fucker.'

Jimmy looked directly into the sergeant's eyes.

There was a special look in them, he recognised only too well. It was the same look he saw in his own eyes, reflected back from the mirror, when his own urges were strong.

'Right Mick, what's the crack with you boys when you're up here, are you allowed out at night to go for a beer?'

'Yeah we can get out, but nowhere local to the army camp. The pubs nearby are off limits and we're not allowed to fraternise with the locals in case conversation turns to argument. A lot of the blokes have got tarts on the go up here though, none of the gaffers bat an eyelid if they go out shagging.'

'This army camp you keep mentioning, is it the old disused one up near Ollerton?'

'Yeah, it's called Proteus Camp. I've been there since the start of this fucking strike. It's a bleeding shithole.'

The distant rumble from the diesel engine of the battle bus approaching interrupted their conversation.

'I'll be in the layby outside Proteus Camp at eight o'clock tonight Mick. I'll be sitting in a dark green Ford Cortina parked up facing away from the gates. I've got a long blonde wig that I'll put on, so if any one sees me from behind they'll think you're being picked up by a tart.'

'Ok Jimmy, eight o'clock tonight, I'll see you later', he said with a malevolent grin.

Jimmy walked over to the battle bus, he'd always known his intuition about the policeman from London would be proved right. He was feeling pleased with himself, he had played Reynolds just right, waiting for him to speak first and disclose his past. It had been a relief when he finally started to talk about what they both were, stone cold killers.

Things were about to get very interesting. For the first time in weeks, Jimmy could feel familiar urges coursing through him.

He knew he had to kill again soon.

The thing that excited him most was that he knew Mick Reynolds was feeling exactly the same. Jimmy had never hunted for a victim before, he had always been opportunistic when it came to killing. He was feeling very excited about the prospect of a new experience.

The meeting with the sergeant couldn't come fast enough for Jimmy Wade.

CHAPTER 34

Ollerton, Nottinghamshire – August 17th 1984

July had come and gone, the year had slipped into August and temperatures during the day and at night had been stiflingly hot. The evenings and nights were almost unbearably sticky and humid. Just turning over in bed was enough effort to ensure most people would break out into a sweat.

As he went into work each day, Jimmy had noticed that even the pickets on the approaches and gates to Warsop Main Colliery appeared to be just going through the motions. The number of pickets had diminished, the venom and hatred shown by the strikers in the early weeks had dissipated too. It was as though the heat and humidity was making everything just too much of an effort.

Two weeks had passed since the night he'd waited for Mick Reynolds in the layby outside Proteus Camp. The decision to wear the long blonde wig had proved extremely prudent as he noticed in his rear view mirror that as Mick approached his car, another off duty copper had come sauntering out of the gate.

Mick had told Jimmy that the off duty cop was one of the younger constables on his PSU. The officer was at least seventy-five yards away and Jimmy had driven away quickly, the last thing he wanted was for the young copper to remember the registration number of his car.

That first night sitting in a quiet booth in the Squinting Cat pub at Clipstone Village had been a revelation for both men. Mick had gone into a lot of detail about the killing of the young woman in London, explaining to Jimmy that in his mind he had imagined he was killing his wife Rita. He clearly relished the chance to confide in Jimmy and told him in great detail what had happened. He bragged to Jimmy that the reason he could get away with murder was because as a police officer, he knew the quickest way to stifle a murder enquiry was to make it impossible to identify the victim. He again described in great detail how this could quite easily be achieved. He also bragged to Jimmy about his awareness of forensic science and other methods the police used to obtain vital clues.

In graphic detail, he explained to Jimmy that depriving a murder investigation of forensic evidence is like sucking the oxygen away from a fire, it will quickly die.

His final nugget of information on how to kill and avoid detection was very simplistic. The victim selected must have absolutely no connection to the murderer.

Mick explained to Jimmy that most murders were committed by people the unfortunate victim knew.

He assured Jimmy that if these three rules were followed implicitly any police investigation would struggle and soon flounder. Jimmy listened patiently, letting Mick incriminate himself further and further. He pretended to be in awe of the burly Londoner. The truth was he had no desire or inclination to go into any of the details of his two killings or the reason for them. He still didn't trust anyone with his secrets, especially a police officer, even if that particular police officer had just admitted to a murder. Everything Reynolds had said so far, could all be bullshit as far as Jimmy was concerned. When Mick spoke about the importance of identifying a victim, Jimmy questioned him on what techniques the police used to identify victims.

Mick confided in him that the two most common methods used to identify people were fingerprints and dental records. If you could deprive the investigation team of these ways of identification things wouldn't be straightforward.

Jimmy only joined in the information sharing once. He offered an opinion to Mick that he thought one of the most important ways to avoid detection was to divert the police into looking elsewhere. Mick readily agreed, telling Jimmy the police loved having enquiries to follow and that if a large enough trail of breadcrumbs was left, the police would always follow it, getting further away from the truth all the time. Mick also explained to Jimmy the tremendous pressure detectives were under, not only to solve a murder, but to solve it quickly.

Jimmy lapped it up, he'd never heard anyone speak about murder and killing in the way the sergeant had. At the moment it was all just talk, as far as Jimmy was concerned the ultimate test for Reynolds would come soon enough.

Only the outcome of that test would decide how long Jimmy remained in the company of the dangerous and calculating police sergeant.

Earlier in the day at the quarry, the two men had made arrangements to meet that evening in the layby near to Proteus Camp, once again Jimmy now found himself in his car waiting for Mick Reynolds to arrive.

It was now nearly nine o'clock, and the daylight had virtually disappeared but Jimmy still wore the blonde wig while he waited patiently.

Glancing in the car's rear view mirror he could now see Mick finally approaching the vehicle. He was carrying a black holdall.

Mick opened the boot of the Cortina and placed the holdall inside. He closed the boot, opened the passenger door and got in the car.

'What's in the bag Mick?'

'With a bit of luck I'll show you later Jimmy', he grinned and Jimmy noticed he had that special look in his eyes.

'I see, have you got something in mind for tonight?'

Mick seemed agitated as he said, 'Our PSU's being stood down for a week from tomorrow. This will be my last night here for a week. I've decided I can't face the prospect of going home to that bitch Rita, so I'm going up north to Newcastle to stay with my sister for the week. It's just that I want, no I need, to do something special tonight. I'm sick of just talking about it Jimmy, I need some action tonight.'

'I feel the same way Mick. I've got something to show you later as well, I think you're going to like it. Let's just play it by ear and see what the night brings shall we.'

Mick nodded and a smiling Jimmy drove the car away from the layby. The two men sat in silence as Jimmy drove the Cortina steadily along Peafield Lane before turning left along the main A60 road towards Mansfield. He then took a left turn at the crossroads onto Old Mill Lane and drove into a small mining village called Forest Town.

Jimmy drove into the car park of The Prince Charles pub. As he parked the car he said, 'I never drink in this pub, so I don't think I'll know anyone in here. It's a bit rough and ready and has a reputation as a pick up joint. The women here aren't exactly tarts but they like their cock and by all accounts aren't too fussy about whose cock it is.'

Mick just nodded, he appeared sullen, brooding, almost trance like. There was a real sense of anger, almost rage, bubbling below the surface and not far below at that.

Before getting out of the car Jimmy paused, looking at Mick, 'Are you alright Mick? Are you sure you want to do this?'

He almost growled a reply, 'Oh yeah, I'm sure, that bitch is really going to get what she deserves tonight.'

'Listen to me Mick you need to lighten up. We're just two blokes having a pint in a pub. At the moment you look like a total nutter. Nobody'll come within a hundred yards of us while you're like that mate.'

'Yeah you're right, sorry Jimmy. Let's go and get a beer shall we?'

Jimmy was shocked at just how quickly the other man's mood changed. It was as if he changed into a different person completely.

As they got out of the car Mick was now laughing and smiling. 'What you having mate?' he said in a loud jovial voice.

'I'll have a Lager and Lime mate, let's go in the public bar. Keep that accent down a bit, I've no idea what the clientele's like in here. It could be full of striking miners for all I know.'

Both men walked into the Public Bar of the pub and walked up to the bar. Mick quietly ordered the beers while Jimmy quickly glanced around at the other customers. In total there were no more than twenty other punters in the bar. He could hear raucous voices from the Lounge Bar next door.

Jimmy leaned forward and said to the barmaid, 'Is there a do on next door luv?'

'Yeah, it's an engagement party, a lot of the regulars are next door. You'd never guess there's a strike on, the way they're spending, it's packed in there.'

She handed over the two beers.

Both men took a long drink from their pints before walking away from the bar to sit in a booth. There was a juke box on the wall which was belting out the latest Wham song. Instinctively Jimmy started to tap his fingers in rhythm to the music as he looked around the room. A group of older men were playing dominoes at a table in the corner. The only other people in the bar were couples, out having a quiet drink. It was as if the pub had been turned around. The people drinking in this bar would, on any other night, be drinking in the lounge. It was obvious there was very little chance of any action in this pub. Jimmy ordered two more pints. The time was fast approaching closing time.

'This is fucking hopeless' growled Mick as his mood changed once more.

'You're right, lets drink this and fuck off'.

Just as they were about to drink up and leave, the door that led from the Lounge Bar swung open. A woman who was obviously quite drunk tottered in on ridiculously high wedges.

She staggered up to the bar and smiled at the barmaid.

'Hello duck, its last orders next door but I can't get near the bar for all those drunken twats. I'll have a large Bacardi and Coke please duck.'

She plonked her black leather handbag loudly on the bar and fished inside for her purse. The barmaid placed the drink on the bar in front of the tipsy woman.

'You alright Mandy? Looks like you've had a good night next door?'

.

The woman took a sip of her drink.

'It's been lovely. I told the silly cow not to go through with it. I've been so much better off since I've been on my own. Men are only good for one thing, and I can get that whenever I want. Variety's the spice of life duck', she giggled.

'You're terrible Mandy', replied the barmaid chuckling.

'No one in there take your fancy tonight then Mandy?'

'Nah luv, they're all twats in there, I'm just going to get this down me, then have a steady walk home.'

'You be careful getting home, you've had a few.'

'I'll be alright duck, I've only got to walk down Pump Hollow Lane, it's not far.'

Both men had been watching intently and listening to the exchange between the drunken woman and the barmaid. Mick's mood once again becoming more intense and agitated.

'This bitch will do Jimmy', he said in a guttural voice that was no more than a low growl.

'I reckon you're right Mick.'

Jimmy now looked closer at the woman.

She was probably coming up to her fiftieth birthday but had good legs that she showed off by wearing the shortest white mini skirt he'd seen for a while. Her top was a black sheer blouse with white buttons at the front. It was unbuttoned quite low and her ample cleavage was being held in check by a lacy black bra that was visible beneath the see through blouse. Her hair was platinum blonde, straight out of the bottle, and the roots were starting to show dark again.

The make-up she wore was garish, trying to hold back the ravages of time and a hard life with lipstick and powder.

All in all, she looked a mess.

Jimmy truly believed that deep down she would welcome what was about to happen to her. It would be a joyous release from her shit life.

In a couple of hours, he'd know this for certain when he looked directly into her eyes at the moment of her release.

Turning to Mick he said quietly, 'Come on Mick, she's nearly finished her drink, we need to get going and be waiting on Pump Hollow Lane.'

Both men quickly swallowed their drinks and walked outside. They were just getting into the car when they heard the bar door open.

'G'night duck!' a now very drunk Mandy shouted to the barmaid as she tottered out.

There was still ten minutes to go before closing time and nobody else was leaving the pub, they were all inside clamouring for last orders.

Jimmy drove the car slowly out of the car park passing the drunken woman. Three minutes later they were parked up in the dark on Pump Hollow Lane. The street lighting here was poor and the road was very dark.

As they waited for the woman to appear at the end of the road Jimmy reached into the glove compartment, he pulled out a plastic document pocket.

'Look at this Mick, remember that deflection theory I was telling you about.'

Mick quickly scanned the short typed document that was in the plastic wallet.

He chuckled malevolently, 'That's fucking brilliant Jimmy.'

'Don't worry, I typed it with gloves on and we'll be taking the plastic wallet with us so there'll be no danger of any prints being left.'

'Sounds like you listened to me well old son', said Mick grinning.

They could now see the woman tottering down the hill towards them, she was making slow progress and was obviously feeling the effects of the alcohol.

Jimmy reached onto the backseat of the car and picked up the blonde wig and put it on.

'Be nice to her Mick, say I'm your wife and that I've come to pick you up. Tell her she shouldn't be walking home alone and that we'll drop her off.'

Mick nodded and wound the window down.

'Hello luv', he said in his best impression of a local accent.

'My wife here says you shouldn't be walking home on your own luv. Can we give you a lift home duck?'

She bent over, swaying slightly as she looked into the car.

It was obvious that drink was affecting her focus as she squinted inside the car. Mick seized the initiative, jumping out of the car he opened the back door.

'Come on luv, let's get you home.'

'Aw thanks duck, it's not far just passed the next crossroads'.

Her reply was very slurred and she almost fell onto the backseat, Mick immediately jumped in beside her.

'Oi what's going on!' she started to say.

Mick punched her hard in the face, the car was silent again.

'No blood in the car', said a calm Jimmy.

Taking off the blonde wig he then drove the car away steadily.

'I know somewhere better to do this', he said.

A fifteen-minute drive later and Jimmy steered the car into a quiet layby just outside Annesley Village.

It was a lonely desolate place, that unless you knew the area would be difficult to find. The entrance into the lay by was almost concealed and was hard to spot, especially at night.

There were no street lights here, the road was very quiet and the lay by was set back behind a row of bushes.

Mick got out of the car taking care to only walk on the hard tarmac, he opened the boot of the car and retrieved the grip bag.

He walked back to the open passenger door and said, 'We'll need these before we go any further.'

He opened the grip bag and pulled out a pair of light blue forensic suits, gloves and overshoes. He handed one set over to Jimmy, 'Get them on before we touch anything else.'

After a couple of minutes both men were standing at the side of the car totally covered in their suits. With gloved hands Mick reached into the bag and pulled out brown Gaffer tape. He quickly wrapped the tape around the woman's head so it covered her mouth. She was starting to stir, slowly regaining consciousness. Mick grabbed two black cable ties from the bag and used them to bind her wrists tightly. She was now fully awake and tried to scream, but the Gaffer tape stifled the scream and the noise was more like a guttural growl.

Both men smiled and Jimmy said, 'I'll bring her, follow me.'

Unseen by Mick, Jimmy tied a length of thin cord loosely around his middle. He grabbed the now terrified woman from the back seat and although she tried to struggle he easily overpowered her. Throwing her over his shoulder, he walked quickly into the woods at the side of the layby.

With the woman over one shoulder, he carried the small

plastic document holder and its contents in one hand while he gripped the legs of the woman with the other.

She was only a small woman and it felt good to him as she wriggled on his shoulder trying to break his grip. After three minutes walking he found a small clearing in the trees.

Jimmy threw the woman roughly down onto the floor.

He placed the document holder on the floor, alongside the woman who was now lying face up.

Mick stood behind him holding the grip bag.

The woman was staring up at him and in the bright moonlight Jimmy could see that her eyes were wide open with fear. He sat astride the woman pinning her bound arms beneath her back. She tried in vain to buck him off but he was far too strong for her to move.

Eventually she gave up and lay still beneath him.

Jimmy put his head a matter of only six inches away from her face and stared into her eyes.

He slipped the thin cord from around his middle and wrapped it once quickly around her neck. Slowly he started to exert pressure by pulling on each end of the thin rope, until the cord was biting into her neck cutting the oxygen off. Her eyes grew wider and she tried to shake her head imploring him to stop. The last thing she would have seen were those intense blue eyes staring into her own. He kept pulling on the ends of the cord until he saw her eyes change from sparkling, bright, wide open, terrified eyes into dull, matt, lifeless eyes that were focussing on nothing.

Slipping the thin cord from around the woman's neck he stood up and turned to face a scowling Mick.

'Have you killed the bitch already?' he growled with some anger in his voice.

'No Mick, she's just unconscious,' he lied. 'This one's all yours. I want to see if you've actually got the bottle to do what you've been bragging about. I love these suits by the way, are these what the coppers will be wearing later when they find her?'.

'Yes, they fucking are, now get out the way and let me show you who's got the bottle for this.'

He stomped forward and aimed a vicious kick at the face of the already dead woman, he then bent forward and removed the brown Gaffer tape from around her head before growling, 'Shut your mouth Rita, you fucking gobby cow!'

Jimmy stood watching as Mick's heavy boots, covered by the overshoes, landed kick after kick into the woman's face.

He was a man possessed, every kick was accompanied by a grunted word.

Kick, 'you!'

Kick, 'fucking!'

Kick, 'bitch!'

Kick, 'Rita!'

The woman's face was now barely recognisable.

After several minutes Mick stopped the frenzied assault and stepped back over to the grip bag. He never acknowledged Jimmy, he was totally oblivious to the other man's presence. He reached into the bag and took out a heavy ballpein hammer. He then picked up the grip bag in his other hand and walked trance like back to where the woman was lying on the grass.

Mick placed the grip bag down at the feet of the dead woman and using the hammer began to rain blow after blow down into the mouth and jaw of the woman until the whole jaw, both upper and lower mandibles were smashed. Jimmy could see teeth flying as the hammer landed.

Finally, he stopped the vicious attack and breathing heavily from his exertions he replaced the hammer back in the bag.

He then took out a resealable plastic bag and a set of small garden shears.

He rolled the dead woman over onto her front, exposing her bound hands. Using the shears, he severed each of the fingers and the thumbs.

The thumbs seemed to be a lot harder to cut through and Jimmy could hear Mick grunting with the exertion.

Finally, he cut off the two black cable ties that had bound her wrists. Meticulously he picked up all the severed fingers and thumbs and put them into the ziplock bag before resealing it. He then placed the bag, the cable ties and the shears back into the grip bag before finally taking out a Stanley knife.

Using the Stanley knife blade Mick repeatedly slashed at the open palms of the woman's hands until they were both a flayed bloody mess. Having returned the Stanley knife, he then took out a black bin liner from the holdall.

He turned to Jimmy and finally spoke, 'Give me a hand to get her stripped off Jimmy.'

'What the hell for? I don't want to touch her like that.'

Mick hissed, 'I'm not going to interfere with her, I'm not a bloody pervert. We need to take her clothes. There could be fibres from your car on her clothes. Better safe than sorry Jimmy.'

Quickly the two men stripped the woman, placing her clothes in a bin liner from the grip bag.

The bloodied and battered body was now jet black and stark white in the bright moonlight.

Her skin white, the blood black.

Mick stepped back, his breathing hard and laboured.

It was now Jimmy's turn to approach the dead woman.

'Now it's time to play some games with the coppers', he grinned.

The first thing he did was straighten the body. The head was a mess, barely recognisable in shape or form, her face had been virtually obliterated.

Jimmy turned the woman so she was lying on her back, then straightened the arms out away from her sides until her body was shaped like a crucifix. He then opened her legs wide. He picked up the plastic document holder he'd placed on the ground earlier and from inside he removed a thin black plastic tube.

He thoroughly wiped the tube on the wet grass before removing a type written note from the plastic document holder. Rolling the note like a scroll, he placed it inside the tube. He put the document holder into the black bin liner containing the woman's bloody clothes, that was sitting on top of the holdall.

He then turned towards Mick and grinned.

Mick also let out a chuckle as he realised where the tube was going. Jimmy carefully inserted the plastic tube into the dead woman's vagina.

'Just by putting that there, we're now sexual deviants Mick. How long will the detectives spend trawling through list after list of sex offenders?' he laughed softly.

Mick nodded knowingly.

Jimmy now reached into the holdall and removed the Stanley knife again.

He knelt at the side of the dead woman and using the sharp blade he cut two words into her chest and stomach.

The first word was carved just above her breasts, the second word below them.

Mick nodded approvingly, 'That will definitely get the detectives in a state of flux. I like it Jimmy.'

Both men then stood back from the mutilated body and surveyed their grisly work. Without saying another word to each other they slowly walked off and left the battered and defiled remains of Mandy on the cold grass, her smashed unrecognisable face looking directly up at the bright moon.

Just before they got back to the car Mick reached into the grip bag and removed the black bin liner that already contained the used Gaffer tape and cable ties, the dead woman's clothes and the digits from her mutilated hands. Once they were standing on the tarmac at the edge of the lay by they removed the forensic suits, the overshoes and finally the gloves, placing everything into the same bin liner. They both quickly checked the area around the car to make sure they hadn't dropped anything. Jimmy opened the boot and Mick placed the grip bag and the bin liner inside.

It was now approaching one o'clock in the morning, Jimmy slowly drove the car back towards Ollerton and the disused army camp.

Neither man said a word throughout the journey.

Stopping the car in the lay by outside the camp, Jimmy finally broke the silence.

'What are you going to do with the bin liner Mick?'

'It's going straight into the boiler room furnace old son, that'll get rid of everything no bother.'

'When will you be back from Newcastle?'

'I'm back on duty here on the 24th. I've only got a week off'.

'I'll see you at the quarry when you get back.'

'You will mate, you will. We make a good team you and me.'

Carrying the grip bag in one hand and the bin liner in the other Mick walked off, disappearing into the darkness and leaving Jimmy alone in the car.

As he watched Mick walking away, Jimmy reflected on what had been a very interesting night.

Previously he'd only killed when he knew he could stage the death to look like an accident.

Tonight was a major change for him.

The two of them had selected the woman totally at random and then killed her in such a brutal and horrific way that her death couldn't be seen as anything other than a cold and calculated murder.

He also realised now how similar and yet how very different he was to Mick Reynolds.

Jimmy realised that the only thing they had in common was that they both enjoyed killing. The mental processes for each of them that led to the act of killing were, however, polar opposites.

Something else was now abundantly clear to Jimmy, killing in this way meant the possibilities were endless.

He no longer had to be so patient.

Jimmy had watched Mick closely as he meticulously managed the scene of the murder so that no clue was left behind. He knew that this new found knowledge coupled with his cold, methodical and calculating mind meant he could now kill whenever he wanted to and more importantly get away with it.

As he drove away, his thoughts turned to how killing as a pair had been so very different. He wasn't sure it was for him, he preferred to work alone.

For the foreseeable future though, it was going to be a welcome distraction from the boredom of this fucking strike.

CHAPTER 35

Fiskerton, Nottinghamshire –
August 17th 1984

Danny Flint and Sue Rhodes were sitting outside a country pub near the picturesque village of Fiskerton on the banks of the River Trent.

It was now a beautiful balmy evening, after what had been another very hot day. Only as the sun neared the horizon had the temperature finally started to become bearable.

The Bradley Arms pub was beautiful.

It was a sandstone building draped with wisteria and other wall flowers. The walls were also adorned with several colourful hanging baskets. Wooden benches and tables had been placed at the rear of the pub overlooking the gently flowing river.

Although it was a popular venue during the summer for a nice cool drink and a stroll along the riverbank, tonight was unusually quiet.

Swallows made the most of the last hours of daylight by swooping low over the river, catching the myriads of insects just above the surface of the water.

Only one other couple were sitting on the benches outside the pub.

Like Danny and Sue, they too were holding hands across the table and staring out across the beautiful river to the countryside beyond.

A month had raced by since Danny had taken his father into the nursing home at Pleasley for the first time.

He had seen Sue almost every day since.

It felt so easy and comfortable, it was like they had known each other for years.

They shared the same interests and although she was slightly younger, there ages were close enough for it to make no difference.

Danny finished his drink and gently squeezed her hand.

'Do you fancy another drink Sue, or shall we have a stroll along the river?'

'Let's go for that walk, shall we. It's a lovely evening and the river looks beautiful.'

The talk was relaxed as they strolled slowly along the path at the water's edge, his arm draped protectively around her shoulders, her arm around his waist.

Danny could not remember when he had last felt this happy.

'What a beautiful spot', she purred.

The sun was sinking slowly down on the horizon and the colour of the wide river had changed to a deep orange hue mirroring the light of the setting sun.

The water flowing nearest the bank, danced over the stones in the shallows and became sparks of flame, reflecting the orange and red rays of the now quickly setting sun.

'It's stunning', he said.

They stopped walking and turned to face each other, embracing each other and kissing slowly.

'I don't want this day to end Danny, come back and stay with me tonight.'

'That sounds wonderful Sue, if you're sure', he smiled

'I'm sure', she said smiling back.

They turned and walked back along the river towards the pub car park.

Their pace a little quicker now as they both anticipated the night ahead.

CHAPTER 36

Mansfield – August 18th 1984

The low intermittent buzzing was incessant.

Gradually the dull noise wormed its way into the consciousness of the sleeping Danny Flint.

Finally, the constant low pitched droning was enough to wake him. He slowly stirred in the large double bed and reached over to the bedside cabinet where he had left his pager the night before.

Danny turned off the alarm and squinted at the number displayed on the small screen of the pager. He became aware of Sue waking next to him and smiled as he felt the warmth of her naked body snuggling into his back.

The night before had been one of the best nights of his life. They had arrived back at the house from their evening out at Fiskerton and no sooner were they through the front door than they were all over each other. They stumbled up the stairs removing items of clothing as they went, before falling onto the top of the large double bed.

The lovemaking had been intense and frenetic the first time, but then slower and more sensual the subsequent times.

It had been almost two o'clock in the morning when they finally fell asleep in each other's arms, exhausted.

Bleary eyed, Danny now looked at his watch, it was only seven fifteen in the morning. The message on the pager was requesting him to contact the control room at Mansfield Police Station.

Today was Danny's scheduled day off, so he knew immediately that something must be seriously wrong if Rob Buxton couldn't handle it. He knew Rob would have arrived at work that morning around six o'clock.

'What is it sweetheart?' said a very sleepy Sue as she slowly caressed his back with her index finger.

'My pager's gone off, I've got to phone the control room at Mansfield. Where's your phone Sue?'

'It's in the hallway at the bottom of the stairs.'

He quickly sat up and got out of the warm bed, he retrieved his boxer shorts, that were lying on the floor next to the bed, where he'd dropped them the night before.

He found his trousers in the hall at the top of the stairs and his shirt and tie halfway down the stairs. Danny smiled as he noticed items of Sue's clothing scattered everywhere too.

Standing in just his boxer shorts he picked up the phone and dialled the number for the control room.

'Hello, it's Detective Inspector Flint, I've received a pager message to contact you.'

The control room Inspector was very matter of fact as he informed Danny the reason for the pager call.

'Yes sir, we've had a radio message from D.S. Buxton. He's asking that you join him urgently at the lay by on the A611 just outside Annesley Village. I'm afraid the body of a woman was found there this morning by a man out jogging. DS Buxton has already requested that Scenes of Crime Officers and a Home Office pathologist attend. I've already sent messages, at Rob Buxton's request, to the other detectives on your team asking them to come in to work early.'

Danny absorbed the message quickly.

'Ok, I'm on my way', he said.

He added, 'Contact DS Buxton for me and inform him that I'll be there as soon as I can.'

With that he put the phone down, he turned and saw a naked Sue standing at the top of the stairs.

'You're not coming back to bed are you?' she said, disappointment in her voice.

He was frantically getting dressed, locating the other items of his missing clothing.

'I've got to go into work Sue, I'm really sorry.'

She turned and went back into the bedroom emerging a few seconds later wearing a cream silk robe. Quickly she made her way down the stairs until she was standing next to Danny.

'Is everything ok Danny?' there was genuine concern in her voice now.

'I don't think it is Sue. A woman's body has been found over at Annesley and it sounds like she's been murdered.'

'Oh my God, Danny that's awful.'

He grabbed his jacket from the bannister rail.

'I've got to go right now, I'm so sorry Sue.'

'No, I understand, you hurry.'

She grabbed him by the lapels of his jacket pulling him close, she kissed him hard on the mouth which he responded to, she felt amazing beneath the silk robe.

'You were amazing last night', she purred.

'So were you Sue, I'm shattered.'

Sue relaxed her arms and he slipped out of her embrace.

'Call me when you can Danny, I love you.'

The three small words almost stopped him in his tracks.

'I love you too sweetheart, I'll call you as soon as I can.'

Danny was then out of the door and running to his car.

He'd left it parked on the street a few houses along from Sue's house. He jumped in and gunned the engine before speeding off down the deserted leafy street.

He put his foot down, with a bit of luck I can be there in fifteen minutes, he thought to himself.

CHAPTER 37

Woods near Annesley Village – August 18th 1984

As Danny approached the lay by on the A611 Annesley Bypass he could already see the blue lights of the police vehicles, parked by the side of the road.

He stopped his own car a little further back from the last marked police vehicle.

A single Panda car was parked actually in the lay by, the other side of the crime scene tape that now cordoned off the entrance.

Rob Buxton had obviously already been busy protecting the scene. As Danny walked quickly towards the layby he saw Rob standing in a full forensic suit, complete with overshoes and gloves, talking to a very young looking police constable at the side of the Panda car. Even from that distance, Danny could tell that the young constable had been sick, he was deathly white and was doubled over.

Waiting behind the tape Danny shouted to Rob, 'Where's it ok to walk Rob?'

'You're ok to walk down to us boss, there's nothing on the road.'

Danny walked down to his sergeant, 'What have we got Rob? The control room said a woman's body has been found?'

'It's a bad one Danny.'

The uniformed officer doubled over and dry heaved again. Danny put his hand on the officers back and said quietly, 'Get up onto the road and get some water son. We'll talk to you in a little while.'

He watched as the young constable gingerly walked out of the lay by and onto the road, where he was helped by his uniform colleagues.

'If he's been right down to the scene, I want his boots and his uniform at some stage', said Danny

Rob turned to Danny and spoke quietly.

'No problem Danny, that's what I was just telling him. Pc Symonds assures me he never went close to the body. He was the first officer here after it was called in, he's only got six months' service in and I'm afraid it's been a bit much for him to take in. It's definitely a murder as you'll see in a minute. Scenes of Crime are here already, Rachel's down at the scene with them and has started the log, she arrived here about ten minutes after me. I've just finished talking to the jogger who found the dead woman, I've got all his details. Andy's still travelling, but he's got the furthest to come. As soon as he arrives I'll set him on getting the statements from Mr Rose, our jogger, and also Pc Symonds. I'll ensure Andy seizes all the clothing and footwear from Pc Symonds and Mr Rose. I think it'd be a good idea if Andy takes the statement from Pc Symonds rather than allowing him to write it himself, Andy won't miss anything.'

'Have we got a pathologist here yet?'

'The on call Home Office pathologist has been called and is on his way, it's Seamus Carter.'

'Well that's some good news at least, Seamus is the best.'

Danny had worked alongside Seamus Carter previously on a number of suspicious deaths. The two men were of a similar age and got on really well. They socialised off duty mainly because of their shared passion for football. Seamus Carter was a massive Nottingham Forest supporter.

'Thanks for getting everything organised so quickly Rob.'

'No problem Danny.'

'Where's the body?'

'Follow the tape, it's a few minutes' walk into the woods. Keep to the left of the tape and you'll eventually come to an area where the trees thin out a bit. The woman's body is in a natural clearing in the trees.'

'Is there another forensic suit in your car Rob? I've come here straight from home.'

'There's a couple of spares in the boot of the CID car, it's just up on the road, give me a minute, I'll get you one.'

As Rob walked off to get the forensic suit, thoughts began racing through Danny's head.

There was no way he could investigate a murder with this small team and still be expected to provide CID cover for the division.

Something would definitely have to give now. A serious major enquiry such as this, had always been his biggest fear.

Rob returned quickly with the suit which Danny put on along with gloves and overshoes.

'This way Danny, stick to the left of the tape, we've kept off the main footpath. Scenes of Crime are interested in some foot marks along there. Rachel's down at the scene itself with the Scenes of Crime team. I've instructed one of the Pc's up at the road to look out for Seamus Carter and to radio me when he arrives, so I can bring him down here.'

The two detectives made their way through the wood being extremely careful and observant as to where they placed their feet. They also deliberately avoided brushing against branches and shrubs along the route. The last thing they wanted to do was destroy any potential evidence by being careless. They eventually came to the clearing and as soon as Danny saw the body of the murdered woman he understood completely why the young Pc Symonds had been so effected.

The scene was one of utter carnage and depravity.

Danny could see the body of the woman lying naked on her back, her arms outstretched in the crucifix position her legs wide open exposing her genitalia.

Her face no longer existed, it had been smashed to a pulp and was now just a black mess of dried blood, matted blonde hair and disfigured flesh and bone.

He saw that both the hands had been mutilated, all the fingers and both thumbs had been severed and were nowhere to be seen. Carefully he made his way nearer to the body and on closer inspection he could see ligature marks around the wrists, she had been bound at some stage.

Perhaps the single most disturbing thing about this horrific sight was the fact that two words had been carved into the flesh of the woman's chest and stomach. The wounds had been caused by a very sharp blade and had started to pare back. The lettering was now distorted, but still legible.

The first word just above her breasts said "SCAB"

The second word on her stomach below the breasts said "LOVER"

'Jesus Christ!', muttered Danny

He turned to see Tim Donnelly, the man in charge of the SOC team, standing at the tree line holding an evidence bag.

'Morning Tim, have you found anything we can use?'

'It's early days sir, but so far nothing. Everything's been taken away.'

'What do you mean, taken away?'

'Well, things we'd usually expect to find at murder scenes, we just aren't finding here. Obviously she's naked but her clothes have been taken away. She was killed here the blood spatter on the plants shows us that all this damage was caused here, but her clothes have been stripped from her afterwards. You can see marks in the blood on her body where it's stopped at her clothing. Which means the clothing was removed after the injuries were caused. You've spotted the ligature marks on her wrists, well whatever she was bound with has also been removed. Weapons have been used and some sort of cutting implement was used to damage her hands, there's no sign of any of them. The fingers and both thumbs severed from her hands are all missing. My preliminary observations of the body reveal no obvious fibres from clothing, but like I say, it's still early days Inspector.'

'Thanks Tim.'

A message came over Rob Buxton's radio informing him that Seamus Carter had arrived. He immediately began to retrace his steps to meet the pathologist and guide him back into the scene. Danny then turned to a very pale looking Rachel, she was standing in her forensic suit at the edge of the clearing clutching a clipboard that contained the log of the scene.

Rachel was staring transfixed at the body of the murdered woman.

Danny asked, 'Are you ok Rachel?'

'I don't understand, how anyone could do this to another human being?'

'I've no answer to that question Rachel. All I know is that we've got to do everything we can to find the monster capable of doing this. We need to find them and lock them up, so they never have the chance to do it again. Have you logged me into the scene?'

'Yes boss, I logged you and the Sarge in, and I've logged him back out again', there was now more than a hint of steel in her voice.

Danny squatted down near to the left side of the body.

He slowly rubbed his chin with his left hand. He was perplexed by what his Scenes of Crime officer had said.

There should be things here.

His thoughts were interrupted by the sound of approaching voices and he recognised the booming voice and raw Irish brogue of Seamus Carter, the pathologist.

Seamus was a bear of a man. He was over six feet five and weighed around eighteen stone, with a mop of red hair and a large bushy red beard. He was a huge man with a big personality to match. As he entered the clearing and saw the body, he slowly exhaled in a low whistle.

'Sweet Jesus! What kind of maniac have we got in our midst? Morning Danny, what can you tell me? Any ideas who she is yet?'

'Nothing yet Seamus, I'm hoping you can maybe help me out with who she is.'

'Working on first impressions from what I can see so far, I think I'm going to struggle. Obviously dental records won't help because of the huge damage to the face, and her hands have been mutilated to stop us obtaining prints. I'll see if I can help you out with a time of death though.'

He set to work with his examination. Twenty minutes later he again stood up.

'Well she was definitely killed here at this location.

Sometime last night, around midnight is my best estimate. Are the undertakers on their way?'

'They're travelling sir', said Rob.

'Good, I want to get the body out of here and crack on with the post mortem as soon as possible. Danny have you noticed there's an object of some kind protruding slightly from the vagina?'

Danny shook his head slowly. Bending down to look closer, he could just about see the object.

'I've no idea what it is yet, that's why I want to get this poor woman out of here as soon as possible', he looked directly at Rob.

Rob said to Danny, 'Undertakers and transport will be here in five minutes' boss.'

'Tim, have you got all the photographs you need of the body in situ?' asked Danny.

'Yes boss we've got everything we need. Once the body's been removed we'll scan this area with a fine tooth comb, if there's anything here we'll find it.'

'Thanks Tim. Seamus are you ok? Is there anything else you need to do while the body's still in situ, or can we move her?'

'I'm fine, thank you Danny. Let's get her over to the mortuary at Mansfield.'

The big Irishman glanced at his watch.

'It's just coming up to eight thirty, shall we say nine thirty at the mortuary?'

'Ok Seamus, I've got to finish up here at the scene first, then I'll join you there as quick as I can.'

Danny tried to remain optimistic for his team, but he was extremely worried. He could already see that whoever was responsible for this brutal killing was showing signs of being extremely forensically aware. The mutilation of the face and hands was obviously an attempt at trying to delay or prevent identification of the woman.

Then on top of all that, there was the macabre message carved into the torso of the woman.

Questions were racing unanswered through Danny's mind.

Was it at all possible that this murder could be politically motivated?

Could a murder as horrific and savage as this one possibly have any connection to the ongoing bitter industrial dispute?

Danny's thoughts then turned to the object, spotted by Seamus, that had been purposefully inserted into the dead woman's vagina.

It was gearing up to be every detective's worst nightmare. There was the frenzied attack, evidence of a calculating and organised killer with the possibility of a sexual or political motive, or both.

Finally, to top it all off, Danny knew he had nowhere near enough staff to investigate it properly.

The undertakers arrived and began the grisly task of removing the body under the close supervision of the pathologist and the Scenes of Crime team.

Danny looked on, wondering how it could possibly be that less than twelve hours ago he'd been the happiest he'd been in years, and now he felt like a three-ton weight was slowly grinding him into the floor.

CHAPTER 38

Mansfield Mortuary – August 18th 1984

'Come in gentlemen', said Seamus Coleman.

Danny and Rob walked into the examination room at Mansfield Mortuary. The last time they were in this room was a couple of months ago when they'd attended the post mortem examination of Albie Jones, the miner who'd been found dead at Warsop Main Colliery.

The pathologist was already wearing a full gown and he pointed at the gowns hanging up.

'Gowns are there gents if you want to put them on.'

It was more of an instruction than a matter of choice and both detectives quickly put on the gowns.

Laid out in front of them on the stainless steel examination table was the body of the woman recovered from Annesley Woods.

Now in this stainless steel clinical setting, under the glaring white lights, the enormous damage caused to the woman's face and head could be clearly seen. The lower jawbone had been exposed and was jutting out grotesquely from the side of the woman's head. The gaping hole that had once been her mouth was now totally devoid of any teeth.

Both eyes had been obliterated and the sockets that once housed them had been smashed. The creamy coloured bone of the skull, that glared white under the harsh lights, could be seen on her forehead, where a large flap of skin had been pared back. The huge fractures on the forehead visible.

'Danny, I don't need to tell you that you're dealing with a monster here right enough', said the big Irishman quietly.

He paused before pointing to the smashed skull, 'The level of violence used to cause all these devastating injuries is way more than was necessary to cause her death. Even if, as I suspect, it has been done to avoid or hinder the identification process its way over the top. Danny, whoever did do this, firstly really hates women and secondly really enjoys the violence.'

Danny tried to remain focused and not be overwhelmed by the grisly injuries.

'Any idea what was used to cause the injuries Seamus?' he asked.

'Now that I've had the chance to have a close look under these powerful lights I can see what appears to be scuff marks around the sides of the head and the remnants of the ears. I would normally associate that type of marking with victims of kicking. I think the murderer started the assault by kicking her around the head and face. Most of the subsequent and more significant damage has been caused by a heavy blunt instrument, my best guess would be some kind of large claw hammer. At the centre of one of the fractures on the forehead is a round indentation, but the width is quite wide. Therefore, a large hammer.'

'What about the injuries to her hands?' asked Rob.

'My best guess would be something like small garden shears or bolt croppers to remove the fingers and thumbs. The damage to the palms of her hands, however, has been caused by a very sharp blade, possibly a craft knife or a

Stanley knife. Whatever was used to slash the hands, was also the same instrument used to carve out the two words on her abdomen.'

He paused, turning to his assistant who was standing ready with the camera.

'Tom have you got all the pictures needed of the injuries to the head and face?'

The young assistant nodded.

Seamus returned his attention to the detectives.

'Ok then gents, shall we see what's been inserted in her vagina. Tom, I want photos of every stage as we remove this item, ok.'

'I'm on it', the assistant said eagerly.

He positioned himself at the foot of the examination table and quickly changed the film in the camera.

It was usual for police Scenes of Crime officers to obtain these photographs but Seamus Carter always preferred to have his own assistant in the examination room. He believed it served as a valuable learning aid for his students to assist him at post mortem examinations.

Using a pair of thin forceps, very slowly the pathologist gently eased the foreign object out of the vagina. The camera constantly clicked throughout this process, with Tom eager to record every detail. Finally, the object was fully extracted and was revealed to be a black plastic tube approximately one inch in diameter and six inches in length.

Seamus picked the object up with the forceps and placed it carefully on a plastic tray. He then carried it over to a bench at the side of the examination room. On this bench was a large magnifying glass that was surrounded by a fluorescent light.

Both Danny and Rob watched on closely as the pathologist examined the object under the magnifying glass.

'This is getting ever more bizarre Danny, there's something inside the tube.'

Using a small set of tweezers Seamus eased a rolled up piece of paper out of the tube. Once again the camera held by Tom was clicking and whirring constantly throughout this process. Eventually and by using great care, Seamus delicately unfurled the paper, then assisted by Tom he placed the sheet of paper on a separate tray.

Danny leaned forward to look at the paper, 'There may be fingerprints on the paper Seamus. I'll need to get it Nin tested as soon as possible.'

Danny now spoke directly to the pathologist's assistant, 'Tom get plenty of photographs of the paper please.'

'Will do sir', came the assistants reply.

The Ninhydrin or Nin test is a process used to obtain fingerprints from paper. It is extremely effective but can seriously discolour the original paper.

Both detectives now examined the paper closely, they could see that on the paper was a type written note.

Seamus said, 'Alright detectives don't keep me in suspense, what's the message from our murderer?'

Rob Buxton read the note aloud,

This scab loving bitch is just the first.

While EVIL Thatcher and her storm trooper coppers are killing the coal fields

I will continue to kill more scab loving whores

The Coal Killer

248

The note had been prepared using a type writer. The lower case letter 'c' was slightly raised above the line of writing.

'Danny have you noticed the typewriter key for the letter 'c' is damaged?' said Rob.

'Well spotted Rob, that'll make the typewriter identifiable at least. The press would have a field day with this. "The Coal Killer", for Christ's sake.'

Seamus returned to the body of the young woman and began the full post mortem examination. As he worked he spoke his findings into a Dictaphone, a comprehensive written report would be prepared later. His work was steady and very methodical. As he worked, various items were handed to Rob for recording as exhibits. The detectives listened intently to the skilled pathologist as he worked and dictated his findings. Both men knew not to interrupt and to save any questions until after he had completely finished his examination.

Finally, the post mortem was complete.

Seamus took off his gloves and turned to Danny.

'Ok Danny, I'll give you a quick summary and go into more detail in my written report, if that's ok?'

'Of course Seamus, fire away.'

'Despite all of the horrific injuries to her head and face, the actual cause of death was asphyxia. She was strangled to death by a very thin cord, probably of a nylon make. Very thin but very strong. There are profound ligature marks on the skin of the neck and because the cord was so thin there is considerable damage to the windpipe. I'm pretty certain that the rest of this woman's horrendous injuries were all caused after her death. Reasonably quickly after her death, but definitely post mortem.'

He continued, 'There's absolutely no evidence of any sexual activity, which is surprising to me, only because of the way the body was staged at deposition. That and the fact that a foreign object had been placed in the vagina. There's no evidence of penetration or semen anywhere. I would estimate that our victim was a woman in her late forties, early fifties. Quite a heavy drinker, and a smoker. There are no tattoos or operation scars that might help you with the identification. I hope somebody's going to miss this poor woman or you're going to struggle to find out who she was. Sorry Danny.'

'Do you have any thoughts on the excessive violence used to cause all these massive injuries Seamus?'

'I'm sorry Danny that's a psychologist's territory. I can give an opinion, but that's all it would be, just an educated guess. Please don't hold me to it.'

'I appreciate that Seamus, but I'd still very much like to hear your opinion.'

'Well bizarrely it's like looking at the work of a number of different types of killers. We've all heard the theories about ordered and organised killers in comparison to the disorganised, frenzied killers. Just looking at the injuries inflicted on this woman, it looks like she's been unfortunate enough to meet all the different types of killer rolled into one. It's either that Danny, or everything we see before us today is just an elaborate game of smoke and mirrors. Sorry I'm not helping much am I?'

'No that's fine Seamus, how soon can I have your report and copies of the photographs?'

'Barring any other call outs today, will tomorrow morning be ok?'

'That would be great Seamus, thanks.'

Danny then turned to Rob, 'Have you finished bagging and labelling all the exhibits?'

'Yes boss.'

'Right then we need to get back to the nick. I'm going to need more staff, there's no way Jackson can refuse now. Let's get back and regroup. Rachel will have finished up at the scene now and Andy should have finished getting the statements of Mr Rose and Pc Symonds. We need to sort out where we're going with this and quickly Rob. You saw the note, there's a very real prospect of this maniac doing this again, and that's a terrifying thought.'

As they walked towards the door of the mortuary Seamus bellowed after them in his booming voice, 'Good hunting detectives!'

Danny and Rob nodded grimly and continued out the door without looking back.

CHAPTER 39

Mansfield Police Station – August 18th 1984

It was now almost two o'clock in the afternoon.

The small CID team were gathered in their office; they had been joined by Tim Donnelly from the Scenes of Crime Department.

Danny raised a hand and addressed the small gathering.

'Right let's get cracking, I've got a meeting with Superintendent Jackson in an hour to get more staff. I'm not taking no for an answer this time. Right Rachel and Tim, what have we got at the scene?'

It was Tim who spoke, 'I'm afraid there's very little at the scene Inspector. We've found footprints leading down to the scene and back up to the layby that we know definitely haven't been made by the police officers who subsequently attended. The significance of this being that the marks found appear to be of shoes or boots that are covered. We see the same type of footprints left by police officers when they're wearing overshoes. We've found absolutely no fibres of any kind on the floor or the surrounding vegetation. Again as a general rule it's something we'd expect to find at a scene such as this one. It's already very evident that your killer's extremely forensically aware and has taken every precaution to prevent leaving any trace evidence. I'm convinced this is also the reason why the clothes of the deceased were removed from the scene by the killer. It's been done purely and simply to prevent us finding fibres that may have been transferred onto her clothes from either the killer or whatever was used to transport her to that location.'

'Thanks Tim, have we got anything at all, exhibit wise, from the scene?'

'We've found a number of broken teeth around the scene which we've bagged up. I don't think they're going to be any use to you for identification purposes.'

'Any observations of the scene from you, Rachel?'

'No boss, other than like Tim, I've never been to such a sterile crime scene. The only other thing worth mentioning is how out of the way the deposition site is, unless you know that area well you'd never know that layby existed. It's hardly visible from the road.'

'That's a good point Rachel. I'd like you, as of right now, to start going through all our missing person's reports. Let the control room know that you're to be notified immediately if anyone reports a female, between forty and fifty-five years of age, missing. We know she was blonde, quite slim and about 5' 2' tall. She liked a drink and was either a smoker or has recently stopped. I know it's not much to go on but it's all we have. Hopefully somewhere out there somebody will be missing a wife, a mum, a sister or a daughter. We need a break and we need it fast.'

'Ok boss, no problem. I'll let the control room know straight away.'

'Thanks Rachel. Ok Andy, tell me about our witnesses please?'

'Our jogger, Mr Nathan Rose, is a twenty-year-old student, currently studying at Nottingham Trent University out at Brackenhurst near Southwell. He's originally from

Stone in Staffordshire. He's currently living at Chapel Terrace, Newstead Village in a rented terraced house he shares with two other students. The other two students have already gone home for the summer, one to Newcastle and one to London. Those two have been back home for the past four weeks and aren't expected back in Newstead for at least another fortnight. Nathan has the loan of a horse at Blidworth, so he's had to stay here to take care of it. He's studying Equine Dentistry at Brackenhurst so his passion is horses. I've checked him on the PNC and he's got no record of any convictions. I've checked his house mates and they're both clean too. This afternoon I made a discreet enquiry at Brackenhurst College. They're closed for the summer holidays, but the secretaries are there this week. The secretary I spoke to knows Nathan quite well, apparently he's a model student who's well into keep fit and athletics as well as everything horsy. Unlike most students he's not interested in drinking. He's very popular at Brackenhurst by all accounts. When I spoke to Nathan he told me that he regularly runs between Newstead and Hucknall to keep fit. He uses several different routes that either go through the woodland or around the farmers' fields. There was no particular reason for choosing the route he took today. I've also seized his running gear and his trainers for comparison with foot marks found at the scene, they are Nike Fireblade.'

Tim Donnelly interrupted.

'We've taken impressions of a training shoe print, but it was in an area well away from the body'.

Andy continued.

'Yeah that would tie in with what he's saying Tim, he told me that he realised it was a body straight away, he made a mental note of his location and then ran to the nearest phone box, which was back in Newstead Village. Having made the three nines call to the police telling them what he'd found, he then ran back to the layby and waited for the cops to arrive. He was waiting in the layby when the Panda car arrived, he then took Pc Symonds into the woods and showed him the location of the body. Nathan told me that he then helped the officer back to the police car as he was being sick. I've checked and the call was made from the telephone box he described. Although embarrassed a little about throwing up, Pc Symonds corroborates everything Nathan Rose has said. I think Rose is a stand-up guy boss, but just to be on the safe side I've fired a check into the local police in Stone, Staffordshire just to make sure there aren't any dark secrets lurking at home. Rose has promised to stick around and will be available if we need anything else.'

'Does he have a girlfriend Andy?' asked Danny

'Nobody special at the moment boss, he's seeing a girl from the college but it's low key, they both have too much going on in their lives at the moment to commit to anything serious, Nathan says they just date if there's a movie they both want to see, that sort of thing.'

'Can Pc Symonds add anything else?'

'Not really boss, but just for the record, I've seized the uniform and footwear he was wearing today in case any fibres are found at a later date.'

'Thanks Andy, good work. Have they both made written statements now?'

'Yes boss I've taken them.'

'Thanks Andy. Rob is there anything else you can add?'

'When I left the scene earlier, I took several different routes to and from the lay by. There isn't a camera in sight anywhere, so we're getting no help in that area. There are no other houses or buildings of any kind within a mile of the deposition site so there's no house to house to be done yet. If we get any further information on who our victim is or where she was abducted from, then we might need a team of officers for house to house enquiries. I'm happy that there's no chance we've missed anything at the scene. The uniform lads along with Tim's team, have done a very thorough fingertip search. Sorry, no pun intended boss, they found nothing apart from the few broken teeth we spoke about earlier. I've had the photos of the typed note, left by the killer, blown up for later use should we ever manage to find the typewriter used. We can maybe get an exact match from the damaged key.'

Once Rob had finished Tim Donnelly spoke up.

'I've had the Ninhydrin test on the killers note fast tracked and the result's back already. Unfortunately, it's a big fat zero. There were no marks of any kind found on the note.'

Danny took a brief moment to absorb all the information he'd just received.

'Right folks, I'm going to see Superintendent Jackson now about staffing levels. I'll also be having a conversation with him about what details we are prepared to release to the press at this stage. My personal view is that for the time being, we at least keep the contents of the note and the fact that words have been carved into the body to ourselves. I can't see any merits in releasing that information to the press right now. Andy did you impress on Nathan Rose that he wasn't to discuss the details of what he saw this morning with anybody?'

'I did boss and he assures me that he's no intention of talking to anybody about it.'

Danny turned to his small team.

'I want all our efforts for the time being to be focussed on the identification of the dead woman. The fact is we've got no worthwhile witnesses and no forensic evidence to follow up, so until we can identify our victim we're struggling. Unless anybody has anything to add or any questions, let's get cracking.'

Nothing was said, the team immediately began getting on with their individual tasks.

CHAPTER 40

Mansfield Police Station – August 18th 1984

'This is bad Danny, really bad'.

Superintendent Ken Jackson was shaking his head as he tried to take in what Danny had just told him.

'If this gets out to the press they'll have a field day. I totally agree with you, we keep both the message carved on the body and the typewritten note to ourselves. I'll go over to the Chief Constable's office this afternoon to brief him. Will you be available to attend that briefing this afternoon?'

'Yes sir, of course I can attend the briefing, but what I really need, immediately, is more staff!'

'From what I've heard so far Danny, until you discover the identity of this dead woman there aren't any manpower intensive enquiries to do, or have I misunderstood that?'

'No sir, you haven't misunderstood me, but I'm confident that with more staff on the ground we'll be able to identify this woman a lot quicker. Believe me, when you've seen the handiwork of this maniac close up, time really is of the essence here. The last thing we can afford to do is drag our feet, and allow another woman to be murdered.'

'Danny don't try to play emotional blackmail with me. As soon as the woman's been identified, I promise you I'll re-evaluate the levels of manpower you need for each enquiry and provide more staff accordingly. The best I can do, in the meantime, is to get two of your detectives recalled from strike duty to run the CID office while your team remains focussed on this murder enquiry.'

'Look sir, with respect, you're missing the point, the more manpower I have the easier it'll be to swamp the area and try to ascertain who this woman is.'

'No you're the one who's missing the point Danny! What I've just offered you is the best I can do at the moment. This strike isn't going away any time soon and our resources are already stretched to the limit. I cannot justify taking any more men from the PSU's.'

Danny was starting to get annoyed and frustrated.

'And how will you justify the death of another innocent woman if this maniac means what he said in the note, and this woman is just the first?'

'That note contains nothing more than the ramblings of a lunatic, I don't put any credibility into that claim and I'm sure the Chief Constable will agree with me this afternoon. I'm warning you Detective Inspector, you'd better moderate your tone this afternoon, is that clear?'

'Oh yes, crystal clear sir.'

'Be back here at three thirty sharp ready to travel over to Headquarters.'

'Yes, sir.'

Danny came out of the office feeling exhausted and walked slowly back to his office. He couldn't believe what he'd just heard, "the ramblings of a lunatic" the Superintendent had said.

They were exactly that, but he'd missed off one word, he should have described the note as the ramblings of a homicidal lunatic.

He slumped down in a chair in the CID office.

'Everything ok Danny? You look shattered', said Rob.

Danny started to explain to Rob about the two extra staff and the rest of the conversation he'd just had with Ken Jackson.

Suddenly Rachel came hurtling into the office.

'I think we've just had a huge slice of luck. The barmaid at the Prince Charles pub in Forest Town has just phoned the nick to complain about a bloke coming into the pub demanding to know where his girlfriend is. He'd threatened to smash the pub up, if the barmaid didn't tell him the name of the bloke his girlfriend had gone off with, when she left the pub last night. The uniform lads have got the guy at the pub now. He's still kicking off and has been arrested.'

'Exactly how is that lucky for us Rachel?' asked Rob.

'Because the barmaid says the woman in question is always going off with different blokes. Her name's Mandy Stokes, she's 47 years old, a blonde and has legs to die for apparently. The sergeant in the control room thought she sounded similar to the missing person reports I asked him to notify me about.'

'Right you two, get straight over to the Prince Charles pub. Let the cops arrest the guy kicking off for a breach of the peace, he can be left in the cells here for us to talk to later. First of all, I want this barmaid talking to properly, fetch her back here. I want chapter and verse on this Mandy Stokes. I'm going with Jackson to see the Chief Constable at Headquarters now to discuss staffing levels and press releases. Rob I want a full update from you the minute I get back.'

'Yes boss!' Rob shouted as he and Rachel legged it out the door.

CHAPTER 41

Mansfield Police Station – August 18th 1984

'I'm not one to moan detective, I just don't know why I had to come down here, that's all I'm saying.'

The complaining voice belonged to Trisha Miller, the barmaid from the Prince Charles pub who had called the police about the disturbance earlier.

She continued angrily, 'I could've told you everything I know at the pub. I bloody hate cop shops.'

Rachel tried to soothe the angry barmaid.

'Look Trisha, I've got a lot to ask you and it's not going to take five minutes. The pub was heaving and this is important, surely you realise that. I can't talk to you in between you pulling pints for the punters, now can I?'

'Ok I get it, but how long's this going to take?'

'I'll try and get through everything as quick as I can. The landlord's fine with it, he's told me to take as long as I need. He's assured me he won't be stopping your money. I'll be as quick as I can, I promise you, but I have to be thorough as well, I can't afford to miss anything out.'

Trisha sat open mouthed for a few seconds, before smiling and saying, 'Bloody hell, I can't believe you've got that tight bastard at the pub to pay my wages while I'm stuck down here, how did you manage that sweetheart?'

'I can be very persuasive when I have to be Trisha, so don't worry about losing any money. I need you to concentrate fully on what we're going to be talking about.'

Trisha Miller shrugged in resignation.

She was edging towards thirty years of age now and had been married since she was eighteen, she had three kids all girls and all between the ages of ten and seven.

After the birth of her third daughter, Trisha had made her husband go for the snip, she was starting to feel like a brood mare.

It had been back in March when she first started working at the pub, she wanted to at least have some money coming in as her bloke had joined the strike.

Trisha found that she really enjoyed the work, it made such a refreshing change to talk to adults instead of children all day, she had no intention whatsoever of giving up the job at the pub after the strike came to an end.

She was still an attractive woman, with a pretty face and bright blue eyes. Her blonde hair was cut in an elfin style. Even after having her three children she still managed to keep her figure. She considered her full breasts to be her best asset and always wore low cut blouses.

Today was no different, and she'd already noticed more than one appreciative glance from the boys in blue at the police station. Leaning back in the chair Trisha took a sip of the coffee she'd been given.

'Ok, what do you want to know?'

Rachel leaned forward placing her elbows on the table.

'Trisha when did you last see Mandy Stokes?'

'Mandy was in the pub yesterday evening; she'd been at the engagement party in the Lounge most of the night. I didn't see much of her in there because I was serving in the Tap Room last night. Mandy only came into the Tap Room to get a drink at last orders because she couldn't get served in the Lounge.'

'How did she seem?'

'She was well on her way to being drunk, let's say she'd certainly had a few, that's for sure.'

'Was she with anybody?'

'When she came into the tap room she was on her own, I don't know if she'd been with anybody in the Lounge.'

'What did she order?'

'That's easy. Mandy always has the same drink, Bacardi and Coke.'

'How many did she have Trisha?'

'In the tap room, just one, it was last orders.'

'Did you have a chat with her or just serve her a drink?'

'We chatted, but only briefly.'

'What about?'

'Basically I asked her if she'd copped off. Mandy said she hadn't and that they were all twats next door. She told me she'd be walking home alone as soon as she'd finished her drink.'

'Did she say which way she was going home?'

'Yeah, she did as it happens. She said she only had to walk down Pump Hollow Lane. I remember it because I'd told her to be careful walking home on her own.'

'Can you remember what Mandy was wearing last night Trisha?'

'She'd got a short skirt on as usual. You can't blame the girl; she's got great legs for her age. I think the skirt was white and she'd got a black see through blouse on.'

'How well do you know Mandy?'

'Everyone knows Mandy, as she's a bugger for the men. That knobhead who came in the pub shouting the odds today, thinks he's her boyfriend. Mandy's got lots of blokes on the go, if you know what I mean detective?'

'Is she very promiscuous?'

'If that means does she shag about, then yes she does!'

'And you're certain Mandy left the pub alone and was going to go straight home?'

'That's what she said and I didn't see anybody leave with her or after her.'

Rachel paused thoughtfully.

'All these men that she sees, have you ever heard any of them make any kind of threat to her face, or threaten her behind her back?'

'No, I've never heard anything like that. All the blokes involved with Mandy know exactly what she's like. I think they just enjoy copping off with her, she must be hot stuff eh?'

Trisha winked at the detective.

'What about the guy we arrested at the pub today?'

'You mean Mr Knobhead, I don't really know him, he's a lorry driver from out of town, I think he stays with Mandy when he's up this way.'

'Was he in the pub last night?'

'I didn't see him, and Mandy did tell me she was going home on her own.'

Rachel had nearly finished.

'Trisha have you ever been to Mandy's house?'

'No, never. I like her, but we're not friends, if you know what I mean. I know where her house is, but I've never been inside.'

'Does Mandy have any kids or other next of kin that live nearby?'

'I think she's got a grown up daughter, but I haven't a clue where she lives. I know her husband left the area when they split up, he went back to Ireland I think. Mandy's lived on her own ever since. As long as I've known her, Mandy's always been footloose and fancy free.'

Not any more, thought Rachel, if Mandy did turn out to be the murdered woman.

'Ok Trisha, thanks. You've been a great help. I need to take a written statement from you, so I can get down on paper what you've just told me about last night. I promise you it won't take long.'

Trisha sighed loudly.

'Ok detective, but before you start, is there any chance I can have another coffee please?'

'Of course you can Trisha. I'll go and grab us some coffee, I'll have one with you while I'm writing your statement.'

At the same time as Rachel was talking to Trisha Miller, just along the corridor in the cell block area, Rob was going into an interview room with Ted Grozier.

He was the lorry driver from out of town who'd been arrested to prevent a breach of the peace at the Prince Charles pub.

Grozier had been technically released without charge now that there was no likelihood of the breach of the peace, he had instigated, reoccurring.

He was now assisting Rob voluntarily with his enquiries.

Ted Grozier was forty-three years old and was quite short and stocky with receding brown hair. He was wearing a pair of bottle green overalls with the name 'Kleenwipes' embroidered in yellow thread on the left breast pocket.

He had a ruddy complexion and the biggest hands the detective had ever seen.

Rob sat quietly in the room and stared directly across the interview desk at Ted Grozier.

'Ted, my name's Detective Sergeant Rob Buxton. I've a few questions for you before you leave the police station, are you happy to stay and assist me with my enquiries?'

Grozier simply nodded.

'Ok Ted, we're concerned that Mandy Stokes appears to have gone missing. I need to find out if there's anything you know that might assist us in finding her.'

'Ok sergeant, if there's any way I can help you, I will.'

Even though technically Grozier had been released from custody Rob had no intention of letting him leave the police station. If Grozier made any attempt to leave, Rob had already made up his mind to arrest him on suspicion of murder. But for now he wanted to try and keep Grozier happy and helping voluntarily.

Rob had noted a strong Welsh accent from Grozier's first reply.

'That's not a local accent Ted, where are you from?'

'I'm from Rhyl in Wales. I drive an HGV delivering toilet rolls all over the UK.'

'Which firm do you drive for Ted?'

'It's a firm called Kleenwipes.'

He pointed to the embroidered name badge on his overalls and continued, 'They're a big company. They provide toilet rolls and tissues to hotels all over the country.'

'Do you drive all over the UK then Ted?'

'Yes, everywhere, it depends on where the orders are. I can be in Scotland one day, then back down to the Midlands the next.'

'So you don't do a regular delivery then?'

'No. I'm all over everywhere me, detective.'

'So Ted, tell me how long you've known Mandy Stokes?'

'I've known my Mandy for just over a year now. We first met when she was on holiday in Rhyl, my home town see.

We had a few drinks together and got on really well. We're both single and well, you know, one thing led to another and we ended up sleeping together. She gave me her address up here boy, and said if ever I was delivering up this way I should call in.'

'Do you see her up here very often then Ted?'

He thought for a moment, and made eye contact with the detective, 'I only deliver up here once in a blue moon. Since we first met in Rhyl, I think I've only seen Mandy about five times. When I found out yesterday that I was coming up to Nottingham today, I called Mandy and arranged to see her. I did my drop at the Grosvenor Hotel in Nottingham at about half past four this morning and then drove straight to Mandy's house. I won't lie to you detective; I was bloody angry when she wasn't at home. I knew she was going to that party last night and I just assumed she'd copped off with another bloke. That's why I was angry, see.'

'I can see why that would get you annoyed Ted. So what time did you arrive at Mandy's house this morning?'

'I got to Mandy's place at around five fifteen, there was no answer when I knocked on the door. I thought that's odd, because normally Mandy's up and waiting for me when she knows I'm coming over. It's always the same routine detective, she does me some nice bacon and eggs, standing there in her little nightie, teasing me with her great legs and arse. I eat my breakfast while she has a cup of coffee and a fag and then we go back to bed. You know what I'm saying detective, you're a man of the world, I can see that, I don't have to spell it out to you, do I?'

'No Ted you don't, I get the picture. Did you go into Mandy's house this morning?'

'Yeah, that's how I knew she hadn't been home. Mandy always leaves a spare front door key under a brick in the front garden, the key was still there so I went in. It was obvious she hadn't been home.'

'Where's this front door key now Ted?'

'It's here.'

Grozier fumbled in his trouser pocket and removed a Yale door key which he handed over to Rob.

'Ted, why did you assume that Mandy had gone off with another bloke last night?'

'Come off it detective, I'm not stupid. I know what my Mandy's like, she's the kind of woman that needs a man in her bed. I'm not daft enough to think I'm the only one.'

'Why get so angry about it at the pub then?'

'I don't know really. The anger, it just came over me I suppose. I think it was just because we'd made a set arrangement and she knew I was coming over. I just thought with her knowing I was coming she would've been at home that's all. I was looking forward to my bacon and eggs I suppose. Not to mention the afters.'

He grinned at Rob.

'Do you know if Mandy has any family local?' asked Rob ignoring the grin.

'All Mandy told me, was that her husband had fucked off back to Ireland years ago and that she had one daughter, who's now grown up and that she doesn't see. I think her daughter lives on the east coast somewhere, at one of the holiday places. Yeah that's right, I think it's Skegness or maybe Mablethorpe. That's why she was having a holiday in Rhyl so she didn't bump into her daughter.'

'Ok Ted, thanks for being so open and honest with me. I'll need to know the name of your Transport Manager at Kleenwipes so I can verify your deliveries and times for today's run and I'll also need the name of the person you spoke to at the Grosvenor Hotel in Nottingham so I can verify what time you left there. I'll then need to take a written statement from you about everything you've told me about Mandy Stokes. Are you ok for time Ted?'

'No problem detective. I'm not picking my next load up until first thing tomorrow morning. I'd planned to be spending the whole day with Mandy.'

He then looked thoughtful and fixed his eyes on the detective, 'Can I ask you a question detective? Why are you lot so interested in my Mandy?'

'We're just a little concerned about her being missing that's all Ted. Now what's the name of your Transport Manager?'

'His name's Brian Davies, I won't be getting into trouble with the firm when you call him, will I?'

'Don't worry about that Ted, I'll make the call myself and tell him you witnessed a road accident or something.'

'Ok thanks detective. The other guy you wanted who works at the hotel, he's an Asian bloke, I know his first name's Manjeet, but I'm not sure of his last name. He deals with all their deliveries and unloading.'

'Thanks Ted, do you want a drink before I start on your written statement?'

'A cup of tea would be great mind. Thanks.'

Rob left the room, leaving a uniformed constable outside the door. He made the two phone calls to Kleenwipes and the Grosvenor Hotel. Both calls confirmed exactly what Grozier had said about the timings of his pick up and deliveries.

He was telling the truth.

Rob returned to the interview room with two cups of tea, 'Right Ted, let's get cracking on this statement shall we.'

The lorry driver picked up the mug in his giant hands, sipped his tea and nodded.

CHAPTER 42

Pump Hollow Lane, Mansfield – August 18th 1984

Rob parked the CID car outside the row of semi-detached houses on Martyn Avenue, a quiet street just off Pump Hollow Lane at Forest Town.

In the car with him were Danny and Ted Grozier.

Grozier pointed to a large HGV that was parked up a little further down Martyn Avenue, 'That's my wagon over there see. I can never park the bloody thing right outside Mandy's house, it's just too long for the bend. That's her house over there, number 34.'

Rob looked over his shoulder into the rear of the car and said, 'Ok Mr Grozier, we may need to speak to you again at some point, but for now, thanks for your help and try to keep that temper of yours a bit more in check.'

'I will detective, I was only gobbing off, see. I would never hurt anyone. You'll let me know when you find Mandy won't you. I really do like her, she's a great girl.'

'We will Ted, try not to worry.'

Grozier then got out of the car and walked up the road towards his HGV. The two detectives also got out of the car and made their way to the front door of 34 Martyn Avenue.

Using the Yale key, he had been given by Grozier, Rob opened the front door.

It was a typical three bedroom, semi-detached house.

There was a lounge that went right through into a small dining room, a kitchen, hall stairs and landing and three bedrooms and a bathroom.

The house was neat, tidy and very clean.

There were no pots and pans in the sink, the kitchen was spotless. There was plenty of food in the refrigerator. Rob took out a pack of bacon and noted that it had a long sell by date. There was also a tray of fresh eggs.

The three bedrooms were all clean and tidy, although the third bedroom was being used more as a large store cupboard than a bedroom.

The main bedroom was a very feminine room. It had been decorated in a dusky pink theme. A large double bed covered with a thick, fresh white duvet dominated the room and there was a large white sheepskin rug on the floor.

The bathroom was a neutral cream colour and was full of women's toiletries, bath salts, hair conditioners and the like.

There wasn't a razor blade or any after shave. It was obvious no man lived at the house.

The detectives did a thorough search but there was nothing to suggest that Mandy Stokes had decided to take a sudden holiday. Rob found an in date passport for Mandy Stokes in one of the bedside table drawers in the main bedroom.

In the box room upstairs Danny found a photo album.

The album was full of pictures of a pretty, petite woman with blonde hair and long legs. In nearly every photo the woman was wearing either a mini skirt or very short shorts.

Danny held up one of the photos.

'This must be Mandy.'

'We can soon get it verified with the barmaid at the Prince Charles, boss.'

'Yeah, let's do that. What do you reckon Rob, do you think Mandy Stokes is our dead woman?'

'I'd put my mortgage on it Danny. Mandy left the pub at around eleven o'clock last night intending to walk home alone, I think the reason she never made it home is because she was intercepted by our killer. She'd made an arrangement to see somebody today that she hasn't kept, she fits the description perfectly and the time of death fits as well.'

'I agree Rob, we can't get a visual identification but let's start doing enquiries with her local GP and get blood group, medical history etc. I recall seeing the dead woman's blood group is AB negative, which is extremely rare. I'll talk to Seamus Carter again; I need to ascertain if the dead woman had ever been pregnant. I don't recall reading about a pregnancy in his report. I might've just missed him referring to it.'

As they left the house Danny locked the front door and said, 'I've made my mind up Rob, I've got to regard Mandy Stokes as our dead woman until proved otherwise. First thing in the morning, as soon as it gets light, I want a full search of this area. Start on Pump Hollow Lane from its junction with Martyn Avenue and work back up the hill towards the Prince Charles pub.'

'Ok boss, I'll get that sorted.'

'I also want all the houses on Martyn Avenue, Pump Hollow Lane and the other two roads on the estate to have a full house to house enquiry. I want a full team on it, I want every house visited as a matter of urgency. I'll go and see Jackson and see if he's as good as his word, we definitely need the extra manpower now. You'd better have a word with Rachel and Andy, there'll be no days off for the foreseeable future. Obviously that goes for me and you as well.'

'No problem boss. Good luck with the extra staff, we're going to need it. I know how stubborn Jackson can be.'

'Stubborn or not, we've got to be given more manpower, this is a murder enquiry for Christ's sake. One other thing Rob, arrange for Andy to be down here at first light with the search teams so he can brief them properly. I want the Special Operations Unit out to do the search, I don't care what strike duties they've got tomorrow, this takes precedence. Andy can brief them and then the house to house teams. I want the house to house enquiries to start no later than eight o'clock in the morning.'

'Ok Danny, I'll get it organised.'

'I know I sound like a broken record Rob and I know I'm fast becoming a pain in the arse!'

'I can't say I've noticed any change Danny!'

'Very funny! I just know that we need to get cracking on this Rob. I'm convinced that we haven't heard the last of this lunatic.'

'I know what you mean boss, and for what it's worth I think you're dead right. I'll get everything organised.'

CHAPTER 43

Pump Hollow Lane, Mansfield – August 19th 1984

It was four thirty in the morning.

The early morning sky was changing from the black of night, to the purple hues that appear just before the sun creeps slowly over the horizon.

The air was refreshingly cool. A group of police officers were standing outside two police Transit vans that were parked at the junction of Martyn Avenue and Pump Hollow Lane. The men spoke in hushed whispers out of deference to the early hour and the close proximity to residential properties.

Two full sections of the Special Operations Unit were being briefed by Detective Constable Andy Wills. The briefing only lasted five minutes, was short and to the point. Andy quickly explained the reason for the search, it was suspected that a woman had been abducted from somewhere along this stretch of the road.

He made it clear to the gathered officers that he was interested in anything, however small, that looked out of place or that looked like it had recently been dropped there. He was also very interested in any signs of a struggle.

Pump Hollow Lane had been closed in both directions for the duration of the search. The entire stretch of road, between the junction of Martyn Avenue and the crossroads where the Prince Charles pub was located, was almost six hundred yards long. The road varied in width along the way being narrower at the Martyn Avenue end.

It wasn't a busy road, especially so at that time of the day and Andy hoped his decision to close the road wouldn't cause too many issues.

Motorists in the area had become used to having their travel plans disrupted ever since the start of the strike. All too often the residents of this and other towns across Nottinghamshire had seen main roads closed without notice to prevent large numbers of pickets getting through to the coal mines.

At this time of day though, traffic would be minimal.

At a single instruction from one of the two sergeants present, the two sections of Special Ops officers spread themselves out in a line that spanned from one side of Pump Hollow Lane to the other.

From hedgerow to hedgerow, the officers were on their knees moving slowly. Intermittently an officer would raise his hand and the whole line would stop. One of the section sergeants would take possession of whatever had been found and then place the object into an evidence bag before completing the relevant exhibit label.

Andy walked slowly with the two Special Ops sergeants, staying behind the line of kneeling officers, as they slowly and methodically searched every inch of the road.

After fifteen minutes of agonisingly slow progress the man on his knees to the extreme far right of the search line stopped and raised his right arm. Once again the entire line stopped, and as before the section sergeant approached the man.

The sergeant turned and shouted.

'Detective, I think you'll want to see this'.

Andy walked briskly over to the far right of the line.

'What have you got Sarge?'

'Just there, right in the bottom of the hedge.'

The sergeant indicated a handbag lying in the hedge bottom. Andy saw immediately that the handbag was clean and looked relatively dry. It was obvious it hadn't been in the hedgerow very long. The handbag was made from black leather and had a gold chain as a strap.

'Do you still have the Polaroid cameras on the vans?' Andy asked.

'We certainly do. I'll get a couple of photographs of it in situ before we recover it.'

'Thanks Sarge.'

The second of the two sergeants indicated for the rest of the men to resume the search while his colleague walked off to retrieve the camera from the van.

Andy looked around him, Pump Hollow Lane narrowed slightly here, the pavements were quite narrow and looking up he could see that there was only one old street light for this whole area. With just the one street light, this particular stretch of the road would be very dark at night.

The sergeant returned and took a couple of Polaroid photographs of the bag still lying in the hedge bottom, before removing it carefully and placing it in a brown evidence bag. He completed the exhibit label and then passed everything to Andy.

Andy carried the brown bag back to his car.

He opened the boot of his car and placed a paper sheet on the floor of the boot before putting on a pair of latex gloves and removing the handbag from the evidence bag.

Andy then carefully opened the handbag and placed the individual items on the paper sheet.

There were only three items in the handbag.

A small black leather purse, a bright red lipstick and a packet of 20 Benson & Hedges cigarettes that contained eleven cigarettes and a slim plastic lighter.

He carefully opened the black purse.

The first thing he saw was a membership card for Blockbuster Video that had the name M. Stokes on the back.

'Bingo!' he said aloud and began to replace everything back into the handbag. He then placed the handbag back into the evidence bag.

Using the radio in his car he left a message with the control room instructing either Det Insp Flint or Det Sgt Buxton to contact him at the search site on Pump Hollow Lane as soon as they came on duty at six o'clock that morning.

CHAPTER 44

Mansfield Police Station – August 21st 1984

It was now the morning of the third day.

Three days had come and gone since the discovery of Mandy Stokes battered remains in Annesley Woods.

Danny had gathered his small team together in the CID office to assess how far the enquiries into her murder had progressed. He looked around the room at his team, they were all exhausted. Every one of them had remained at work since the discovery of the body, taking naps in between enquiries at work. Phone calls had been made regularly to their loved ones explaining why they were staying at work and not coming home.

The handbag found on Pump Hollow Lane during the fingertip search carried out by the Special Operations Unit had been positively identified by Trisha Miller, the barmaid at the Prince Charles pub.

She was certain that it was the bag Mandy Stokes had with her in the pub on the night she disappeared. Trisha could remember in detail the way a drunken Mandy had noisily placed the bag on the bar as she ordered her drink.

Specifically, she recalled the gold chain link strap that had rattled so noisily on the hard wooden bar of the pub.

Danny now addressed the team.

'I'm certain now that Mandy Stokes is our victim. The enquiries that have been made with her GP over her medical history and the fact that her blood group matches our victim have convinced me. I don't think we'll ever get a cast iron identification, but all the evidence we have suggests that Mandy was abducted from Pump Hollow Lane and taken to Annesley Woods where she was murdered. It occurs to me that not realising she'd dropped her handbag was the first mistake our killer has made. He's been so careful, so forensically aware that if he'd seen her drop the bag there's no way he would've left it behind.'

Andy then spoke up, 'Nothing else of any relevance was found on the search boss, I've been back there at night and where the bag was found is the darkest part of the road, the level of street lighting is really bad.'

'There's nothing from the house to house as yet boss', said Rachel.

Rob spoke next, 'I've tracked down all of Mandy's casual lovers that we know about, and spoken to them all. They can all account for their movements that night and all their alibis check out. I've also confirmed that Ted Grozier was picking his load up in Cardiff at 12.30am on the morning Mandy was killed, which rules him out completely.'

Danny paused taking in the information he had been given.

'Thanks everyone. Your efforts have been amazing; I know the hours you've all put in. The good news is we're now officially dedicated to this murder enquiry full time. The superintendent has finally agreed to take one more Dc and a Ds off the PSU's to help take care of the everyday work generated by the CID office. This will stay the same for the duration of the strike or until we solve this murder. So, from today all your efforts will be focussed on catching this killer.

I know we don't have much to go on, but there are some enquiries still outstanding.'

Andy said, 'I'm still trying to identify the paper the note was typed on. I've sent it to the lab for analysis. I'll keep chasing it so I can then get a list of suppliers. I'm also trying to identify the make of the typewriter used from the impressions made by the keys.'

'Good work Andy, make sure you keep at them', said Danny.

Rachel said, 'I'm still working my way through the guest list for the engagement party at the Prince Charles pub, so far everyone remembers Mandy being there but nobody remembers her being with anybody else.'

'How many have you still got to talk to Rachel?'

She quickly looked down at the list of names and addresses in front of her.

'I've spoken to twenty-seven of them, but there's at least another forty-six still to get through.'

'Rob, can you give Rachel a dig out on that enquiry, let's get these people seen as a matter of urgency please. While we're at it lets talk to Trisha Miller again and see if she can remember anything about the punters in the tap room that night. Up to now we've only concentrated on the engagement do in the lounge. Let's make it a priority to identify as many punters as possible from the tap room and talk to them as well. Any one of them may have seen Mandy leaving with someone.'

'Ok boss we're on it', said Rob.

'I've got to go over to Headquarters again this morning to talk to the Chief Constable about the television appeal that's scheduled for broadcasting this evening on the local news at half past six. I don't think he's going to want any of the items that relate to the strike forming part of the release, but we'll see. It's twenty past eight now, I want everyone back here at six o'clock this evening before the press appeal is shown on the TV. You never know the phones might start ringing with new information. It's going to be another long day folks.'

CHAPTER 45

Warsop, Nottinghamshire – August 31st 1984

As the month of August drew to a close the number of miners regularly going into work at Warsop Main Colliery had grown to fifteen.

It was still the same routine every morning getting the men in and out of work. The only difference, was that the taxi's being used to pick up the men in the morning had now been replaced by two hired Transit vans.

Sgt Mick Reynolds was still in charge of the Metropolitan Police PSU that escorted the miners into work every day.

As soon as the small convoy reached the standby point at the disused quarry, all the miners and the police officers would get out of the vans to stretch their legs before the 'battle bus' arrived.

The police officers would also use the time to start getting their protective clothing on. All the men, miners and police officers alike, took the opportunity to have a quick hot drink and a cigarette and every morning, without fail, Mick Reynolds would seek out Jimmy Wade.

The two men would disappear to a quiet corner of the yard to talk and smoke a cigarette over a cup of tea while they waited to make the journey into the colliery.

The other police officers in the PSU had thought it all a bit strange. They knew their sergeant was a closed book and kept his cards very close to his chest, but they found it slightly weird that he could find so much to laugh and joke about with the striking miner.

On one occasion one of the young constables made a comment in the van about 'the odd couple'. Unfortunately, his careless remark was overheard by the sergeant. The young cop received an almighty dressing down by a clearly livid Reynolds. After that incident nobody else had dared to comment out loud again. The men all came to the decision that if he wanted to be friends with the scab miner, let him get on with it. Today was no different, the two men stood well away from the rest of the gathering. They were both smoking cigarettes and sipping hot tea well out of earshot.

'It's September tomorrow for Christ's sake. I say we find another one now, Jimmy.'

'The dust hasn't settled from the last one yet Mick, we'd be crazy to go again already.'

'That's just where you're wrong Jimmy old son, it's the perfect time. They've got nothing, they know nothing. You saw the appeal they put out on the TV, it was pathetic. They're shit scared, they never once mentioned the connections to the strike we left. You saw it Jimmy, not a word about the note, nothing about the state of the body and no mention of 'The Coal Killer' name we left in the note. Trust me Jimmy, the Chief Constable will be more bothered about all that getting out into the public domain, than he'll be about finding us.'

'Mick I reckon just to be on the safe side, we let the dust settle for another week, then we go again.'

Mick sighed and shrugged his shoulders, finally accepting that he wasn't going to be able to change the other mans mind.

'Ok Jimmy if you insist. My deployment here finishes next week on the 7th September. I'll be going home for a week the following day; I won't be back up here until the 15th. I'm happy to do as you say and wait another week as long as we go again before I've got to go back. How about the night before on Thursday 6th September?'

'Ok Mick you're on. I'll check out a couple of different venues this time. Last time was all a bit hit and miss. I want to make sure we go to a busy venue next time, where we can just blend in and where there's plenty of targets to choose from.'

He smiled and fixed Mick with those cold blue eyes.

'It's my turn to actually do the killing this time though Mick, you hogged all the fun last time.'

Mick smiled and let out a small chuckle.

'Whatever you say Jimmy, whatever you say.'

CHAPTER 46

Retford, Notts – September 4th 1984

The long hot summer didn't look like ending any time soon. The first week of the new month had brought record temperatures, along with long, hot and humid nights.

Tempers everywhere were fractious, and none more so than at the home of DC Andy Wills.

Since the very beginning of the strike, Andy had worked very long and very unsociable hours. As well as the long hours worked, there was also a three quarters of an hour commute to get to work and back every day.

The pressure of these long days, spent away from home, was starting to mount up and cracks in his personal life were starting to appear. Andy, like the other officers that remained in the CID, had taken only one day off a week since March. After the murder of Mandy Stocks, in the second week of August, he hadn't been able to take a single day off.

Andy's wife Sally tried to be patient and had done her best to be understanding of his demanding job, but now she was getting to the end of her tether.

Andy had, as usual, left the house at seven o'clock that morning. It was now nine thirty at night.

What was he trying to do, kill himself?

He'd telephoned earlier in the day to say he was having another busy day and that he'd try to be home sometime around nine o'clock that night.

Suddenly, Sally saw headlights flash across the lounge wall and heard a car pull onto the driveway. The door of the car slammed shut, and she heard footsteps walking slowly across the gravel drive. After a few seconds she heard the noise of the key in the front door.

Andy opened the door and was surprised to see his wife standing there, arms folded, in the hallway.

'Hello sweetheart, how was your day?' he asked.

Although a pleasant enough greeting, the glibness of his comment was enough to finally tip, an already seething, Sally over the edge.

'How was my day, how was my fucking day? You don't have a clue what day it is, do you?'

The importance of the date instantly dawned on Andy.

It was the 4th of September, their wedding anniversary.

'Of course I know what day it is sweetheart, it's our wedding anniversary.'

'And what wonderful events have you got planned to mark this special day, husband dear? Are we going to the theatre to see a nice show? Perhaps a lovely meal at a Michelin star restaurant? Are they flowers you've brought me?' she asked sarcastically.

Andy hated it when his wife got angry. He always felt like he was in the witness box at Crown Court being cross examined. When she was angry and upset Sally could not help slipping into Barrister mode, it was her way of lashing out.

'I'm really, really sorry Sally. You know how it's been for me at work at the moment. What with this murder enquiry on top of the bloody strike, we're all working flat out, it's not just me Sal.'

Sally was warming to her theme now, 'It's one day Andy, it wouldn't have killed you to ask for one bloody day off. You do remember you've got a wife, don't you? I think you're way too preoccupied with the bloody police force, the bloody CID!'

'Sally, listen to me.'

'Listen to you, why should I?'

'Let me explain Sally.'

'I swear I'd see more of you if you'd got a bloody mistress on the side!'

Andy was desperately trying to control his own temper, he was tired and irritable and the last thing he needed now was a slanging match with his wife. He loved Sally more than anything else in the world, but his own professional pride made him stay at work until the job was done.

Andy persevered he knew he had to try and make her understand, 'Give me a break Sally, you knew what my job entailed three years ago when we got married. You helped me with my application to join the CID as you thought it'd help me get promotion. You've helped me study for my promotion exams and helped me celebrate when I passed. I know what you want for both of us, trust me we'll get there. I know it's been shit since March, and the hours have been horrendous, but this strike isn't going to last forever and the work I'm doing is being appreciated, trust me it will help in the long run. Once this bloody strike's over and things get back to normal, the promotion boards will soon come around again and I'll be right up there for promotion to sergeant. Trust me sweetheart, please.'

She listened patiently, smiled and then let rip, 'I didn't sign up for this bullshit Andy! What sort of an organisation makes people work, from stupid o'clock in the morning until daft o'clock at night, every day for three weeks. It's not on and something's got to give. I want you to transfer off the CID straight away!'

'That's not going to happen Sally, it's totally unfair for you to even ask me that. Right now we're in a race against time to catch a monster that butchered a young woman for the sake of it. When I say butchered, I mean just that. The woman was killed and mutilated in the most horrendous way you can imagine, for no other reason than to fulfil some sick fucker's lust for violence. So here it is Sally, no I won't be quitting the CID. I'm a detective, it's my job, it's what I do. I'm back on duty at seven in the morning, I'm very tired and I need to sleep, so goodnight. We'll talk this through properly tomorrow.'

Sally shook her head and said softly, 'If you're not prepared to change things Andy, then I will.'

'What's that supposed to mean Sally?'

'We've all got choices to make in life Andy, and you've got a very simple one to make right now. You can either choose me, your wife, or your precious fucking job!'

'Sally, do NOT give me ultimatums, you might not like the answer, I'm going up to bed!'

Andy turned and slowly made his way up the stairs, he could hear his wife sobbing in the hallway below. He hoped with all his heart that she hadn't meant what she had said.

Andy loved the very bones of her, but he couldn't just stop, he couldn't quit the CID. He knew that if they didn't catch this madman, it would only be a matter of time before he struck again.

Andy didn't know it then, but he was about to be proved right, much quicker than he could ever have imagined.

CHAPTER 47

Ollerton, Nottinghamshire – September 6th 1984

Mick threw the black holdall into the boot before opening the front passenger door and getting in next to the blonde with the long hair.

'Hello Jimmy, my old son, I swear with that wig on and with those sparkling blue eyes you get more gorgeous every time I see you.'

He laughed raucously.

'Not funny Mick, not funny at all', said Jimmy

As soon as he had driven the car away from the lay by outside Proteus Camp, Jimmy took off the wig and threw it onto the back seat of the car.

'So Jimmy, what delightful establishment have you got lined up for us tonight?'

'We're going to a pub called The Archer. It's at Rainworth village about seven or eight miles from here. It's nine o'clock now, we should be at Rainworth and in the pub for around nine thirty.'

'Why The Archer?'

'I've been a couple of times already this week Mick, and there's a Northern Soul disco on tonight. Apparently for these music nights the place gets rammed with birds. The pub itself is sort of out in the sticks but it's within walking distance of both Rainworth and the next village Blidworth.

I reckon come closing time we'll be able to intercept some silly tart walking home on her own. Then it's down to us to do what we do best.'

'I can see you've been busy old son. It all sounds very promising, very promising indeed.'

Both men laughed.

'Let's go for a pint in a different boozer first Jimmy, I'm dying of thirst.'

'Yeah, why not.'

'Is there somewhere on the way to Rainworth?'

'Not really, but we can get a quick pint at the Robin Hood pub in Rainworth itself. You'll have to keep your gob shut in there though Mick, there'll be lads in there that are definitely out on strike.'

'No problem Jimmy, I'll keep quiet and let you get the beers in.'

'We'll have a swift one in there, then we can park the car just up the road from The Archer and wait to see what little darling comes our way.'

'It's a marvellous plan Jimmy, I'll have a nice cold pint of lager when we get there, cheers!'.

CHAPTER 48

Blidworth, Notts – September 6th 1984

June Hayes had been looking forward to going out all week.

The other women at the Pretty Polly hosiery factory had spent all week talking the very shy June, into having a night out with the girls. All the women caught the mini bus, that took them from Rainworth over to the factory at Sutton in Ashfield, every day. The other women that caught the mini bus all lived in Rainworth, June was the only one that lived in Blidworth. Every morning she walked from her house, over to the Joseph Whittaker School in Rainworth to catch the bus.

The driver of the mini bus always made a point of going through Blidworth first on the way home though, so he could drop June off outside her house. The girls on the mini bus were quick to point out to June that The Archer pub was only a twenty-minute walk from her house in Blidworth, and was only five minutes further down the road than the Joseph Whittaker school.

Reluctantly, she finally agreed to go on the night out. Arranging to walk to the pub and meet the other girls in there at seven thirty.

For the rest of the week the conversation on the bus was all about the Northern Soul disco at The Archer.

The girls discussed at length what they would be wearing, the single women and some of the married ones had spent the week speculating on what men from the two villages would be there. Much to her own surprise, June found herself really looking forward to finally having a night out, where she could let her hair down and have some fun.

Her husband Dave was all for it and had readily volunteered to look after their two children for the night, a boy of eight and a girl of six.

Dave was a self-employed plumber, so although not directly involved in the strike, his work had suffered badly as people in the community put off having jobs done. As the strike went on and on, so there was less and less money around in the village and surrounding areas. Without the emergency work that was, more often than not, paid for by insurance companies his little plumbing business would have gone bust a long time ago.

Dave did appreciate the extra hours June worked at the factory, trying to make ends meet. He encouraged her to go out, telling her she thoroughly deserved to have some fun with the girls.

He watched her closely as she got ready to go out.

June was thirty-two years old on her next birthday and was still a very sexy woman. He hardly ever saw her fully made up these days and now as he watched her get ready he was still wowed by her appearance.

She had let her stunning long red hair down for the night, it was usually tied up ready for the factory. Her eyes were the brightest, most beautiful green eyes he'd ever seen. There were fine lines at the corners of her eyes that only appeared when she smiled and that made her eyes even more beguiling.

Her figure was fuller now, after motherhood, but was still very attractive. June oozed sex appeal, which was heightened even more by the fact that she had absolutely no idea how sexy she actually was, or of the effect she had on most men.

As her husband watched her get ready to leave the house he thought to himself just how lucky he was, he absolutely adored his stunning wife.

'Have a lovely night sweetheart', he said as he tried to kiss her.

She turned her head right at the last moment.

'Don't smudge my lippy', she laughed.

He kissed her gently on the cheek.

'Are you sure you don't want picking up from the pub later? I think I should June, it'll be late.'

'No Dave, I'll be fine. You can't leave the kids on their own in the house just to come and fetch me.'

'They'd be fine for ten minutes June'

'Definitely not Dave, it's way too risky. If anything happened to them I'd never forgive myself.'

'Well get a cab home then, I don't think you should walk at night.'

'Don't be daft Dave, we can't afford a taxi. It's only a fifteen-minute walk, twenty tops, I'll be fine. I walk it every day to catch the bus to work. Now stop fussing or you're going to make me late.'

As she walked up the path he shouted after her, 'I love you sweetheart.'

' I love you too', she said.

As he watched her walk away from the house he thought how amazing she looked in her figure hugging navy blue jumpsuit.

June only ever felt comfortable in trousers and never wore skirts or dresses. This was because both her legs, from the knees down were terribly scarred.

The scarring was the result of an unfortunate accident at home when she was a very young toddler. Her mother had stood her straight into a bath that had been run by her father. By a tragic oversight she failed to check the temperature of the bath water first.

The burns caused by the scalding hot water were terrible and meant that as she got older June had to endure numerous operations to apply skin grafts to the badly burned and disfigured areas of her legs.

June counted her blessings every day that her mother hadn't simply laid her down in that scalding hot bath.

It was purely an accident, but June's mother had never really forgiven herself for disfiguring her daughter so badly. This guilt subsequently affected the relationship between mother and daughter. Those same feelings of guilt played heavily on her mother's mind right up until the day of her death, when June was only eighteen. As June walked from her house towards The Archer pub thoughts of her childhood and the terrible burns were a long way far from her mind.

As she strolled along, she was happily singing her favourite Northern Soul songs. 'Skiing in the Snow' was her favourite track of all time and she found herself belting out the lyrics at the top of her voice as she walked. This was followed by her loud rendition of the Smokey Robinson classic 'Tears of a Clown'. By the time she reached the pub June was virtually skipping along, she couldn't wait to meet her friends inside and start dancing.

She could already hear the beat of the Northern Soul music booming out from the pub.

June knew she was really going to enjoy tonight.

CHAPTER 49

Blidworth, Notts – September 6th 1984

June Hayes couldn't remember the last time she had enjoyed herself so much. The music in the pub had been fantastic, all the girls had been dancing around their handbags on the small dance floor. Her workmates from the factory had been brilliant fun and they'd all danced for most of the night.

June had smiled to herself when she saw a couple of the younger single girls kissing men as they enjoyed the last slow dance of the night. It had taken her back to when she first met her husband Dave, back to that special giddy feeling of a new romance.

She felt warm and happy, the warmth may have had something to do with the three glasses of Mateus Rose wine she'd drunk throughout the evening.

When the bar staff finally called last orders, the girls from the factory all booed loudly. Feeling under pressure to carry on, the DJ continued to play music until finally switching the decks off at twenty past eleven.

June and her friends were now standing outside the pub laughing, chatting and saying their goodbyes.

'Are you sure you'll be alright walking home on your own June?' asked one of her friends.

'Of course I will. It's not far and there's plenty of street lights along the way.'

She spread her arms wide, giggled and said, 'Who'd want to come after an old bird like me anyway?'

'Just be careful June, you must've seen on the telly what happened to that poor woman they found over at Annesley. They still haven't caught anybody for that yet.'

'I'll be fine Glo, Annesley's miles from here. If anyone comes after me they'll get one of these shoes up the side of their head, they don't call 'em killer heels for nothing!'

June waved one of her high heel shoes above her head and laughed, 'Don't worry, I'll see you lot bright and breezy on the bus in the morning. Can't say I'm looking forward to the noise of that stocking machine tomorrow morning though.'

The women all agreed with that comment as they started walking off their separate ways.

June slowly started on the twenty-minute walk from The Archer pub to her house. Only five minutes had gone by when she noticed how different it felt walking home in the dark, to how it had been walking down to the pub.

She had been happy, singing on the way down the hill, the sun had been shining and the countryside either side of the lane looked beautiful.

It was totally different now, for a start she was walking up the hill and after a night of dancing her feet were killing her.

Her progress was slow.

She looked up and saw a really bright moon, the light from the moon made her feel a little better as the street lights were dismal and were spaced around a hundred yards apart.

Because of the long distance between street lights there were areas of the path where it was really dark, she quickened her pace slightly through these darker areas.

June shivered involuntarily, as for the first time she felt the night chill. The warmth from the wine drank earlier was quickly wearing off. A single cloud obscured the moon and suddenly it was very dark.

Looking along the straight road she grimaced and let out an audible sigh, realising how far she still had to walk.

Another five minutes passed and she was now well away from the last of the houses at the Rainworth end of the road. Joseph Whittaker School was also way behind her, she was now on the stretch of road where it narrowed and became little more than a country lane.

Here there was nothing but fields either side of the road.

For the moment June wasn't concerned, she had walked along this road a thousand times or more. She could think of many occasions when she had walked along the road in the dark during the cold winter months. The bright moon was now frequently covered by passing clouds, everywhere becoming instantly darker as the moon disappeared. Once again she shuddered involuntarily.

It wasn't fear, she wasn't scared. It was more a feeling of apprehension, that she experienced every time a cloud flitted across the moon.

Ahead of her in the distance she could now see the slight bend in the road, she knew that just after that bend the houses of Blidworth village would start to come into view.

Using the street lights dotted ahead to judge the distance, June calculated that after another three or four minutes of walking she would reach the bend.

The sound of a sharp crack that sounded like a twig snapping broke the deathly quiet.

The noise had come from directly behind her.

Instantly all of June's senses became alert, she tried to quicken her pace a little, but her high heels wouldn't allow her to go much faster.

She listened intently, desperately trying to hear another noise. Suddenly there it was, above the silence she heard the unmistakeable sound of footsteps approaching her from behind. Real fear began to seep through her body now, quickly she glanced over her shoulder.

There was nothing there.

Inwardly she scolded herself and said quietly under her breath, 'Calm down June, stop being stupid nobody's there.'

Her breathing was shallow and her heart was racing.

She walked on, quicker now.

Tears were starting to sting her eyes and she felt clammy all over. Another couple of minutes passed by, she was nearly at the bend.

Suddenly she heard the sound again, definitely footsteps.

June didn't want to, but she had to look back.

Forcing herself to look, she turned her head quickly, just as she did so, the moon slid from behind a cloud bathing everywhere in bright moonlight.

To her horror she clearly saw a man.

He was about eighty yards behind her and was crouched over, very close to the hedgerow.

She watched in horror as the man moved away from the hedgerow across the grass verge and onto the pavement. He was now walking quite quickly and because he was crouched over, he resembled a large ape.

Immediately June turned her head to face the way she was going and began trying to walk even faster.

She could hear the man's footsteps clearly on the path behind her now. It was obvious he knew she'd seen him and he was now intent on catching her up.

The footsteps sounded close and a terrified June again glanced over her shoulder. To her horror she saw that the man was now no more than fifty yards away.

She felt tears start to well in her eyes, and a panicked sob escaped her lips. Quickly she kicked off her shoes and picked them up before walking on barefoot. The hard, cold pavement made her feet hurt like hell but at least she could walk faster now.

The first house was no more than a couple of hundred yards away. She was terrified and thought about breaking into a run just to reach the bend and the sanctuary of that first house.

The footsteps behind her were getting louder, the man was getting closer. June didn't dare to look back again and was just about to break into a desperate run when she heard a car approaching from behind her.

Now she did risk a glance over her shoulder, to her relief she saw that the man had stopped and was waiting for the car to pass him.

She knew this was her chance.

As the car approached she stepped to the side of the road and waved her arms, frantically signalling for the driver to stop.

June prayed the driver of the car would see her and stop.

She could still see the stalker some thirty yards behind her. He was now standing stock still, like a statue. The approaching cars headlights illuminated the man from behind. She could see he was staring at her.

The man watched impassively as the car passed him by.

June desperately tried to stop it, waving her arms and shouting.

To her horror the car did not stop and sped by, her heart sank. Her eyes initially followed the car as it sped by, quickly she turned her head again to look back down the road.

June saw that the man had begun to walk slowly towards her again. She turned and began to run for her life.

As she turned to run she saw that the car was now about forty yards ahead of her. Brake lights were coming on; the car was stopping.

Sprinting now, she ignored the pain in her feet and desperately ran towards the stationary car that had stopped and was now only about fifteen yards in front of her.

The driver of the car reached over and opened the front passenger door. As the door swung open the interior light of the car came on and for the first time June got a glimpse of the driver.

Thank God, long blonde hair, the driver was a woman.

June reached the car and desperately yanked the passenger door open wider.

She blurted out loudly, 'Help me please, there's a man after me!'

Suddenly to her horror June realised that the driver of the car was also a man.

'I know that darling!' the driver snarled, 'He's with me.'

As she turned away from the car door to run, she was terrified to see the man who had been following her was now right behind her.

June was trapped between the open car door and the man. She screamed loudly and swung one of her high heels at the man's face. The shoe narrowly missed its mark, the stalker pushed her roughly backwards against the car. She hit the side of the car with such force that it knocked all the breath from her body and she felt her knees buckle.

June could now feel strong hands pushing her into the back of the car. She was pushed down onto the back seat and managed one more piercing scream before she saw a bunched fist heading straight for her.

Suddenly everything went black.

'Close the door Mick for Christ's sake, and keep her quiet. Let's get out of here.'

'Just a second Jimmy, she's dropped her shoes.'

Having retrieved the shoes with the killer heels, Mick got into the car, climbing onto the back seat after the woman.

Jimmy could hear whimpering noises coming from the back seat and then the taut screech of Gaffer tape being removed from the roll. The gag was applied and everything went quiet.

'All sorted Jimmy', growled Mick.

'Thank Christ for that', muttered Jimmy as he slowly drove the green Cortina away.

About a hundred yards away, on a small hill in the fields off to the left, looking down over the road stood Stan Briggs.

Briggs had heard the piercing scream made by the woman and turned in the direction of the noise. He saw the car and heard the door close, he then heard one more scream before the car was driven off at speed towards Blidworth.

'Another bloody domestic', he muttered to himself.

He picked up the dead rabbits on the string and his high powered, silenced, .22air rifle. He shouldered the rifle and tied the rabbits to his waist. Lastly he picked up the large lamp that he'd used to transfix the rabbits, making them remain still as he shot them.

Stan Briggs was nearing fifty-six years of age, he had thought his lamping days were behind him, but as a striking miner times were now very hard and he'd been forced to revert to his youth, back to the old poaching method to supplement food for his family.

He was on private land and he knew that poaching was illegal, but he had to provide meat for his wife, kids and grandkids. Stan decided the three rabbits he'd already shot would have to be enough for one night. The cold night air was starting to seep through his camouflaged overalls. He felt cold and damp and was ready for a hot cup of tea.

As he slowly trudged across the muddy fields back towards his home in Rainworth, the woman's screams were already forgotten.

CHAPTER 50

Woods near Blidworth Village – September 7th 1984

It had just turned midnight.

June Hayes was conscious again. She was shivering with the cold and could feel the damp grass on the bare skin of her back. The realisation that she was now totally naked shocked her and she whimpered.

Her mouth felt bruised, she tried to lick her swollen lips beneath the tape that covered her mouth, but winced at the pain it caused. She ran her tongue along the bottom edges of her front teeth and could tell by the rough texture that a couple of them were broken.

Her head was throbbing, the pain travelling in waves from the back of her head to the area immediately behind her eyes. Slowly as more of her senses returned she looked around urgently with terrified eyes.

June could see she was surrounded by tall trees. The moon kept dancing from behind the clouds, intermittently shining through the leaves of the trees way above. The moonlight also afforded glimpses of the small clearing in the trees, where she now lay.

Her hands were tightly bound behind her back and she could feel whatever was being used to bind her wrists starting to dig deep into her skin. She tried to raise her head off the floor, but went dizzy as a rush of pain swept over her.

Ignoring the pain and dizziness, June looked down along her body, she had been stripped naked and was bound around her ankles as well as her wrists.

The gag across her mouth felt sticky and had a strong smell of glue. Now fully aware of her situation, panic rushed through her, questions bursting into her head.

Where were the men who had brought her here? Would they be coming back to rape her? Had they already raped her while she was unconscious?

Her friends warning, as she left the pub, about the murder of the woman at Annesley then came crashing into her consciousness. June felt tears sting her eyes and trickle down her cheeks and she started to shiver violently as the cold of the damp grass seeped in.

Suddenly, an overwhelming sense of anger gripped her and with a renewed strength and determination she struggled against her bindings and forced herself to sit up.

As she finally managed to sit up, she was confronted by an image that terrified her to the bone.

June felt the warmth between her legs as her bladder loosened at the terrifying sight in front of her.

Illuminated clearly, as a cloud slipped past the bright moon, were two figures silently watching her.

They stood ten yards away and were dressed from head to foot in light blue nylon suits with hoods, they had covers on their shoes and their hands were a ghostly white, she realised they were wearing gloves.

They looked like surgeons preparing to operate.

The stark, white light of the moon gave the figures an ethereal glow.

A strangled scream erupted from her throat, but was stifled by the Gaffer tape. Thoughts of her husband and two young children came into her mind. In that instant, June knew for certain that she'd never see any of them again.

One of the figures bent down and she watched in horror as he silently reached into a black bag at his feet.

Fleetingly the moon disappeared and the figures evaporated in the darkness, then just as suddenly they were both standing there again, bathed in white light as the moon emerged from behind the clouds once more.

Her eyes widened in fear when she saw that the figure who had bent down to the bag was now holding a set of small gardening shears.

Without making a sound the figure slowly walked towards her watched intently by the other one. The fact that everything was done in deathly silence only heightened the feeling of utter dread she now felt.

Suddenly she felt gloved hands on her naked shoulders as the man pushed her back down onto her back. He then turned her over roughly, so she was now lying on her side. She struggled gamely but felt a heavy blow to her kidneys.

The fight and anger were quickly replaced with a feeling of total helplessness and June lay unmoving on the damp grass, quietly sobbing.

Her hands were now exposed and she felt the coldness of the metal shears against her thumb. A lightning bolt of pain shot up her arm as she felt the blades of the shears slice off her thumb. She felt two more fingers being severed before the pain caused her, mercifully, to black out.

The figure watching tutted loudly, 'Now look what you've done Mick, I told you the pain would be too much for her to stand'.

'She'll be back with us soon enough, you'll see. It's so much more satisfying when they're awake to feel it.'

'Sort the fingers and her hands out now, while she's out of it. We'll be here all night at this rate.'

'Who put you in charge Jimmy?'

'Just do it Mick, or I'll finish her off now and the fun will be over, got it.'

Grumbling to himself Mick severed each digit from the hands of the unconscious woman before picking them up and placing them in a re-sealable Ziplock bag.

He then walked back to the grip bag and took out the Stanley Knife. Returning to the woman he made long, deep lacerations across the palms of both her hands until the skin resembled a lattice work.

The unconscious woman was then rolled over onto her back again. Carefully he turned her head to one side so she didn't swallow her tongue. The two men then stood together watching her in silence as they waited patiently for her to come around.

Fifteen minutes passed before she stirred again, another five before she was fully awake. Her hands felt strange and when the realisation of what had happened became apparent June felt herself gag, the acid of the wine consumed earlier burned her throat as she almost vomited. Forcing herself, she swallowed the burning bile.

It was either that or choke.

With a feeling of dread, she saw that the other figure was now moving towards her. Bizarrely, she noted that he was slightly taller and appeared thinner.

He knelt beside her and moved close enough for her to see his face clearly. He smiled at her benignly saying, 'Don't worry this will all be over soon. I know that all you want is to leave this place. Do you sweetheart, do you want to leave this place?' he asked softly.

June nodded vigorously ignoring the pain in her head.

She thought he'd meant leaving these woods, leaving these monsters, returning home to her loving family.

It was not what Jimmy Wade had meant at all.

He slowly showed her the thin nylon cord that he gripped in both hands and smiled again.

The reality of his intentions now rushed into her head, she shook her head from side to side, pleading with her eyes.

She looked directly into those cold, unfeeling, unblinking blue eyes imploring him not to hurt her any more.

Very slowly he wound the thin cord once around her neck. Her eyes widened with terror as she felt the cord tighten around her throat as he exerted a slow gradual pressure. Slowly Jimmy Wade continued to squeeze the life from her, watching her beautiful green eyes intently as he did so.

After five minutes it was over and he stood up quickly removing the cord from around her neck.

June Hayes was dead.

'At last. What a performance. Do you mind if I have a play now?', a voice growled from the shadows.

Jimmy took a step back from the woman, turned and walked away allowing Mick Reynolds to approach the dead woman. He knew what was coming next and was totally disinterested, almost bored by it.

Standing just ten yards away from the dead woman, he looked up at the moon as he heard the orgy of violence begin.

Jimmy could see no point to it. He knew there was absolutely no chance this woman wouldn't be missed, she was obviously married and would quickly be reported missing from home.

Deep down Jimmy knew that Mick Reynolds was completely mad, the only reason he tolerated him, was so he could fulfil his own needs and achieve that special feeling that only came as he actually extinguished a life.

Having achieved that already, he was now feeling extremely bored.

'Hurry up Mick, we need to get out of here, it'll be starting to get light soon.'

There was just a grunt of acknowledgement.

'Nearly done, have you got the letter and the Stanley Knife so we can leave another message for the cops?'

Jimmy nodded and walked back towards the shattered remains of June Hayes to play out the final part of their macabre ritual.

CHAPTER 51

Mansfield Police Station –
September 7th 1984

'Good morning sir, its Sgt Clark at the front counter. I've got a Mr David Hayes here. He's insisting on speaking to someone from the CID urgently. Apparently his wife June didn't come home from a night out with the girls, at The Archer pub in Rainworth last night.'

'Ok Sarge, I'll be up there shortly with DS Buxton.'

It was the phone call Danny had been dreading ever since the body of Mandy Stokes was discovered at Annesley.

The investigation into her horrific murder was going nowhere fast, no new leads or lines of enquiry were coming through and time was passing quickly by.

The appeal for information that had been shown across all the television networks had yielded nothing of any note.

It was now four weeks since Mandy Stokes had been brutally murdered. A feeling of dread washed over him as he walked quickly towards the front desk of the police station. Rob walked in silence at his side. Neither man said anything, but both were already thinking the worse.

Another murder, another dead woman.

At the front counter Danny saw a man sitting alone, he looked dishevelled, his skin colour was grey and looking at his eyes it was obvious he hadn't slept.

'Mr Hayes, I'm Detective Inspector Flint and this is Detective Sergeant Buxton, the sergeant tells me you want to speak to the CID.'

'Yes Inspector, it's about my wife June, she never came home last night.'

Danny showed David Hayes into an interview room where they could talk in private.

Once everyone was seated Danny said, 'You're saying your wife didn't come home last night, is that unusual for her?'

'My wife's never stayed out Inspector, she didn't come home last night and that's just not like her.'

'The Sgt has told me your wife was at The Archer pub last night, what was the occasion?'

'There was no occasion, it was just a night out with the girls from work.'

'Does she go out with the girls from work regularly?'

'No, it's the first time she's had a night out in months, my wife's a stay at home mum, we've got two young kids.'

'Where does your wife work Mr Hayes?' asked Rob.

'June works at the Pretty Polly factory over at Sutton in Ashfield. It was just a night out with the other girls who catch the laid on transport every morning from Rainworth to the factory.'

'What were the arrangements for your wife to get home last night?'

David Hayes put his head in his hands and looked down at the floor. In a faltering voice cracking with emotion he said, 'She said she'd walk home, I knew I should've picked her up. This is all my fault.'

Trying to placate the man's obvious fears Rob said, 'We don't know anything's wrong yet Mr Hayes. Is it possible your wife just didn't fancy the walk home and stayed with one of her friends for the night?'

'I thought that myself sergeant, but I've phoned the factory this morning at half past eight, all the girls that were out last night are at work except June. She wasn't on the mini bus this morning. That's when I knew something was seriously wrong. I've taken the kids to school and then came straight here to report her missing.'

Danny glanced at his watch, it was now just after nine o'clock, 'How far is it from The Archer pub to your house?'

'Probably half a mile, three quarters at the most, we live at the end of Blidworth that's nearest to Rainworth.'

'How long should it have taken your wife to walk home?'

'It should only take twenty or so minutes.'

'Do you know what time your wife left The Archer?'

'I've spoken to Glo, her best friend at Pretty Polly, she told me that June left the pub at about half past eleven and she saw her start to walk home. June should've been home way before midnight. Earlier this morning while the kids were still asleep in bed, I walked all the way along the route she would've taken last night, I can't find anything. There's no trace of her Inspector, something awful's happened, I know it has. People don't just disappear into thin air.'

David Hayes then fixed Danny with a glassy eyed stare before saying, 'Inspector, have you caught that nutter who killed the woman in Annesley Woods yet?'

'Let's not jump to any conclusions Mr Hayes, there could be any number of reasons why your wife didn't come home last night. I'll get Det Sgt Buxton to run you home so he can obtain all the details we'll need about your wife. I'll organise a proper search along her route home and start making some enquiries at the pub. Have you contacted any of the local hospitals yet Mr Hayes?'

'No I haven't, do you think she might be there?'

'It's possible, she may have had an accident. I'll call them all now and let Rob know the outcome, so he can tell you straight away.'

Danny stood up, 'I know its difficult Mr Hayes, but try not to worry. We're going to do everything we can to find your wife June.'

Again the man seemed to visibly crumble in front of Danny.

'Thanks Inspector.'

Danny left the room leaving Rob to take David Hayes back to his home address.

The main reason Danny had arranged for Rob to take Hayes home, was so he could search the family home thoroughly.

Danny had to keep an open mind, June Hayes could have made it home safe and well and then fallen foul of domestic violence, as her husband flew into a jealous rage about his wife having a night out with the girls.

Having spoken to the distraught husband, Danny doubted this was the likely scenario in this instance.

He needed to organise manpower for a search, there was a body out there somewhere. Every instinct in his body was screaming to Danny that June Hayes was already dead.

After leaving the interview room, Danny went straight to Jackson's office. He needed the superintendent to authorise the manpower needed for a search.

Just an hour later and arrangements had been made via Strike Control to release three PSU's from their duties on the dispute. They would be tasked to assist in the search of the surrounding farmland and woods adjacent to the route June Hayes would have taken on her way home last night.

Three PSU's meant a total of thirty-three men, Danny was satisfied that a large area of the surrounding countryside could be searched properly by that number of officers. He would have liked more but was thankful he'd managed to get that many.

Danny returned to the CID office where he briefed Andy and Rachel about the disappearance of June Hayes.

'Rachel I want you to go straight to the Pretty Polly factory over in Sutton and speak to all the women June Hayes was out with last night. Start with her best friend, this Glo. From what the husband says it appears that Glo may've been the last person to see her. I definitely want a full and detailed statement taking from her, but play it by ear for the other women, statement them if necessary. If there's anything startling that comes to light, like a secret lover etc. let me know straight away.'

'No problem boss, I'll get over there right now, unless there's something else you want me to look at as well?'

'No that's more than enough to be getting on with Rachel. I don't know how many of the factory girls were out last night, I suspect it'll be quite a few. I also want you to talk to the mini bus driver who takes the women to the factory every day. He could be a gold mine of information, I bet he listens to all the juicy gossip.'

'Right you are boss.'

'Keep me posted if there are any developments ok.'

Rachel stood up, grabbing her coat, a set of car keys and a bundle of statement paper she hurriedly left the office.

Danny turned to Andy, 'Andy I want you to stay here and do all the background checks on the husband and the Hayes family in general. I want you to find out everything you can about our missing person June Hayes, and her husband Dave. I want to know everything there is to know about the Hayes family unit. Have either of them ever had an extra marital affair? Have there been any previous domestics? Do they have money troubles? the works.'

'Ok boss, no problem.'

'Sorry Andy, I'm not trying to teach you to suck eggs, you know what I want.'

'I know boss, I'll shout Rob up for a chat once he's got over to Hayes house and get all the details from him.'

'I'm going over to Blidworth now to help organise the search with the Inspector from the Special Operations Unit. Superintendent Jackson has arranged for him to come over and co-ordinate the searches being carried out by the Foreign Force PSU's. Once I've spoken to him I'll join Rob up at the Hayes family home. We'll then make a start on the enquiries at The Archer pub. Andy I want you to make sure we all keep in touch by radio. My gut feelings telling me that we've another murder on our hands. I hope I'm wrong of course, it could just be that June Hayes was hit by a car last night and is lying unconscious in a ditch somewhere. Either way time is of the essence.'

Danny walked out into the car park and took two or three deep breaths before climbing into the CID car.

He sat quietly in the car, it felt like the world was closing in around him. As he drove out of the police station he was already rehearsing in his mind how he was going to break the worst news imaginable to David Hayes.

CHAPTER 52

Warsop Main Colliery – Sept 7th 1984

The Metropolitan Police PSU had just finished escorting the working miners through the picket lines at Warsop Main Colliery. The usual cries of "SCAB!" were still ringing in their ears. The men had just begun removing the protective clothing they wore every morning and beginning to think about yet another fried breakfast when the radio in the Transit van crackled into life.

'Mike Alpha One Zero, over.'

Three times the call sign was repeated before a disgruntled Sgt Reynolds answered the radio.

'Go ahead control, Mike Alpha One Zero over.'

He answered the radio begrudgingly because he was desperately hoping his PSU wouldn't be given another task to carry out. Today was the last day of their deployment, they would be heading back to London first thing tomorrow morning for a well-earned week of rest days.

The answer he was dreading came soon enough as the Control Room operator's voice came over the radio again, 'Mike Alpha One Zero resume immediately from Warsop Main Colliery and travel to Blidworth Police Station. Upon arrival at that location liaise with Insp Richardson of the Special Operations Unit.'

Mick let out a low groan before saying, 'Will do control, what's the commitment? We're standing down for a week this evening and obviously we've got a lot of kit to get stowed, Mike Alpha One Zero over.'

'Mike Alpha One Zero, we're aware it's your last day. You're required to assist in the search of countryside around the Rainworth and Blidworth area for a missing woman, over.'

'No problem control, we're just finishing off at Warsop Main. Show us travelling to Blidworth police station.'

There was a loud chorus of moans and groans from the men in the back of the Transit.

'All right you lot shut it! Is everybody here?'

'We're three missing Sarge, they went to get a brew.'

That's all I need, thought Mick, he knew exactly where the missing woman was. He and Jimmy had left her in a small clearing just off a bridle path in the woods. He hoped that he didn't get that area to search with his PSU. He didn't want any connection to the woman.

He quickly located his missing men, 'Come on you three, look lively we've got a search commitment to get done before we can pack up and go home.'

The moans came thick and fast from the three men who had anticipated an early finish ready for home.

Mick rounded on them sharply, 'Stop whining and get your gear on board. The sooner we're there and get it done, the sooner we can get packed up ready for home.'

The three men reluctantly binned their coffees and climbed into the back of the Transit van.

As the Transit was driven towards the rendezvous point Mick subconsciously reached into his trouser pocket and felt the two small gold rings inside.

Making sure the van driver was watching the road, Mick surreptitiously removed the rings from his pocket to look at them. One was a small, gold wedding band, the other a gold ring with a single solitaire diamond.

When he came to dispose of the items removed from the site of last night's killing he'd seen the two rings still on one of the fingers he'd severed.

He removed the rings before throwing the severed digits into the furnace.

As he looked down at the tiny rings sitting in the palm of his hand, Mick smiled. The memories they instantly stirred felt delicious, he felt an overwhelming surge of excitement. He played with the rings, slipping them on and off his own little finger, before quickly replacing them back into his pocket. For the time being, at least, his secret double life was safe.

As the police van was driven nearer to Blidworth police station he was praying his PSU wouldn't be tasked to search the area between Blidworth Lane and the main A60 road that ran between Mansfield and Nottingham.

CHAPTER 53

Blidworth Police Station –
September 9th 1984

For two days the police search had concentrated on the area of open countryside between the villages of Rainworth and Blidworth. The police had meticulously searched vast areas of the open gorse land that lies between the two townships.

On the first day of the search the Metropolitan Police PSU, led by Sgt Mick Reynolds, searched the area immediately behind The Archer public house until finally being stood down at last light.

Reynolds had known the search in that area was a pointless exercise but he still bullied and cajoled his men to carry out as thorough a search as was possible.

All the Metropolitan Police PSUs in that particular serial had now gone home for a week of rest days, they would not be back in the Nottinghamshire coalfield again until September 15th.

The search for the missing woman had been carried on by PSUs from Hampshire Constabulary. Once again the search areas were concentrated towards the village of Rainworth.

All the searches so far had drawn a blank.

It was now entering the third day that June Hayes had been missing, everybody in the community was starting to fear the worse.

Danny had travelled to Blidworth Police Station at half past six that morning to meet with Jim Richardson, the Special Ops Inspector, so they could discuss the areas to be searched that day. The search was going to be extended, moving further out from The Archer public house, the location June Hayes had last been seen alive. The intention today was to move the search area more towards the village of Blidworth.

While ever June Hayes was only missing there was still hope.

Both men sipped steaming hot cups of coffee as they examined the Ordnance Survey Maps of the area.

Jim Richardson pointed at the map saying, 'Right Danny, I propose we extend the search into this area of woodland today. If we get the search teams to gradually spread out from Blidworth over towards the A60 we might have some joy. It seems a natural direction of travel away from the point of abduction.'

The two men had long ago dismissed any other scenario than an abduction. The SOU Inspector continued, 'We haven't got many PSU's at our disposal today Danny, but some of the villagers will no doubt turn out to help. It's another huge area and some of the terrain's quite difficult. There's a large area of pine forest here that I think we should start with. I'll deploy the PSU's in there first thing this morning, then we'll extend the search out into the general woodland later this afternoon.'

Danny nodded his agreement to the search plan.

The discussion was taking place in a mobile control and command centre that had been set up in the car park of Blidworth Police Station.

The mobile control centre also served as the Incident Room for this enquiry. If a body was discovered, the incident room would then be transferred to the police station at Mansfield, but for the time being the mobile control centre would suffice for a missing person enquiry.

A general press release had gone out on the evening of the first day asking for anyone with information to contact this mobile control centre. It had been constantly manned around the clock.

There had been five bogus sightings of June Hayes reported so far. All of these sightings had to be investigated thoroughly before they could be discounted. It was yet another drain on an already limited resource, that of manpower.

Danny again carefully studied the search areas identified on the map, 'That looks good to me Jim. I'll leave you to co-ordinate the search teams this morning and I'll liaise back here with you at two o'clock this afternoon.'

'Yes of course Danny, no problem. I know you're running a skeleton crew doing the enquiries. So any way I can help, I will.'

'Thanks Jim, I really appreciate that. What time are the PSU's arriving for the briefing?'

'Any time now, I told them to be here no later than seven. I want them out on the ground as soon as it's properly light at about seven thirty.'

'How many have you got today Jim?'

'Only three again, thirty-three men in total.'

'Ok, I'll see you at two this afternoon. Contact me on the radio if you find anything in the meantime.'

'Of course Danny'.

Danny made his way out to the car park and sat in his car.

Again he allowed himself the luxury of a few minutes to gather his thoughts before beginning the fifteen-minute drive back to Mansfield. He had another briefing with his own staff scheduled for seven thirty before updating the Superintendent at nine o'clock.

As he drove his car along the country lanes he made a mental note to call his girlfriend Sue, he needed to have a proper conversation with her, not just a two-minute chat.

It seemed as if his whole life had been taken over at the moment by the pressure of work.

Danny had only seen his father Frank, in the new care home, a couple of times in the last three weeks.

He had a fledgling relationship with Sue, who again he hadn't seen properly for over two weeks.

It was a blessing that Sue was caring enough to be a regular visitor to the care home, her daily visits had helped his father enormously to settle into his new surroundings.

Her thoughtful attitude had allowed Danny the time to concentrate solely on trying to find the killer in their midst.

CHAPTER 54

Ricketts Lane, Blidworth –
September 9th 1984

The two teenagers had been up since six o'clock that morning. They quickly ate their breakfast and made their way straight to the stables.

Lizzie and Polly Thornley, like a lot of teenage girls, loved horses more than anything else in the world. Both girls were nearly fifteen and had been riding the horses kept at their father's livery stables, since they were eight years of age.

The twins were not identical to look at, but were definitely identical when it came to their interests.

The girls loved riding and especially show jumping.

This morning they were both up early to muck out the stables, they would then have the opportunity to exercise two of the horses liveried at the stables.

The exercise for the horses would be a steady hack through the local woods along one of the many bridle paths situated around the village of Blidworth.

The women who owned the horses couldn't always get in to ride them due to work and family commitments. Whenever this was the case it was left to Lizzie and Polly to exercise the horses on their behalf.

The horses they were going to ride this morning were two of their favourites. Both horses were mares and a beautiful chestnut colour, they stood almost seventeen hands and both animals had lovely temperaments.

They had been trained as dressage horses and were very sensitive to each little command given by the teenagers.

Both girls were excited about taking the horses out and were really looking forward to their hack through the woodland between Blidworth and Papplewick Village.

Their father's business, Thornley Livery Stables, was located just outside Blidworth on a stretch of land that lay between the village and the small upmarket town of Ravenshead, not far from the main A.60 road.

There was a secluded bridle path that ran virtually the whole way from Blidworth to Papplewick. It was very seldom used by anyone and for that reason, was the Thornley girls' favourite.

It was a beautiful clear morning and the sun was just creeping over the horizon when the girls set off from the stables. They wore identical gear of black riding helmets, blue quilted anoraks over chest protectors, beige coloured jodhpurs and black boots.

The horses they were riding may have good temperaments but it was never worth riding without the proper protective clothing on.

A horse could be spooked at any time for any reason.

Their father had always instilled in them that it was better to be safe than sorry.

After saddling the two horses, the young girls mounted their rides and set off at the walk, out of the livery yard.

The two girls were chatting happily as they rode the horses out of the yard and along the secluded bridle path.

After ten minutes, the girls had reached a stretch of the bridle path that passed directly below Ricketts Lane, the path here was bordered on both sides by a tall hawthorn hedgerow.

The horses were so big however, that both Lizzie and Polly could see over the top of the hedgerow and into the woodland beyond.

Suddenly Lizzie gasped and said, 'Whoa!' as she pulled on the reins to stop the horse.

Polly who was riding just behind Lizzie immediately stopped her horse.

'What's the matter Lizzie, why've you stopped?'

'Polly come here and look over the hedge into the clearing.'

Polly could tell by her sister's voice that Lizzie was afraid.

She guided her horse next to Lizzie and looked over the hedge.

Immediately she saw what had made her sister gasp. Lying face up on a small area of grass in the woodland she could see the naked body of a woman.

'Oh my God Lizzie! Come on we need to get back and tell dad what's up here.'

The two girls immediately turned the horses around and trotted them back to the stables.

Polly was shouting as they entered the stable yard, 'Dad! Dad!'

Having heard the girls shouting, their mother came out into the yard from the house. The girl's father emerged from one of the stables with a face like thunder.

'Whatever do you think you're doing shouting like that, you know better than that, the horse could spook and throw you off, be quiet right now.'

Once the girls had halted their horses. Polly handed the reins of her horse to Lizzie. Dismounting quickly, she ran the short distance towards her father. Jack Thornley could see instantly that something was wrong, he saw how pale Polly looked and could tell she'd been crying.

'Whatever's the matter girl?' he said.

'Dad, there's a dead woman in the woods up near Ricketts Lane!'

'Whatever are you talking about, a dead woman in the woods, talk sense girl', said their mother.

'I'm not messing about mum, there's a dead woman in the woods, she's got no clothes on and her face is horrible.'

The girl was now crying loudly.

Lizzie also dismounted and walked the two horses towards her father.

'It's true dad, I saw the woman as well, it's horrible.'

'Right girls, get them horses seen to and stabled. I'm calling the police. Will you be able to show them where this woman is?'

It was Polly who answered her father.

'Can you go dad, I'm too scared. I don't want to go back up there, it's horrible, I don't want to see it again.'

'Me neither', sobbed an equally upset Lizzie.

'Alright, calm down girls. Exactly where is this woman?'

'Go along Ricketts Lane, as far as the Lightning Oak. Once you reach the oak tree go down the bank and onto the bridle path where the hawthorn hedges are tall. The woman's in the woods on the other side of the bridle path.'

'Ok girls, I know where you mean. Now get these horses unsaddled and stabled before you do anything else. I'll call the police and take them up to the Lightning Oak.'

Both girls were still sobbing as they led the horses into the stables, followed by their concerned mother.

Jack Thornley ran inside the house to call the police.

CHAPTER 55

Ricketts Lane, Blidworth – September 9th 1984

The telephone call from Jack Thornley had come into Mansfield Police Station just after eight o'clock as Danny was finishing briefing his staff.

It was the call Danny had always known would come, but it still felt like a hammer blow when the control room passed the call down to the CID Office.

It had been Rob who had answered the phone.

'Danny, a woman's body's been found', he said quietly.

'By the search teams?' asked Danny.

'No, by a couple of young lasses' horse riding over near Blidworth.'

'Who called it in Rob?'

'It was the young girl's father a bloke by the name of Jack Thornley, he owns the livery stables just outside Blidworth.'

Without saying another word all four detectives dropped what they were doing and ran out of the station.

Taking two cars, the four detectives travelled at speed to Thornley Livery Stables at Blidworth where they were met by a very concerned and worried looking Jack Thornley.

Within minutes of arriving at the stables and speaking to Mr Thornley, Danny and his small team were following him as he drove his Land Rover up onto Ricketts Lane.

Still on Ricketts Lane but about two hundred yards from the main A60 road, he stopped the Land Rover in a lay by.

At one end of the lay by was a very old, gnarled oak tree that still bore the black scorch marks of a lightning strike.

The two CID cars pulled in behind the Land Rover.

'The girls tell me the dead woman's in the woods down here. I'm afraid you'll have to go on foot from here.'

Danny turned to his team, 'Andy wait here and start a log, if the information's right and it's a body, we can use this layby as the rendezvous point. Rob get some tape from the car and mark the route we're taking in please.'

Both Andy and Rob nodded.

Rob was back quickly with the tape and tying it to a tree he started to mark their descent from Ricketts Lane down onto the bridle path where the girls had been.

'The woman might be difficult for us to see', said Jack Thornley.

'Why's that?' asked Rob.

'My girls were on horses that are seventeen hands high, so they were able to see over these hawthorn hedges. They told me the woman was in some sort of clearing in the trees beyond the far hedge.'

Danny, Rob and Rachel began to bend at the waist trying to look under the hedgerow as they moved slowly from left to right along the bridle path.

Suddenly Rachel stopped and held her hand to her mouth.

'Over here boss, she's over here!'

Rachel turned and took two paces away from what she'd seen and dry heaved, retching loudly.

Danny and Rob ran over, 'Rachel, are you ok?' asked Danny.

She said nothing and just pointed behind her.

Danny and Rob bent over so they could see below the hedgerow. Instantly they saw the mutilated remains of the naked woman.

'Christ Almighty!', muttered Rob.

'Right Rob, take Rachel with you and get back up to the cars. Take Mr Thornley with you as well please. Rachel are you ok?'

Rachel looked as white as a sheet, 'I'm ok boss, it was just a shock, that's all. I'm sorry.'

'Rachel, don't apologise you've done nothing wrong. I want you to go back with Mr Thornley and speak to his girls. I want statements from both of them, whenever they're able, just take your time with them, they've had a massive shock too. Rob when you get back up to the cars, get Scenes of Crime travelling. I want Tim Donnelly in charge of the team. I want the Home Office pathologist travelling as well, if at all possible I want Seamus Carter on this. No, scratch that, not if at all possible, I insist on Seamus Carter coming out to this scene. The whole thing looks exactly the same as Annesley to me. Last thing Rob, get on the radio to Insp Richardson and tell him to meet me here, we're going to have to re-deploy our search teams. Tell him, from me, that I want all his search teams on standby at Blidworth Police Station.'

'Ok Danny'.

Rob turned to Rachel, 'Come on Rachel, let's get you back up onto the road.'

Danny shouted to Rob as he made his way back up the banking, 'Once you've got the circus travelling Rob, bring a couple of suits and overshoes back down with you, we'll try to find the easiest way through the hedgerow to get to where she is.'

'Ok Danny'.

Ten minutes later Danny and Rob were walking slowly along the hedge line, trying to find a suitable gap to get through.

Both were now wearing forensic suits, gloves and overshoes. Rob continued to mark the route with tape. About twenty yards along the bridle path from where they'd first seen the body, Danny saw an opening in the hedge.

The opening was about five yards across. Carefully both men scanned the area for any sign that the offender had used the same gap.

At the nearest point they could see some indentations in the mud and the grass had been flattened a little.

Rob taped off that area and the two detectives carefully skirted around and entered the grassy area from the far side, keeping away from the area where the grass had been laid flat.

Tying the tape to a small tree Rob then allowed the tape to trail behind them as he and Danny made their way into the area where they had seen the body. There were small saplings everywhere and larger trees further in.

Suddenly the ground rose a little and there in the middle of a grassy clearing was the dead woman.

'Oh for fucks sake', whispered Rob.

'I know Rob, it's fucking identical. I can see that from here.'

Carefully they got as close as they could to the body.

There were marks and indentations in the grass immediately around the body, where obviously the killer had been walking.

From where he stood, a distance of about eight feet away, Danny could see the woman was lying face up, she was in the same crucifix position with her arms stretched out wide and her legs slightly open.

The hands had been mutilated in the same way as Mandy Stokes. The head injuries were horrendous and appeared worse after being out in the open, exposed to vermin and the elements for three days.

The same two words had been carved into the woman's torso, but the wounds had started to pare back with decomposition and were barely legible.

'What's the betting the bastard has left us another note boss.'

'It wouldn't surprise me Rob. There's no sign of any clothing anywhere'

'I can't see any, but this is definitely June Hayes boss.'

'Why are you so sure?'

'Look at the legs below the knees.'

'You're right Rob, I can see the scarring now, that's mentioned in the statement you took from her husband isn't it.'

'Yeah she was scalded as a kid, the scarring's on both legs from the knee down.'

'Right stay here Rob, I'm going back up to meet and brief the Scenes of Crime team and Seamus Carter as soon as they get here. I'll talk to Inspector Richardson on the radio and get the search teams organised for as soon as Scenes of Crime have finished with the scene. I'd like you to manage the scene again Rob, you know, chapter and verse, what was at the Annesley scene.'

'Makes sense Danny, no problem.'

'As soon as I've briefed Tim and spoken to Seamus, I'll go straight over to Blidworth and see David Hayes. I want to inform him personally that we've found a body. I don't want him hearing anything through the grapevine.'

'I don't envy you that job Danny.'

'I'll make sure there's a policewoman available to meet me at Blidworth Police Station, she can help to look after the two children while I talk to their dad.'

Carefully Danny retraced his steps and made his way back up on to Ricketts Lane to await the arrival of Scenes of Crime and Seamus Carter. He quickly spoke to Insp Richardson on the radio and appraised him of the situation and that a search team would be required at this location shortly. Having finished the radio call Danny leaned on the bonnet of his car and took several deep breaths.

This was fast becoming a nightmare.

Two women killed brutally in the same identical way. God knows what the note left by the killer, if there was one, would say this time.

No new leads or lines of enquiry of any consequence from the first killing. He prayed the killer had been more careless this time and left something of some evidential value behind at the scene.

Danny exhaled and then said aloud, 'I won't hold my fucking breath!'

CHAPTER 56

Mansfield Police Station – September 9th 1984

It had already been a very long day.

In half an hour's time at seven thirty, Danny and Rob would be making the short walk from the police station to the mortuary. Danny had arranged to meet Seamus Carter, the Home Office pathologist there. He and Rob could then observe the post mortem examination of June Hayes and take any relevant exhibits.

The deposition site at Ricketts Lane had proved to be just as frustratingly sterile as the one at Annesley Woods.

Nothing at all of any evidential value had been found.

Indeed, had it not been for the scarring on the legs of the dead woman they would have, once again, been struggling for a formal identification.

The scarring from both the original injury and the subsequent skin grafting all matched perfectly to the medical records of June Hayes.

There were signs at the Ricketts Lane scene, identified by Seamus Carter to Rob, that once again there was an object inserted in the dead woman's vagina.

Seamus could only estimate that the time of death had been somewhere between midnight and four o'clock am on 7th September. He was unable to be any more specific due to the amount of time that had lapsed and the level of decomposition.

Rachel had patiently interviewed both Polly and Lizzie Thornley at length, one after the other. She had taken detailed statements from them individually, in the presence of their mother and father.

It had been a long drawn out process as both girls had been traumatised by what they'd seen and frequently broke down in floods of tears.

Rachel could empathise with their feelings and had struggled hard not to shed a few tears herself alongside the youngsters. Eventually, after several hours two very detailed and informative witness statements had been obtained.

Rob had managed the crime scene at Ricketts Lane until the body had been removed and Scenes of Crime had finished. He had then, together with Insp Richardson, co-ordinated a fingertip search of the area.

Nothing had been recovered.

Danny had spent most of the day with David Hayes.

Initially he'd broken the terrible news to him, then very patiently and gently he coaxed every last piece of information he could glean from him about his wife's medical history.

This process had also taken a long time, Danny was only too aware of how upsetting and traumatic a time this was for the entire Hayes family.

Danny and the policewoman who had gone with him to break the news, only left when David's brother and sister in law arrived from Matlock to stay with him and the children.

Now back in the CID office Danny addressed his team, 'Ok, I know this is exactly what we've all been dreading. Another murder of an innocent woman, obviously carried out by the same sick individual. Once again there's absolutely nothing for us at the scene. Andy and Rachel, get a quick bite to eat and then get yourselves up to The Archer pub at

Blidworth. I want you to talk to as many of the regulars as you can. I know it's been a few days since the Northern Soul night, but I guarantee there'll be people in there this evening that were in that night. I need you to find me something. I don't care if it's rumour, speculation or Fantasy fucking Island, we need a break to kick start this enquiry. Our killer isn't going to stop any time soon. If we don't catch him this is going to keep happening. More women will die. I'm going with Rob to the mortuary shortly. Once we've finished there, Rob will join Rachel and Andy up at the pub while I'm thrashing out the detail of tonight's press release. I think it's important we get something out to the public tonight. I know you're all knackered, but I want you all to make phone calls home and let your other halves know what's happening. Ok let's go.'

At seven thirty on the dot Danny and Rob walked into the mortuary, waiting for them was Seamus Carter.

In the centre of the room lying on a stainless steel bench were the putrefying remains of June Hayes. Once again under the stark white lights the detectives saw exactly how defiled and mutilated her body was.

In silence Danny and Rob donned the protective overalls and this time slipped masks over their faces, both men dabbing Vicks vapour rub just below their nostrils on their top lips. The smell of decaying flesh in the room was already overpowering and both men knew the stench would only get worse once Seamus commenced his examination.

'First things first then gents, let's see what little insight into his depraved tiny mind, the killer's left for us this time?'

Danny nodded wearily and watched closely as Seamus removed the object from the vagina.

Using exactly the same method as he had with Mandy Stokes the pathologist removed the rolled up paper from the black plastic tube.

'Everything looks identical, obviously you'll need to get it tested but the tubing looks as though it's been cut from the same material, the paper also looks the same as before.'

Slowly he unfurled the rolled up paper.

Typed on the paper was a chilling message which Seamus read aloud,

```
I warned you the first one wouldn't be the last

Thatcher and her Police boot boys haven't stopped

They continue to kill the coal fields

So I will continue to kill scab loving whores

Until the next time Detectives

'The Coal Killer'
```

'Looks like he's making this personal now Danny' said Seamus.

Danny said nothing

Finally, after a minute's silence taking in the contents of the note, Danny said softly, 'Ok Seamus, let's get this done shall we.'

At the end of the full autopsy Seamus took a deep breath.

'In my opinion Danny, this has definitely been committed by the same individual who killed Mandy Stokes. The wounds to the hands are identical, the same instruments have been used. The level of violence is escalating though.'

'How can it have escalated? The wounds are the same.'

'When Mandy Stokes was killed all the wounds to the hands had been made post mortem. This poor woman was alive when they severed her fingers and mutilated the hands. The injuries to the face and head however have all once again been caused post mortem.'

'Jesus Christ,' whispered Rob.

Pointing to the dead woman's neck area, Seamus continued, 'The cause of death is exactly the same. Strangulation with the same type of thin cord. Once again there's no evidence of any sexual activity apart from the insertion of the tube containing the note into the vagina. The note has the same dropped letter C, so undoubtedly the same typewriter was used.'

'Thanks Seamus.'

'I'll get my report over to you as soon as possible Danny.'

Danny nodded wearily, 'Thanks.'

'I know I said it last time Danny, but this bastard will keep doing this until you catch him and make him stop.'

'Tell me something I don't know Seamus', said an exhausted Danny.

CHAPTER 57

Mansfield – September 10th 1984

Jimmy Wade hadn't forgotten about the beautiful, enigmatic detective that had visited him at his home asking questions about the death of Albie Jones.

He had watched her slim elegant fingers caress the mug when she drank the coffee he'd made her. He remembered how she had looked longingly into his eyes.

He'd seen her full red lips pout as she blew the hot coffee, he had tasted the lipstick ring she left on that mug.

Jimmy enjoyed fantasising, again and again, how her young voluptuous body must look beneath the business suit she'd been wearing. He imagined the lacy black underwear, the stockings on those long slim legs.

Jimmy wanted her in every way.

She aroused him, sexually.

Just thinking about her, he was once again starting to feel the same familiar lustful stirrings.

He also wanted her in that most exquisite special way.

He had looked into her beautiful eyes and he knew that she yearned for that beautiful release from her hum drum boring little life.

Once he finished playing games with that ignoramus Mick Reynolds, he would return to the planning, capture and subsequent demise of the beautiful detective.

He'd quickly grown tired of allowing the insane sergeant to play his gross sadistic games with the pitiful women they found.

He was excited at the thought of moving on. It would soon be time for him to call on Detective Rachel Moore.

The plans he'd set in motion were slowly coming to fruition. Very soon it would be time to call a halt to his current life, and start afresh.

Jimmy was weary of the Neanderthal policeman. It had been fun, a distraction, but it was never destined to be a long term thing.

He'd learned a lot from the sergeant, but the whole thing was only ever intended to be an experiment.

The time to move on had arrived, he needed to concentrate on Rachel Moore.

Her time to shine was approaching fast.

CHAPTER 58

Wembley, London – September 14th 1984

It was the day before Mick Reynolds was due to travel back to the coal fields of Nottinghamshire to resume his duties policing the miners' strike.

His mood was dark.

He cut a brooding, menacing figure as he paced up and down the lounge of his three bedroomed semi in Wembley.

His foul mood had been caused by two things, the prospect of another month of boredom in Nottinghamshire and the culmination of a week spent in the company of his nagging bitch of a wife Rita.

She'd spent the entire week, moaning at him to take her out for a drive in the car. The weather had been glorious, the country was in the grip of an Indian Summer, the sun was shining and the days were pleasantly warm. She'd constantly nagged to be taken out here, there and everywhere. He was never going to agree to that, he was fully aware the police were searching for his Ford Sierra.

He knew he had to get rid of the Sierra sooner rather than later. But it had been impossible to arrange the disposal of the car, while ever he kept having to go north for strike duty.

Again the strident voice of his wife Rita screeched from upstairs, 'What's the point of having the frigging car if we never go out in the bleeding thing?'

'It needs repairing. How many more times have I got to tell you the same thing, ya daft cow!'

He could hear her stomping down the stairs.

Here it comes, he thought, as she stormed into the lounge.

'What's wrong with the bloody car?' she demanded.

'The big end's gone. I've told you a dozen times already!'

He shouted back, trying hard to control the rage building inside him.

She sneered sarcastically, 'Oh! The big end is it? Well I bet that's the first time anyone's ever said that to you, eh darling?' she chuckled spitefully.

'Fuck off ya evil bitch!'

'I'm a bitch am I, is that what you call your tarts when you're fucking them?'

'What ya talking about, tarts?'

Their voices were getting louder and louder as each tried to out shout the other, 'Do you think I'm fucking stupid Mick, I know you go and see tarts. They're the only silly bitches that would accept your poor excuse for a cock!'

'Shut it Rita, I'm warning ya!'

'They're the only women you don't have to satisfy aren't they, you just pay them, don't you Mick. You fucking sad act!'

Mick Reynolds then did something he had never even dreamed of doing before.

He punched Rita full in the mouth as hard as he could. The force of the blow knocked her to the floor.

'Shut ya poisonous mouth, bitch!'

Rita was as shocked as she was hurt.

'Bastard!' she yelled through gritted teeth, as she sat stunned on the floor.

She could already begin to taste the blood in her mouth as she slowly got to her feet. She pointed an accusing finger and was just about to tell Mick what she thought of him, when he stepped across the room towards her raising a clenched fist. She quickly changed her mind about saying anything and cowered away.

'Rita get the fuck out of my house', he said quietly but with real menace.

She went to respond, but he held up his hand and said, 'If you open your fucking poisonous mouth again, I'll kill you right here, right now.'

The last sentence was said in barely a whisper and for the first time in their relationship Rita was afraid, really afraid.

She had never seen her husband act this way. There was a dark and dangerous look in his eyes that she'd never seen before. It was as though something inside him had finally snapped.

Grabbing her door keys, coat and a handbag Rita fled out of the house and ran down the street.

Mick slammed the front door behind her and went back into the lounge. He sat on the settee breathing heavily, he could feel beads of sweat trickling down his face.

Slowly he felt himself calming down.

He smiled to himself, he felt great.

Mick knew Rita would be back as soon as he left the house to travel back to Nottinghamshire but right then he didn't care, he had drawn the line. If she ever crossed that line again, he knew he'd kill her on the spot. There'd be no second chances, he knew he'd been only a fraction of a second away from killing her today.

Mick walked out of the lounge, went upstairs and started to pack his kit ready for deployment.

CHAPTER 59

Wembley, London – September 14th 1984

After fleeing the house to escape from her enraged husband, Rita had run to the phone box at the end of the street. Breathless and panicked she phoned her best friend Sue Jessop.

Rita arranged to meet Sue at The Green Dragon pub on Wembley High Street in ten minutes.

Both women now sat in the scruffy public bar of the pub slowly sipping their drinks. The pub was a proper shit hole, the old wooden floor was sticky underfoot and the whole place reeked of stale, spilt beer and cigarette smoke.

It was a hard drinker's pub, the sort of place you went to if all you were interested in was getting drunk.

The only other customers in the bar were two old geezers sitting at the bar drinking pints of Double Diamond with Bells whisky chasers.

An indignant Sue Jessop sipped her gin and tonic and said, 'Rita, you're coming over to my flat in Peckham and you're staying with me until that animal's gone back up bloody north. I'm not having any arguments.'

Sue Jessop was forty-three years old, a divorcee with one grown up son.

The boy had left home on the day of his sixteenth birthday to join the Army. Truth be told, the boy would probably have joined the French Foreign Legion if it meant he could get away from his mother.

Sue Jessop was a mess, she dressed like a twenty-year-old, had peroxide blonde hair with jet black roots and chain smoked John Player Special fags.

She was very short and about two stones overweight.

By far the biggest problem with Sue was that she thought men found her irresistible. The procession of different men, who only ever wanted sex, into her bed every weekend had been the main reason her son wanted to leave home so badly.

She was now right up on her soap box, as she poured out advice and sympathy to her equally slutty best friend Rita.

'You don't have to put up with any of that shit Rita love. That man's lucky to have you. Look at you darlin' you're bloody gorgeous. How dare he lay a finger on you. You should go to his bosses and get him sacked.'

'What good would that do, you stupid cow. It's his job that keeps me in money.'

'You can't accept it Rita, trust me girl, if a man hits you once he'll sure as hell do it again.'

'I must admit Sue, he scared the shit out of me today. I've never seen him like that before, he wasn't like my Mick at all. He's usually such a soft twat. When he said he'd kill me I really thought he meant it.'

'What are you gonna do Rita?'

'I've got to stay with him Sue. I've got no choice, it's my home and he gives me everything I want. Just do me a favour, if ever you don't hear from me for more than a few days, please go to the police station and tell them everything. Will you do that for me?'

'Fuckin 'ell Rita, are you that scared?'

'I don't know Sue, maybe I'm being a bit over dramatic but there was definitely something in his eyes today. When I go home, I'll call you every other day for a chat, it's what we do now anyway. If for some reason I don't call you and you can't contact me then you'll know something's happened. Just go to the cops and tell them something's wrong.'

'Of course I will darling, us girls have got to look out for each other. Shall we have another before we go back to mine?'

'Gin and tonic for me Sue, thanks.'

'Coming right up darling!'

CHAPTER 60

Rainworth, Nottinghamshire – September 14th 1984

Rob Buxton was standing at the bar in the lounge of the Jolly Friar pub on the outskirts of Rainworth village.

He glanced at his watch and took another sip of the half pint of lager he was nursing while he waited for Jamie Towle to arrive. Jamie had phoned the incident room the day before saying he'd got information on the recent murders.

He was a striking miner and had point blank refused to walk into the Mobile Incident Room parked in the car park of Blidworth nick.

Instead he'd agreed to meet, early doors, at The Jolly Friar pub. The small pub was on the very edge of the village and was usually a quiet place. Jamie knew there was less chance of him being seen talking to the police if he arranged to meet them there.

Rob was given the task of meeting Jamie and had arrived at the pub ten minutes before the agreed time.

The pub was empty. That wasn't unusual, ever since the strike started to bite the local pubs had suffered.

Any drinking by striking miners was being done at the Welfare as the men mulled over the progress, or lack of it, of the strike.

Rob was glad the place was empty, it would make it easier for Jamie Towle to speak to him openly. He took his lager and sat in one of the small booths that formed part of the lounge bar.

He sat well away from the bar and faced the door so he could see Jamie Towle when he walked in.

Another five minutes ticked slowly by then Rob saw the door to the lounge bar open quietly. A skinny youth who still looked too young to drink in pubs looked inside.

Seeing the pub was empty, except for Rob, he walked in.

The youth was dressed in scruffy jeans and a Donkey jacket that looked two sizes too big for him. His hair was long and greasy and he had a face full of acne.

Jamie Towle quickly looked around the bar and immediately saw the detective sitting in the booth. After having one more quick furtive glance around him, he walked straight over to Rob, ignoring the bar and the barman, who glared markedly at him.

In an overly aggressive manner he said, 'You the cop?'

'I'm DS Buxton are you Jamie Towle?'

'Yeah that's me, let's get this done quick I don't want anyone seeing me talking to you lot.'

'Ok Jamie, let's get things straight, you asked me to come here, here I am. Sit down and let's talk properly. Exactly what information have you got for me?'

Jamie sat down, leaned forward and in a conspiratorial whisper said, 'It's this bloke at the Welfare, all he does is talk about the two women who've been murdered. He's just a bit weird that's all.'

'What do you mean Jamie? In what way is this man weird?'

'He's weird coz he's a total fucking nutjob, you know what I mean! He said the other day if he couldn't kill Maggie Thatcher some other tart would have to do. I'm not the only one who thinks he's strange. Half the miners at the Welfare keep their distance from him, he gets really nasty and violent when he's had a few beers.'

'Have you seen him get violent yourself Jamie?'

'Yeah I've seen it, when he's had a drink he just goes mental, he'll fight anybody.'

'Does he work down the pit?'

'Yeah, he works at Rainworth. He's the same when he's at work down the pit, people avoid him.'

'Is he on strike?'

'Yeah, and he fucking hates scabs. I mean we all hate scabs, but he really hates them. He's always saying how we should start taking them out. That's what I mean, I'm telling you he's fucking nuts.'

Jamie paused looking around him again, before continuing, his voice now even more of a whisper, 'Then the other morning he comes into the Welfare wearing overalls that are like camouflage. Well, there's blood all over the front of them. One of the other blokes in the Welfare asked him what he'd been up to, and he just told him to fuck off and mind his own business. He's getting on a bit now, he must be fifty odd, but a lot of the blokes are still shit scared of him. The rumour is that he's got weapons as well.'

'Weapons?'

'Yeah, some of the blokes in the Welfare reckon that he's got guns and a load of knives.'

'Ok Jamie, what's this man's name and where does he live?'

'Me talking to you like this, it's not going to come back on me is it? If people around here find out I've been talking to the cops, I'll get battered.'

'No it won't come back on you Jamie; I won't be telling anybody we've spoken. So if you don't say anything to anyone you'll be fine.'

'I won't be making any statements and I definitely ain't going to Court.'

'That's fine too Jamie, just give me the name.'

'Stan Briggs, his name's Stan Briggs.'

'Where can I find this Stan Briggs?'

'He lives at 15 Hardcastle Road in Rainworth but he spends most of the day at The Welfare.'

'Thanks Jamie, who else lives with him at Hardcastle Road?'

'It's just his old lady who lives with him now, he's got two daughters who live in Blidworth with their husbands. I know the husbands, they're on strike too. They don't like Stan either, they think he's mental. I think both his daughters have got kids as well.'

'Thanks for telling me all this Jamie, can I give you some money for a drink or something?'

'I don't want your money copper. I ain't a grass, but it ain't right what's happened to them women either. I'm out of here.'

Jamie then stood up and took off out of the pub like a scalded cat.

Rob waited for two minutes then he also left the pub, leaving the now flat, half-drunk glass of lager on the table.

He walked back to his car and drove out of the car park and set off back towards Mansfield.

As he drove the car along Python Hill, away from the pub, he passed Jamie walking along the street. Neither man acknowledged the other.

Rob made a left turn onto Little John Avenue and then took another left onto Hardcastle Road.

He noted that the houses with odd numbers on Hardcastle Road all backed onto fields. The fields at the back of these houses all led directly towards the rear of The Archer pub.

Rob slowly drove his car to number 15 Hardcastle Road.

It was a large semi-detached house, identical in design to every other pit house in the village.

The house was very scruffy and run down.

Hardcastle Road was a cul de sac and number 15 was the last house on the street. The other half of the semi-detached was almost derelict with an overgrown garden and a couple of smashed windows. It appeared as though number 13 hadn't been occupied for a long time.

There was a rusting wreck of a car on the front garden of number 15. The grass where the car had been abandoned was as high as the wheel arches of the car.

The paint on the front door and window frames of the house was flaking off. There were filthy dirty net curtains hanging in all the windows.

Rob turned the car around in the cul de sac and again drove slowly passed the house. This time he looked down the side of the house. He could see a large coal bunker which was empty.

Looking beyond the coal bunker Rob noted there was a falling down fence at the back of the property. He could also see there was clear access onto the fields behind the house.

'Ok Stan Briggs, let's see what we know about you already, shall we?' he said quietly to himself as he drove his car out of Hardcastle Road.

CHAPTER 61

Mansfield Police Station – September 15th 1984

It was six o'clock in the morning and a full section of the Special Operations Unit were being briefed by Danny and Rob at Blidworth Police Station.

Rob cleared his throat and the men stopped talking and listened as he began the briefing, 'Right gents our target today is a man named Stan Briggs. There's an up to date photograph of Briggs in your briefing pack. We've received information that he may be connected in some way to our recent murders. The address on the warrant is 15 Hardcastle Road at Rainworth. Briggs was a nasty bastard in his youth, he's got two previous convictions for Sec 18 wounding. He's also got numerous convictions for ABH, three of these have been for assaults on women. There's numerous calls logged to his home address following domestic disputes. Basically Stan Briggs is violent and is no fan of women. Our information is that he hates scabs with a passion and has recently tried to incite violence against working miners. He's also been heard recently making threats against women, connecting the threat to the strike. He was heard to say, "If I can't kill Maggie Thatcher some other tart will have to do".

We're particularly interested in locating and seizing a set of overalls with a camouflage pattern, that may or may not be blood stained, any weapons, any typewriters or any other article you think may be connected to our two recent murders. I want to be on the road by ten past six and at the address no later than six fifteen. Any questions?' asked Rob.

A voice from the back of the gathering spoke up, 'Are there any firearms registered to the address?'

'Our information from the source is that Briggs does have access to firearms. Our records indicate that he doesn't legally own any firearms or shotguns, but as we all know that doesn't prevent the possibility of him having an illegal weapon. This is one of the reasons I want a very rapid entry to the house. Hopefully Briggs will still be in bed asleep and you'll be able to contain him before he stirs. Any other questions?'

There were no other questions.

Five minutes later and the two vans containing the Special Operations Unit were being driven out of the police station followed by a car containing the two detectives.

'How good's the information Rob?' asked Danny.

'It was good enough to get a warrant from the Magistrates, but it's not the best. It's uncorroborated and the word of an untested informant, but we've got to act on it. Let's face it Danny there's not much else coming in, you never know, it might just be spot on.'

'We'll soon find out Rob, won't we.'

The house at 15 Hardcastle Road was in darkness when the small convoy of police vehicles pulled up quietly outside.

Quickly the men from the SOU surrounded the house.

As soon as he was satisfied that all exits to the house were covered, the sergeant in charge indicated to the man with the sledge hammer to knock the front door in.

With one almighty blow landed directly onto the mortise lock the front door flew open. Immediately other officers ran through the door and up the stairs.

Danny and Rob remained outside on the road and saw lights coming on in various rooms and heard shouts emanating from the first floor of the house. Less than a minute later the sergeant in charge of the raid emerged from the front of the house.

'The house is secure Inspector; your man's getting dressed upstairs. He's secured but he hasn't been arrested yet.'

Danny turned to Rob, 'Do the honours Rob, arrest him on suspicion of murder, it might just focus his mind away from the strike.'

The SOU sergeant spoke up, 'That might be a very good call sir. When we grabbed him, the first thing he started spouting on about was Thatcher's boot boys.'

Rob looked knowingly at Danny before walking into the house and up the stairs to the main bedroom.

Stan Briggs was a very angry man, he was now fully dressed and had been handcuffed behind his back, he was threatening anybody who could be bothered to listen.

Rob looked closely at Stan Briggs. Yes, he was obnoxious and yes he was violent, but was he a murderer?

Right now he looked pathetic, his puffy, bloated face red from shouting.

He was a very scruffy, short, stocky man. He'd not shaved for days and his hair was long and lank. His clothes were unwashed and smelled.

Basically, the man was a shambolic mess.

The house was even more of a shithole inside than it was on the outside. It smelled of damp and mould, stale fried food and cigarette smoke. There was rubbish and old unwashed clothes piled everywhere.

Rob looked at Briggs, took hold of his right arm and said

evenly, 'Stan Briggs you're under arrest on suspicion of the murders of Mandy Stokes and June Hayes.'

Rob then cautioned Briggs.

There was a long silence before Briggs spluttered a response, 'Did you say murder? This has got to be a fucking joke. I've never killed anybody.'

Briggs was suddenly very subdued and had stopped shouting.

Rob took him downstairs and through the kitchen.

Briggs wife, dressed in a shabby old dressing gown, had rolled herself a cigarette and was now smoking it in the kitchen. Rob heard her talking to the officers who were starting the search of the property.

'What exactly is it you're looking for, he's not one of the great train robbers, you know', she said wearily.

Rob escorted Briggs out of the house and walked him towards Danny and the waiting car.

'Are you his boss?' asked Briggs quietly.

'I'm Det Insp Flint, why?'

'You've got it all wrong chief. I'm not a murderer this is a huge mistake.'

'Let's get you over to the police station at Mansfield, then you can tell me everything you know about the murder of Mandy Stokes and June Hayes.'

There was now a level of panic in Briggs voice.

'I don't know anything; I've never heard of either of those women.'

The return journey to the Police Station was made in silence. The only noise in the car came from Briggs sitting in the back, constantly muttering the word "No" to himself.

At Mansfield, Briggs was immediately taken to the cells

where he complained to the sergeant in charge of the cell block.

'This is all wrong Sarge!' he whined.

Briggs was put in a cell and Danny and Rob made their way to the CID office. They had a quick cup of tea while they waited for the Special Ops team to arrive with the result of the subsequent house search at 15 Hardcastle Road.

'What do you think Danny?'

'I honestly don't know Rob. Like you I heard the comment he made, that's also on the note, but looking at him?' He shook his head.

'I hope the search of the house yields something boss. This killer's so careful and meticulous at the scenes. Everything's obviously planned in minute detail, it's hard to imagine him being so different in the way he lives his everyday life.'

'I know Rob, that's exactly what's bothering me the most, our killer's extremely organised and Briggs on face value looks like the most disorganised man I've ever seen. Let's just wait and see what the SOU lads bring back from the search. You never know your luck in a raffle.'

The two men then set about planning the interview they were about to have with Briggs. Initially they had to plan as though nothing was found at the house.

When the SOU team arrived at Mansfield having completed the search, they had good news.

The sergeant walked into the CID office with the search log in his hand.

'I'll give you the highlights of what's been seized, then you can have the search logs. We've recovered the camouflaged overalls and there's what looks like a lot of blood on the front and both sleeves of them. We've got two very sharp filleting knives, a.22 silenced air rifle, a headlamp attached to a car battery and most surprisingly of all an Olivetti typewriter. The last item being found in one of the unused bedrooms in amongst a load of other junk.'

'Did the wife say anything to you about any of the items recovered at the house?' asked Danny.

'I asked her specifically about the typewriter boss, she told me it belonged to one of her daughters and that Briggs had borrowed it at the start of the strike. I didn't ask her about the other things we've recovered. They all look pretty straightforward to me, that's a full poaching kit we've recovered. My guess is that the blood on the overalls will turn out to be from poached rabbit's.'

'Ok Sarge, thanks. It was another very professional job this morning, will you thank your men for me.'

'Will do boss, all the recovered items have been booked into the property store, everything's labelled up and the statements from the officers who found the items will be on your desk by the end of the day.'

'Thanks Sarge.'

As soon as the sergeant left the room, Rob grabbed a plain piece of paper and was on his feet racing out the door, quickly followed by Danny.

At the property store Rob got out the Olivetti typewriter recovered from Hardcastle Road quickly inserted the sheet of paper and typed out a random sentence.

'Bollocks!' he exclaimed before continuing, 'It types perfectly Danny. Look at the letter 'C' it's aligned correctly.'

'I can see it is', said a very disappointed Danny.

An hour later, Danny and Rob were sitting opposite a very quiet and subdued Stan Briggs in an interview room.

A uniformed constable was also standing at the back of the room having brought Briggs from the cells to the interview room.

Danny started the interview.

'Ok Mr Briggs first things first. Tell me your movements on the night of Thursday 6th September?'

'I was at home with my old lady most of the night.'

'What does "most of the night" mean?'

'I was at home until about ten o'clock at night, then I went out.'

'Where'd you go?'

'Just out, I went for a walk.'

'Exactly where did you go for a walk?'

'I walked around the streets, nowhere in particular.'

Danny looked at the desk and shook his head slowly, finally looking up and staring directly into Briggs eyes.

'Why are you lying?'

'I'm not lying.'

'Don't waste my fucking time Briggs, we both know you weren't walking the streets of Rainworth, now where did you go?'

Briggs let out a long sigh.

'I might as well tell you, you'll have found all my gear anyway. I was out on the fields at the back of my house.'

'Doing what exactly?'

'I was fucking poaching. I was out lamping for rabbits. I've got to get food for my daughters and their little ones. They've got no money coming in now, thanks to that cow Thatcher.'

'Exactly where were you poaching?' asked Rob.

'I was only out for about two hours, I remember it was freezing that night and I started to get cold.'

'Where were you Briggs!' said Rob, raising his voice.

'Alright, alright. I was on the private farmland behind The Archer pub.'

Danny looked directly at Briggs.

'Let me get this straight Briggs, you were on the fields behind The Archer pub between eleven and eleven forty-five on Thursday 6th September?'

'Was that the night all the music was on at the pub?'

'YES!'

'Yeah, that would be about right, I got three small rabbits early doors about ten thirty, then I didn't see anything else. I gave up just after I heard the couple arguing.'

'What couple?'

'Well I think it was a couple, they must've had a row or something, because I heard the woman scream.'

'Exactly where were this couple?'

'Down on the road that runs from the pub towards Blidworth.'

'Whereabouts on the road?'

'Up towards the Blidworth end, I was up there at that time'

'What did you see?'

'After I heard the scream, I turned around and looked in the direction it came from. I saw the car and I heard the door being slammed shut. I heard another quieter scream from inside the car, then the car was driven off quickly towards Blidworth. Like I said they must've had a row. She was probably talking when she should have been listening, you know what women are like.'

'I want you to think very carefully Briggs, how far away from all this commotion were you?'

'A good seventy-five yards easy, but I was looking down from the top of the hill so I had a good view, the car was sort of in between the street lights so it was quite dark where it was.'

'Did you get a better look at the car as it was driven off passing the street lights?'

'I suppose I did, slightly.'

'Can you remember what type of car it was?'

'It looked like an old one. It definitely wasn't a modern car the shape looked old. I remember it was a dark colour, but it's hard to tell the colour in them orange street lights.'

'Did you see the woman who screamed?'

'No, I never saw her. I just heard the scream.'

'Did you see the man in the car?'

'No'

'Have you ever seen that car before?'

'No'

Danny nodded to the uniform PC who was standing in the interview room, indicating for him to keep an eye on Briggs.

He and Rob then walked out of the interview room.

Once outside the room Danny said, 'Briggs isn't our killer, he saw our killer abducting June Hayes!'

Rob nodded.

Danny said, 'Rob arrange for the blood to be tested but I'm pretty certain it'll turn out to be rabbits blood like the SOU Sgt suggested. Get a statement from Briggs and spend as much time as you can on the car he saw. Take him around garages if you have to. I want to know what type of car he saw. Make, model and colour. If we can find that car we may just find our killer.'

CHAPTER 62

Mansfield Police Station – September 29th 1984

All the optimism Danny felt about finding a witness to the abduction of June Hayes had now evaporated.

Two weeks had flown by since the arrest of Stan Briggs and the subsequent discovery, during interview, that the poacher had witnessed the moment June Hayes was abducted and bundled into a car on her way home from a night out at The Archer pub in Rainworth.

After making a witness statement Briggs had been released. Disappointingly he was unable to specifically identify the type of car used by the killer, despite the best efforts of Rob Buxton to jog his memory.

The only thing Briggs had been able to say with any degree of certainty was that it was an older car, possibly a Ford Cortina and dark in colour.

Danny was now sitting in the CID office with his team discussing the sparse evidence they had and more importantly if there was anything else they could do to progress the enquiry.

It was Rob who spoke up first, 'I've been on the phone to the lab this morning, they've finally completed all the tests on the camouflage overalls we recovered from 15, Hardcastle Road. As we suspected from the outset, the blood isn't human, it's from an animal, most likely a rabbit. The typewriter's also been fully examined and there are no recent repairs to any of the keys.'

'Thanks Rob, I think it's fair to say that we can now discount Briggs from this enquiry other than as a witness, albeit a reluctant, woman hating one', said a weary Danny.

He paused before continuing, 'Are we missing something here people? Is there something blatantly obvious staring us in the face?'

The team were silent for a minute or two before Andy spoke up, 'There's one thing that's nagged at me about both of these murders, that's the total lack of forensic evidence at either scene. We've all moaned about it but have we asked the question, why? Who'd have the knowledge to commit crimes like these and leave absolutely no trace of forensic evidence? Who'd even know what we look for at scenes and the processes we use to obtain it?'

Rachel now carried Andy's theme on, 'Add to that the deliberate acts taken under the guise of a frenzied assault to obliterate the identity of the victims.'

'What do you mean, under the guise of a frenzied assault?' asked Danny.

'Well the cause of death in each case has been strangulation, the rest is all window dressing in a sense. Albeit very careful and calculated window dressing, I'll grant you. The identification of the victims could have been made difficult without going to such lengths. I think it's all staged, he wants us to think he's out of control and that his motive for killing is hatred, personally I think that's the opposite of the truth.'

She continued, 'And what about the messages left on the body and the typed notes? Am I the only person in this room who doesn't believe there's any political motive to these murders? I think all that's a massive red herring left deliberately to throw us off the scent.'

Andy spoke again, 'Who's got the forensic awareness?'

Danny had listened carefully to his two junior officers then said, 'I'm going to say out loud what I believe you're all thinking anyway. Should we be looking for a Police Officer?'

Rob replied, 'It's a good question Danny. Scenes of Crime have already said they've found marks from overshoes at both murder scenes where they can be sure no police officers or Scenes of Crime personnel had been.'

'Do you think our killer was wearing a forensic suit when he killed these women?' asked Danny.

'It would certainly explain a lot boss.'

A thought suddenly came into Danny's head, 'Rob, how many police officers from foreign forces are currently working in Nottinghamshire?'

'Thousands Danny, and they're chopping and changing every week. They're arriving from virtually every police force in the land on mutual aid. I think there's over five hundred officers deployed from the Metropolitan Police alone, obviously they're not all here at the same time.'

'How many remain in Nottinghamshire for the duration of their deployment?' asked Danny

It was Andy who answered the question, 'All of them that are based too far away to be deployed from their home force on a daily basis. That's most of them.'

Danny stroked his chin and thought for a long time before saying, 'Right, Andy and Rachel, I want you to start contacting the Personnel Departments of all Forces that are currently providing mutual aid in the shape of Police

Support Units to this Force. I want you to start obtaining comprehensive lists of police officers that have been seconded to Nottinghamshire from all these foreign forces. It's going to be a hell of an undertaking and I'll need you to be very discreet in your enquiries. I don't want it known outside of these four walls what we suspect. If the public got wind of this enquiry it would be a public relations disaster. The level of bad feeling between the community and the police is already the worst I've ever known. I want accurate lists drawing up. I want you to include officers that have only been deployed in Nottinghamshire for a few days. I want the dates each individual has been in the County. Once we've got all that information, we can then cross check it with the dates of our murders. That will narrow down the suspect list massively.'

'That's a huge task Danny', said Rob.

'I don't see any other option Rob. I think you're all on the right track. I think we could be looking for a serving, or recently retired, police officer with a good knowledge of the investigation of murder and a good understanding of forensic evidence and how we obtain it. I believe it will also be an individual who still has ready access to forensic suits. I think it's time to move this investigation forward, we've no significant leads or lines of enquiry outstanding at this time, so I want to get started on this enquiry today. I think our killer's name will be somewhere on one of those lists'

CHAPTER 63

Warsop Main Colliery – October 8th 1984

The strike was crumbling.

The number of miners returning to work across the country was growing steadily, the number going in to Warsop Main Colliery had now reached twenty-four.

The levels of picketing at the gates to the mine had also declined. The usual number of pickets each day was now down to around fifty. The strike was quickly losing all impetus and was dying a slow death.

Once in a while pickets from the Yorkshire coal fields would get through the intercept points and boost the numbers picketing the mine. As the numbers of pickets had reduced, the policing of them had intensified. Pickets were getting arrested and put before the Courts for the least little thing. Once before the Court, stringent bail conditions were imposed that meant if an arrested picket returned to the mine entrance again he would risk being sent to prison.

The strike was being slowly and mercilessly crushed to death by the judiciary.

At the disused quarry the groups of miners and police officers milled about as usual while they waited the twenty or so minutes before the two battle buses arrived.

While waiting for the busses, Mick Reynolds immediately sought out the company of Jimmy Wade.

Once he found him, Mick steered Jimmy furtively out of earshot of the rest of the gathering.

'Are you deliberately trying to avoid me Jimmy?' said a disgruntled Mick softly through gritted teeth.

'Of course not Mick, what makes you say that?'

'We haven't had one of our little chats for a while, that's all.'

For the last couple of days Jimmy had stood in amongst the groups of other miners to deliberately avoid having a conversation with the irritating cockney sergeant.

Jimmy had grown tired of Mick's constant moaning about Rita, his wife, and how he'd dealt with her the last time he was home and that if she stepped out of line again he was going to finish her once and for all.

'I think it's time we went out on the prowl again Jimmy. We need to let them know we're still here.'

'Haven't you seen the paper Mick, the cops are looking for an old Ford Cortina that's a dark colour. I'm sorry Mick, but at the moment it's not an option to go anywhere. We have to lie low for the time being. I can't risk driving my car around now, I've got it safely locked up in my garage.'

'Don't be so soft Jimmy old son, we'd be fine. I'm telling you I need to go again!'

Jimmy could see that the Sergeant was getting angry, so he tried to placate him.

'It's not that I don't want to Mick, but there's so many of your lot everywhere, we'd be bound to get a pull and then it really would be game over.'

'Are you too scared Jimmy?'

'Grow up Mick, I don't want to spend the rest of my life behind bars just to please you, now fuck off!'

Jimmy started to walk away.

Mick shouted after him, 'I don't need you Jimmy, I'll go myself!'

Angrily Jimmy spun around to face him, 'Don't be an idiot Mick, all we've got to do is just bide our time.'

'We'll see shall we, I'm not waiting any longer. I need to do one more up here so the next time I'm home in London I can do Rita as well. That bitch has had it coming long enough.'

'What about your rules Mick? I thought one of them was never kill anyone you know?'

'This is different. I've been planning this for ages. I've found a place to dump her where she'll never be found.'

'And why do you have to do one up here to kill Rita? It's madness.'

'I need to do one more here so I'm ready for her, you don't understand Jimmy.'

'Bloody right I don't understand. You're talking like a crazy man Mick. You need to get a grip of yourself, we need to wait. I'm going to swap my car soon, then we can go out again.'

'When?'

'When you get back after your next rest days, I'll have swapped the car; I promise you we'll go out again then.'

'I go back to London on rest days from the 20th of this month. I'm back up here on the 27th. Are you saying we can definitely go out on the 28th?'

'It's a deal, we just need to be careful and take our time. One more thing Mick, no more talk about killing your old lady Rita when you're back home, that would be madness at this moment in time.'

'Can't promise that old son', he grinned.

The battle buses were now powering up the lane to the where the men had gathered. Once the transport had come to a stop, Jimmy took the front seat on the first bus.

He watched through the front window of the bus as Sgt Reynolds mustered his men into their police Transit vans.

Jimmy was deep in thought now, he was glad he'd made the preparations. It was nearly time to move them forward. The time was coming for him to deal with the police sergeant who was quickly becoming a dangerous liability.

Jimmy didn't trust Reynolds, he knew he was crazy enough to go out on his own and risk getting caught. He also knew that eventually Mick would kill his wife and then it would seriously come on top. Jimmy had made his mind up, the problem of Mick Reynolds had to be sorted out once and for all. They'd be going out again on the night of the 28th alright and there would definitely be a killing.

Jimmy grinned at the prospect.

Sitting in the front seat of the police Transit, Mick Reynolds was also thinking.

Who the fuck does Jimmy Wade think he is?

Mick considered himself to be the brains and the driving force behind their little ventures. He made the decisions when it was ok to go, not Jimmy Wade.

'Fuck Jimmy Wade!' he mumbled to himself.

His mumbled words were lost in the noise of the Transit van as it was driven at speed along the country lane.

By the time they reached the entrance to the mine Mick had made his mind up. With or without Jimmy Wade, he was going to have one more bitch before he went back to London.

CHAPTER 64

Edwinstowe – October 19th 1984

Mick Reynolds checked his watch again.

It had just turned nine thirty at night as he slipped silently out of his bed. He had to be careful, he was in the Nissan hut he shared with the rest of his PSU.

He looked around at the men, they were all still sleeping. They had a four o'clock start the next morning and there was nothing else to do anyway. He was carrying a small grip bag as he carefully closed the door of the Nissan hut and made his way stealthily across the disused army base.

Mick was wearing a black jacket, black jeans and gloves and in his pocket was a black ski mask. He also had his warrant card in his jeans pocket just in case he was stopped by some overzealous local copper.

Having made his way carefully out of the camp without being spotted he walked down the long driveway to the main road. It was a really dark night, the night sky was full of cloud, there was no moonlight whatsoever. It felt like a storm was coming, there was definitely the feeling of rain in the air.

Once on the main road he knew it would take just over three quarters of an hour to walk from the entrance of the army camp to the small village of Edwinstowe.

There were no street lights along the road until he reached the outskirts of the village. As he walked along the dark road dressed from head to toe in black he felt totally invisible. He'd made a couple of visits to Edwinstowe over the last week or so to check out the geography of the village and to pick out likely places where he may find a young woman walking alone at night.

He had a loose plan in his mind and as he neared the village he could feel a tingling excitement racing through his body. His intention was to grab a woman off the street and drag her into the woodland that surrounded the village.

Once in a quiet location he could then take his time and make sure he removed any evidence.

As he walked towards the village he cursed Jimmy Wade quietly under his breath.

'Fuckin yellow bastard', he muttered.

Just under an hour later and he had reached Edwinstowe without any major dramas. There was only one incident, when he'd had to dart back into the hedgerow to allow a car to pass by.

Having reached the village, he made his way, unseen, to the Forest Tavern pub, right on the outskirts of the village. He found a good place to observe the front door of the pub from behind a privet hedge opposite.

For just over half an hour he stood in the same position, watching the front door of the pub. Mick had chosen the small white walled pub because of its proximity to the surrounding woodland. It was the last building at this end of the village, the road went out into the dense woodland immediately after the pub. There was a large beer garden at the side of the pub that overlooked the woods.

As he patiently waited he thought to himself what a beautiful spot it must be in the summer.

He checked his watch, it was now almost eleven o'clock, last orders would be being called. Mick slipped further back into the shadows cast by the large privet hedge across the road from the pub.

He could hear voices laughing and joking now and he saw groups of people starting to leave the pub.

Mick cursed silently as he saw that the people leaving the pub were all couples. After the last pair left, he saw the front door of the pub close and heard the bolts slide across.

He cursed his luck and was just about to leave his hiding place and head back to Proteus camp, when he heard the bolts on the front door slide back again. Moving back into the shadows he watched as a young girl stepped out of the door.

'Goodnight Tony', she said.

He heard a male voice reply, 'Goodnight Sarah, see you tomorrow evening.'

Bar staff, thought Mick.

Perfect.

He now watched intently, his eyes glistening in the dark, as the young girl stood near to the gate of the beer garden and lit a cigarette. She was standing with her back to the woodlands on the edge of the beer garden. This was going to be easier than he'd thought, as he watched the girl he licked his lips in anticipation, she was young, probably around nineteen.

She was very petite, just over five feet tall with long blonde hair that was tied back in a ponytail.

As she stood beneath the single white street light he could see that she was an extremely pretty girl.

'I bet you're popular with the punters', Mick said softly to himself.

He could see she was wearing tight blue denim jeans and a cream coloured blouse underneath a thin dark blue cardigan and black flat shoes.

As she took a long drag on the cigarette she glanced down at her wristwatch.

'Shit!' he whispered to himself.

He'd suddenly realised that the girl was waiting for somebody or something. Maybe she'd called a taxi to take her home. He knew he had to move fast.

Silently he slipped out from behind the cover of the privet hedge unseen, he then manoeuvred until he was directly behind her. He could now approach her from the direction of the woods.

He slipped the black ski mask on and crept stealthily over the beer garden towards her, carrying the small black grip bag in his left hand.

He got within five yards of her and caught a faint smell of her perfume, as it was carried towards him on the slight breeze. The perfume smell was then replaced by the smell of tobacco as she exhaled smoke from her cigarette.

He could hear the young girl humming a song which he recognised from the charts.

Mick was now only a couple of strides away from the girl.

He felt empowered as he realised she still had no idea of his deadly presence. He paused momentarily, then as the girl took another long pull on the cigarette he pounced.

Placing the grip bag on the floor he stepped forward two strides and punched the girl once, hard on the back of her head. The force of the punch sent the cigarette flying out of her mouth. The cigarette travelled in a high arc before landing in the gutter.

The girl's legs buckled beneath her and she crumpled in a heap, knocked out cold from the force of the blow.

He immediately reached down and started to drag the unconscious girl back across the beer garden to the woods.

Mick was about to bodily pick the girl up off the floor so he could carry her off, when he heard footsteps running towards him as he struggled to lift the girl.

He looked up and saw a young man hurtling up the street towards him. The youth was quite slight and skinny, he looked to be of a similar age to the girl.

He was approaching very fast though and Mick could now hear the youth shouting, 'Get the fuck off her!'

Mick let the girl drop onto the floor, as the youth was almost upon him, he then stepped forward and met the onrushing youth with a hard punch to the face, knocking him backwards onto the floor.

The shouting and commotion from outside had raised people in the pub, the lights inside were again being turned on.

As the youth started to gamely get to his feet Mick stepped forward and kicked him hard in the face. The force of the kick spun the youth over onto his back and knocked him unconscious.

Mick could now hear the bolts on the pub door being drawn back once more.

'Bollocks!' he muttered under his breath, before picking up his bag and sprinting away in the direction of the woods beyond the beer garden. Once he reached the cover of the woods Mick stopped briefly and watched as the landlord emerged from the pub.

The landlord saw the two unconscious teenagers on the floor and immediately shouted to his wife to call the police and an ambulance.

Mick turned away from the pub and briskly walked off into the woods.

He knew he could get back onto the road that led back to the army base a little further on.

It was time to get back to Proteus Camp.

As he walked away he replayed the events of the night in his mind and he cursed the outcome. Another couple of minutes and he would have carried the girl into the woodland where he wouldn't have been disturbed.

Now he was well away from the pub he took off the ski mask and dropped it into his small black grip bag. He made his way from the woods back out onto the road that led from Edwinstowe to Ollerton.

As Mick walked slowly along the road he stayed close into the hedgerows in case any cars came along, he again cursed Jimmy Wade for being too scared to join in tonight's activity.

As he walked Mick fantasised about what he would be doing right now if he and Jimmy had both been there.

Suddenly, his attention was snapped back as he saw blue lights approaching fast from the direction of Ollerton. Quickly he dropped down into the ditch that ran alongside the road and from his concealed position he watched as the police Panda car raced by.

He waited a minute then got to his feet and began to jog slowly back towards Ollerton. Ten more minutes passed before Mick silently slipped into the army camp. Once inside the camp it was easy to make his way unseen back to his own Nissan hut. Quietly he opened the door and slipped inside the hut.

Everyone inside was still fast asleep.

He glanced at his watch before undressing.

It was now nearly one o'clock in the morning, three more hours and he would be getting up. He knew he wouldn't be able to sleep, he could still feel the adrenalin pumping through him.

As soon as he closed his eyes, his mind was full of images of him raging over the smashed and battered body of the dead young barmaid.

He opened his eyes again and placed his hands behind his head as he stared at the ceiling of the hut.

'Who needs to fucking sleep anyway', he growled softly.

CHAPTER 65

Edwinstowe – October 20th 1984

The two detectives stood outside the Forest Tavern at Edwinstowe. It was still early morning and everywhere was covered in a heavy dew, the sky was grey and brooding. The clouds above looked full of rain, there was definitely a storm coming.

'It's a nasty attack Danny, do you think it's our killer?' asked Rob.

'I really don't know. Compared to the other two attacks, this seems a bit disorganised. It's way too risky, too haphazard.'

'It's certainly a weird one.'

'What about our victims, what are they saying?'

'The barmaid, Sarah Featherstone, can't give us any description whatsoever, all she remembers is standing outside the pub having a cigarette waiting for her boyfriend, then wham! The next thing she remembers is coming to in the ambulance. She never saw or heard a thing.'

'What about the boyfriend Rob, can he help us out?'

'I've just spoken to him at the hospital before driving over here, his name's Steve Pepper. The hospital kept him in overnight because he took such a nasty whack to the head.

The doctor thinks he was kicked in the head near to the temple, he wouldn't let me speak to Mr Pepper until first thing this morning. All he can tell us is that he saw a figure dressed in black from head to foot standing over his girlfriend. He thought the man in black was trying to pick her up off the floor. He can recall shouting and running at the figure and he remembers getting punched in the face and falling backwards to the floor. He says he tried to get up but as he was on his hands and knees he was hit again and knocked out. He didn't come around until they were at the hospital.'

'Can he give any sort of description of the attacker?'

'Not really Danny. He says the guy was bigger than him, not taller but stockier and that he was wearing one of them black woollen ski masks.'

'He sounds a brave young lad Rob.'

'Yeah, he is. He was more concerned about his girlfriend's welfare, when he came to the first thing he asked was how she was. He's a Forestry Commission worker at the moment, but he's recently applied to join the police. The poor kid's only just turned eighteen.'

'Ok Rob, is there anything else?'

'Oh yeah sorry Danny, there's one other thing. Steve also thinks he saw a black bag near the feet of his attacker.'

Danny paused deep in thought, 'That changes things Rob. I was ready to treat this as a random attack that's not connected to the two murders, now I'm not so sure. Maybe the bag is significant. Perhaps that's where the forensic suit and tools he uses are kept until he's somewhere quieter, where he won't be disturbed. It's possible the attacker was trying to pick the girl up off the floor and take her into the woods, where God knows what would have happened to her. I think maybe we've had a lucky escape here, thanks to the bravery of Mr Pepper. Remind me to write him up a commendation letter, you never know it might help him get on the force at a later date?'

'Will do Danny. Neither of the witnesses made any mention of a car being involved though.'

'That could've been parked up anywhere, for him to go back to later. The car's something else that's been bothering me Rob. If our theory's right, where would a deployed officer, from out of the County get hold of an old car?'

'It's a good question Danny, perhaps they've already got links in this area. Maybe it's not a cop that's on deployment. Maybe it's one of our own.'

Danny shuddered involuntarily as that thought was digested inwardly.

'Rob, can you organise a press release to go out later this morning. The usual stuff, women to be vigilant etc. Don't link it to the other attacks and don't mention the bag or some bright journalist might link them anyway.'

'Ok Danny will do. I've left Andy and Rachel back at the station, they're hard at it talking to the foreign forces personnel departments.'

'Thanks Rob, I know I keep dumping work on you but I really do have to go and see my father over at the nursing home today. I haven't been over to see him for weeks. Thank God, Sue's been over to see him every day.'

'She's a very nice lady Danny. How's that all going by the way?'

'Apart from the fact that since all this started, we've hardly had five minutes together, it's going very well Rob, thanks for asking', he laughed.

As they walked back to their cars Rob said, 'Danny there's something I do need to talk to you about. I'm starting to get a little concerned about Andy. He doesn't seem himself lately, I've noticed he's coming to work unshaven and a couple of times he's been wearing the same shirt for a few days. I know that's not the end of the world, but it's just not Andy. We both know he's normally very sharp and smart with his appearance.'

'Do you think he's having problems at home?'

'I don't know Danny, possibly. At work he's as focused as ever, but something's definitely changed. Would you take him to one side and have a word with him, when you get back from seeing your Dad?'

'Of course Rob, I'll talk to him over a beer at the Railway after work.'

'Thanks Danny, he's a hard worker and a bloody good lad, but something's not right.'

'I'm sure I'll get to the bottom of what's bothering him over a beer or two.'

Both men had reached their cars that were parked near the centre of the small village.

'See you later Rob.'

Rob nodded before getting in the car and speeding off.

Danny took a moment and sat quietly in his car. He chastised himself for not spotting that Andy was maybe having problems, he should be the one to look after the welfare of his staff. It shouldn't be down to Rob to inform him that something was amiss.

He started his car and drove off.

CHAPTER 66

Mansfield – October 20th 1984

The lounge bar in The Railway pub was almost empty.

An old man sat in the corner next to the roaring open fire eating a bag of pork scratchings. He was eating them at the rate of one scratching every five minutes.

He was washing them down equally as slowly with his pint of Mansfield Mild.

Danny and Andy walked into the pub and closed the door hurriedly, the cold autumnal nights were really setting in and the warmth of the fire was definitely welcome.

Both men walked straight to the bar.

'Evening gents, what can I get you?' asked the landlord

'My shout Andy, what you having?'

'Guinness for me boss, thanks.'

'Make that two pints of Guinness then please Billy.'

'Coming right up Mr Flint.'

The Railway pub was very often frequented by detectives as the police station was less than a hundred yards away. The landlord of the pub, Billy Steele, knew most of the detectives by name.

As he waited for the Guinness to settle, Billy said, 'I heard you nicked someone for the murders of those poor women, is that right?'

'That's right Billy, we did make an arrest, but unfortunately he wasn't our man. We're still looking.'

Billy placed the two black beers on the bar.

'Good luck, gents. I hope you get the bastard locked up soon. Could you do me a favour Mr Flint, when you go over to your seats just check and make sure old Fred's still breathing. I haven't seen him move for twenty minutes now!'

'Will do Billy.'

Danny and Andy both chuckled as they took their beers and moved away from the bar.

'Let's sit over here Andy.'

'Ok boss.'

'We're off duty Andy, just call me Danny, ok.'

'Ok, Danny is everything alright?'

'That's what I wanted to ask you Andy. You don't seem yourself lately.'

'Is there a problem with my work?' Andy asked defensively.

'Not at all, you're work and your effort is the same as it always is, exemplary. No, I mean in yourself, you don't seem like your old self.'

Andy now slowly turned his glass on the beer mat, before lifting the glass and taking a long drink of the black beer. He carefully placed his glass back on the beer mat before looking directly at Danny, 'Sally and I have separated,' he said flatly.

Danny was shocked.

'What do you mean, separated? A temporary thing or permanent?'

'She says it's only temporary, but I don't know. It's the hours we're all working Danny, I'm never at home. Because I live over at Retford, most days I leave the house just before seven o'clock and if I get home at all it isn't until after nine o'clock at night. The straw that broke the camel's back, so to speak, was a few weeks ago when I completely forgot our wedding anniversary. I didn't get in from work until gone nine o'clock that night. Then the next day June Hayes was reported missing. I've hardly been home since.'

He took another long drink of the Guinness, then continued, 'One night last week I got home and found a note from Sally saying she'd moved out and gone back to her parents' house in Gainsborough. The note said she was going to stay there until I knew what I wanted, a marriage or a career in the police force.'

'Bloody hell Andy! Why haven't you said anything to me before?'

'What can I say? I'm not working any harder or putting in any more hours than the rest of us. This is my job, it's what I do. I thought Sally would understand that's all.'

'Andy, you need to sort this out right now. I want you to go home tonight, get tidied up, get a shave and drive over to her parents' house at Gainsborough. You need to be doing everything you can to save your marriage mate.'

'It's not that simple Danny.'

'It is that simple Andy, trust me I know. I had exactly the same situation, I chose not to fight for my marriage and just let it go. I've regretted that decision every day since. If you love Sally, which I know you do, you'll go home and sort this out now. This isn't a request Andy; this is an order. Go home and speak to Sally, take two weeks off work and get your marriage back on track.'

'It's going to be difficult to talk to her at her parent's house, her father's never really liked me anyway.'

'Then take her away on holiday somewhere. Get away from this fucking strike and these fucking murders. Andy you're a valued member of the team and I'll miss your hard work and endeavour, but this is way more important. Sort this out and it'll make you and Sally stronger.'

'Danny I'm not taking two weeks off and leaving you all in the shit. I know how much work there is for me and Rachel still to do. There's a shitload of stuff with the foreign force enquiries alone.'

'You won't be leaving us in the shit Andy, I've got two more detectives starting on the team tomorrow. The Superintendent's finally relented and agreed that we need more staff. I'd planned to feed them into you and Rachel in the morning to help with the foreign force enquiry.'

Andy suddenly looked alive, he sat up straight, 'That's great news Danny, are you sure it's ok for me to take two weeks off though?'

'I'm sure Andy, now finish your pint and get going.'

'I've had enough of the beer thanks Danny. If it's all the same to you I'm going to get off home.'

He stood up and made for the door, pausing just before he went out.

'See you in two weeks' time Danny, thanks.'

He left the pub leaving Danny alone to finish his pint.

Danny wondered how Rachel would take the news that she was now on her own doing the foreign force enquiry.

There were no more detectives coming tomorrow.

He hoped Rachel would understand.

CHAPTER 67

Bristol University – October 23rd 1984

Seamus Carter hated seminars with a passion.

As he walked into the Brunel Lecture Hall at Bristol University he immediately knew it was going to be a tortuous day for him.

Carter was a large man and he sighed audibly as he saw the rows of small hard plastic chairs all lined up in rows, facing the stage where a small lectern stood to the left of a large white screen. He could see a cable running from the lectern across the stage and then down through the middle of the twenty or so chairs to a portable overhead projector.

'Oh great, death by overhead!' he groaned aloud.

'I don't think it'll be quite that bad', said a woman's voice with a chuckle.

Seamus turned around, startled.

He hadn't been aware anybody else was in the room.

Walking towards him was a very pretty blonde woman, in her early thirties with a broad smile on her face.

'You must be Seamus Carter', she said.

He grinned and said, 'Was it my bad mood that gave it away?'

'Oh that and the fact that I can't think of any other pathologists that are six foot five inches tall with a shock of red hair and a beard that would put Grizzly Adams to shame.'

They both laughed before Seamus said, 'I'm sorry, I don't want to appear rude, but I don't think we've met.'

'No I'm sorry, I should've introduced myself, I'm Emily Cook. I graduated from this University a couple of years ago. Professor Mason who is giving the lecture on facial mapping today was my professor.'

'Oh, now I understand why you said it wouldn't be too bad. Is he an interesting chap, this Professor Mason?'

'He's more than interesting, Professor Mason is a brilliant man. He recently helped me out with the identification of a woman who'd been murdered in Peckham. I cover most of the South London area, when I'm on call.'

'Now I know who you are, so I do. You took over from old Jock McArdle in London when he retired didn't you?'

'That's right I did, and I've enjoyed every minute so far.'

'I've heard good things about you Mrs Cook.'

'It's Ms Cook, but call me Emily, please.'

'I'll gladly do that Emily, and you must call me Seamus. Do we have a deal?'

'We certainly do Seamus.'

'I'm very interested in hearing a bit more about your Peckham case, I'm fascinated by facial mapping but I've never had the opportunity to employ the technique.'

'I know the Peckham case will be forming part of the professors' lecture today, so I won't steal his thunder and spoil it. Why don't we listen to the lecture and then go for a bite to eat and a drink, there's a very nice Italian Restaurant just up the road. We can have a proper civilised conversation over a plate of delicious food and a nice glass of red.'

'Emily, that sounds a terrific idea', gushed the big Irishman.

All of a sudden Seamus Carter decided he was a massive fan of seminars.

The lecture itself from Professor Edwards was very informative, and mercifully for Seamus's back it wasn't too long. He had found himself listening intently to the description of the injuries suffered by the victim in the Peckham murder. The mutilation of the hands, the severing of the digits. The massive injuries to the face and jaw.

The injuries were almost identical to the two murder victims he'd recently performed post mortems on in Nottinghamshire. The conversation with Emily that evening was going to be even more interesting than he'd first thought.

An hour after the seminar had finished, Seamus opened the door for Emily to enter "Giovanni's", the small Italian restaurant, a short walk from the University.

Having been shown to a table for two by the waiter, they sat down and perused the menus. After enquiring whether Emily preferred red or white wine, Seamus ordered a bottle of Valpolicella Reserve red wine.

Emily ordered the Spinach and Ricotta Cannelloni, while Seamus ordered the Pollo a la Creme chicken dish. While they waited for their food to be prepared they sipped the velvety red wine and talked quietly about the lecture.

'Emily I'm fascinated by your Peckham murder case, is it still unsolved?'

'Yes I believe so. I can check with the Detective Inspector in charge of the case. Why do you ask?'

'I've recently carried out two post mortem examinations on murdered women in Nottinghamshire, where I've seen almost identical injuries to the hands and fingers as well as massive trauma to the heads, especially the jaw. Tell me what was the cause of death of your Peckham victim?'

'The actual cause of death was a massive brain haemorrhage caused by repeated blunt force trauma to the skull.'

'You see, from what you've told me so far and what I heard in the lecture, that's the only difference right there. The two women I examined had both been strangled prior to the injuries being caused. Tell me Emily, is it just the one victim you've seen with these injuries?'

'Yes only one, she was a young prostitute. There was something very strange about the case though.'

'Strange?' echoed Seamus.

'Yes strange, it was like looking at two text book murder scenarios in one go.'

'I'm sorry if I'm being a little dense, but I don't understand Emily.'

'Well there were definite elements of rage involved, but there was also an element of cold calculation. I also know that the detective in charge was bemoaning the total lack of evidence found at the scene.'

'What do you mean, no evidence?'

'There was absolutely no forensic evidence left, either at the murder scene or the deposition site, it really was quite an unusual case.'

Seamus stroked his bushy beard thoughtfully before saying, 'Emily I really think that the Peckham murder and the two murders in Nottinghamshire could be linked, there's so many similarities. I think it would be a good idea if you pass onto me the details of the detective in charge of the Peckham case, so I can put him in touch with the Detective Inspector dealing with the murders in Nottinghamshire.'

'No problem at all Seamus, if you think there could be a connection, I'll get that information to your office first thing in the morning.'

'Any way Emily, I think that's more than enough talk about work for one night, so it is. Now would you like another glass of this lovely red wine, before you tell me all about yourself and your new life in London?'

'That would be lovely Seamus, thank you', she said smiling widely.

Seamus looked across the candle lit table and hoped this would be the first of many meals with the beautiful Emily Cook.

CHAPTER 68

Peckham Police Station, London –
October 26th 1984

On the third ring Glyn Johnson answered the telephone in his office, 'Hello. Detective Inspector Johnson, can I help you?'

'Good morning. My name's Detective Inspector Danny Flint, Nottinghamshire CID. I'd like to talk to you about the unsolved murder of a young girl in Peckham. The victim's name is Jenny Taylor.'

Brusquely Glyn answered the request.

'Give me your contact number Detective Inspector Flint and I'll call you straight back. I'm not being funny here, but I ain't about to start discussing a murder case over the phone with somebody I've never even heard of before. No offence.'

Equally brief and to the point Danny answered, 'None taken, I'd be exactly the same. As I said, my name's Detective Inspector Danny Flint. I'm stationed at Mansfield Police Station in Nottinghamshire. My direct line will be in the Police Almanac on your desk. Talk to you shortly.'

Glyn hung up the phone and muttered, 'Cheeky bugger!'

He opened his desk drawer and rummaged through the contents until he found the beige coloured book that listed the telephone numbers of every police station in the UK.

Quickly thumbing through it he found the pages for Nottinghamshire Constabulary. He scanned the pages and found the number for the direct line into the CID office at Mansfield Police Station. He picked up the phone and dialled the number. It was answered on the first ring.

'Detective Inspector Flint.'

'Danny its Glyn Johnson from Peckham, what can you tell me about Jenny Taylor?'

'Glyn, thanks for getting straight back to me. I had an interesting telephone call from a pathologist last night by the name of Seamus Carter. He told me that very recently he attended a seminar at Bristol University where he bumped into Emily Cook, the Home Office pathologist who I believe covers your area. The seminar he attended was a lecture about facial mapping by Professor Mason and the case of Jenny Taylor formed part of that lecture. From what Seamus told me last night, it would appear that the injuries suffered by Jenny Taylor are almost identical to the injuries found on two murder victims up here in Nottinghamshire.'

'That's interesting Danny. Have you got a suspect in mind for your cases'?

'No Glyn, both our cases are still unsolved.'

'These injuries you mentioned on the victims in your cases, what were they specifically and how are they similar to those inflicted on Jenny Taylor?'

'Our victims suffered mutilations to both hands and massive injuries to the head and face. According to Seamus these injuries are identical in every way to those found on Jenny Taylor. The only thing that differs is the actual cause of death. Our women were strangled using a thin nylon cord. Jenny Taylor, I believe, died as a result of a massive brain injury caused by blunt force trauma to the skull.'

'That does sound remarkably similar. Tell me something Danny, have you got much to go on evidentially with your cases?'

'Forensically, we've got absolutely nothing.'

'The scenes were totally sterile, right?'

'Totally.'

'Have your Scenes of Crime people found any foot marks?'

'Yes at both scenes.'

'Don't tell me, they were footmarks covered by overshoes. Am I right?'

'Spot on Glyn. This goes no further, but between you and me, I've started looking at the possibility that a serving police officer is responsible for our two murders.'

'Ditto Danny, that's exactly what we've started to look at down here on the Jenny Taylor case as well. I'm looking at serving or recently retired police officers. Unfortunately, my investigation has ground to a halt down here. My guvnor's are slowly pulling the plug on the Jenny Taylor enquiry, unless something drastic comes to light this murder will stay unsolved. Danny would you mind if I travelled up with my skipper Craig Fraser, to see you and your team. That way we can compare notes and see exactly what common ground we have?'

'I think that would be a good idea Glyn, when can you get up here?'

'I'll have to clear it with my guvnor down here first and tidy a few things up, but I should be able to get up to you on the 29th. If I give you a call later with the time we'll be arriving, could you arrange for somebody to pick us up from the railway station in Nottingham?'

'No problem Glyn, I can arrange that. I look forward to seeing you on the 29th.'

Glyn hung up the telephone and sat back in his chair.

'Interesting', he said aloud.

CHAPTER 69

Wembley, London – October 27th 1984

'What time you going back up to Nottingham Mick?' asked a very timid Rita.

She'd stayed away from the house all week, only popping in and out when she absolutely needed to. Something about her husband had definitely changed.

He stalked around the house in his dirty vest and pants, just lying on the sofa watching TV. He hadn't been out all week, refusing to tidy up after himself, he'd not had a wash or shave all the time he'd been home.

Only once had she dared to make a comment about the state of the house. He had simply glared at her before walking over and raising his hand, feigning to slap her.

Rita had cowered away and quickly slipped out of the house without saying another word. She'd stayed with her best friend Sue Jessop at her flat over in Peckham every night.

Lying on the settee, Mick angrily responded to Rita's question now growling, 'What the fuck's it got to do with you when I'm going back?'

'I'm sorry love, I was just going to iron your shirts, that's all.'

He sneered at her now.

'Iron my shirts, you've changed your fucking tune haven't you. I don't know Rita darlin' I reckon I should've given you a slap years ago.'

Rita was fighting the urge to make a comment back, she knew he was goading her, but she was terrified of him in this menacing mood.

'There's no need for that love, you know I care about you', she said.

'All you care about, you dirty slag, is your next shag pressed up the wall of some dark alley behind some dingy pub in the East End!'

She could bite her lip no longer and before she thought about the consequences, she snapped back at him, 'Yeah, well at least I don't fuck tarts!'

'You're a fucking tart Rita. Don't think for one minute that I don't know you've been dossing down at that fat slag, Sue Jessop's flat. I bet you've both had a different bloke every night!'

Rita desperately tried to bite her tongue, but it was too much for her and she railed back, 'Yeah, well who could blame me! All I've ever wanted was a proper man, not some ugly retard with a cock the size of an acorn, and that's when it's fucking hard!' she screamed.

Mick jumped up from the settee and with one powerful hand he grabbed Rita by the throat, pushing her backwards until she slammed hard against the lounge wall.

The force with which she hit the wall caused ornaments to fall from the mantelpiece above the fireplace.

'Apologise you bitch', he snarled.

'If you don't say sorry in the next ten seconds, I'll kill you right now!' he said through gritted teeth.

Desperately she tried to say the word but his powerful hand was gradually crushing her windpipe.

A noise escaped her mouth but it was just an inaudible rasp.

'Sorry, what did you say love?' he laughed and then squeezed harder.

'I can't fucking hear you!' he mocked.

He put his other hand around Rita's throat and now squeezed in earnest, slowly lifting her off the floor. He watched as her eyes bulged and her tongue started to protrude from her mouth. Her head was getting darker and darker. He could feel her feet kicking his legs and her hands pounding his head and shoulders.

Still he squeezed.

Eventually her feet and hands became still and his hands and arms grew tired. After ten minutes Mick slowly relaxed his grip, Rita had been dead for the last four.

He let go of her completely and she dropped lifeless to the floor.

'Finally, some peace and fucking quiet!' he roared.

He stepped over her body and walked from the lounge into the hallway. He opened the door that led from the hallway into the attached garage.

The dark blue Ford Sierra was there.

He grabbed the car keys from the hook above the work bench at the back of the garage and unlocked the boot. Lifting the boot lid, he removed a few items, clearing the entire boot space.

He then walked out of the garage and back into the lounge, he rolled Rita's body out of the way with his foot and carefully replaced the ornaments that had fallen onto the floor from the mantelpiece.

Trance like he walked from the lounge into the kitchen and got a glass of cold water from the tap. He drank the water quickly, before picking up the kettle and filling it. Mick then took a mug from the cupboard and threw a tea bag in.

While the kettle was boiling, he walked back into the lounge. Grunting loudly, he lifted his wife's body off the floor and over his shoulder. Rita was quite heavy and he struggled at first with her dead weight. He carried her into the garage and threw her down into the boot of the car, he grabbed an old dust sheet from the back of the garage and threw it on top of her body.

He slammed the boot shut.

'Good riddance, bitch!' he said under his breath.

Mick then locked the boot of the car and hung the car keys back on the hook before leaving the garage.

Closing the interior door, he walked into the kitchen and finished making his mug of tea. Calmly he sat at the kitchen table and took a sip of the hot drink.

Ten minutes ticked by as he slowly finished his tea. He placed the mug on the table and looked at his watch. Three hours to wait before he would be travelling north, back up the M1 motorway, back up to Nottinghamshire.

Mick couldn't wait to see Jimmy Wade and tell him the news about Rita. He'd tell him before they went out for some proper action tomorrow night.

He would deal with Rita's body, when he came back on rest days next time. He knew exactly where he intended to dispose of her body.

Mick sat at the table and closed his eyes and began to plan it all out in his head.

First, he'd buy an old van for a couple of hundred quid, then he'd chuck Rita's body in the van and drive down to the old tin mine in Cornwall. He was confident that her weighted body would never be discovered down the flooded mine shaft. Once he'd dumped her body he would scrap the van down there in Truro, then catch the train from Cornwall back to London.

He would then scrap his own Sierra to avoid any implication into the prostitute's death. The last thing he'd have to do, would be to buy a brand new motor with the proceeds of all the overtime he'd worked during the strike.

It was a perfect plan.

Rita would just have to stay in the boot of the car for now. After all, it wasn't like she was going anywhere.

That thought made him chuckle.

At last he was free.

CHAPTER 70

Ollerton, Nottinghamshire – October 28th 1984

Mick was in a buoyant mood.

He quickly climbed into the front seat of the dark green Ford Cortina that was parked in the layby outside Proteus camp.

'Hello Jimmy, it was good to see you again at the quarry today old son. Have you missed me?'

He frowned before continuing, 'You didn't say much today, was that because you were shocked when I told you about Rita?'

'This was you Mick, wasn't it?' said a disgruntled Jimmy without looking up.

'What was me?'

Jimmy thrust a copy of the local Observer newspaper towards Mick. The newspaper headline read "Woman attacked in Edwinstowe".

'Yeah it was me, so what?'

'I thought we agreed to wait until tonight.'

'No you agreed. Anyway I thought you said you were going to change the motor?'

'No need to, the cops are looking for a silver Nissan now.'

'How come?'

'Because the smart one in this team, made an anonymous phone call saying he'd seen a silver Nissan speeding away from the lane where we dumped the second woman, that's how come.'

'Sweet, good thinking Jimmy.'

It was a lie. There had been no phone call to the police. Jimmy was prepared to risk using the Cortina for one more night.

'Talking of Rita, what were you babbling on about at the quarry earlier? Have you really done her in Mick?'

'Oh yes! I couldn't stand another minute listening to her nagging, grating voice.'

'I thought we'd agreed that you would hold off doing her in at this moment in time.'

'I never agreed to that. I told you, I couldn't promise anything. She just wound me up once too often.'

'What've you done with her?'

'If you must know I throttled the bitch. Look its fine Jimmy, nobody's going to miss her and nobody's going to find her. Just relax will you, everything's fine and dandy.'

'I don't like it Mick.'

Mick glared at Jimmy.

'You don't have to like it old son, it's done. Get over it!'

Mick didn't want to risk Jimmy getting so annoyed that he cancelled tonight, so he said in an acquiescent manner, 'Alright Jimmy, I'm sorry. I know I shouldn't have snapped with Rita, but I just couldn't help it, ok.'

'You've got to stay in control Mick, I know what it's like when the urges are strong, but you've got to remember the most important thing is not getting caught.'

'Ok Jimmy, you're right and I'm sorry. Trust me though, I've taken care of everything down there, Rita won't ever be found. Now where are we going tonight?'

'Oh, I've got a proper treat for you tonight Mick, we're going over to a small village called Newstead. I've been watching a woman who walks a little terrier dog, on her own, through the grounds of Newstead Abbey at night.'

'Silly bitch!' grunted Mick.

'You're going to love this one mate, she's really fit.'

'Nice one Jimmy, this is more like it, the two of us back in the groove.'

The journey over to Newstead Village was made in silence. Jimmy was constantly on the lookout for police cars or a road block.

Luckily they saw neither.

After half an hour Jimmy drove the car into Newstead village. He drove straight through the village and turned into the grounds of Newstead Abbey. After two minutes he pulled off the main lane and turned onto a very narrow, very bumpy dirt track.

Finally, he stopped the car.

'Bloody hell Jimmy, this bird must have a death wish walking down here on her own.'

'No Mick, she walks along the lane up the top, but I don't want her to see the car. The plan is we wait up there by the side of the lane grab her, kill the dog and then bring her down here to have some fun. What do you think?'

'It sounds perfect to me Jimmy. Tell me about the woman, is she a blonde?'

'Yes Mick she's a blonde.'

'Great stuff, I'll get the bag out of the boot.'

'There's no need Mick. We can leave the bag in the car. We're bringing the woman back down here away from the lane, remember?'

'What about the dog? We'll need something to deal with the dog.'

'Don't you worry about the dog Mick; I've got some stuff here to deal with that.'

Jimmy held up a small brown bottle and a rag.

'One whiff of this stuff and the little rat will be history. You concentrate on grabbing the woman Mick, let me worry about the dog.'

'How long before she gets here Jimmy?'

'She'll be along soon enough. We need to get up to the lane.'

Both men got out of the car, it was very cold and a frost was starting to form on the ground.

'Fucking hell it's brass monkeys out here Jimmy!'

'For Christ's sake, keep the noise down she'll hear us.'

'Sorry guvnor!', Mick said in an exaggerated sarcastic whisper.

They crept stealthily through the woods until they were ten yards from the main lane.

'Wait here Mick, I'll see if she's coming, I won't be long.'

'Ok.'

Jimmy disappeared into the dark woodland.

Mick hadn't felt this excited about any of the others. He felt aroused and had already decided that before he killed this woman, he was going to have some fun with her. The more he thought about all the deviant acts he was going to do to the silly cow, the more aroused he became. It was her own fault, fancy walking down here at night on her own, she was asking for it.

His mind had wandered so much that he never heard Jimmy stealthily approaching him from behind.

Suddenly, a chloroform soaked rag was clamped firmly over Mick's mouth and nose. He struggled briefly, but Jimmy was strong and held the rag firmly in place.

Within a few seconds Mick had slumped into unconsciousness and fell to the ground in a heap.

'Now for the hard part', Jimmy said aloud.

Mick was quite short, but he was a stocky man. Getting a good grip on his clothes Jimmy hoisted him over his shoulder into a fireman's lift.

He retraced his steps finally dropping Mick down onto the floor about twenty yards in front of the car. Once again he clamped the chloroform soaked rag over Mick's mouth and nose, then walked over to the car. Jumping in, he quickly turned the car round and flicked the headlights on. The beams of the headlights picked out a rope with a hangman's noose swinging from an oak tree.

The rope had been tied off onto a lower branch and the noose was hanging about four feet off the ground.

After a hard struggle, Jimmy managed to manoeuvre Mick's head through the noose. Mick was still totally unconscious; he was now hanging from the noose with his arms dangling by his side.

His knees were still resting on the floor taking most but not all of his weight.

Jimmy could hear a gurgling sound coming from Mick as the rope of the noose began to dig into his windpipe. He quickly walked over to where he had tied the end of the rope off. Carefully he untied the rope and took up the strain of the weight of Mick's body.

Using all his strength Jimmy hauled on the rope until Mick was completely suspended from the rope, his feet were no longer touching the ground.

Jimmy pulled again, hoisting the dead weight further off the floor, until the sergeant's feet were about one foot above the ground.

Maintaining the tension on the rope, Jimmy tied it off again on the lower branch of the tree. Once the rope was fastened securely he stepped back and watched, grinning, as Mick began to thrash around.

He had obviously started to come around as the effects of the chloroform began to wear off.

Mick was now kicking his legs and his hands went up to the rope that was now biting hard into his neck. Desperately he tried to claw his fingers behind the rope to allow some air to get in.

His thrashing limbs, illuminated by the cars headlights, caused shadows to dance against the surrounding trees.

Jimmy chuckled as he watched the sergeant dancing at the end of the rope like some crazed puppet. Finally, the thrashing stopped, replaced by a few twitching movements. Eventually even they stopped and everything became still, the arms had once more dropped to the side of the hanging body.

Mick Reynolds slowly swung from side to side at the end of the rope. Jimmy walked over to take a closer look.

It was grotesque.

Mick's head was nearly black and looked swollen. His eyes were bulging almost out of their sockets and his bloated swollen tongue was already protruding slightly from his mouth.

'You just wouldn't listen would you?' said Jimmy to the dead man.

He put gloves on, before he reached into his pocket and took out a black plastic tube, placing it in Mick's inside coat pocket. He had typed out the final message from the "Coal Killer" earlier that day.

There was one other thing left to do. Reaching up he found what he was looking for under the dead man's jumper. Quickly he removed the object, stashing it in his own coat pocket.

Jimmy walked back to the car and grabbed Mick's grip bag from the boot. He quickly checked the contents to ensure there was nothing in there that would incriminate him. He was unconcerned that there were two forensic suits in the bag. Anybody finding him would just assume that the sergeant had carried a spare. He placed the bag next to the carefully staged overturned wooden crate.

It looked perfect, it looked like the sergeant had taken his own life.

Jimmy had only used the bare minimum chloroform to incapacitate Mick and he hoped that all traces of it would have worn off by the time the body was discovered.

Having left the grip bag by the side of the hanging man, Jimmy returned to the car and threw the chloroform bottle and rag inside the already open boot.

From inside the boot he retrieved a full petrol can.

Returning to the hanging man he splashed a little petrol on the sleeves of the dead man's coat.

Jimmy then walked back to the car, his precious Cortina, and began splashing petrol in the boot, in the foot wells and finally all over the engine.

He quickly removed the registration plates from the front and the back of the car. He'd already removed the chassis plate, engine number and the Vehicle Identification Number plate earlier that day. He couldn't risk removing the registration plates until now, he knew exactly where he was going to dump those later.

Having filled the car with petrol Jimmy took a step back before lighting a rag he'd taken from his pocket. He then threw the lit rag into the car, there was a loud whooshing noise as the car erupted into a ball of flame.

Once again Jimmy chuckled as the hanging body of Sgt Mick Reynolds, illuminated this time by the car fire, caused eerie shadows to dance in the surrounding woodland.

He walked over and pushed the legs of the hanging man, making the dance even more animated.

Finally, Jimmy picked up the two number plates he'd removed from the car and walked off through the woods.

He'd played here as a child and knew these woods like the back of his hand. After ten minutes walking he came to the edge of the wood.

In front of him was an open field.

The field was rock hard with the frost, so Jimmy was unconcerned about leaving footprints. He walked straight over the field towards the small copse in the middle.

At the centre of this tiny copse was a small, deep pond.

The pond held a specific childhood memory for Jimmy Wade and he smiled as he looked at the black water, that reflected the bright full moon like a mirror.

Jimmy hurled the two number plates into the middle of the pond.

He stared in wonder, as ripples disrupted the solid disc of the reflected bright moon into a myriad of exploding white stars.

Silently he watched until the water settled down again and the moon became a whole entity once more.

He then left the small copse and walked back out across the frosty field, this time heading in the opposite direction, back towards Newstead village.

Jimmy planned to walk as far as the first phone box in nearby Annesley and then call a taxi to take him back to Mansfield Woodhouse.

As he walked he felt free, totally unburdened. No more Police Sergeant Mick Reynolds to worry about.

His thoughts immediately turned to Detective Rachel Moore, he knew it would be her time very soon.

The careful planning for the future was starting to come together now and he couldn't help smiling as he walked briskly towards Annesley.

CHAPTER 71

Peckham Police Station – October 29th 1984

The West Indian cleaner paused at the door, her hand shooting towards her mouth, she gasped, 'Bloody hell Glyn, you gave me such a fright man!'

It was seven o'clock in the morning, Glyn and Craig were already at their desks in the Peckham CID office, both were busy clearing paperwork.

Glyn looked up at the startled cleaner, 'Don't worry about it Florence, sweetheart. I won't be making a habit of it. You can leave this room today.'

'Thank you for that anyway, kind sir', she smiled before moving on along the corridor.

Glyn took another sip of his black coffee and then reached for the telephone. He dialled the number for the Mansfield CID office on the off chance that Danny Flint had also started his day early.

The phone was answered on the second ring.

'Good morning Danny, it's Glyn Johnson here, sorry it's a bit early.'

'No problem Glyn, it's good to hear from you, are you still ok to travel up here?'

'Yeah, well that's the reason for my call Danny. Myself and DS Fraser have come on duty early today to clear the decks. We intend catching the midday train from St Pancras. It's due to arrive at Nottingham Midland Station at approximately two thirty this afternoon. Will you be able to arrange for someone to meet us there?'

'No problem Glyn, it will probably be Dc Rachel Moore. Shall I get her to wear a pink carnation?'

Glyn laughed, 'That's not a bad idea Danny, I'm sure we'll spot each other. Just tell her to look out for one devastatingly handsome black dude and one ugly Scottish dwarf!'

'Charming', muttered Craig.

'Nice one, we'll see you later and have a chat over a few beers', said Danny

'Sounds like a plan Danny, see you later this afternoon.'

No sooner had Glyn put the phone down than it started to ring again.

'Bloody hell, don't people realise it's only seven in the morning!'

Sweeping up the phone he answered the call tersely, 'DI Johnson!'

'I know it's early guvnor, but I saw you come in. Its Sgt Collins at the front desk.'

'Bloody hell Sarge, I've come on early for a reason. What's so important that it can't wait?'

'Sorry guv, I've got a woman by the name of Sue Jessop in reception, she says her best friend's missing and she reckons she's been done in. I wouldn't normally bother you straight away guvnor, but the missing woman's married to a cop over at Wembley nick.'

'Can't we send her over there then, and let Wembley deal with it?'

'That's the problem, this Sue Jessop's saying it's the husband who's done her in and she's too scared to go into Wembley nick, coz that's where he works.'

'Bloody hell, this just keeps getting better. What's the misper's name and who's the cop?'

'Her name's Rita Reynolds and his name's Sergeant Mick Reynolds.'

'Ok Sarge, I'm on my way down.'

'Thanks guvnor.'

Glyn turned to Craig and said, 'Come on Craig we'd better go downstairs and listen to this load of old shit before we book the train tickets.'

Craig said nothing, the two men grabbed their jackets and made their way out the door.

'See what happens when you come in early Craig.'

'I know guv, that's why I always try my hardest to be late.'

'Yeah, ain't that the truth', chuckled Glyn.

Five minutes later and Craig was showing Sue Jessop into the interview room where Glyn was waiting.

'Good morning, Mrs Jessop is it? I'm Detective Inspector Johnson and this man here is Detective Sergeant Fraser. I understand you've got some concerns over a friend of yours?'

'That's right I have. It's my best friend Rita Reynolds, she's married to one of your lot. He's an arsehole and he punched her in the face the last time he was home.'

'What do you mean the last time he was home?'

'He's always away on this bloody miners' strike thing.'

'So how do you know your friend was punched by her husband?' said Craig.

'I saw her straight after she'd run out of the house, her face was a right mess.'

'Why didn't she report it?'

'Look, I'll be straight with you, Rita's no angel and she gives Mick a hard time sometimes, but that's still no excuse to belt her one is it?'

'No it certainly isn't Mrs Jessop. Why are you so concerned about Rita's wellbeing this morning?' asked Glyn.

'Well he came home last week, and he's been a proper swine to her all week. Anyway after he smashed her face in the last time he was home, Rita made me promise that I'd phone her every evening and every morning to make sure she was ok.'

'That's a bit drastic isn't it Sue?'

'Rita's terrified of him, he threatened to kill her last time and she thinks he meant it.'

'When did you last speak to Rita?'

'Well she'd been staying at mine for that week he was home, but she went back over to her house on the morning of the 26th.'

'That was three days ago Sue. Why haven't you been in before?'

'I don't know, coz he's a copper I suppose. I was too scared to go into Wembley nick. I went over there twice but bottled it, I just daren't go in. That's why I've come here today and not Wembley. I don't want to be talking to his mates, do I?'

'Why did he hit Rita last time he was home?' asked Craig.

'Rita says it was nothing, apparently it was all to do with the fact that he wouldn't take her out for a trip in the car.

They've got a lovely dark blue car and he refuses to use it. Anyway, he wouldn't take her out for a ride, they ended up arguing and Rita gave him some grief about seeing prostitutes.'

Glyn now leaned forward and placed his elbows on the desk.

'Hang on a minute Mrs Jessop, did you say this Police Sergeant sees prostitutes?'

'Yeah the dirty sod. Apparently, well according to Rita, he's down the red light areas all the time. He likes to get off with the tarts. Rita reckons the younger the better, filthy perv!'

'Do you know what sort of car they've got Mrs Jessop?'

'Nah, I'm useless with cars. I've only seen it once. It's quite big, almost brand new and it's dark blue. That's all I know about the car.'

Glyn was thoughtful for a moment.

'Ok Mrs Jessop, where does your friend Rita live?' he asked.

'It's on Miller Street over at Wembley, number 29 I think. It's a nice semi, with a garage n' everything.'

'Is there anything else you can tell us Sue?' asked Craig.

'Yeah, I've got a key for their front door. Rita gave it to me two weeks ago in case anything was wrong.'

She took the Yale key out of her coat pocket and offered it to Glyn.

'Blimey! She must've been worried to give you a key Mrs Jessop', said Glyn.

'Rita isn't worried, she's terrified. Mick's a proper nasty bastard! Sorry, I know he's one of your lot, but he is. I hope she's alright.'

Glyn took the key, 'Well thanks for coming in Mrs Jessop, we'll have a drive over to Miller Street and make sure everything's ok.'

'Will you let me know that Rita's ok please?'

'Of course we will Mrs Jessop, give the Detective Sergeant a phone number where we can reach you.'

'Thanks, I'm so worried about her.'

Craig stood up and escorted Sue Jessop out of the police station.

When he returned to the interview room, Glyn was still sitting there. He was rubbing his chin and looked deep in thought.

'Penny for 'em guvnor?' asked the tough Scot.

'I'm probably clutching at straws here Craig, but a big blue car, prostitutes, a copper who's violent towards women. I think me and you need to get over to Wembley and check this out.'

'Ok guv, I'll make a quick call and find out what shift Sgt Reynolds is working today.'

Fifteen minutes later, Craig walked back into the office.

'Right guv, I've done some ringing around. Sgt Mick Reynolds returned to Nottinghamshire on the night of the 27th. He's doing four weeks on and one week off. The call sign of his PSU is Mike Alpha One Zero. They're currently being billeted at a place called Proteus Camp near a town called Ollerton. It's actually a disused army camp that the local Army Cadets use. It's a bit of a shithole by all accounts.'

'Right come on Craig, let's get over to Wembley and check out Reynolds house.'

'Do you want me to contact Wembley nick and let them know what we're doing?'

'Nah, not yet, Sue Jessop might be giving us a load of old pony. We've got a front door key, let's check it out ourselves first. It'll only take five minutes. Straight in, make sure the wife's ok, straight out.'

'Right you are guvnor, I'll grab some car keys. I reckon I know where Miller Street is. If I remember rightly it's in quite a nice area not far from Wembley Stadium.'

It took forty-five minutes to drive over to Wembley, the rush hour traffic was just starting to build up.

Finally, Craig parked the car directly outside 29 Miller Street.

'Looks a nice place guvnor.'

Mimicking Sue Jessop's description of the house, Glyn replied, 'Yeah, it's got a garage n 'everything.'

The two detectives got out of the car and walked up the path to the front door. Glyn tried the key in the Yale lock, he turned the key and with a gentle push opened the front door.

As they walked in Glyn shouted, 'Anybody home!'

It was a typical semi-detached house.

The front door opened directly into the hallway, the lounge door was off to the right, the stairs went straight up from the hallway and just past the stairs was the kitchen door. Glyn walked into the lounge and Craig went straight upstairs.

'Guv, you'd better come up here and have a look at this!', he shouted down from upstairs.

Glyn climbed the stairs three at a time and found Craig in the small third bedroom, 'What is it Craig?'

'Over here, have a look in the bottom of this wardrobe.'

Glyn stepped forward and saw a stack of four or five blue forensic suits still in their plastic packets. At the side of them in a clear plastic packet that had been torn open, lay black tie wraps.

On the other side of the suits were two rolls of brown Gaffer tape.

'Get Scenes of Crime out here to photograph this lot Craig. I'm going back downstairs to check out the garage, it looks like there's an internal door that leads into the garage from the hallway.'

Glyn went downstairs and through the internal door into the garage.

Immediately the stench hit him.

Ignoring the foul smell, Glyn saw the dark blue Ford Sierra.

'Craig, you'd better get down here mate, I think I've found Rita!'

Craig came downstairs and walked into the garage, 'Bloody hell guvnor, I see what you mean. That smell's only going to be one thing, a body. Have you seen any keys for the car?'

Both men quickly looked around the garage and Glyn saw the keys on the hook above the workbench.

'Before we do anything Craig, nip out to the car and grab us a pair of gloves each.'

'Ok guv.'

Craig was glad to get out of the garage, even it was only for a minute, the smell was already unbearable. The heating was on full in the house and there was a small radiator, near the back of the car, in the garage.

While he waited for Craig to return with the gloves Glyn looked closely at the registration plates that were on the Ford Sierra.

He could see that the plates had been tampered with using black electricians tape.

The actual number beneath the tape was B 623 FJH.

The black tape had been cleverly used to change the number 3 to an 8 and the letter F to an E, changing the registration number to B 628 EJH.

Glyn got out his notebook and compared the tampered registration plate to the number Lee Skipton had scribbled down the night Jenny Taylor had been abducted and killed.

They were identical, this was the car Skipton had seen Jenny Taylor getting into on the night she was abducted and murdered.

Craig returned with the gloves.

'Craig, look at the plates. This is the car that was used to abduct Jenny Taylor.'

'Bloody hell guvnor, we've cracked it!'

Having put on the gloves, Glyn grabbed the car keys from the hook and opened the boot.

Both detectives involuntarily took a step back, as the action of the boot opening wafted the stench directly up towards them.

'Jesus Christ!' said Craig.

The light in the garage was dim, it was hard to see into the boot properly.

Glyn held his gloved hand over his mouth and nose.

'Craig, there's a light switch over there near the door, flick it on mate'.

Craig flicked on the switch and a light bulb directly over the work bench came on. With the light now on, Glyn could see there was a bundle in the boot covered by an old dust sheet. He could see that parts of the dust sheet were moving.

Glyn reached into the boot and pulled away the dust sheet.

The sight that greeted him was horrific.

Although it had only been a few days since Rita had been dumped in the boot of the car, the central heating, that came on automatically in the house, was so high that her body had started to decompose very quickly.

Her face was black and grotesquely bloated distorting her features. Her tongue had swollen so much that it resembled an arm trying to escape from her mouth. Glyn could see maggots moving around her face, crawling in and out of any orifice they could find. It was the maggots crawling around the head and face, that had caused the dust sheet to appear to be moving slightly.

The stench of putrefying flesh was overpowering.

Having opened the boot to confirm their suspicions, both Glyn and Craig quickly moved out of the garage and then out of the house.

Once outside the house, both men took deep breaths filling their lungs with the cold morning air, trying to remove the cloying stench from their nostrils.

'Fuck me guvnor, what a mess!'

'I've seen some bad sights in my time Craig, but bloody hell, that's right up there with the worst.'

'I know what you mean, I think I'll be smelling that stench for the rest of the week.'

Glyn took a minute to take a few more deep breaths of fresh air.

'Get back on the radio Craig, I want a full Scenes of Crime team turning out and I want a Home Office pathologist travelling immediately. If at all possible I'd like it to be Emily Cook.'

'Ok guv, I'm on it.'

'Craig, I'm going to need you to manage the scene here for a little while. I've got to get back to the nick and make a phone call up to Nottinghamshire. Sergeant Mick Reynolds is definitely our man for the murder of Jenny Taylor as well as this woman I'm assuming is his wife Rita. We need to get him nicked immediately, if not sooner. He may well also be responsible for two more murders up there. They've got be told what we've found down here.'

'No problem guv, I can sort it out here. Can you send me a couple more blokes, to help with the bagging and labelling?'

'Ok Craig will do. As soon as I've made the call up to Mansfield CID, I'll be back here myself. First I need a chat with Danny Flint, we need to get things moving up in Nottinghamshire.'

CHAPTER 72

Mansfield Police Station – October 29th 1984

The telephone in the CID office at Mansfield Police Station was ringing off the hook. Rob ran back into the office and picked up the phone, 'Hello, DS Buxton. Can I help you?'

'It's Detective Inspector Johnson from the Met, is your guvnor around?'

'He is sir, just a second.'

Rob placed the receiver on the desk and ran down to the canteen where Danny was just taking the first bite of a sausage sandwich.

'Boss, there's a phone call for you in the office, it's that D.I. from the Met who you spoke to earlier.'

Danny grabbed the sandwich and raced back to the office, picking up the phone he said, 'Hello again Glyn, what's up?'

'Danny, we've had a major breakthrough down here. We've just found the body of a dead woman in a house in Wembley. It would appear, on first look, that she's been murdered and we've found forensic suits, black cable ties and Gaffer tape all at the scene.'

'Forensic suits still at the scene? We've never found any at the scenes. Was your suspect disturbed?'

'Sorry Danny, I'm not being very clear. I've just left the scene and I'm still a bit hyped up.'

'Don't worry Glyn, take your time.'

'The house where we found the body is the deceased's home address. She'd been stuffed into the boot of the family car. I think her name's Rita Reynolds. The man she's married to is a serving police officer, Sergeant Mick Reynolds. The forensic suits were all still in their packets, there were five of them.'

'Go on Glyn.'

Danny was now trying hard to restrain his own growing excitement at what he was hearing.

'Danny, this Sergeant Reynolds has been in charge of a Metropolitan Police PSU in Nottinghamshire for the entire duration of the miners' strike. The PSU call sign is Mike Alpha One Zero. Reynolds and his PSU have been billeted at Proteus Camp near Ollerton in Nottinghamshire, they're still there now.'

'Bloody hell Glyn! This has got to be our man.'

'It certainly looks promising Danny. I've already contacted the strike control room and they've informed me that call sign Mike Alpha One Zero is currently escorting working miners into Warsop Main Colliery. They're due to stand down at around nine thirty this morning.'

Danny's brain was going into overdrive.

'Glyn do me a favour, get back onto the control room and tell them to instruct Mike Alpha One Zero to return to Proteus Camp as soon as they stand down from Warsop Main for a special commitment. We'll start travelling out to Proteus Camp immediately.'

'Ok Danny, will do. Obviously we won't be travelling up to Nottingham today as planned. We've got a major crime scene to sort out here. Keep me posted as soon as you get Reynolds nicked.'

'Will do Glyn, I'll arrest him on suspicion of the murder of Jenny Taylor for starters, we can always arrest him for the murder of his wife later, if your body's identified as being Rita Reynolds. In respect of our outstanding murders, I'll wait until I know exactly what we've got to connect him to the killings up here. First things first, let's get him in.'

'Ok Danny, that sounds like a plan. I'm going back over to Wembley now to meet the Detective Inspector from that nick to sort out a plan to deal with this latest murder, technically it's not on my area but I think it's so obviously linked to the murder of Jenny Taylor that I'll be taking charge.'

'Ok Glyn, talk to you later.'

Danny put the phone down.

Both Rob and Rachel were staring intently at him having heard one side of the conversation.

'What's happening boss?' said Rachel.

'I think we might've just identified our killer.'

'Come on Danny, spill the beans', said an excited Rob.

'Rachel, have you started your enquiries with the Metropolitan Police personnel department yet?'

'Yes sir, I finished the Met yesterday, I'm starting on North Yorkshire today.'

'I want you to forget about North Yorkshire now. I want you to go back to the records of the Met and dig out everything we know about the deployment of Police Sergeant Mick Reynolds from Wembley Police Station. He's been on duty up here, off and on, since the start of the strike. I want to know exactly when he was up here and when he was back down in London. His PSU call sign is Mike Alpha One Zero, I want to know from the strike control room exactly when that call sign was actively on duty and when they were stood down. Can you manage all that?'

'Yes sir, is this Sgt Reynolds our killer?'

'I don't know yet Rachel, but it's looking good. I'll give you a full update when we get back.'

He grabbed his jacket and coat from the back of the chair.

'Come on Rob we need to get to Proteus Camp at Ollerton, I'll brief you on the way.'

Rob grabbed his coat and a set of car keys.

Five minutes later and the CID car was being driven at speed through Forest Town as it headed towards Ollerton.

'Ease off the pedal a bit Rob, let's get there in one piece.'

'Sorry boss.'

Rob eased back on the accelerator.

'Danny, I heard some of your conversation with the Met DI, but not all of it, what's happening?'

Danny took a deep breath, 'Ok Rob, this is what's happened. It would appear that Sgt Reynolds has killed his wife and dumped her in the boot of the family car in the garage at their home. The Met cops have found forensic suits still in the packets, cable ties and Gaffer tape all at the house. They strongly believe Reynolds is responsible for killing his wife as well as a prostitute in London.'

'Jenny Taylor, the murder in London that Seamus told us about boss. The one that had the similar MO to the murders of Mandy Stokes and June Hayes.'

'That's right, Jenny Taylor. If the dates and times of Reynold's deployment tie in with the dates and times of our two murders, then maybe we can link him to the deaths of Mandy Stokes and June Hayes. All that painstaking work by Rachel and Andy could prove vital.'

'Bloody hell boss, a serving cop. The shit's really going to hit the fan when this gets out to the media.'

'I don't give a toss about the media Rob, I just want this nutter off the street. If it turns out he's a nutter who's also a cop, so be it.'

'Dead right Danny, what's the plan once we've got hold of him?'

'We'll arrest him on suspicion of the murder of Jenny Taylor to get him in and hold him at the police station. Once he's locked up then the hard work, trying to link him to both the murders here and the murder of Rita Reynolds and Jenny Taylor in London, can begin.'

They were now on the main road between Clipstone and Ollerton and the road was clear. Once again Rob gunned the engine and the car accelerated away. Within ten minutes they were driving along the lane that led to Proteus Camp.

A police sergeant from Hampshire Constabulary was standing at the gate.

Danny showed the sergeant his warrant card and asked him for directions to the Metropolitan Police PSU billets. In particular the billet for Mike Alpha One Zero.

The sergeant checked a list on the clipboard he was holding and directed them towards the far end of the camp and Hut 23.

Rob parked the car on the hard standing nearest to a Nissan hut that had the number 23 painted in white on the side wall.

Danny was surprised to see a uniform Chief Inspector waiting outside the door of the hut. As soon as their car came to a stop the Chief Inspector walked purposefully over. Danny wound the car window down as the senior officer approached.

'Good morning gentleman, my name's Chief Inspector Delaney, I'm the liaison officer in charge of the Metropolitan Police Mutual Aid. I've been informed by strike control in London that there's a situation I need to be informed about.'

Fucking jungle drums have been beating already, thought Danny.

'It's a little bit more than a "situation" sir. My name's Detective Inspector Flint, I'm here at the request of Detective Inspector Johnson from Peckham Police Station in the Met, to locate and arrest Sgt Mick Reynolds on suspicion of the murder of Jenny Taylor.'

The Chief Inspector rubbed his chin thoughtfully before saying quickly, 'Very good Inspector, kindly let me know when the Sergeant's under arrest please.'

He started to walk away.

Danny shouted after him, 'Before you go sir, would you arrange for this hut to be padlocked for the time being. I'll also need an empty hut we can use to temporarily house the rest of the PSU in. We're obviously going to need to search this hut without it being disturbed.'

'Hut 24, next door to this one is empty at the moment, you can use that. The PSU normally using it left yesterday, to begin a week of rest days. I'll arrange for a padlock for this hut to be brought over to you immediately.'

'Thank you sir.'

Chief Inspector Delaney then quickly strode away.

Danny wound the car window up.

'That was all a bit bizarre', said Rob.

'I think that's the closest Chief Inspector Delaney has been to police work for a few years Rob. I reckon the words "arrest" and "murder" used in the same sentence, seemed to shit him up more than a little, don't you think?'

'Yeah, I think you're right. I reckon he's gone straight back to the canteen to finish his bacon and eggs.'

Both men chuckled and then settled down to await the arrival of Police Support Unit, call sign Mike Alpha One Zero and Sergeant Mick Reynolds.

CHAPTER 73

Proteus Army Camp – October 29th 1984

Thirty minutes had ticked slowly by since the Chief Inspector had hurriedly left the two detectives.

Five minutes after he beat a hasty retreat, a very young constable turned up with a gleaming new padlock and a bar to go across the door of the hut. The bar was quickly put in place and the padlock fitted. The constable handed Danny the two keys for the lock and scooted off.

Almost immediately after the padlock was fitted it began to rain heavily. Danny and Rob were thankful they had grabbed their overcoats as they ran out of Mansfield nick.

Rob was sitting in the driver's seat, constantly flicking his handcuffs closed before opening them again, clicking the metal teeth along the ratchet of the locking mechanism.

The rain was beating loudly on the metal roof of the car and the car windows were starting to steam up because of the warmth being generated inside the vehicle.

Using his sleeve to wipe the condensation from the windscreen Danny saw two unmarked dark blue Transit vans approaching.

Both the vans had metallic grilles attached to the windscreens.

Danny could see the windscreen wipers of the leading van swiping rapidly from side to side beneath the metal grilles. The two vans came to a stop and parked on the same hard standing as the CID car.

Danny stared intently at the front passenger seat of the lead van waiting for Sgt Reynolds to get out of the vehicle.

The side doors of both vans opened and six officers clambered out heading straight for Hut 23. There were howls of protest as the men realised they couldn't get into the hut and out of the rain. Quickly getting drenched by the downpour, the men returned to the vans.

The driver of the first van then got out and started to head towards the door of the Hut. Danny and Rob got out of the car and approached the constable.

Danny showed the officer his warrant card.

'I'm Detective Inspector Flint, this is Detective Sergeant Buxton. We need to talk to Sgt Reynolds.'

'He's not here guvnor', said the driver.

'What do you mean he's not here?'

'Just that guv, I'm not being awkward. He went out last night with that blonde tart of his, and didn't come back. I've been covering for the daft sod all day. She must be good that's all I can say, coz he's gonna be right in the shit when he gets back.'

'What's your name constable?' asked Rob.

'Oh don't say I'm in the shit for covering for him, he'll be back later. It's the first time he's missed a shift.'

'Your name?'

'Pc Ken Drury. Look, I don't need to be in the shit over this. I need the money this strike's bringing. You ain't gonna send me back to Wembley are you?'

Danny held his hands up to placate Pc Drury saying, 'Ken, calm down. Nobody's sending you back to Wembley.

You and the rest of the lads will have to use the hut next door temporarily. We've had to seal off this hut. Is there a room I can talk to you and the rest of the PSU? I want to know everything you can tell me about this blonde woman that your sergeant's been seeing.'

A relieved look came over the face of Ken Drury.

'There's a small room at the end of each of the huts that's got a table and chairs in, you can use that if you like. What shall I say to the lads about the hut being temporarily out of bounds?'

'Tell them we're from the Complaints Department and that if we don't get full cooperation we'll make sure this entire PSU is sent back to Wembley. We've already spoken to Ch. Insp Delaney and told him we're here about Sgt Reynolds and his activities with this woman.'

Pc Drury then walked back over to the vans and spoke to the men sitting inside.

Drury was followed by the two detectives.

Danny introduced himself and Rob to the men and reiterated what Pc Drury had told them already, that they were investigating Sergeant Reynolds for a clandestine affair he was having with a married woman.

Rob told the men to use hut 24 for the time being.

Once they had made their way into that hut, Rob then unlocked the padlock securing hut 23 and walked in followed by Glyn and Pc Drury.

Rob looked around the room, 'Ok Ken, which is Sergeant Reynold's bed space?' he asked.

The officer stepped forward and pointed, 'The skipper uses this bed.'

The bed he indicated was the nearest to the small room they would be using to talk to the officers.

Danny took Pc Drury into the small room, 'Take a seat Ken, I'll be with you in a minute.'

Danny left the room and closed the door.

'Rob I want a Scenes of Crime team out here to photograph the sergeants bed space, then I want every bit of the bedding and all his kit bagged and tagged.'

'Yes boss.'

Danny took Rob further away from the door to the small room before adding, 'We need to get Mick Reynolds circulated urgently. Make contact with Rachel back at the station and tell her to get him circulated as wanted on the PNC as soon as possible.'

'Ok Danny.'

Danny then walked into the small room where he'd left Ken Drury.

'Sit down Pc Drury. You're obviously quite tight with your sergeant, or you wouldn't have covered for him today. How long have you known him?' asked Danny.

'Mick Reynolds has been my skipper at Wembley nick for the last six years, we were Pc's together for three years before that.'

'Are you surprised he's been seeing this woman?'

'Not really guvnor, I know things haven't been great between him and his old lady for some time now. Between you and me she leads him a dog's life.'

'How long's he been seeing this other woman?'

'I honestly don't know the answer to that question. He's a bit of a closed book is Mick; he plays his cards very close to his chest. He's never told me about her or anything. I only know about her coz one of the lads saw him getting in her motor at the end of the lane here.'

'Who's the constable who saw him getting in her car?'

'Tony Jones, one of the younger lads. I told him to keep quiet and not to go blabbing it around. I didn't want it to become common knowledge among the lads. I was trying to prevent the skipper getting into strife over it.'

'How do you know Pc Jones saw this?'

'Coz Tony told me what he'd seen. It was quite a few weeks ago. Tony had been going to the shops in Ollerton for a walk. It gets bloody boring in here all the time. So anyway, he sees the skipper walking up the lane about sixty or seventy yards in front of him. He told me that at first he was gonna run to catch him up, but then he couldn't be arsed.'

'Go on Ken.'

'Well when Tony gets to the end of the lane, he looks along the layby and sees the skipper getting into the passenger side of this motor.'

'Who was driving, did he say?'

'You'll have to ask him that guv, all he said to me was that it was a bird with long blonde hair.'

'Ok Ken, that's all for now. Send in Pc Jones to see me next. I know I don't need to tell you this Pc Drury, but don't say anything to the other lads about our conversation. The least they know the better. I don't want to drop your mate Mick Reynolds any deeper in the shit than he already is.'

'Ok guvnor, no problem. I'll send in Tony.'

'One last thing Pc Drury, where do you think Mick Reynolds is now?'

'Knowing that randy bastard, he's probably in bed somewhere shagging that blonde. He's always talking about skirt. What he wouldn't want to do to this tart or that tart. You know what I mean guv. When we're driving around, there isn't a single bird he doesn't clock, he's woman mad.'

Danny knew everything would be out soon enough, but he didn't want the rumour mill to go into overdrive until after they'd located and detained Sgt Reynolds.

Rob popped his head around the door, 'Scenes of Crime are here Danny.'

'Alright get them into the hut. I want the entire bed space photographed. Anything suspicious they find I want photographing in situ before it's recovered. Then I want everything removed from Reynolds bed space. Blankets, sheets, pillow cases I mean everything. I want the entire contents of his locker emptying and bagging up properly. Make a full inventory while they're bagging everything Rob, so we can go through it all back at Mansfield. You crack on with that while I talk to Pc Tony Jones.'

A couple of minutes passed before there was a knock on the door.

A young fresh faced cop stuck his face around the door.

'Sir, Pc Tony Jones, you wanted to talk to me?'

'Come in Pc Jones and sit down', said Danny.

The young officer who looked fresh out of training school came in and sat down.

'How much service have you got Tony?'

'I was only two weeks out of my probation when all this lot started. This is my first PSU duty. I've only been training once. I've got to tell you sir; it's boring the tits off me.'

'Tony I'm going to ask you some questions about your sergeant. I know you're young in service, but don't try and avoid answering any of my questions thinking you're doing him a favour. Do you understand?'

'I understand sir. I'll answer if I can.'

'Good lad. I want to ask you about this woman you saw your sergeant with a few weeks back.'

'The blonde?'

'Have there been others?'

'No sir, I don't know sir. I mean, I only saw him with a blonde.'

'Look Tony, you're not in any trouble, ok. Just listen to the questions I'm asking and answer them if you can. No one's trying to trip you up.'

'Ok sir, sorry.'

'Right tell me about this blonde woman?'

'I can't remember when it was for sure, but it's quite a few weeks ago now. I was walking into town to get some biscuits from the shop one evening. Anyway, as I'm walking along the lane up to the road, I see the skipper in front of me. He's a bit too far ahead, for me to run and catch up with him. The skipper then turns off the lane and into the lay by. By the time I got up to the lay by he was already getting in the car being driven by the blonde.'

'How far away from the car were you Tony?'

'Forty or fifty yards I guess.'

'What time was it?'

'It was getting quite late but it was still light.'

'Could you see the driver?'

'Honestly sir, all I could see was long blonde hair. She never turned around so I never saw her face. As soon as he got in the car they drove off quickly.'

'Are you sure there's nothing else you can tell me about her?'

'Positive sir, sorry.'

'Ok Tony, what about the car?'

'That's a bit easier, it was an old Ford Cortina. I'm sure of that sir, my dad had one when I was a kid.'

'What colour was it?'

'It was a dark green colour. That British Racing green you see on older cars.'

'What else can you tell me about the car? Could you see the plates?'

'I was close enough to see them, but I honestly can't remember the number. Sorry sir.'

'Anything else about the car that springs to mind?'

'Only that it looked in mint condition for an old motor.'

'Did you speak to Sgt Reynolds about what you'd seen?'

'Bloody hell! No way sir. I told Ken Drury, he's the driver of our van. He told me to shut the fuck up and not to repeat it or I'd be shipped back to Wembley.'

'So you haven't told anybody else on your PSU?'

'No sir.'

'Do you have any idea where your sergeant is right now Tony?'

'Haven't got a clue sir, he just wasn't around this morning when we set off for Warsop Main pit.'

'Has the sergeant ever missed a shift before?'

'No, definitely not. He goes out some nights and doesn't get back until late, but he's always been back for the shift to start, except for today that is.'

'How late?'

'I've seen him come back into the hut a few times, during the early hours of the morning.'

'Thanks Tony that'll be all, don't talk to your colleagues about what we've discussed. Do you understand?'

'Yes sir.'

Pc Jones then left the small room.

Danny knew it was probably going to be a pointless exercise, but he nevertheless spoke to every one of the officers on the PSU individually. Not one of the Pc's had any idea where their sergeant had spent the night.

A couple of them confirmed what Pc Jones had already said, that they'd noticed the Sgt slipping out of the huts during the evenings. None of them could remember when.

By the time Danny had finished the interviews with the PSU officers, the Scenes of Crime team were just bagging up the last of Sgt Reynolds belongings and bedding.

'Have we got everything Rob?'

'We've left nothing Danny, I've logged everything as we've gone along.'

'Anything of note?'

'Definitely boss. There's four forensic suits still in the wrappers, a roll of Gaffer tape and an open packet of black tie wraps. There's also a black woollen ski mask stuffed at the bottom of a bag full of dirty washing. One last thing boss, I found these in a small tin at the bottom of his PSU bag.'

Rob indicated a small evidence bag in his hand that contained a small gold wedding band and an engagement ring and said, 'We've never recovered the rings worn by June Hayes boss.'

'Was everything photographed in situ before recovery?'

'Yes.'

'The black ski mask? Are you thinking Edwinstowe last week Rob?'

'Who knows boss, it could well be, there's plenty of dark clothing to go with it.'

'I'll need to get the rings over to Mr Hayes as soon as possible for identification.'

As they left the Nissan hut Rob secured it again with the padlock.

'Rob, I want this entire PSU stood down until we find Reynolds. You never know they could all be covering for him. I doubt it, but I don't want this lot allowed off this camp, until Reynolds is found and arrested.'

'Ok Danny, what about all their gear in hut 23?'

'If we haven't found Reynolds by the morning they can enter the hut one at a time, under supervision, to remove what they need. Hopefully we'll have Reynolds in custody before the morning.'

'I'll fire a phone call in to strike control to get that organised as soon as we get back to Mansfield nick.'

'Thanks Rob. I need to let Glyn Johnson know that Reynolds is still on his toes. I don't think he'd make his way back to London, but you never know.'

Danny thought for a moment then said, 'The key to all this is finding the mystery blonde. The description of the car she drives isn't a million miles away from the one Stan Briggs gave us. Find the car, the blonde or both and we'll get Reynolds. Let's get on with it.'

Danny and Rob, helped by the Scenes of Crime team then loaded the CID car with the bagged items from Reynolds bed space.

Once the car was loaded with the exhibits, Rob started the engine and drove slowly out of Proteus Camp.

CHAPTER 74

Mansfield Police Station –
November 3rd 1984

It had been five days since Danny and Rob had gone to Proteus Camp intending to arrest Mick Reynolds for the murder of the young prostitute in London.

During those five days there had been no sightings of either Reynolds or the old style dark green Ford Cortina.

Danny and Glyn were in constant touch over the hunt for Reynolds. Between them they'd organised a nationwide press appeal to try and help track down the man, the papers were now labelling as Britain's most wanted.

Danny had taken the two rings found in Reynolds' PSU bag to David Hayes. A distraught Mr Hayes had positively identified them as his wife's engagement and wedding ring. Danny then had to explain to David Hayes that he was unable to release the two rings back to him until after any future trial.

In spite of this damning evidence the police had still not publicly linked Reynolds to the Nottinghamshire murders of Mandy Stokes and June Hayes. They had, however, released to the press, that Reynolds was wanted in connection with both the murder of his wife Rita and the young prostitute Jenny Taylor.

Danny, Rob and Rachel were working tirelessly around the clock trying to establish the links that would implicate

Reynolds in the murder of Mandy Stokes as well as that of June Hayes.

Through her meticulous and painstaking enquiries Rachel had been able to establish that not only was Sgt Reynolds in Nottinghamshire at the times of the murders but that he had also been off duty and kicking his heels at Proteus Camp.

The same was also true of the assault on the two teenagers at Edwinstowe. Danny was hopeful that Scenes of Crime may find blood matching either of the two young victims on some of the clothing seized from Reynolds bed space at Proteus.

Danny was liaising constantly with Glyn Johnson, both detectives were certain they had identified the man responsible for the murders both in London and Nottinghamshire.

Glyn assured Danny that he was already in a position to charge Reynolds with the murders of Jenny Taylor and Rita Reynolds.

Danny looked at the wall clock in the CID office. It was five o'clock in the evening.

'Ok, Rob, Rachel, that's enough for today. There's nothing more we can do this evening, I want you both to go home, put your feet up and have a meal with your families. Let's be back here at seven in the morning to start a fresh day. One other thing Andy phoned me earlier today, he's back tomorrow, so the team will be back together.'

'Trust him to come back now all the works done and we know who the killer is', laughed Rachel.

'I know it's typical, now get off home both of you.'

Rob instantly grabbed his jacket saying, 'That's great Danny. I could do with seeing the wife and kids before they go to bed. See you in the morning.'

Rob was up and out the door quickly, leaving Danny and Rachel alone in the office.

'What about you Rachel, what's your plans for tonight?'

'The usual stuff, get home, eat a frozen meal for one while I watch a bit of telly and then bed.'

'Look Rach, I've just phoned Sue, she's cooking at my house tonight, why don't you join us for a home cooked meal before you go home?'

'Are you sure you two wouldn't like to spend the evening together, you know just the two of you?'

'Rachel come and eat with us. Dinner's going to be ready for six o'clock. Me and Sue can still get an early night later, if you know what I mean.'

'Only if you're sure Sue won't mind boss.'

'I'll let you into a secret Rachel, it was Sue's idea to ask you.'

'In that case, what's for dinner?'

'Her famous beef stew and dumplings I think.'

'Why's it famous?'

'I've absolutely no idea.'

He laughed, as he held the door open for Rachel before switching off the lights in the office.

As the two cars left the police station car park another car slipped in behind Rachel's Mini. Neither Rachel nor Danny paid any attention to the small Datsun that followed them up to Danny's house.

Jimmy Wade stopped the Datsun and watched as the two detectives walked up the pathway towards the house.

As he watched he said aloud to himself, 'Being very friendly towards your staff aren't you Inspector Flint?'

As the detectives approached, the front door to the house was opened. Wade could see it was a woman who'd opened the door, he'd seen her before and recognised her as Insp Flint's significant other.

Wade relaxed a little, again speaking aloud, 'That's ok then Inspector.'

To his surprise Jimmy realised that he'd begun to feel angry when he thought the Inspector had designs on Rachel Moore. It was his intention to follow Rachel to her home tonight and make one last recce before he paid her the visit that would ultimately end in her death. Accepting how he had felt earlier, when he thought Rachel would be spending the night with her boss, he had come to a decision.

Jimmy had decided that he would allow himself some intimate time with Rachel when he visited her that final time, he felt he owed it to himself. He couldn't deny that he found the policewoman very attractive. He knew that with the plans he'd already put in place, it would be ok for him to pleasure himself fully, before finally killing her.

It had been a long time, since he last enjoyed any proper intimacy with a woman. Especially one as attractive as Rachel Moore.

He licked his lips in anticipation.

CHAPTER 75

Newstead Abbey grounds – November 4th 1984

Winter had arrived with a vengeance.

The ice cold wind was driving the freezing sleet into the face of Tommy Dawson. The old man pulled his check woollen scarf tighter around his neck and took his grey flat cap off, before putting it back on again, this time making sure it was tighter on his head.

The black Donkey jacket that covered the thick Aran jumper he was wearing, helped to keep out the biting wind.

His gloved hands held on tightly to the leather dog lead.

It was just beginning to get light; the night sky was fading fast but dawn hadn't quite broken yet.

The small wire haired terrier was pulling hard on the lead.

He yanked the dog lead back sharply and snapped, 'Sam, stop bloody pulling lad!'

The dog stopped pulling for a few seconds, before resuming the tug of war he was having with his master.

It was six thirty in the morning and Tommy was making his way from Newstead village to Newstead Abbey.

Every day since he'd retired from Annesley Colliery a year ago, the ex-miner had taken an early morning walk into the grounds of the Newstead Abbey estate. It mattered not to Tommy, what the weather was like.

His constant companion on these daily walks was his little dog, Sam.

Tommy pulled hard on the lead again trying to control the little dog before saying, 'I know Sam, it's time for you to have your run.'

Bending down he unclipped the lead from the collar letting the little dog off the leash. Tommy grinned as Sam immediately darted off into the woods.

He shouted after the small dog, 'You'll do well to find any squirrels to chase today lad!'

Tommy whistled a melodic tune as he continued his slow stroll along the tree lined lane that ran through the centre of the Abbey grounds.

He never tired of the beauty of this place.

For a man who had spent his entire working life underground at Annesley Colliery, it was now a simple pleasure to spend a small part of every single day walking through this beautiful estate.

Each of the seasons brought its own beauty.

The spring held the promise of new life. Everywhere new leaves would be beginning to show, the light pastel green colours were always beautiful to see. The bluebells would cover the floor of the woodland with their deep blue and purple hues.

Summer was full of birdsong and colour as the forest burst into life. Rabbits and squirrels were abundant and Sam had hours of fun desperately trying to catch them.

Tommy's favourite season was the autumn as the leaves changed colour. Every morning he would be treated to a dazzling display of deep reds and golden yellows. A cold crisp morning in September or October with the sun shining down onto the colourful leaves was hard to beat.

Today was a proper winter's day and was extremely cold.

The bitterly cold wind made the sleet feel like shards of freezing ice biting into his skin. Slowly the sun crept over the horizon and Tommy watched as the sky gradually changed colour above the leafless branches of the trees.

Suddenly, Tommy could hear his small dog a long way off in the woods.

The dog was barking fiercely.

'Where are you lad!' he shouted.

He continued to walk along the lane, he felt grateful that the sleet was easing and had nearly stopped.

The dog continued to bark.

The light was getting better now as the sun cleared the horizon. Tommy could see a small track that ran from the lane off into the woods. The noise of Sam's barking was coming from the end of the track.

He shouted after the dog, 'Come on Sam, stop playing silly beggars. We need to head for home now. I'm ready for my tea and toast.'

The dog carried on barking incessantly. Losing patience Tommy shouted, 'Come on Sam, get here now!'

He took off his gloves and put his fingers to his mouth, using them to make a shrill whistle.

Still the dog carried on barking.

Tommy realised the dog wasn't going to come back on his own. He put the gloves back on his freezing cold hands and set off down the track towards the sound of the barking.

The sleet had now stopped altogether and as Tommy made his way into the woods and out of the chill wind he immediately felt warmer.

The long grass underfoot was sodden though, and Tommy could feel his boots and the lower part of his trousers quickly becoming saturated.

The wet trees were dripping icy water and whenever Tommy brushed against a branch he was showered with freezing cold rainwater.

He shouted after his dog again, 'Come on Sam, stop messing about now old lad. Your Tommy's getting soaked here!'

The dog just continued to bark.

Tommy knew instinctively that something was wrong, Sam was not usually a yapping dog. He continued to walk along the track further into the woods, the sound of the barking was closer now.

He was about to shout the dog's name again, but the sight that now confronted him took his breath away.

After the shock passed, Tommy said out loud, 'Good God Almighty!'

About ten feet away and directly in front of him was a rotting corpse hanging from the branch of an oak tree.

The neck of the dead man had stretched and looked to be almost a foot long. The head was tilted at a grotesque angle to the neck and looked ready to separate from the body at any time. The feet of the corpse were now just brushing the floor.

In between barks, the little dog was growling and tugging at the trouser leg of the rotting corpse.

'Get away from there Sam, get here now boy!' shouted Tommy.

Slowly the dog cowered towards him, unsure of the tone in his master's voice.

Tommy grabbed the dog by the scruff of its neck and clipped the lead back onto the collar. With the dog finally under control Tommy had a closer look around the macabre scene. He could see a sodden leather bag and an upturned crate near the feet of the hanging man.

He yelled at his dog that was still barking, 'Shut up Sam!'

Finally, the dog stopped barking and sat quietly at his master's feet.

'What else have we got here then Sam?' said Tommy as he walked around.

Looking beyond the corpse, Tommy could see the charred remains of a burned out car. He walked around the hanging man towards the torched car. Carefully he walked slowly around the car, finally stopping again behind the hanging man.

A gust of wind suddenly blew into the small clearing and was enough to cause the corpse to begin gently swinging on the creaking branch.

Feeling uneasy Tommy said aloud, 'Come on Sam lad, let's get out of here. We need to fetch the police I reckon.'

Tommy knew there was an old gate lodge that was occupied about half a mile along the lane. He walked quickly through the woods along the track and back up onto the lane. After a brisk ten-minute walk along the lane, Tommy stood outside the front door of the small stone lodge.

He began to hammer urgently on the wooden door.

The resident of the lodge, Frank Bennett, was a farm labourer who worked on the nearby Harris Farm.

After repeated banging on the front door, eventually it was opened.

'Bloody hell! It's you Tommy. Don't you know what time it is? What's all the commotion about?', said a shocked and bewildered Frank.

'Have you got a phone here Frank?'

'Yeah I've got a phone, what's the problem?'

'Frank, call the police straight away and tell them to drive up to the lane about half a mile back towards Newstead. I'll wait for them there.'

'What's up Tommy?'

'I've found a body in the woods. There's a bloke who's hung himself. There's a burned out cortina down there as well.'

Tommy started to walk off, heading back along the lane.

Frank shouted after the old man, 'Tommy you're not making this up are you?'

Tommy turned around and shouted angrily back, 'Don't be so fucking stupid Frank, of course I'm not bloody well making it up. Get the bloody cops out here now, as quick as you can!'

Tommy turned and continued to walk back along the lane.

The sun was creeping up into the sky and the weak light was getting stronger.

Tommy had just reached the entrance to the track again, when he heard the sound of a car being driven along the lane from the direction of the Abbey. He turned around and began to wave his arm indicating to the driver of the police car to stop.

As the car came to a stop alongside him, Tommy could see there were two officers in the car. He knew the policeman who was driving the car, Pc Steve Jarvis regularly patrolled Newstead Abbey and Newstead Village.

Pc Jarvis got out of the Police car, 'Hello Tommy, what's all this about a dead body?'

The policeman bent down and made a fuss of Sam as he waited for Tommy to reply.

'Hello Mr Jarvis, it's just down this track here. There's a bloke who's hung himself. There's a burned out car down there as well.'

Sam immediately started barking again.

'Sam, bloody well be quiet now!' said Tommy, firmly pulling on the lead.

The dog fell silent and Tommy continued, 'It was the dog that found the body, when he went for his run.'

Pc Jarvis turned to the younger officer and said, 'Wait in the car Nick and monitor the radio. I'll go down and have a look.'

Pc Jarvis turned back to the old man, 'Come on then Tommy owd lad, show me where this body is.'

Tommy walked back into the woods down the track with the police officer following. After five minutes they had reached the hanging man.

'Bloody hell Tommy, it looks like he's been here a while.'

Tommy nodded, he was starting to feel cold now in his wet clothes. All he wanted was to get home for his cup of tea and a slice of hot buttered toast.

A shivering Tommy pointed out the torched car to the officer, 'Looks like an old Ford Cortina to me Mr Jarvis, what do you reckon?'

'I think you're right Tommy, come on let's get back up to the car.'

They walked out of the woods along the track back to the lane.

Pc Jarvis spoke to the other officer, 'There's a body down there alright Nick, and a burned out motor that looks like an old Ford Cortina.'

'Steve we're supposed to be on the lookout for a Ford Cortina. Do you remember the briefing the other morning? That Met copper they want for the murders in London, he's supposed to be driving a dark green Ford Cortina.'

'Bloody hell Nick, you're right. Get on the radio and tell the control room what's down here and tell them to get the CID out of their beds.'

Tommy sniffed loudly.

Pc Jarvis looked at him and saw he was shivering, 'You alright Tommy? You look frozen to the bone pal?'

'Sam and me, we're both ready for our tea and toast.'

'I'll bet you are owd lad, its bloody freezing this morning. Hop in, I'll nip you home. Byron Terrace isn't it Tommy?'

Tommy climbed into the back of the police car clutching Sam tightly on his lap.

'It's number sixteen, that's grand, thanks ever so much Mr Jarvis.'

'It's no bother Tommy, we've got time before the CID get out here. We'll drop you off for your tea and toast and then get back up here. The CID might want to talk to you later though.'

Tommy laughed, 'I'll be in all day Mr Jarvis; they can come over any time. I'll have the kettle on, they can have a brew with me.'

The police car sped off down the lane to take Tommy and Sam home.

Left alone in the woods, the hanging man continued to drift slowly from side to side in the breeze.

Soon the only sound in the woods was the dripping rainwater and the creaking of the oak branch straining under the weight of the dead Sgt Reynolds.

CHAPTER 76

Mansfield Police Station – November 4th 1984

It was six thirty in the morning, the shift was just about to start, Danny was sitting alone in the CID office sipping a coffee. The office door opened and in walked a suntanned and smiling Andy Wills.

'Hello Andy, how was the break?'

'Just what Sally and I needed boss, thanks.'

'Did you manage to have a good talk and sort things out?'

'We certainly did. We've had ten glorious days in Cyprus at Sally's parents' villa in Paphos. You were right Danny, all we needed was to spend a bit of quality time together to talk things through and get back on track.'

'I take it that Sally's behind you and supporting your career again then Andy?'

'The news is better than that Danny. It turns out the reason she was having a crisis about the two of us, was because it'll soon be the three of us.'

'Do you mean?'

'Yes Danny, I'm going to be a Dad. Sally was all over the place emotionally when she found out she was pregnant. All it needed was reassurance from me that we'd be a proper family and that I'd commit to being a proper father. I assured her that I'd like nothing better than being a dad, I've always wanted children, she knew that anyway. I even talked to her about Rob, how he works long hours and still manages to be a fantastic father.'

Just at that second the door to the office opened and Rob walked in.

'Did I hear my name?'

'You did Sarge, I was just telling the boss my news, I'm going to be a dad.'

Rob stepped forward and warmly shook Andy's hand.

'That's fantastic news Andy, congratulations.'

Danny stood up and also shook Andy's hand saying, 'Yes, congratulations Andy, I'm glad things are all sorted.'

'I think I'm the one who should be thanking you, boss. I've heard on the grapevine the extra staff you told me about never actually existed and that you've been running the enquiry with just you, Rob and Rachel. I'm really grateful for what you did Danny. I'm going to buy Rachel the biggest bunch of flowers as a big thank you for taking on all my work as well as her own without complaining. I really do appreciate it. Thanks.'

Danny shrugged, 'It's all sorted now Andy, that's the main thing. Anyway, have you heard the developments here?'

'Of course I have, it's all over the news. As soon as I got off the plane from Cyprus I saw it. I thought that's bloody typical, trust me to miss it. Have you arrested Reynolds yet?'

'Unfortunately not, he's still on his toes. It's only a matter of time though.'

Andy walked over and grabbed the kettle, 'I'll fill this up and make us all a brew.'

Rachel walked into the office just as Andy was leaving with the kettle in his hand.

'Ah, perfect timing, I've missed my tea bastard!' she laughed.

'That's charming, and just when I was singing your praises as well', laughed Andy.

Ten minutes later and they were all sat in the office with a cup of tea discussing the joyous news of Andy's impending fatherhood. There was a knock on the office door and a young police cadet stepped nervously into the CID office.

'Excuse me Sir', he said timidly.

'Come in son, what's the problem?' asked Danny.

'The sergeant in the control room asked me to nip down and tell you there's been a suicide at Newstead Abbey. A man's been found hanged in the woods not far from the Abbey.'

Andy put his mug of tea down saying, 'I'll go boss.'

The young cadet continued, 'The sergeant told me to make sure I tell you, that there's a burned out Ford Cortina near to the dead body as well.'

Danny was already grabbing his coat, 'We'll all go, exactly where is it, son?' he asked the cadet.

'The local Panda car is already at the scene, they're parked on the lane between the Abbey and Newstead village, sir.'

'Ok thanks, son.'

Within seconds all four detectives had abandoned their drinks and run out of the office, leaving a very bewildered police cadet standing on his own in the CID office.

CHAPTER 77

Newstead Abbey, Nottinghamshire – November 4th 1984

The two CID cars raced to Newstead Abbey.

Entering the grounds through the gated entrance off the main A.60 road they sped past the beautiful lake and the abbey building itself.

Heading along the lane towards Newstead village they quickly saw the Panda car parked at the side of the lane.

The two uniformed officers who had been sitting in the Panda car now got out of the vehicle. The CID cars skidded to a halt behind the Panda car, Danny and his team got out of the cars.

Danny walked over to the two officers, 'Where's the body and the burned out Ford?' he asked.

'It's down here sir', said Pc Jarvis.

The uniformed officer walked down the track in front of Danny and Rob. Andy and Rachel remained on the lane talking to the other officer.

'The body's just through here.'

Pc Jarvis stood to one side and allowed the two detectives to pass by him into the small clearing where the body was hanging from the tree.

Danny turned to Pc Jarvis, 'Have you asked for Scenes of Crime to attend?'

'Yes sir, just after I informed the control room what was here. I've not cut him down yet for obvious reasons.'

'No you did right, how long do you think he's been here?'

'I've seen a few suicides in these woods, going on the state of him I'd say he's been here about a week.'

'Right as soon as Scenes of Crime have got their photographs we'll get him down. Get back on the radio and put a call in to control, I want the on call undertakers attending to remove the body. I also want the Vehicle Examiners here to check over the vehicle.'

'Will do sir.'

'Who found the body?' asked Rob.

'Tommy Dawson, he's an old retired miner from the village who walks his dog down here every day, apparently it was the dog that found it.'

'Why isn't Mr Dawson still here?'

'I took him home Sarge, he's an old man and he was freezing. I took him home so he could get a hot drink, is that a problem?'

Danny intervened, 'No it isn't a problem, where does he live?'

'He lives at 16, Byron Terrace in Newstead Village sir.'

'Ok thanks, make the calls to the Control Room requesting the Undertakers and the Vehicle Examiners please. Would you also, on my behalf, tell Dc Moore and Dc Wills that I want them to go straight to 16 Byron Terrace and interview Tommy Dawson at his home. Thanks.'

'Will do sir.'

Pc Jarvis exchanged glares with Rob before walking off up the track.

As the constable disappeared back up to the lane, Rob shook his head, 'He knows better than that, he should've kept the witness here so we could question him.'

'No Rob, for once my good friend, you're dead wrong. The Pc did exactly the right thing taking the old man home to get warm. For one thing we don't want a witness with hypothermia and for another he'll now think the police are the best thing since sliced bread and will bend over backwards to help.'

Rob held his hands up, 'If you say so Danny.'

'I do. Now let's have a proper look at what we've got here. What do you think first impressions?'

'Looks like suicide, you can see the box he's used to stand on, his feet are only touching the floor now because over the week his neck has stretched.'

'Have a look at the knot that fastens the rope to the lower branch.'

'I don't see anything unusual Danny.'

'I agree I can't see anything odd about the knot, but look at how deep the foot marks are below the knot. Why'd you reckon they're so deep?'

'I don't know; the ground does look really wet there.'

'Or could it be where someone else has used a lot of effort to hoist the body up?'

Danny then turned his attention to the upturned crate and the bag.

'Let's have a look at what's in the bag at his feet?'

Rob walked over to the wet bag. Taking a pair of gloves out of his pocket he quickly put them on before carefully opening up the bag.

'The bag's absolutely sodden Danny; we won't be getting any prints off it that's for sure. Everything inside's wet through as well.'

Opening the bag, he carefully picked out two forensic suits still in the plastic packets.

'These are dripping wet too. There's also black cable ties, a roll of Gaffer tape, a hammer, garden secateurs and a Stanley knife in here Danny. The suits, ties and Gaffer tape look the same as the ones we recovered from Reynolds bed space at Proteus Camp.'

'Looks like we've finally found the elusive Sgt Mick Reynolds then', said Danny.

Pc Jarvis then returned to the clearing followed by Tim Donnelly, 'Scenes of Crime are here sir, your detectives have gone off to see old Tommy. Do you still need me and Nick to remain up on the lane?'

'Yes please, I'd like you to wait on the lane until the undertakers and the vehicle examiners arrive. That will free us up to examine the scene properly?'

'Of course sir, no problem.'

'Once they've both arrived you can both resume. I'll need your statements before you go off duty today as well please', said Danny.

Pc Jarvis nodded and once again made his way up the track.

'Hello Tim, can you get busy with your camera so we can get the body cut down. I'm also interested in some deep foot marks around the area below the knot used to tie the rope to the lower branch. They look deeper than maybe they should be just to tie a knot off.'

'Of course Danny.'

Immediately the Scenes of Crime officer began to take photographs of the scene. The first pictures he took showed the entire scene, then gradually he made his way towards the body. Finally taking close up shots of the knots in the rope, the upturned crate and the corpse.

Standing right next to the corpse Tim pointed at the dead man's jacket, 'Have you seen this Danny?'

'Seen what Tim?'

'There's a black tube sticking out of his jacket pocket. I'm not a betting man, but it looks the same as the tubing we found inside the murdered women.'

Danny walked over and looked at the tubing that was just protruding out the top of the dead man's jacket pocket.

'Have you photographed it?'

'Yes, I've got a few shots of it in situ.'

Danny now slipped on gloves and removed the tube from the jacket, 'The tubing's soaked, but I can see there's a note inside.'

'I'd strongly advise against taking the note out of the tube here Danny. You should do it somewhere dry, the last thing you want is for the note itself to get wet. If the paper's still dry inside the tube, we might be able to NIN test it. I'll dry the tube and bag it up properly with a view to saving the paper.'

'Thanks Tim, I'll leave you to it. Have you got all the photos you need?'

'Yes thanks boss.'

'Right then let's cut the body cut down.'

Tim Donnelly was the tallest so it was he who reached up with the knife and sliced through the rope. Danny and Rob had the unpleasant task of supporting the soaking wet corpse while Tim severed the rope. He made the cut well away from the knot that formed the makeshift noose.

Finally, the soaking wet rope gave way and Danny and Rob lowered the rotting body to the floor.

The remainder of the rope was then removed from the tree and placed into a sack and labelled up. The contents of the bag, the bag itself and the crate that had all been beneath the corpse were also placed in exhibit bags and labelled up.

All the exhibits would need to be dried out slowly and carefully at the specialist drying area back at the police station.

Pc Jarvis again returned to the clearing, this time followed by the undertakers and two men in blue overalls.

'The undertakers and the Vehicle Examiners are here now sir.'

'Thanks Pc Jarvis, you've done a cracking job today. You can resume your patrol now.'

'Thanks sir.'

'Don't forget I'll need your statements today.'

'No problem sir.'

The undertakers quickly placed the sodden, decomposing body into a black plastic body bag and carried it back up the track to their waiting hearse.

'Mansfield Mortuary please gents', said Rob.

He had already arranged for the Coroners Officer to be waiting for the arrival of the body at the mortuary.

The two Vehicle Examiners walked over to Danny.

'Hello Danny, long time no see.' The voice belonged to Peter Cameron.

'Pete, how are you?' replied Danny.

'I'm good thanks, it's been a good many years since I tutored you as a young cop fresh out of training school. You're a Detective Inspector now? Well done you.'

'Thanks Pete, how's working part time with the Vehicle Examiners suiting you?'

'It's great, the money supplements my Sergeants pension perfectly. You know me I've always loved motors. Anyway, enough of all this chit chat, what do you want us to look at Danny?'

'You're right Pete we'd better get on. It's good to see you looking so well though. The motor I want you to have a look at is over there.' Danny pointed over to the burned out wreck.

Quickly Pete and his colleague were all over the vehicle.

'Well Danny, it's definitely a Ford Cortina Mk 1. There's a little bit of paint over the rear wheel arch that hasn't been touched by the fire. Its dark green, possibly similar to British Racing green.'

'Can you identify the car Pete?'

'I'm struggling to do that Danny, obviously there's no registration plates on the vehicle and it would appear that the VIM plate, chassis number and engine number have all either been removed or ground off. Without any of them, there's no way we can identify who the owner of the car is, sorry Danny.'

'It's not your fault Pete, can you arrange for a full lift to get the car removed and taken to Force Headquarters.'

'Yeah, I reckon we'll be able to get the tow truck down this track so it shouldn't be a problem Danny.'

'Was the car torched deliberately?'

'Definitely. Petrol's been used to burn this; you can still smell it.'

'Thanks Pete. Give me a call when the car's arrived at the forensic bay at Headquarters please. Oh and Pete will you pass on my regards to your wife, Maggie for me.'

'Will do Danny, it's good to see you again.'

Danny then turned to Tim, 'Have you finished Tim? Have you got all the photos of the car you need?'

'Yes Danny, we're all done.'

'Right let's get back to Mansfield and see if there's anything else we can glean from the body.'

CHAPTER 78

Mansfield Mortuary – November 4th 1984

Stewart Henson, the Coroners Officer, was waiting for Danny and Rob when they walked into the mortuary.

'Good morning gents, I've stripped the body and laid all the clothes out separately in the drying room next door. We can look at them after you've viewed the body if you like.'

'That sounds like a plan Stewart. First things first though, have you found any identification on the body?'

'Oh yes, it's your man alright. I found his Metropolitan Police warrant card in his left trouser pocket and also one of his shirt epaulettes showing his Police number.'

'Only one?' asked Rob.

'Yes, there's only one epaulette. He might've lost one or got changed in a hurry, who knows? He was still wearing a police uniform shirt but non uniform jeans and a jumper. Anyway the body's ready if you want to view it.'

Danny and Rob followed Stewart into the same examination room where they'd watched the post mortem examinations of Mandy Stokes and June Hayes.

Laid out on the stainless steel table was the naked body of Police Sergeant Mick Reynolds.

'There are no marks of violence on the body at all.'

Stewart turned the body so that the detectives could view the back as well as the front. This was no easy task due to the level of decomposition that had already taken place.

'The neck's abnormally elongated due to the length of time the body's been suspended, a few more days and the head may have become detached completely. It's been really windy of late and I think the body's taken quite a buffeting from the elements.'

'Lovely', said Rob.

Stewart continued, 'There are some marks around the bottom of the legs and around the face and neck. These are consistent with the attention of vermin such as rats and birds, probably Carrion crows.'

'What time's the post mortem?' asked Danny.

'It will be later this afternoon.'

'Have you spotted any signs of possible foul play Stewart?'

'Nothing at all, I've seen countless hangings, this looks like suicide plain and simple to me.'

'Can you let me have the pathologists report as soon as possible for the Inquest?'

'Of course Danny, do you want to see the clothing now?'

Danny and Rob followed the man dubbed Dr Death into the adjacent drying room. The dead man's clothes were all stretched out on benches. The heating was high in this room compared to the cold of the examination room. They could smell the familiar odour of death, emanating from the clothes that until recently were covering a rotting corpse.

On the benches were a pair of black lace up Dr Marten shoes, black woollen socks, a pair of white Y fronts, a white vest, a police uniform shirt with one epaulette attached, a navy blue woollen jumper, a pair of dark blue denim jeans and a black Reefer style coat.

Also on the bench was the short length of rope that Stewart had now cut from around the neck of Reynolds. The knot was still intact. The pathologist would want to examine the rope and the knot later to compare it against any surface or underlying injuries he found during the Post Mortem.

'Anything startling on the clothing, apart from the warrant card and the epaulette?' asked Rob.

'No, not really. There were some sodden paper tissues in one of the trouser pockets. The only other thing worthy of note is that on both sleeves of the coat, there's a faint smell of petrol.'

'Really? How on earth can you smell petrol above the other stench?' asked Rob.

Stewart grinned at Rob's question, 'I suppose it's all a matter of what you get used to sergeant.'

'I'll ask Tim to come down and swab the sleeves. He can test it later to see if it's petrol. The car was torched before he killed himself so it's not unreasonable to believe he may have splashed some on his jacket', said Danny.

'I hear you might have a suicide note Danny?'

'That's the next stop Stewart, Tim's drying it out slowly for us. It'll be interesting to see what's on it.'

The two detectives left the mortuary and made the short walk back to the police station. They walked straight through the station and into another specialist drying room. This time it was at the exhibits store where Tim was already busy working on the exhibits recovered from Newstead Abbey.

'There's nothing else in the bag, other than what you've already seen. The make of the forensic suits is identical to those found at Proteus Camp. The cable ties match the ones found in the opened bag at the camp too', he said.

'Thanks Tim, what about the note?' asked Danny.

'I'm almost ready to take it out of the tube now. The tubing material looks identical as the two found on the women, I'll be checking it to make sure. I want to photograph the note once it's out of the tube, then send it straight for NIN testing to check for any possible fingerprints.'

'Ok Tim, let's have a look', said Danny.

Tim slowly removed the paper from the tube and unfurled it very carefully. Once again there was a typewritten note on the paper and once again the letter 'c' was slightly below the line of type.

Placing the notepaper on a tray Tim stood back to allow Danny and Rob to read the note.

```
I cannot continue on this path of destruction

I killed Rita and I know I'll be caught

I killed the others because Rita drove me to it

The girl in London and the two women here

The Coal Killer was a fantasy I made up

I cannot go to jail

Death is the only way out for me
```

'It looks like it's been typed on the same typewriter', said Rob.

Danny scowled, 'Send it for testing Tim, but don't expect to find any prints. Come on Rob.'

Five minutes later and the two detectives were sitting in the CID office.

'Thank Christ that's over Danny, what a sick fuck', said Rob.

'I'm not buying it Rob.'

'What do you mean?'

'It's been bothering me ever since I saw those deep foot marks below the branch the rope was tied to. The examination of the vehicle heightened my suspicions and now the note has just confirmed it.'

'What are you talking about Danny? Confirmed what?'

Danny picked the phone up, 'Hello Seamus, it's Danny here, can you do me a huge favour. We've recovered the body of the police sergeant suspected of committing our murders. He's apparently hung himself. There's no obvious signs of foul play, but I'm not convinced. Would you be able to carry out the post mortem at Mansfield later today?'

There was a long pause.

'Thanks Seamus, I owe you one.'

Danny hung up, then dialled again, 'Hello Stewart, I've arranged for Seamus Carter to do the post mortem on Reynolds later this afternoon, are you able to be there to observe?'

Again a pause, this time shorter.

'Thanks Stewart, you're a star.'

'Ok Danny what's going on?'

'Doesn't it seem at all strange to you Rob, that someone who's intent on killing himself would go to all the trouble of obliterating every identifying feature of the car?'

'He may have done it to protect this blonde woman, whoever she is.'

Danny continued, 'And if you're going to kill yourself why take a bag with two forensic suits, cable ties, Gaffer tape and weapons?'

'Maybe they were already in the car and he got them out before he torched it.'

Danny shook his head, 'Why would he do that? You mentioned the blonde, do you think she knows more about our two murders than we think? I guarantee you Rob, there'll be no marks on the typed note. So why take the trouble to ensure there are no fingerprints on the note if you're intending to kill yourself?'

'So what you're in effect saying, is that you think Reynolds death isn't a suicide?'

'I don't know yet Rob, but I want Seamus to have a bloody good look and make sure. I'm not prepared to write this investigation up as closed just yet.'

Danny then picked up the telephone again, 'Hello Glyn, it's Danny. We've found Mick Reynolds, unfortunately he's now in our mortuary. It looks like he's topped himself, he's hung himself in woods at a place called Newstead Abbey.'

There was a brief pause.

'There's a note we found with the body in which Reynolds confesses to killing Rita and a girl in London. I'll send you a full report and photographs of the note. I think that's going to be case closed for you Glyn. I've still got a couple of questions I need answering about the two murders up here. Sorry we couldn't find him alive Glyn.'

Another pause, this time longer.

'Yeah, I know what you're saying, definitely the coward's way out. I'll need to liaise with you further anyway, I need to see all your paperwork regarding the enquiry into the deaths of Rita Reynolds and Jenny Taylor ready for the Coroner's Inquest into Sergeant Reynolds death. Take care Glyn, I'll talk to you again soon.'

CHAPTER 79

Peckham, London – November 4th 1984

In the CID office at Peckham Police Station, Craig watched as Glyn slowly replaced the telephone back on its cradle.

'You look shocked guvnor, is everything all right?'

'That was Danny Flint on the phone from Nottingham, they've finally found Mick Reynolds, he's bloody well topped himself. The cowardly bastard has hung himself in the woods up in Nottingham.'

'Bloody hell!'

'That's not all Craig, Danny says they've recovered a suicide note from Reynolds body, and that in the note he's admitted killing both his wife Rita and a young girl in London.'

'Well the young girl's got to be Jenny Taylor, hasn't it?'

'God I'm pissed off Craig, that bastards took the easy way out and won't ever have to answer for his crimes.'

'I know where you're coming from guv, but at least nobody else's gonna get hurt by him, the cases here are solved and we can start to close the enquiry's down.'

'That's all very true Craig, but we'd got more than enough evidence to secure convictions against him for both the murders here. Danny's asked me to prepare a report summarising our enquiries into the murders of Jenny Taylor and Rita Reynolds ready for the Coroner's Inquest that'll be held up in Nottingham.'

'I can crack on with that guv, I've got everything I need on my desk anyway.'

'Thanks Craig. It sounds to me like Danny's not happy about something up in Nottinghamshire though. He's just said to me he still needs a couple of questions answering.'

'Wonder what that's all about?'

'I don't know, I'll call him in a few days' time and find out, I'm curious is all.'

'Anyway guvnor, I know you're a little bit pissed off at the way that bastard Reynolds has dodged his final reckoning, but there's something else that we do need to pay attention to as a matter of urgency.'

'Pub?' said Glyn.

'Pub!' said Craig.

CHAPTER 80

Mansfield – November 11th 1984

It had been a week since the body of Sgt Mick Reynolds had been found hanging from a gnarled oak tree in Newstead Abbey.

Danny had finally received all the outstanding forensic test results. As he'd expected there were no marks of any evidential value found on the typewritten note left on the Sgt's body.

The burned out car had been forensically examined at Police Headquarters and no identifying features were found that could help trace the owner.

Sitting in the lounge at Sue's house, Danny leaned forward on her sofa and grimaced. He shook his head in disbelief as he watched the press release being delivered on TV by Superintendent Ken Jackson.

Jackson was smiling, telling the audience that women in the area could once again feel safe and that the hunt for the killer of Mandy Stokes and June Hayes was over. He praised the efforts of the police and thanked the public for their assistance and support.

Danny remained perched on the edge of the sofa, he was not impressed.

'What the hell's he doing?' he yelled.

Sue had picked up on Danny's angry mood as he watched the broadcast, 'What's wrong Danny?' she asked.

'I can't believe Jackson's sitting there in front of the cameras spouting all this rubbish. He doesn't know what he's talking about and what's more he hasn't even had the courtesy of speaking to me about the progress of the case first.'

'But surely it's good news Danny. That monster you've been working every hour God sends to find, is dead.'

'You're right Sue, Sgt Mick Reynolds is dead, and yes, I'm sure he was a monster, but I don't think this is all over yet. I've got a nasty feeling we're being fed a line here somehow. There are too many things that don't make sense to me. Jackson should've spoken to me first before going public like this. I only got the last of the forensic results back late this afternoon and those results have only confirmed my nagging fears about this case.'

'I don't get it Danny; do you think women are still in danger?'

'I just think not everything's as crystal clear as Jackson would want us to believe, and yes Sue, I really think women may still be in danger.'

'But Reynolds is dead, surely that's it, it's all over.'

'I hope you're right Sue, I really hope you're right.'

Gently Sue pulled him back from the edge of the sofa and cuddled him.

'Well I for one think it's good news. Now the case is closed I might get to see a bit more of you.'

'I'm not arguing with that Sue, there's nothing I want more than to spend more time with you, but I'll be seeing Superintendent bloody Jackson first thing in the morning. I want to keep the murder team working. I just know something about this isn't right, the case shouldn't be closed yet.'

Sue knew that Danny wasn't going to lighten his mood, so she just snuggled into him, trying her best to calm him down and take his mind off his anxieties.

CHAPTER 81

Mansfield Police Station – November 12th 1984

Danny had waited patiently for Superintendent Ken Jackson to arrive at the police station that morning.

When he arrived Danny had followed him straight into his office and closed the door.

'Sir, we really need to talk. That press release shouldn't have been made without you at least having the courtesy to speak to me about the progress of the case first.'

As he hung his jacket on the coat hook on the back of the office door Ken Jackson made eye contact with Danny and glared angrily, 'I really don't see what your problem is Danny?'

'My problem is, you should've spoken to me first. I'm not happy about closing down the enquiry into the murders of either Mandy Stokes or June Hayes at this time, sir!'

'Exactly what aren't you happy about Danny? You've got a dead suspect who's left a suicide note with a full confession for Christ's sake. The Met have closed their enquiries. They're quite happy that Reynolds was the man responsible for the death of his wife Rita and Jenny Taylor.'

'With respect sir! I don't really give a flying fuck what the Met have done. The murders in London, although linked in some ways, are totally different to what we've got here!'

Ken Jackson having retreated behind his desk had remained standing. He scratched his head and slowly walked over to the office window, he gazed out deep in thought.

'Exactly what are these issues that you're not happy with? Explain them to me Danny, so I can understand what the hell it is you're talking about.'

Danny took a deep breath and began, 'I think the person responsible for murdering Mandy Stokes and June Hayes is still out there.'

Jackson spun around now his anger mounting, 'You're losing the plot here Inspector! What on earth gives you that idea?'

'Sir, I'm of the opinion that Reynolds didn't kill the women by himself. I believe he's always worked alongside somebody else, I'm convinced it's this second person who's actually carrying out the murders.'

'I've never heard anything so ridiculous Danny! What possible evidence have you got to support this ludicrous theory of yours. I've gone on TV telling the public that they're safe and that the killer's been found, and now you're standing here telling me this rubbish!'

'That's why, with respect, you should've spoken to me before last night's TV broadcast!'

'Look Danny, the Chief Constable himself ordered that TV bulletin to be broadcast last night. In case you hadn't noticed, the Nottinghamshire Police Force has been getting some severe criticism lately, embarrassing questions have been asked. Why hadn't we found Reynolds until he was dead? Why hadn't we solved the murders here before he killed his wife? The whole thing's been a public relations disaster, the media are having a feeding frenzy at our expense. I'm not prepared to go to the Chief Constable this morning and say, "Did you see the press release on TV last night sir? Oh, and by the way sir, really sorry sir, but actually the real killer's still on the loose sir." Not a chance Inspector!'

'Even if it turns out to be true?'

Supt Jackson walked back around his desk and sat down, trying to calm himself down. He looked squarely at Danny and said, 'Ok Danny, sit down and tell me exactly what evidence you've got to back up this fantastic theory?'

Danny sat down opposite the superintendent and began to speak quietly, 'There are a number of things that have bothered me throughout this investigation sir. The first was the massive injuries to both victims, the rage displayed causing those injuries was enormous, but conflictingly, the cause of death in both cases was strangulation. It was as though the rage was either being staged to throw us off the scent, or there were two individuals involved in the murders. One of them motivated by rage, which would have been Sgt Reynolds. The other motivated by something else completely, a cold calculating killer. Two individuals, with different motivations, working together to carry out horrific murders.'

Danny continued, 'As the investigation progressed and Reynolds was identified, other things came to light that supported this theory.'

'Such as?'

'Such as the blonde woman described by the young Pc at Proteus Camp. Who is this woman? The young cop only saw long blonde hair from behind, so how do we even know for sure this person's a woman. This blonde, male or female, is still outstanding and has yet to be traced.'

Danny took a breath and pressed on, 'Then there's the car. There was a green Ford Cortina seen by the Pc at Proteus Camp, and also by Stan Briggs on the night of the Hayes murder. A green Cortina was subsequently found burned out at the side of Reynolds body. Who actually owned that car? Why would someone about to take their own life be bothered about obliterating every identifying mark on that vehicle, it doesn't make any sense.'

'Is that it or do you have more of this nonsense?'

Danny threw his hands up in despair, anger creeping into his voice, 'Yes there's more, if you can be bothered to hear it Sir!'

'Carry on Inspector, I'm all ears!'

'We've done an awful lot of background checks into Mick Reynolds, before his deployment on the strike he'd never been to Nottinghamshire. Think for a second about the remote locations used by the killer as deposition sites for Mandy Stokes and June Hayes. Then think about the location where Reynolds body was discovered. How would Reynolds possibly know about these locations? Surely this fact alone, suggests the involvement of somebody else. Somebody that has good local knowledge.'

Danny paused to allow that point to sink in before continuing, 'Then there's the fact that the suicide note found on Reynolds body was typed, using the same typewriter as the notes left on the murder victims. We've still not recovered that typewriter. I've checked with the Met, there isn't a typewriter at the Reynolds home and Detective Inspector Johnson has had every typewriter at Wembley Police Station checked. I've even checked every typewriter I can find at police stations throughout the County that his PSU have visited, as well as every typewriter at Proteus Camp. There are no typewriters with a dropped letter C anywhere. My question to you is a simple one. Is Reynolds the author of the notes? Or could it be that the typewriter used for the notes is still in possession of this second individual?'

Ken Jackson shook his head slowly.

Danny ignored the negativity emanating from his senior officer and continued, 'Finally the suicide note itself found on the body of Reynolds has been NIN tested. There's absolutely nothing on the paper, not a mark of value anywhere. Would a person typing their own suicide note be bothered about leaving fingerprints on the paper used, when he's about to kill himself?'

Danny leaned forward having finished outlining his theory. After a long pause Jackson steepled his fingers beneath his chin and said, 'That's all very interesting Inspector, but that's all it is, an interesting theory, supposition at best on your part. I've read the pathologists report and there's nothing to suggest Reynolds death was anything other than suicide.'

'Sir, in his report, Seamus Carter said he could find nothing that would indicate anything other than suicide, but he also said it wouldn't have been impossible for somebody else to hang Reynolds. Don't forget the very deep foot marks that were found below where the rope was tied to the lower branch. They could've easily been made by somebody using a lot of effort to raise a dead weight.'

'That's only your opinion about the foot marks Danny, more supposition that you're using to help promote your theory of a second killer. Did Seamus Carter say it wouldn't have been impossible for somebody else to hang the Sergeant in answer to a specific question put by you Inspector?'

'Yes he did, but...'

Jackson cut him off, 'Then it means nothing. The bottom line is this; Carter thinks Reynolds death was suicide. I'm sorry but I can't agree with you Inspector. The reality of this situation is, we're fortunate that this man took his own life rather than continue his killing spree because, let's face it, you and your team were no nearer catching him, were you Inspector?'

Jackson had subtly gone on the attack.

Danny countered by saying, 'Sir, let me remind you of the enquiry I'd instigated, tracking the movements of visiting officers. I'm confident that enquiry would've eventually led us to Reynolds.'

With a self-satisfied smile Jackson said, 'Yes Inspector, that's exactly my point, it would have led us to Reynolds. Not to some phantom blonde haired maniac who's still out there, waiting to strike!'

Danny sat back in his chair, he knew what was coming next.

'Inspector, as of today the murder enquiry team's disbanded. You'll resume normal CID duties. I don't want you, or any of the detectives under your command wasting any more time on these murder enquiries. As far as Nottinghamshire Police are concerned they're solved. Case closed, move on.'

Danny stood up to leave, as he was going out the door he paused and said angrily, 'There's none as blind as those who want to be. I hope for everyone's sake you're proved right about this, sir!'

Without even looking up from the paperwork on his desk Jackson had the last word, 'Think about taking some leave Inspector!'

CHAPTER 82

Mansfield Police Station – November 12th 1984

Danny was fuming as he walked back into the CID office, he looked around at the detectives in the small office and said angrily, 'Rob, Rachel, Andy as of this moment you'll all resume normal CID duties. There'll be no further enquiries carried out into the murders of Mandy Stokes and June Hayes. I'll take care of the paperwork for the Coroner's Inquest into Reynolds death and I'll close the files on Mandy Stokes and June Hayes.'

For the first time since the strike started, Danny walked through the general office and into his own office, closing the door behind him.

After ten minutes there was a polite knock on the door.

'Come in', he shouted.

Rob opened the door, walked in and said quietly, 'I'm guessing Jackson didn't go for your theory then Danny?'

'Shut the door and sit down Rob.'

As soon as Rob had closed the door and sat down Danny spoke again, 'That man's a fucking idiot. He always takes the line of least resistance. I spelt it out for him chapter and verse, but he wouldn't listen, worse, he didn't want to listen. As far as the Force is concerned its case closed, move on. He actually said those words to me Rob!'

'So that's it then boss, 'The Coal Killer' enquiries are to be put to bed.'

'Be honest with me Rob, do you think this is all over? Tell me straight if you think I'm being paranoid.'

'I can see some merit in every point you raise, such as the local knowledge needed for the deposition sites, the anomalies with the suicide, the car, the blonde all of it makes sense.'

'I sense a "but" coming Rob.'

'You're right, there is a "but", Danny. I think we've got to accept what Seamus Carter told us, that Reynolds death was suicide. My other problem with your theory is this Danny, even if there's a second individual involved in these crimes, what's his connection to Reynolds?'

'That's a very good point Rob, and I really don't know the answer. There's got to be a connection between Reynolds and the second man somewhere, it's just finding it.'

'If there's a second man, Danny.'

'Anyway, it's all hypothetical as there are to be no more enquiries made, so it's back to work as normal for everyone. Will you do me a favour Rob, ask Andy and Rachel to come in here for a minute.'

Rob nodded and left the office. Seconds later the door opened again, Rachel and Andy walked in. Danny indicated for them both to be seated, 'Grab a chair both of you. As from today, the official line is that the investigation into the Coal Killer murders is now closed. We're not to spend any more time on enquiries into the two murders. I just wanted to personally thank you for your tireless work and the hours that you've put in. I know it hasn't been without impact on your personal lives. I'll be seeking a Chief Constable's commendation for both of you.'

'Thanks boss', said Andy.

'That's great, thanks boss. Do we start on the old shift pattern again then, or are we staying on the rota we started when the strike began?' asked Rachel.

'I think we'll be reverting back to the strike hours, so generally day shifts but with plenty of overtime.'

Rachel smiled, 'My brother's coming up to stay for a week on the 14th. Would it be ok to book a week's leave from that date? We plan to do some walking up in Derbyshire?'

'No problem at all Rachel, Andy you can cover if anything drastic comes in, can't you?'

'It's the least I can do boss, Rachel covered all my work for a fortnight.'

'That's sorted then Rachel. You can take leave for a week from the 14th. Just drop an Annual Leave request form on my desk and I'll sign it through.'

'Thanks boss, will do.'

'That's that then folks, and thanks again both of you, for all your efforts.'

Rachel and Andy left the office, leaving Danny alone thinking about what Rob had said to him.

Connection was the key.

Rob had been right when he'd asked what was the connection between Reynolds and the second killer. The thought had suddenly come into Danny's mind, what if the connection was somebody Reynolds had met while on strike duty. Suddenly feeling very enthused, he stood up and stuck his head around his office door.

'Rachel could you get me a list of all the deployments undertaken by Mick Reynolds PSU, Mike Alpha One Zero please, I need it for the Coroners file.'

'Of course boss', said Rachel

Danny closed the door, no more enquiries to be done my arse. Jackson could go fuck himself, he thought.

CHAPTER 83

Mansfield, Nottinghamshire – November 13th 1984

Jimmy Wade had been waiting a long time for this day to arrive, the anticipation inside him was growing steadily, he felt like a volcano about to erupt.

His Datsun car was parked just around the corner from the block of flats where Rachel Moore lived with her cat. He'd spent hours watching her, stalking her, getting to know her routine.

Jimmy hadn't bothered going back into work after dealing with the idiotic police sergeant. Everything was now in place, there was absolutely no reason or any need for him to keep going down the mine. He'd purchased the Datsun second hand, it was a runner and was cheap enough to be discarded later.

The painstaking preparations he'd made to get to this point were all now in place. Rachel Moore was the last piece of his perfect jigsaw.

Thinking about her made the anticipation he felt, even stronger. It had been a long time since he'd enjoyed a woman properly, intimately and Jimmy fully intended to enjoy Rachel in every way before finally dispatching her to a better place than this one.

Patiently he sat waiting in the car, biding his time, watching the communal entrance to the block of four flats.

Glancing over his shoulder, he saw the large suitcase on the back seat of the car, there was another bigger case in the boot. After tonight, if all went to plan, he would need a long break. He looked down at his watch, it was almost three o'clock in the afternoon, still a few more hours to wait before she'd be due to arrive home.

Suddenly, the opportunity he'd been waiting patiently for, seemed about to happen. An elderly woman walked slowly towards the communal entrance carrying a couple of heavy bags, full of shopping.

Instantly Jimmy jumped out of the car. Having locked the car door, he strode purposefully over saying, 'Here, let me help you with those heavy bags?'

'That's very kind of you, thank you. I live on the top floor and it's a bit of a struggle getting the bags up the stairs. Would you mind carrying them up the stairs for me darling?'

Perfect thought Jimmy.

'No, not at all', he said, quickly taking both the bags of shopping from the old lady, he took a step back to allow her to open the communal door with her key. He followed the old lady slowly up the stairs to the first floor until he was standing outside her door.

The old lady's flat was directly opposite Rachel's flat.

'That's lovely, thank you so much. I can manage them from here', she smiled.

Jimmy smiled back and said, 'No problem at all, be seeing you.'

He turned and walked noisily back down the stairs.

Once downstairs he opened and then slammed the communal door shut, remaining on the inside. Very quietly he stepped under the stairwell. He waited until he heard the old lady close and lock the door to her flat, then stealthily he crept back up the stairs, taking his wallet out as he did so. He removed a plastic credit card, before returning the wallet back to the pocket of his windcheater jacket.

Jimmy quickly put on a pair of the light blue latex gloves that Reynolds had introduced him to. The fact that the gloves were police issue gave him an additional thrill.

Very carefully, he slipped the thin plastic card between the door frame and the Yale lock. After a few seconds of wriggling the card, he felt the Yale latch slide open.

He slowly pushed open the door and stepped inside Rachel's flat, before closing the door softly behind him.

A quick check was made inside the flat to make sure there were no unexpected visitors. Happy he was alone in the flat he returned the plastic card to his wallet. Suddenly he was startled by something brushing against his leg.

It was Rachel's black and white cat. Instantly he roughly grabbed the cat and shut it inside what appeared to be the second bedroom.

Jimmy hated cats with a passion and was tempted to throw the animal out of the first floor window. He quickly discounted this action, the bloody thing might hang around outside and then Rachel would wonder how it had got out of the flat. No, the small bedroom would have to do.

Satisfied nobody was in the flat, Jimmy began to have a close look at all the rooms.

There was a small kitchen just off the hallway that was clean and tidy, there were no dirty dishes left in the sink. He opened the well-stocked fridge and thought about helping himself to some fresh orange juice. He decided not to and walked along the hallway through an interior door. This led into a spacious room, that was used as a lounge and dining area. At the end of the room nearest the kitchen was a small teak table and four chairs. Beside the table and chairs was a large teak wall unit with a stereo at one end and a large, heavy, cut glass vase at the other. There were no flowers in the vase. A large record collection and a vast number of books took up the remaining space on the wall unit.

The other end of the lounge was dominated by a dark brown leather, three seater sofa. It was covered in beige coloured scatter cushions and looked extremely comfortable.

He could see that the end of the sofa nearest the colour TV was obviously where Rachel spent most of her evenings. There was a noticeable indentation where she sat and there were a couple of the scatter cushions strategically placed to aid her comfort while watching the TV.

At the side of the sofa, was a carefully placed small teak coffee table. It still had last night's coffee mug on a bamboo coaster. In front of the sofa was a very large, cream coloured, sheepskin rug.

Closing his eyes briefly, he instantly imagined himself with Rachel, writhing around on the rug in the throes of passionate lovemaking.

From the lounge he made his way into the bathroom. Again, neutral colours made up the bath, toilet and basin. There was a large chrome shower head above the bath with a glass screen at the side of the bath.

An image of Rachel standing in the shower with lather from her scented body gel cascading down her naked body, came crashing into his brain.

Quickly he checked his imagination and walked into the main bedroom.

It was exactly how he had imagined her room would be.

The room was dominated by a huge double bed, covered with a very thick, ivory coloured duvet. There were two large ivory colour pillows at the top of the bed. Smaller chocolate brown scatter cushions made of silk were haphazardly placed on the bed. The headboard was a brass frame, with bed knobs on the pillars. At either side of the bed were small cream coloured bedside cabinets with matching lamps. The lamp shades were a very subtle light beige and the stands were an intricately carved mock ivory.

There were cream coloured fitted wardrobes down one entire wall of the bedroom and a matching chest of drawers on the other side of the room that had a stand-alone vanity mirror sitting on the top. In front of these drawers was a matching stool.

Jimmy could now imagine Rachel sitting naked on the stool applying her make-up, before getting dressed every morning.

Regaining his concentration, Jimmy opened the top drawer of the chest of drawers and pulled out the contents, spreading them all over the ivory duvet.

All of Rachel's silky underwear was now on display for him to inspect. He lingered over the black bras and panties for twenty minutes, picking them up and allowing the silky material to slide slowly across his face.

He glanced at his watch, it was nearly four thirty.

Not long to wait now.

'Hurry home Rachel', he said aloud.

CHAPTER 84

Mansfield Police Station – November 13th 1984

Danny looked at his watch and said, 'Rachel, why are you still here?'

'I've just got to finish this report before I go home boss.'

'I thought I'd signed a leave pass for you to be off for a week, from tomorrow. Isn't your brother coming up from Plymouth today? You don't want to leave him stuck outside on the doorstep do you?'

'He isn't due to arrive until about six o'clock this evening. What's the time now boss?'

'It's getting on for five thirty Rachel, time you weren't here. Your brother will curse you, if you're not at home to welcome him.'

Rachel laughed out loud, 'I doubt it, not our Joe. He'd just let himself in and make a brew. He's very self-sufficient like all Royal Marines. The first thing I did when I got the flat was give him a key, that way whenever he gets some leave and fancies a base to go walking, he can come up and stay, without worrying what shift I'm on.'

'Rachel, get yourself home. Whatever that report is, it'll keep, and if it won't keep I'll get Andy to sort it in the morning. Go home, enjoy a week with your brother, then come back refreshed and raring to go.'

Rachel put down the paperwork, 'Thanks boss, you've talked me into it. It's only an intelligence report for a sighting of a suspect motor we saw yesterday, Andy will know which one it is.'

'Don't worry, I'll make sure Andy gets it sorted out. Enjoy your leave Rachel, you've earned it.'

'Will do boss, see you next week.'

Rachel grabbed her coat and walked out to the car park.

Throwing the coat onto the seat beside her she started her car and drove out of the car park. Her head was already full of the different walks she'd be doing with her brother in the coming week.

Edale and Kinder Scout in the Derbyshire Peak district would be the first. They always liked to start a week's walking with the long climb up Jacobs Ladder on to the moors. The view from the top of the climb was breathtakingly beautiful and helped to raise their spirits at the start of the week.

Eventually she pulled her Mini onto the car park next to Bateman Court and made her way into the block of flats.

Wearily she trudged up the flight of stairs until she reached her front door. Unlocking the door, she walked in, flicking the light on as she entered and calling out for her cat, 'Come on Mr Tibbs where are you?'

She walked straight past the kitchen and opened the door into the lounge diner throwing her coat onto the back of the nearest dining chair.

Jimmy Wade was waiting silently in the main bedroom. He heard the key in the lock and heard her shout out for the cat before opening the lounge door.

He could now hear her footsteps walking towards the bedroom.

With a growing sense of excitement, he watched as the brass door handle moved slowly down.

The door opened.

He saw her eyes widen in terror when she finally saw him standing directly in front of her. She was too startled to react to the threat and although she saw the punch coming she couldn't move quickly enough.

He punched her once, hard on the forehead, directly above the bridge of her nose. The force of the blow was enough to stun her and knock her backwards into the living room. She fell onto the sheepskin rug and lay there dazed.

Quickly he was upon her, trying to grab her wrists, trying hard to feed them into the cable ties.

Rachel regained her senses and was now fully aware of what was happening, she began to fight back in earnest.

A strong and fit young woman, she refused to curl up and submit to this maniac.

Rachel began lashing out with fists and feet, fighting hard for her life, she felt her fists connect with her attacker's face, instinctively she raised her right knee sharply upwards forcing it hard into the groin of her attacker and heard him gasp as pain racked through him.

Wade now realised he had a fight on his hands, he dropped the cable ties, concentrating solely on subduing her. After the painful blow to his groin all thoughts of sexual activity had quickly disappeared from his mind. All he wanted now was to control the bitch so he could savour the moment of killing her.

Fighting desperately against her much bigger and much stronger assailant, Rachel knew she was losing.

She cried out at the top of her voice, 'Help me!'

Wade instantly let go of her wrist, and punched her hard in the face.

The blow landed heavily, flush on Rachel's left cheek bone.

Once again she was momentarily stunned, he used this pause in her fight and straddled her arms with his legs, pinning her to the floor. Regaining her senses again, Rachel started to buck and thrash wildly with her legs trying to dislodge him.

Wade was too heavy and too strong, she was pinned to the floor and couldn't move. His weight was crushing her chest and she struggled to breathe, she could feel his hands around her throat now.

Frantically Rachel tried to twist her head from side to side, trying to prevent him getting a good grip.

It was useless, she couldn't stop him and could now feel his hands closing around her throat. Then she felt him starting to squeeze. All the fight suddenly left her, she couldn't offer anything else and just remained still.

Rachel stared up at her attackers face and looked into his piercing blue eyes. Her last thought was that she knew who he was, that she'd stared into those piercing blue eyes before.

Even as her eyes rolled back, Wade continued to strangle her. Rachel was completely still now and he knew she was dead. Finally, he released the pressure on her throat.

Slowly he started to edge back along her torso until her arms were no longer beneath his legs. He was now sitting on her waist. Her arms lay limp at the side of her body.

He calmed his breathing down, then slowly began to unbutton her sheer maroon coloured blouse, exposing the black lacy bra beneath.

When he'd undone the last button he opened the blouse fully, pushing the black bra up towards her neck exposing Rachel's large firm breasts.

He removed the latex gloves he was wearing, stuffing them into his jacket pocket. Slowly he cupped his hands around her breasts, gently caressing them. He then bent forward and kissed each nipple, saying softly, 'Stupid girl, this would've been so much better if you hadn't struggled so hard.'

Suddenly, Jimmy heard the sound of a key being inserted in the door, behind him.

He jumped off Rachel and stood behind the door that led from the hallway into the lounge, grabbing the heavy, cut glass vase from the wall unit.

He heard the front door slam. A man's voice said, 'Hello Rach, I'm here. Where are you sis?'

The door opened and a short, powerfully built man stepped into the lounge.

Rachel's brother Joe instantly saw his sister lying on the floor in front of him.

He shouted as he moved towards her, 'Rachel, what the fuck!'

Jimmy stepped out behind him and crashed the heavy vase onto the back of his head. The glass vase smashed into a thousand pieces and Joe was knocked out cold.

Knowing the commotion would have alerted the neighbours Jimmy ran out of the flat, down the stairs and across the street to his waiting car.

He jumped into the car and drove quickly away, leaving the carnage in the flat behind him. It would take him less than a quarter of an hour to reach the M1 motorway.

His visit to Rachel Moore hadn't gone exactly to plan, he deeply regretted not being able to have sex with her. He had thought of little else for weeks. He consoled himself with the fact that he had succeeded in killing the beautiful, enigmatic detective that had consumed his thoughts for so long. That had to be a good thing. It would now be a new beginning for him in every sense.

As Jimmy Wade eased his car into the southbound traffic on the motorway, back at Bateman Court, Rachel's brother Joe was starting to come round from the enormous blow to the back of his head.

Slowly he shook his head and the fog started to clear from his brain. He looked around his surroundings and saw his sister lying motionless on the floor.

Quickly he reached over and felt her neck for a pulse. It was very weak but it was there, Rachel was still alive.

His head throbbing with pain he dragged himself over to the telephone on the wall unit. He pulled the phone onto the floor and trying hard to focus, dialled 999.

His head began to swim once again as the operators voice came on the line.

He spoke in a soft faltering voice, 'I need an ambulance and the police right now. I'm at 4, Bateman Court, Mansfield. My sister's been attacked and she's unconscious.'

Having made the call for help Joe dragged himself back across the floor to where Rachel was lying. Tenderly he pulled his sister's bra back down until it was once again covering her breasts.

Using all the reserves of his considerable strength, to overcome the pain in his head, he rolled Rachel over into the recovery position. He then remained at her side, holding her hand and talking constantly, waiting for the ambulance to arrive.

Every so often he checked for a pulse, it was still there, very weak, but it was still there.

He repeated over and over again, 'Keep fighting Rach, hang in there Sis, I'm right here with you.'

CHAPTER 85

Mansfield, Notts – November 13th 1984

The blue lights of the gathered emergency vehicles splashed across the concrete walls of Bateman Court.

Danny and Rob parked their cars across the road and quickly walked towards the block of flats. An ambulance cranked up the two tones as it sped away from the flats, back down the hill, heading towards Mansfield.

A uniform police woman was standing at the communal door to the flats, notebook in hand.

'Oh shit', muttered Danny.

Rob got out his warrant card and showed it to the young policewoman.

'Ds Buxton and DI Flint', he said quickly.

'It's the flat upstairs, on the left'

Danny muttered under his breath, 'I know which bloody flat it is.'

At the top of the stairs waiting outside Rachel's flat was a very worried looking Andy Wills. He'd been returning to the police station from an enquiry at Rainworth when he heard the call on the radio. He'd driven directly to Bateman Court and arrived first on the scene, seconds before the first Panda car.

'What's the news Andy?' asked Danny.

'She's still alive boss, just.'

'Thank God for that, who called it in?'

'Her brother Joe, he walked in and found her unconscious, he stepped forward to help her and was whacked from behind. By the time he came around the attacker was long gone.'

'Where's Joe now?'

'He's gone in the same ambulance as Rachel, he wouldn't leave her, he's talking to her constantly, telling her to hang in there and keep fighting. He needs checking over as well boss, he's had a really nasty blow to the back of his head.'

'Did the ambulance crew say anything Andy?' asked Rob

'Nothing at all Sarge, they were too busy working on her. She's in a really bad way boss, its touch and go I'm afraid. They've just this second left for Kings Mill Hospital.'

Danny took a deep breath, 'Rob get things started here, I want Scenes of Crime out here sharpish. I want officers talking to the neighbours in the flats, and also up and down the street. I'm going to the hospital to see how Rachel's doing and find out what the prognosis is. I'll also talk to Joe down there once he's been seen by the doctors.'

'Ok Danny, I'm on it', said Rob as he walked back to the car.

'It's all very strange boss', said Andy.

'What do you mean?'

'Well, when I first got here, I had a quick look through the flat and nothing appears to be missing. There's a lot of valuable stuff that would've been nicked in a burglary. Her knicker drawer's been tipped out onto the bed, her underwear's strewn all over the place. Rachel's blouse was totally unbuttoned as well boss.'

'What are you thinking Andy?'

'It looks more like a sex attack than a burglary to me.'

'Ok Andy, that's a line of enquiry we can look at later.

Right now crack on with the enquiries I've asked you to do, concentrate on the neighbours in the flats first.'

'Ok boss.'

Danny turned back to Rob as he walked back towards him, 'Are Scenes of Crime on their way yet?'

'I've just fired another call into them boss, they're travelling. It's Tim Appleby who's coming out.'

'Ok, if the Scenes of Crime team find anything let me know straight away, Rachel's one of our own and we're going to find whoever did this to her.'

Danny started down the stairs.

Rob shouted after him, 'Let us know how she's doing Danny.'

Danny looked up and saw the look of concern on the faces of the two detectives.

Danny nodded and was then running to the car. He gunned the engine and sped off down the hill towards the hospital. Ten minutes later he ran into the Casualty Department at Kings Mill Hospital.

He took out his warrant card and was just about to ask the receptionist where Rachel and Joe had been taken when he saw Sue walking quickly towards him.

'Oh Danny, I'm so sorry', she said.

'Rachel's not dead is she Sue?'

'No she isn't, she's alive, I don't quite know how though. The ambulance crew had to revive her in the ambulance, helped by her brother. Her heart stopped, she didn't have a pulse for over two minutes before they got her heart started again. Its touch and go Danny, they've rushed her straight up to the Intensive Care Unit.'

'How's she doing now Sue?'

'Like I said its touch and go Danny, they've stabilised her but she's in a coma.'

'Thank God she's still alive.'

'I saw her when they first brought her in Danny, she's got a couple of really nasty injuries to her head and face, but she's been strangled almost to death Danny. Somebody's tried to kill her and then had a bloody good go at killing her brother Joe.'

'Where is Joe?'

'He's in the treatment room next door. The wound he received is very bad, my colleague's putting quite a few stitches into the back of his head. I'll tell you something Danny these Marines are tough. By rights, with the blow he's taken, he should still be out for the count. It's a good job he came around pretty quickly or Rachel would be dead. He's basically kept her alive until the ambulance got there.'

'I need to talk to Joe as soon as I can Sue.'

Sue took his arm, gently restraining him as he walked towards the treatment room, 'Take your time Danny, I know you want to find who did this, but don't forget he's just taken a tremendous whack to the back of his head. Tough or not, he could get forgetful or drowsy at any time, so go easy.'

'Ok Sue, I will. After I've spoken to Joe will I be able to go and see Rachel on ICU?'

'I'll take you up to ICU as soon as you're ready.'

'Thanks Sue.'

Danny stepped forward and kissed her gently on the lips, before walking into the treatment room.

Joe Moore was sitting on the treatment couch, his blue denim shirt was covered in blood and he had dried blood on his face and hands. He didn't flinch as the attending doctor put another stitch into his head wound.

'Joe, I'm Danny Flint. Rachel's boss.'

'How's my sister Inspector?'

'I've just spoken to the doctor Joe, and Rachel's stable now. She's in the Intensive Care Unit, I'm sorry to have to tell you she's in a coma.'

Relief washed over his features and he said quietly, 'She's still fighting then.'

'Yes Joe, your sister's still fighting. She's a very strong and determined young woman.'

The doctor stood up from behind Joe saying, 'That's all done Mr Moore, I'd like to keep you here at the hospital overnight for observation, that was one hell of a clout you took, I've put twenty-two stitches in that cut.'

'Don't worry doctor, I'm not leaving this hospital without my big sister.'

As the doctor walked towards the door to leave he looked directly at Danny saying, 'Not too many questions detective, Mr Moore needs to rest.'

Danny nodded.

Joe waited for the doctor to leave then said, 'Ask as many questions as you like Inspector, I'm fine.'

Danny looked at the young Marine.

Joe was twenty-three, around five feet seven inches tall and looked about three feet wide. He was a very stocky, very powerful man. Danny knew from what Rachel had told him, that Joe had been a Royal Marine for five years and had fought in the Falklands War.

Fortunately, he was extremely fit and a very tough young man.

'What can you tell me Joe?' asked Danny.

'I arrived at the flat around six fifteen I guess. I've got keys so I let myself in the communal door, then into her flat. I walked into the living room and saw her lying on the floor, I thought she was dead Inspector.'

'Call me Danny, what happened then Joe?'

'Ok Danny. So I remember, I shouted her name and started to bend down towards her, the next thing I know I'm on the floor as well. Someone must have been hiding behind the lounge door and gave me a right clout.'

'Do you know what it was that hit you Joe?'

'Rachel's got a big glass vase on her wall unit, its heavy crystal. I've got some flowers in my car to put in it. I always bring flowers for my sister. Anyway, I'm guessing whoever hit me used the vase. When I came around I was surrounded by smashed glass. The flat door was wide open, whoever whacked me was long gone.'

'How was Rachel when you first saw her?'

'She was out cold Danny, totally unresponsive. Her pulse was very weak.'

'I've just come from the flat and one of my detectives said when he arrived he noticed Rachel's blouse had been unbuttoned. Did you do that Joe to find a pulse?'

'No Danny I didn't. Her blouse was unbuttoned and her bra had been pushed up around her neck. I reckon I disturbed whoever did this, just as he was copping a feel of my sister, the sick pervy bastard.'

He went silent, then he said softly, 'I promise you one thing Danny. You'd better find whoever did this before I do. If I get to him first, I'll just bury the bastard.'

Danny nodded his head as he saw the tears well in the eyes of the tough Marine.

'Come on Joe, let's go and see your sister.'

He helped Joe off the treatment couch and walked slowly outside the room into the corridor.

Sue was waiting outside.

'Do you want to go to ICU now Danny?'

'Yes please Sue, Joe's coming along too, he needs to see his sister.'

'Are you sure you're ok Joe, you really do need to rest', said a concerned Sue.

'What I really need doctor, is to see my big sister.'

They took the lift up to the Intensive Care Unit, then stood in silence at the foot of the bed where Rachel now lay.

She was connected to several machines that were breathing for her, monitoring her heartbeat and other vital signs. There was total silence in the ward apart from the noise of the machines hissing and beeping as they kept Rachel Moore alive.

Sue addressed the two men quietly, 'Rachel's in a coma because her brain was starved of oxygen during the attack. We can't say how long she'll remain in this state. Unfortunately, it's not an exact science, all we can do is monitor her progress.'

Joe looked down at his sister and said, 'Rachel's a fighter doc, she has been all her life. I know she'll come through this.'

'I need to get back up to the flat now Joe, I take it you're staying here?' said Danny.

'Definitely, I won't be leaving here without my sister Danny'.

Sue put a reassuring hand on Joe's arm, 'You won't be able to stay on the ICU ward Joe, but I can find you a room just along the corridor. I'm on duty all night and I need to monitor your vital signs anyway, so I'll keep you updated if there's any change in your sister's condition.'

'Ok thanks doctor.'

Joe then turned to Danny saying, 'Danny you'd better find this bloke quickly, I meant what I said earlier.'

'I know you did Joe.'

Danny left the hospital and drove back to the flat.

When he arrived the policewoman was still guarding the communal door.

'Is Ds Buxton inside?' he asked.

She nodded saying, 'I'll sign you in again sir.'

'Thanks.'

Danny walked up the stairs two at a time.

He paused at the door to Rachel's flat and watched as Tim Appleby went about his work. He was busy taking swabs of blood droplets that were on the sheepskin rug. Tim looked up and saw Danny standing there.

'Found anything Tim?' he asked.

'I've found some glove marks here and there, looks like our offender was wearing gloves.'

Danny looked down at the remains of the heavy crystal vase. The base was still quite intact.

'Have you printed that glass yet Tim?'

'That's my next job Danny.'

'The offender has definitely picked that up before he smashed it onto Rachel's brother's head.'

Rob appeared from the bedroom, 'I thought I heard your voice Danny, how's our girl doing?'

'She's stable, but in a coma, still on the critical list.'

'Bloody hell, what about Joe?'

'He's fine, he's had quite a few stitches in his head but he's a tough sod.'

'It's a bloody good job he turned up when he did.'

'Tell me about it Rob, have we got anywhere with the neighbours?'

'We might have something there Danny, the old lady who lives opposite Rachel's flat told us a young man helped her up to her flat with some shopping earlier today. Andy's with her now getting a statement. I've got a police sketch artist travelling to try and get a likeness from her. He might be a perfectly innocent guy who was just helping the old lady out.'

'Yeah and he might just be the bastard that's done this!'

'One of the uniform lads doing the house to house around the corner, has found another possible witness. This guy lives in one of the houses just down the road from Bateman Court. The witness says he saw a Datsun car parked up for a few hours earlier today. He saw a man run to the car and drive off at speed back towards Mansfield at around six thirty.'

'Any description of the man he saw?'

'It appears to be very similar to the description of the man given by the old lady.'

'Ok get the artist to talk to him as well, any details on the car?'

'No boss, just a dark coloured Datsun, no registration plate, nothing.'

'Make sure we get a proper statement from that man as well Rob.'

'Ok boss will do. I'm really struggling to get my head around this, why would anybody want to attack Rachel?'

'I don't know Rob, I really don't. Let's get the artists impressions sorted, then tomorrow morning, all of us can start trawling through the sex offenders lists to see if any are likely. We're going to have to start rattling a few trees first thing tomorrow. I'll see you, Andy and Tim for a de-briefing in our office at eight o'clock sharp. I'm going back to the hospital now to get a written statement from Joe while everything's fresh in his mind. I'll let you know if there's any change with Rachel. See you in the morning Rob.'

'Ok Danny, see you tomorrow.'

CHAPTER 86

Mansfield Police Station –
November 14th 1984

The mood in the CID office was a sombre one.

It was still only seven thirty in the morning, when Danny walked into the room. Already waiting in the office were Rob, Andy and the Scenes of Crime officer Tim Appleby.

'There's a cuppa in the pot Danny', said Andy.

Danny poured himself a hot cup of tea before sitting down at Rachel's desk.

He took a swig of his tea, then said, 'Thanks for getting here promptly everyone. Let's start with you Tim, what have we got from the flat?'

'There are definitely three blood groups found at the scene, I've cross checked with the hospital for Rachel and Joe's blood groups. It means our offender is blood group O positive. It also means he may have sustained injuries to his face and that Rachel fought back bravely. I've checked with all casualty departments across the county for any males presenting with facial injuries that are blood group O positive.'

'Anything so far Tim?'

'Nothing, but I've asked them to call this office should anyone present throughout the day matching those parameters.'

Tim continued, 'I've also lifted what looks like a partial thumb print from the base of the vase. The print's too large to be Rachel's and I've checked with Joe at the hospital and he hasn't touched the vase. This partial print is currently being checked against our systems. I've also lifted a lot of glove marks throughout the flat, in particular the drawer containing her underwear. The significance of this being, at some stage our offender took off his gloves.'

Danny interrupted saying, 'Joe told me last night that when he first saw Rachel on the floor her bra had been pushed up revealing her breasts. I reckon our attacker took off his gloves and was having a proper grope before he was disturbed by Joe coming into the flat.'

Tim continued, 'That's definitely possible Danny, I've now got Rachel's clothing from the hospital to test for fibres today. I'll also test for the powder used in latex gloves to see if there are any traces on her clothing.'

'Good work Tim, let me know about the powder as soon as possible please.'

'Will do Danny.'

Danny turned to Andy, 'Right Andy, what about the description of the man seen by the neighbour in the flats?'

'The neighbour, Edith Balshaw, describes the man as being about six feet tall, with short blonde hair. He was dressed smartly in a black windcheater jacket and blue jeans. Edith reckons he's about the same age as her grandson who is mid to late twenties. The most striking thing she remembered was the man's eyes, she reckons she hasn't seen eyes that blue since Paul Newman.'

'How did she get on with the Police Artist?'

'Pretty good, this is the image they came up with.'

Andy passed the picture around the table.

'Did this man say anything to the neighbour?'

'Nothing of note boss, he asked if she needed a hand with her heavy shopping bags, that's all.'

'Did she see where he'd come from?'

'I asked that question and all she could say was that she thought it was from behind her, from down the road a little way.'

'Is that where the other witness saw the car parked, the Datsun?'

'Yes Danny exactly.'

'Ok what about that witness?'

'He describes the man he saw as being around thirty, six feet tall, slim build with short blonde hair wearing dark clothing.'

'Any good with the artist?'

'Didn't come up with anything, he reckoned he was too far away to get any sort of look at the man's face.'

'Ok Andy, what about the car?'

'He did his best, but all he can say is that he thinks it was definitely a Datsun and was dark coloured, possibly dark blue. He thinks it may have been a Datsun Cherry.'

'Have you got statements from both witnesses?'

'Yes boss.'

'Ok Andy, that's great work. What time did you get off last night?'

'I don't know boss, sometime around three o'clock I reckon.'

'Like I said, good work Andy. I want you to get that artists impression printed and circulated out to all patrols along with as much information about the car as we have.'

'Yes boss.'

'Andy don't be too late getting off today. You're no good to me exhausted. This could well turn out to be another long and protracted enquiry. That goes for everyone in this room. I've been assured by Superintendent Jackson that manpower is not an issue on this case, so don't think we've got to do everything ourselves.'

'Right Rob, sex offenders. Have we compiled a list yet?'

'Yes boss, I've been in touch with all the collators across the divisions. They're compiling lists of all the sex offenders that live on their respective areas, they are going to fax the completed lists over to us. There are detectives en route to us from Worksop and the City Divisions. I'll team them up into pairs, then we can gradually work through all the names on the sex offender lists. I've warned the cells that it might get busy later, when we start dragging their sorry arses in for questioning.'

'It's a good start, well done all of you. Before you go I've an update from the hospital. Sue spoke to me just before I came into work. Rachel's condition has remained stable overnight and there's been no change, which I'm assured at this stage is a good sign. Joe's had a restful night and is now at his sister's bedside talking to her about fell walking. I don't need to tell you what needs doing, so get cracking and let's get this bastard locked up.'

CHAPTER 87

Mansfield Police Station – December 14th 1984

It was now a month since Rachel Moore had been brutally attacked and left for dead in her own home.

She was still unconscious, still in a coma.

Her brother Joe had been granted special leave from the Royal Navy in order to stay at his sister's bedside. He had been living at Rachel's flat for the past three weeks.

A search made on the partial thumb print, lifted from the smashed crystal vase in Rachel's flat, had yielded nothing. The attacker's prints were not on any database held by the police.

Detectives drawn from every Division had spent over two and a half weeks working through the sex offender lists provided by the Divisional Intelligence Officers from across the Force.

Twenty four men, all with previous convictions for attacking women in their own homes had been arrested and questioned at length.

The criteria for arrest had been left extremely loose, even if the men only vaguely fitted the description provided by the witnesses, they were brought in for questioning.

The result of all this time consuming, painstaking, labour intensive work had been nothing. No positive leads or lines of enquiry were forthcoming.

Once again Danny could feel the pressure of working a case with very little evidence to go on. Today as he walked into the control room, he was in a very despondent mood.

'Anything for me Sarge? I'm just nipping out to get a turkey cob from the Railway pub', he said.

'Sorry sir, I didn't know you were in the building. I've been looking for someone from the CID to talk to a bloke at the front counter. I've been phoning the CID office but nobody's picking up.'

'They're all out on enquiries. What's this bloke's problem?'

'His name's Dave Smedley, he says he wants to talk to someone about a miner who died underground at Warsop Main pit back in March.'

'Did he say the name of the dead miner?'

The sergeant looked at his note pad and said, 'Jones Sir, Albie Jones.'

'Ok Sarge, I'll talk to him, I dealt with Albie's death.'

Danny walked out to the front office and looked at the man waiting there, 'I'm Detective Inspector Flint, I understand you wanted to talk to me about the death of Albie Jones.'

'That's right Inspector I do.'

'And who might you be?'

'My name's Dave Smedley. On the day Albie Jones died at the pit, I was the Deputy in charge of the men working on the face.'

'I didn't think Albie was working on the face that day.'

'He wasn't Inspector, but he was in my work detail working further down the loader gate. I really need to talk to you about the events of that day.'

Danny was intrigued, he showed Dave Smedley into an interview room, where both men sat down. It was obvious to Danny that Dave Smedley was extremely nervous.

'Is it ok if I smoke Inspector?' he asked.

Danny nodded, then declined Smedley's offer of a cigarette. Dave Smedley lit his cigarette and took a long drag, inhaling the smoke deep into his lungs before exhaling. His hands holding the cigarette were shaking, he looked a very worried man.

'Right Mr Smedley, you've obviously got something you want to get off your chest. What is it you need to tell me about the death of Albie Jones?'

'Before I say anything Inspector, I want you to know that at the time Albie died, nobody ever suggested that his death was anything other than an accident. There was never any question of a criminal enquiry.'

'Why exactly is that important Mr Smedley?'

There was a long silence, Smedley took another long pull on his cigarette before stammering, 'Because at the time, when I was questioned by the Mines Inspectorate, I lied to them.'

'You did what?'

'I lied to them. I've left the coal industry now so they can't take my Deputy's papers off me. That's what I was scared of you see. I'd broken the rules that day, but I couldn't say anything about it or I would've lost my papers. I'm not proud of what I did and now I need to tell somebody the truth.'

'What exactly did you lie about Mr Smedley?'

'I told the Mines Inspectorate that I'd escorted an injured miner all the way to the pit bottom, and that I'd passed Albie Jones twice. I told them Jones was alive both times I saw him. All that was a lie, I never escorted the injured miner, he walked out by himself. I never saw Jones alive at that time.'

Danny was thoughtful for a moment, then he said, 'Yes, I remember this now. There was a miner on your team who had an eye injury, he had to leave the face and go topside to get it treated'.

'That's right Inspector.'

'And you're telling me now that the miner with the injury to his eye, left the pit bottom and walked out on his own unsupervised?'

'That's it exactly.'

'Why haven't you said anything before?'

'I wanted to, I was in two minds whether or not to come clean to the Inspectorate about the whole lying business. Then, when the strike started I was shipped off down to Wales, they were short of Deputies to carry out the essential safety maintenance down the mines there. I only came back here last month and I've now resigned from my job at Warsop Main colliery, I reckon the coal industry in Britain's finished, I've started looking for new work.'

'Why say anything at all Mr Smedley? You could've just kept quiet about everything.'

'The reason's simple Inspector, what I did that day has bothered me ever since. There was something strange about the miner who walked out of the pit that day. I went to see him after the shift at his house to make sure he'd stick to the story. I swear that he already knew Albie was dead. This is the part that's bothered me ever since, because there's no way he could've known about the death. Albie wasn't found until the afters shift came down the pit later, way after he would've walked past him on the loader gate. The only way he could've known about Albie, was if he was already dead when he walked passed him to get to the pit bottom.'

'There is one other explanation Mr Smedley.'

'What's that?'

'The miner who walked out the pit that day was responsible for the death of Albie Jones.'

'Oh my God!'

Smedley put his head in his hands, he was visibly shaking.

Danny leaned forward glaring at Smedley, 'Remind me again, what was the name of the miner with the injured eye Smedley?'

'His name's Jimmy Wade.'

'You said you went to his house that night. Where does Jimmy Wade live?'

'He lives on Marples Avenue at Mansfield Woodhouse, I think it's number 56.'

'Thank you Mr Smedley. You should thank your lucky stars that at the time, Mr Jones death wasn't a criminal investigation. If it had been I'd be locking your lying arse up for a very long time. I want a full written statement from you right now!'

'I'm sorry Inspector. I never meant any harm, I was just trying to protect my job and my livelihood.'

'Where do you live Smedley?'

Dave Smedley gave Danny details of his home address before asking sheepishly.

'How long will the statement take, my wife's waiting outside?'

'It will take as long as it takes.'

'I'm sorry I lied, I truly am.'

'Yeah, me too', said Danny as he stepped out of the interview room.

He turned to the desk sergeant and said, 'Do me a favour Sarge step in the interview room and sit with him until I can get a detective up here to get his statement. He's not under arrest, but I don't want him walking out of here. Is that clear?'

'Yes sir.'

Danny walked quickly back to the CID office where he found Andy and Rob eating lunch.

He said, 'Sorry Andy, can you leave that and go up to the interview room at the front desk. There's a bloke called Smedley in there. He's got information relating to the death of Albie Jones, a miner, who died at Warsop Main pit. I want a full witness statement taking from him. I don't care how long it takes I want every detail, ok?'

'No problem boss. I remember that job, it was at the beginning of the strike wasn't it.'

'That's the one Andy, apparently when Smedley was questioned by the Mines Inspectorate he was less than forthcoming about the truth of what occurred that day.'

'I'm on it boss.'

Andy took a last bite of his sandwich, scooped up a large stack of statement forms and strode out the door.

Rob was just about to have the second bite of his own cheese and ham sandwich, when Danny said, 'Come on Rob, get your jacket we're going out. Bring that sarnie with you.'

Rob grabbed his jacket and put it on while he held the cheese and ham sandwich in his mouth, still chewing a mouthful of sandwich he mumbled, 'Where we going Danny?'

'We're going to 56, Marples Avenue, Mansfield Woodhouse. We need to ask Jimmy Wade some questions about the death of Albie Jones at Warsop Main Colliery in March.'

'The roof fall that caused the massive head injury?'

'The very same, I'll fill you in on all the gory details on the way to Woodhouse. Chuck me the keys, I'll drive while you finish your sandwich.'

Rob threw Danny the car keys and said, 'Didn't Rachel speak to Jimmy Wade at the time we were looking into the death?'

'Yes she did, if I remember rightly he's the guy that gave her the creeps.'

'That's right, I remember her saying she thought he was laughing at her, like it was all a big game to him.'

'Well let's see if he's still laughing today, shall we?'

Danny drove the CID car slowly out of the car park and headed for Mansfield Woodhouse.

CHAPTER 88

Marples Avenue, Mansfield Woodhouse – December 14th 1984

Danny parked the car on Marples Avenue, a short distance from number 56, he paused before getting out.

'What are you thinking Danny?' asked Rob.

'I'm thinking that I may have missed a massive opportunity. I could kick myself for not following Rachel's intuition about this Jimmy Wade character.'

'I wouldn't beat yourself up Danny, it was so manic during the early days of the strike, we worked with what we'd got at the time. Without that little nugget from Smedley, how could we have known any different back then?'

'You're right Rob, come on let's go and talk to Wade.'

As they approached the house they saw an old Vauxhall Viva parked on the driveway. Danny walked alongside the car and noticed a baby seat on the back seat of the car.

'I thought Wade lived here alone?', he said.

'That's what it said in Rachel's report, but that was back in March boss.'

'That's very true, I guess things could have changed since then.'

Danny knocked loudly on the door.

The door was answered quickly by a young woman in her mid-twenties with a small child in her arms. Danny showed the harassed woman his warrant card and said, 'Police. We need to speak to Jimmy Wade.'

The woman left them standing on the doorstep and shouted back into the house, 'There's a couple of your lot at the door Ray!'

Seconds later a man appeared at the door.

'Detective Inspector Flint. What are you doing here sir?'

'It's Pc Turner isn't it?' said Danny.

'Yes sir, Ray Turner. I transferred to Mansfield from Canning Circus, just before the start of the strike. I'm sorry where are my manners, don't stand on the doorstep its freezing, step inside. You'll have to excuse the mess but we haven't been here long, we're still unpacking.'

The two detectives stepped into the lounge over the toys strewn across the floor.

A clearly embarrassed Turner shouted to his wife, 'Bloody hell Sandra! Don't these kids ever pick anything up?'

Sandra bustled into the room quickly picking up the children's toys.

'Please sit down, can I get either of you a hot drink?' she asked.

Declining the offer of a drink Danny and Rob sat down on the settee, Ray sat opposite in the armchair.

'It's not every day the CID call, what's the problem sir?' he asked.

'How long have you lived here Ray?' said Danny.

'We only took possession of the keys on November 13th, that's why we're still in a bit of a mess.'

'Who'd you buy the house from?'

'We bought it from a bloke named Wade, we were dead lucky. It was only on the market for a couple of weeks, it was a real bargain. I only got it because I've got a mate who works in the estate agents Wade put it up for sale with. Anyway my mate let me know that the house was for sale, fully furnished and at a rock bottom price. Apparently this bloke Wade wanted a quick sale.'

He continued, 'Anyway, I asked my mate to take the details out of the estate agents window until me and Sandra could have a look. Well, as soon as Sandra saw the house that was it, she loved it straight away. We put an offer in that same day and it was accepted.'

'Can you remember when you and Sandra viewed the house Ray?'

Turner paused, attempting to recall the date, 'I think it was sometime back in October. I do remember there wasn't a chain because we were only renting and Wade was leaving the UK. Everything went through pretty quickly. Sandra's dad's quite well off and he gave us the cash for a deposit, so clinching the mortgage was easy.'

'Leaving the UK?' asked Rob.

'I'm sorry?' said Turner.

'You just said, Wade wanted a quick sale as he was leaving the UK?'

'Yeah that's what he said Sarge. He told me he was a miner and that he was pissed off with Thatcher. I'm not a hundred per cent sure, but I think he mentioned South Africa.'

'What did Wade look like?' asked Danny.

'I only saw him the once, when we had the viewing. Everything was done through the solicitors after that. From memory, I'd say he was about six feet tall, slim build with short blonde hair and probably mid to late twenties. Is there a problem sir, we're not going to lose the house are we?'

'No Ray, you're not going to lose the house.'

'Thank God for that sir, I was beginning to get worried. Sandra loves it here and I know I submitted the General Report requesting permission to live here, that all got signed through ok.'

Rob raised his hand to stop Turner talking and said, 'Ray stop worrying, there really isn't a problem with the house. All I need from you is your friends name, and the name of the estate agents he works for?'

'The estate agents are Proctor and Lewis in Mansfield, my mate's name is Johnny Lowe. I play football with him at the weekends. He's not going to be in any bother is he Sarge?'

'No Ray he isn't. he's done nothing wrong.'

'Can you remember the name of the solicitors Mr Wade used for the conveyancing?' asked Danny.

'Not off the top of my head sir, but I'll have some paperwork here somewhere. I'll dig it out and give you a call if that's ok. In fact, I'm on evening's tonight so I'll be coming into work in a few hours' time anyway. Do you want me to drop the details off in your office?'

'That'll be great if you can Ray, I think that's all I need for now, thanks. What're your new neighbours like?'

'They're fine, I've got old couples either side. They love the kids, so it's all good.'

'It's a nice house Ray, I hope you'll all be happy here.'

'Thanks sir, me too. Is Jimmy Wade wanted or something?'

'No he isn't. We just need to ask him a few questions that's all.'

Danny and Rob stood up, Ray also quickly stood up to show the detectives out. At the front door he said, 'If that's everything then sir?'.

'That's everything Ray, sorry to have disturbed you.'

'No problem sir.'

As soon as Ray had shut the door Danny strode over the open plan garden and knocked on the neighbours' front door. Eventually the door was answered by an elderly man who said brusquely, 'No thanks, whatever you're selling. I never buy anything at the door!'

'Just a second sir, we're the police. I need to ask you a few questions, it won't take long.'

The man carefully studied the warrant card being held up as Danny said, 'It will only take a few minutes, I promise you.'

'Spit it out then man, what do you want to know?'

No offer of a hot drink here then.

Danny indicated the house next door and said, 'I wanted to ask you about your next door neighbour.'

'That noisy bloody lot, screaming kids, marvellous, that's all we need at our time of life.'

'I meant your previous neighbour, Mr Wade.'

'Oh Jimmy. He was a good lad, no trouble at all, not like this new bunch of howling banshees.'

'Do you know where Mr Wade's moved to?'

'He's gone abroad somewhere, Canada I think. I'm sure he told me he'd got a job near Niagara Falls, that's in Canada isn't it?'

'Yes that's in Canada. Has Mr Wade gone over there for good?'

'How should I know. He didn't tell me everything you know; Jimmy was really quiet not like….'

'Not like your new neighbours. I know, you said. Well thank you very much sir, you've been very helpful.'

The old man started to close the door, just before it closed completely Danny put his hand on the door to stop it.

'Sorry sir, there's just one more question, what sort of car did Jimmy drive?'

'Jimmy had a lovely old car. A dark green Ford Cortina Mk 1. It was in mint condition, beautiful. They don't make cars like that anymore. The car was originally owned by his grandfather, I think it was Jimmy's pride and joy.'

'Sounds amazing. What's happened to the car now Jimmy's gone abroad?'

'He said something about selling it to a dealer down south, got top dollar for it as well apparently. The only problem was, he had to sell the car a few weeks before he left. He came home one evening with some shitty Jap crap motor he'd bought. It was bloody horrible, a shitty dark blue colour and noisy as hell.'

'Ok thanks, that's very helpful. Don't let all the heat out of your house will you.'

The two detectives walked slowly back to the car.

'Are you thinking what I'm thinking Rob?'

'Oh yes! A dark green Ford Cortina is just way too much of a coincidence.'

'Let's get back to the station, I need to find out whether Jimmy Wade was working or on strike until he left the country. We already know that Sgt Reynolds and his PSU were involved in escorting working miners into Warsop Main Colliery. If Wade was a scab and going into work, it's possible we've just found our connection.'

CHAPTER 89

Mansfield – December 14th 1984

Soon after returning from Wade's old house on Marples Avenue, Rob quickly ascertained that Jimmy Wade was on the list of working miners and had indeed been escorted into Warsop Main Colliery each day by the PSU commanded by Sgt Mick Reynolds.

Rob's enquiries revealed that Wade was one of the first miners to break the strike, the first time he went back into Warsop Main Colliery was on June 25th.

Armed with that information, Rob immediately drove to Proteus Camp where he spoke at length to Pc Ken Drury, the driver of PSU Mike Alpha One Zero.

The sergeant of any PSU always sits in the front seat of the Transit van next to the driver. Rob knew that if anybody had information on Reynolds, it would be Drury.

Pc Drury explained to Rob, that Sgt Reynolds regularly held conversations with one of the working miners. These conversations happened daily and were always out of earshot of other officers or other miners. Drury described how the sergeant and the miner would talk while they drank coffee and smoked cigarettes waiting for the battle bus to arrive.

Drury described the miner as being six feet tall, mid to late twenties, with short blonde hair.

He also recalled how Reynolds had totally overreacted one day, when a younger member of the PSU had jokingly commented about the sergeant's new best friend, the tall, blonde miner.

Drury explained that Reynolds had gone way over the top with the young officer and threatened to throw him off the PSU and send him back to Wembley Police Station that very night. After that incident nobody paid any attention to the sergeant and the miner. Drury told Rob from that day onwards all the younger officers on the PSU referred to the pair of them as "the odd couple".

After speaking to Pc Drury, Rob then drove straight to Warsop Main Colliery where he established that Jimmy Wade had not been in to work at the pit since October 28th, the same date Sgt Reynolds had last been on duty.

From that date onwards, both men had effectively disappeared. At least they had until the body of Sgt Reynolds was found at Newstead Abbey.

When Pc Ray Turner came on duty that evening, Danny spoke to him and ascertained that the name of the solicitors used by Jimmy Wade for the conveyancing of the house was Shaftsbury, Morton and Binks.

Pc Turner had brought with him a letter from the solicitors. The signature on the bottom of the letter was that of Richard Morton, one of the partners of the firm.

Danny and Rob had left work at ten thirty, satisfied that there was now more than enough evidence to prove a link between Mick Reynolds and Jimmy Wade.

Danny felt vindicated that his theory about a second killer still being at large was now looking more likely.

Before leaving work that night, Danny called Dave Smedley on the telephone. He needed to know if Smedley had any information or knowledge of Wade's current whereabouts. Smedley assured him that he hadn't seen Wade since the day he'd been seconded down to Wales and that he definitely hadn't seen him recently.

Finally, Danny circulated Jimmy Wade on the Police National Computer.

Wade was now officially wanted in connection with the suspicious death of Albie Jones at Warsop Main Colliery in March 1984.

CHAPTER 90

Mansfield – December 15th 1984

Danny and Rob were sitting in an unmarked car parked opposite the office of Mansfield estate agents, Proctor and Lewis. They'd been there since eight o'clock that morning.

All the lights in the office had just come on and a young girl was busily unlocking the front door.

'Looks like they're opening up now Danny', said Rob.

'That means all the staff must be in there, let's go and have a chat with Mr Johnny Lowe.'

The two detectives walked into the shop and were met by the girl who had been unlocking the front door, a young attractive brunette.

'Can I help you?' she asked politely.

'We'd like to speak to the manager please' said Rob.

'Yes of course, can I say who wants to see him?'

'It's a private matter, thanks. I'm sure he'll see us', said Danny.

The girl hurried towards the back of the shop.

Danny scanned the faces of the other members of staff and saw a young man sitting behind a desk towards the back of the office, the youngster never once averted his gaze and was staring hard at Danny and Rob.

He looked to be in his early twenties, very tall and very skinny, his jet black hair was cut short and neat. He was wearing an ill-fitting dark blue suit, a white shirt and a blue and white spotted tie. The young man stood up and walked straight over to Danny.

'You're the CID right?' he said before continuing, 'I think you might want to talk to me? My name's Johnny Lowe, my mate Ray told me you'd be coming in to see me. I'm not in any bother am I?'

Just at that moment Vince Proctor, the manager and part owner of the business, came out of his office at the very rear of the shop. He walked across to the two detectives and said in a friendly voice, 'Good morning, I'm Mr Proctor. I own the business; can I help you gentleman?'

Vince Proctor was in his early fifties and had been an estate agent all his working life. He had joined the firm of Lewis estate agents when he left school. He gradually worked his way up until, in the mid-seventies, Mr Lewis offered him a partnership in the business.

Proctor now had a small drink problem and was starting to show the tell-tale signs of alcohol abuse. He had a very rotund stomach, florid cheeks and a bulbous, ruby red nose.

His grey hair was receding and he wore wire framed round spectacles that perched precariously on the end of his nose and gave him an owl like appearance.

Danny answered quietly, 'Good morning Mr Proctor, we're from the CID. I'm sorry to bother you at your place of work but we need to ask your employee Mr Lowe here, a few urgent questions about the sale of a property he recently handled. Would it be ok to have a word with you both in private? In your office, perhaps?'

'Of course gentleman. I'd much prefer it if we didn't discuss matters out here.'

Proctor then growled at the young salesman, 'Follow me Lowe.'

Proctor then walked back to his office followed by Johnny Lowe and the two detectives.

Once in the privacy of the office Danny and Rob showed their warrant cards to Mr Proctor. After examining the warrant cards Mr Proctor gestured for Danny and Rob to be seated.

Having taken a seat Danny said, 'Thanks very much Mr Proctor I do appreciate this. First and foremost, I want to point out that Mr Lowe has not acted wrongly or dishonestly in any way and we're not here to accuse him of any wrong doing.'

'Well that's good to know Inspector, because Mr Lowe's one of my best sales people. Which property is it you're interested in?'

'I need to ask him a few questions about the sale of 56 Marples Avenue at Mansfield Woodhouse.'

Mr Proctor then looked markedly towards Johnny Lowe indicating that he should start talking.

Lowe took a deep breath and said, 'Yes, 56 Marples Avenue at Mansfield Woodhouse. A three bed semi. I remember it well because it sold so quickly.'

'Who was the vendor?' asked Rob.

Lowe looked at Proctor and asked, 'Is it ok if I go and get the paperwork from the filing cabinet?'

'If it will help you answer the questions, go and fetch it', said Proctor.

Lowe darted out of the office and returned less than a minute later with a thin Manila file.

On the front of the file was stencilled 56 MARPLES AVENUE- J. WADE.

Lowe opened the file and read aloud, 'The seller was Mr Jimmy Wade.'

'What was the price?' asked Rob.

Referring to the file again, Lowe replied, 'Initially he asked me just to value the property. The house was immaculate and he wanted to sell it fully furnished. The house was full of top of the range fixtures and fittings. The average price we're achieving for a three bedroomed semi in that area is around the £31,000 mark. I told Mr Wade that I could easily get him £35,000 for his property.'

'So what price did you sell it for?'

'Mr Wade told me to put it on the market for £27,950. I argued and told him he could get a lot more for the property, but he was having none of it. He just wanted a very quick sale.'

'Did he say anything about why he wanted such a quick sale Johnny?' asked Danny

'I know there was no chain on his side, let me think for a second.'

He rubbed his chin thoughtfully, before saying, 'That's it, I've got it. Mr Wade was moving to America. I remember him saying how totally pissed off he was with the mining industry and the UK in general. He wanted a complete change.'

'How did you market the house?'

'To be honest, I didn't bother marketing it. Look, the house was such a bargain I knew I could sell it without spending anything advertising it. I knew my mate Ray Turner was looking to purchase a house, he was fed up of being stuck in rented accommodation after transferring to Mansfield Police Station. I just phoned him and told him about the house. He asked me not to put anything in the window or the newspaper and to let him and his missus have a look at it first.'

'Is that normal practice?'

Mr Proctor interjected, 'No it isn't normal practice Inspector, but I encourage my staff to think on their feet and to achieve a sale in any way they can. Our biggest expense as a business is advertising, so if a property can be sold quickly without advertising, that's very definitely a bonus and something I'd always encourage.'

'That's all I did. I knew Ray would probably have the house once he saw it. I arranged with Mr Wade for them to view it the next day. Sure enough Ray put an offer in for the asking price on the same day, the sale went through like lightening. It's the easiest commission I've made all year.'

'One last question Mr Lowe, when did Wade approach you to sell the house?'

Again Lowe quickly skimmed through the papers in the file before saying, 'He first came in to the office on September 10th, everything was finalised and the keys given over on November 13th. It could've gone through even quicker than that, I think it was his solicitor who delayed it for a few days at the beginning of November.'

'Does it say on your file who Mr Wade used to do his conveyancing?' asked Rob.

Lowe turned over the last page in the manila file and said, 'Here it is. Shaftsbury, Morton and Binks over in Newark. He had Richard Morton handling his affairs, one of the partners.'

'Do you deal with that law firm very often Mr Proctor?' asked Danny.

'We do Inspector; they're one of the oldest legal firms in the County. They now employ twenty-four solicitors, who all handle conveyancing, so it's very unusual for one of the partners to be hands on these days.'

'Thank you Mr Proctor. You and Mr Lowe have both been very helpful', said Danny.

The two detectives then left the shop and walked back to the car. As they walked Rob said, 'Newark?'

'Newark, and don't spare the horses!' said Danny.

CHAPTER 91

Newark, Nottinghamshire – December 15th 1984

'Good morning, we're here to see Richard Morton please', said Danny.

The receptionist didn't bother to look up from her typewriter and continued typing as she said, 'Do you gentlemen have an appointment?'

Her desk and typewriter were across the office from the small reception window and Danny found himself raising his voice over the click clack noise of her typewriter keys.

With more than a little note of irritation in his voice he replied, 'No, we don't have an appointment Miss, but this is an urgent police matter and I would very much appreciate your cooperation.'

He held out his warrant card for her to see.

The secretary stopped typing and looked over at the warrant card, inspecting it thoroughly before saying, 'It's not Miss its Ms, and you really do need to make an appointment. Mr Morton's a partner of this law firm and he doesn't see anybody without a prior appointment.'

There was a note of annoyance in her voice now.

'Yes Ms I understand that, and I'm a Detective Inspector investigating two murders, now do what you have to do and get us in to see Mr Richard Morton, NOW!' said a clearly agitated Danny.

Visually irritated the woman then stood up sharply and marched across to the window and said, 'Who shall I say wants to see him?'

'I'm Detective Inspector Danny Flint and this is Detective Sergeant Rob Buxton.'

The receptionist stared hard at the warrant cards again being held out by the two detectives. She quickly scribbled down the names on her note pad and stalked through a door that led off her office.

'What a Rottweiler', said Rob.

Danny smiled and nodded in agreement.

After three minutes the door opened and the Rottweiler reappeared, only now she was more like a poodle. All of a sudden, she couldn't have been more gracious.

'Mr Morton will see you immediately Detective Inspector', she purred before continuing, 'Can I get either of you refreshments, a cup of tea or coffee perhaps?'

Danny looked at Rob with a hint of a smile before replying, 'No thank you.'

In the broadest Yorkshire accent, he could muster, Rob said brusquely, 'Coffee, white one sugar. Ta luv!'

'No problem Sergeant', she said quietly, but through gritted teeth, before adding, 'I'll buzz you in gentlemen, Mr Morton's office is the first door on the left. I'll bring your coffee through shortly Detective Sergeant.'

'Thank you Ms', said Rob emphasising the Ms so it sounded like Mzzzzz.

The door lock buzzed open and they walked into the private offices of Shaftsbury, Morton and Spinks.

Richard Morton was waiting at his open office door.

Morton was now sixty-three years old and was considering retirement. He was a very short man. He was still extremely smart and wore a charcoal grey pin stripe suit, a crisp white shirt with gold and black onyx cuff links, a maroon paisley pattern tie that was held by a tie slide that matched the cuff links. His black brogue shoes were highly polished. Although nearing the end of his working life Richard Morton was still as sharp as a tack.

He was very slim and fit and still had a full head of slate grey hair. There was no smile of welcome, he just fixed both the detectives with a hard look from his cold grey eyes and asked, 'Which one of you is Detective Inspector Flint?'

'I am Mr Morton, thank you for seeing us without an appointment', said Danny.

'Ms Faversham, my secretary, gave me the impression that I'd little choice in the matter', he said his face breaking into a grin for the first time.

'A formidable woman, your Ms Faversham', said Danny returning the smile.

'Oh, you caught her on a bad day that's all, she's a lovely woman and a fantastic secretary.'

Morton waved the two detectives into his office saying, 'Sit down gentlemen, please.'

Just as they sat down Ms Faversham came into the office carrying a cup of coffee on a small tray. Also on the tray was a small plateful of assorted biscuits, a milk jug and a sugar bowl containing a variety of white and brown sugar cubes. She placed the tray down on the coffee table in front of Rob and said quietly, 'There you are Detective Sergeant, please help yourself to milk, sugar and a biscuit.'

'Thank you very much', said Rob with a smile.

Ms Faversham then beat a hasty retreat from the room.

Morton sat down behind the large walnut desk that dominated his office. The desk was positioned directly in front of the only window in the room. It was a large sash window that almost took up the entire wall. Through the fine net curtains Danny could see that the view from the window was spectacular, overlooking the ruins of Newark Castle at the side of the River Trent.

The walls were panelled with a dark coloured wood similar to the large desk. One wall was made up of floor to ceiling bookshelves, the shelves were stacked with a huge collection of law books.

In one corner of the room stood a very large free standing safe that was metallic blue in colour. On the front of the safe in brass lettering was the maker's name, Chubb. Beneath the name was a large brass handle and a black combination dial.

The only other furniture in the room was a large red leather Chesterfield settee, which matched the red leather Captain's chair that Morton had behind the desk. In front of the settee was a dark wood coffee table upon which, sat the coffee and biscuits. Rob and Danny had sat at each end of the Chesterfield and Rob busily put milk and sugar into his coffee.

Morton turned to Danny and said, 'What was so urgent that you had to see me today Inspector?'

'I need to ask you some questions about a conveyancing job you undertook recently. My understanding is that you dealt with this matter personally.'

'As I thought, you want to speak to me about Jimmy Wade.'

'Yes we do, how did you know that?'

'Years ago, when I was a very young boy, my family lived at Newstead village, my father was a pitman. To cut a long story short Inspector there was a connection between my family and the Wade family. So when Jimmy Wade came to the firm requesting that we represent him for the conveyancing of his house sale, I overhead him talking to one of our juniors. I enquired as to whether he was related in any way to the Wade family from Newstead. When he informed me that he was the grandson, I offered to do the conveyancing myself.'

'That still doesn't explain how you knew we wanted to talk to you about Jimmy Wade today Mr Morton.'

'Patience Inspector, please. I completed the conveyancing with the minimum of fuss as you would expect, it was very straightforward sale. When Jimmy Wade came into settle his reduced bill he left something with me, his instructions were very clear. I must only hand it to you Detective Inspector Flint, but he stipulated clearly that I was only to pass this on to you, if you ever come to my office making enquiries about the house sale.'

Rob who had been sipping his coffee quietly, now hurriedly placed the cup on its saucer and leaned forward and asked, 'What was it he left with you Mr Morton?'

Morton waved his hand towards Rob in a dismissive gesture, before saying, 'I'm sorry sergeant, I mustn't talk to anyone about this, except Detective Inspector Flint, as I'm bound by client confidentiality rules. If Detective Inspector Flint has no objections about you staying here, then I'm able to talk about this matter in front of you, but I mustn't refer to you in any way. So if you wish to stay in the room I must ask you to respect this and stay silent.'

Rob bristled, clearly annoyed at the stinging rebuke, but Danny said, 'It's ok Rob, that's a fair comment. I would like my Detective Sergeant to stay, he'll remain silent and just observe. Now what exactly was it that Jimmy Wade left with you, that he so clearly wanted me to have Mr Morton?'

Morton stood up and walked over to the Chubb safe in the corner of the room. He quickly twisted the combination dial first one way and then the other. Finally, he yanked hard down on the brass handle and pulled open the safe door.

He removed a white A4 sized envelope from the centre shelf before closing the door, pulling the handle back up and spinning the combination dial.

He then walked over to Danny and handed him the envelope.

Danny took the envelope and said, 'Before I open this letter Mr Morton, are you prepared to stand in a court of law, if necessary, and confirm that this envelope was given to you by Jimmy Wade?'

'No court would ever ask me to do that and violate my Legal Privilege, Inspector. At any subsequent Court proceedings that fact would never be contested, you may open the envelope.'

'Are you aware of the contents?'

'Definitely not Inspector. It was sealed when he gave it to me. There are three signatures on the back over the seal, they are my own, Mr Wade's and Mr Travis a solicitor who works here at the firm.'

'Could I borrow the letter opener on your desk to open the envelope please Mr Morton?'

'Of course Inspector.'

Morton handed Danny a thin bladed silver letter opener that had a thistle motif on the handle.

Danny reached into his jacket pocket and retrieved a pair of latex forensic gloves.

After quickly putting on the gloves Danny slid the thin blade into the envelope, opening it carefully.

Inside the envelope were two more envelopes. A small brown envelope and a letter sized envelope.

Danny opened the brown envelope and found a small key.

He then opened the second envelope and found that it contained a hand written note.

Detective Inspector Flint
Your answers lie with the key.
Lloyds Bank, Market Place Branch, Nottingham
Safety Deposit Box 212

The note was unsigned.

Danny read the note aloud and then said, 'Does that mean anything to you Mr Morton?'

'I can only assume it means that Mr Wade has left something for you in a safety deposit box at that branch of Lloyds Bank in Nottingham.'

Danny stood up, Morton also stood and walked around from his desk.

'Thanks for seeing us today Mr Morton', said Danny.

'No problem Detective Inspector. I'm intrigued, will you be able to let me know what's in the safety deposit box?'

'If it's anything you need to know about Mr Morton, rest assured I'll be in touch.'

Morton held out his hand, Danny quickly removed the latex gloves and accepted the outstretched hand. They shook hands.

'You understand why it has to be this way don't you Inspector?'

Danny nodded, 'I do Mr Morton, legal privilege and all that. There's one last question, when exactly did Jimmy Wade come in to settle his bill?'

'He came to see me on the morning of November 13th, he paid his bill in cash and gave me the envelope and his instructions then.'

'Thanks Mr Morton.'

The two detectives left the building and hurried to their car, Danny gripping the envelope.

They got in the car and Rob started the engine.

As he drove out of the car park and across the bridge that spanned the River Trent, Rob asked, 'I take it we're going to Nottingham?'

'Just as fast as you can get us there Rob!' said Danny.

CHAPTER 92

Nottingham City Centre –
December 15th 1984

They parked the CID car at the back of the main Central Police Station in Nottingham city centre and walked briskly down onto the Old Market Square. The city centre was heaving with shoppers, they weaved their way across the bustling square and into the main branch of Lloyds Bank. Outside the front door of the bank, it was crowded both with customers of the bank and with patrons of the Flying Horse pub which was next door.

Once inside the bank, Danny walked up to the first cashier who was free, showing his warrant card he said quietly, 'I need to see the Branch Manager straight away please.'

The young cashier nodded, left her seat and made her way through a door, into the private offices of the bank. She returned almost immediately followed by Mr Frederick Spooner the Branch Manager.

Mr Spooner asked to see the detective's warrant cards again, before allowing them through the armoured door into the back of the bank.

Once out of earshot of any members of the public Mr Spooner said, 'How can I help you Detective Inspector?'

'I have a key for a safety deposit box that is stored at this branch. It's imperative that I inspect the contents of this box immediately.'

Frederick Spooner was fifty two years old, a very dour man who lived a bachelor life. A man who lived only for his job, he led a life that was devoid of all excitement, he was a grey man in every sense of the word.

Spooner was clearly troubled; this was a highly irregular request. In all his considerable years in banking he'd never known the police to make such a request.

'I'm sorry but don't you need a warrant or something Inspector?'

'No Mr Spooner, I don't. I was given the key and instructions to go with it, from the solicitor who was acting on the instructions of the man who set up the safety deposit box.'

Spooner huffed, shrugging his world weary shoulders.

'I don't know; this is all highly irregular!' he said.

'But all highly proper Mr Spooner, so can we get on with this please, time really is of the essence here.'

The Branch Manager rubbed the area of his forehead that sat just above his nose, he then pinched the top of his nose and squeezed his eyes closed as though trying to alleviate a headache. Suddenly he opened his eyes as though he had made a momentous decision.

'Very well Inspector, what's the number of the box?'

Danny held up the key and said, 'The safety deposit box number is 212, and this is the key for that box.'

'Follow me please, we have to go down to the vaults.'

Danny and Rob followed Spooner down two flights of stone stairs and into the vaults. Once inside Spooner opened a large metal door revealing a room where the safety deposit boxes were stored.

The room was about twelve feet long and eight feet wide. Both of the longer walls contained floor to ceiling safety deposit boxes. In the centre of the room was a large table that was bolted to the floor. The room was lit with a single very bright fluorescent tube strip light.

The boxes themselves were black and made of brushed steel. In both corners of the room at ceiling height, were two closed circuit security television cameras that were pointing at the opposite wall to the one they were mounted on. These cameras covered both banks of security boxes but did not have any view of the table in the centre of the room. This was to ensure the privacy of clients who wished to use the table to inspect the contents of their individual boxes.

Spooner retrieved safety deposit box number 212 and placed it on the table. Using a key from his pocket he unlocked the first of the two locks mounted on the top of the box.

'I'll leave you to inspect the contents in private Inspector. I've unlocked my lock; you'll need to open the other lock with the key in your possession. I'll be outside the door if you need anything else. When you've finished just call my name, I'll escort you out of the bank.'

'One last thing Mr Spooner, do the cctv cameras record?'

'They certainly do detective, but they're on a forty eight hour loop. The system will only store images for two days, after that it automatically records over any previous recordings.'

'That's a shame, but thanks anyway.'

Spooner then walked out, leaving the detectives alone in the vault.

Danny and Rob each took a pair of latex gloves from their pockets and quickly put them on. Danny took the key from the envelope and put it in the lock. One quick twist of the key to the left and the lock opened.

The strong box itself was eighteen inches high, by two feet wide and two feet in length. Slowly Danny lifted the lid, he was breathless with anticipation. As the lid was raised Danny saw a white A4 size envelope, obviously sitting on top of bulkier items below. Printed on the front of the envelope, in black felt tip pen, were the words,

FAO – Detective Inspector Danny Flint

Danny removed the envelope and placed it on the table next to the box, then reaching inside the box he carefully removed the contents one by one and also placed those on the long table. The safety deposit box contained,

A small Olivetti typewriter

A long blonde haired wig

A single police uniform epaulette that had Sgt's chevrons on

A length of black plastic tubing

A four-foot length of thin nylon chord

A set of Ford Cortina M*k 1 car keys*

Danny picked up the envelope and opened it.

Inside was a single sheet of white A4 paper on which was a typed note, Danny removed the sheet of paper and read the note to Rob.

Detective Inspector Danny Flint

I've enjoyed the chase and you've been a worthy adversary.

Just the fact that you're reading this letter proves that.

I had some fun with that oaf of a Police Sergeant, but he was a moron who wouldn't listen. We had our way with the two women, first at Forest Town and then again at Blidworth. We could have gone on and had many more, if he hadn't been so stupid.

Oh well! That's all over and in the past now, I left the good Sergeant hanging about for you to find near the Abbey.

Hopefully you've found him by now.

We had a right laugh over 'The Coal Killer'

Didn't you like the name?

I was disappointed you never gave the name to the press.

I've gone now, disappeared like a phantom, don't bother looking because you'll never find me.

I'm far too clever for you to track me down Inspector.

Is it South Africa, Canada or America? Ha Ha Ha!

Thank you for sending the lovely Rachel to see me about dear old Albie.

I really enjoyed my visit with her before I left.

A beautiful feisty woman but she had to die too!

Sorry about that.

Not really!

Anyway it's been fun Detective

The Coal Killer — aka Jimmy Wade — aka?

Danny's face was set like stone, he put the note down on the table next to the contents of the box.

He suddenly erupted and shouted, 'Bastard!' before hurling the now empty box across the room, clattering it into the opposite wall.

Turning to Rob he said, 'It was this bastard all the time Rob, and he thinks he's killed Rachel.'

'I know Danny, look at the letter 'c' on the note. This is obviously the typewriter they used, the blonde wig, the epaulette, the nylon cord, the keys for the car. He thinks it's all a bloody game.'

'The question is Rob, where is he now? We've got to find him because he'll do this again and again, until he's stopped!'

'Where do we start boss? He's well and truly covered his tracks. He's obviously not Jimmy Wade anymore, somehow he's managed a change of identity.'

'It's hard to know where to start Rob, but we've got to try and find him. Get the local CID to come down here and get this lot bagged and tagged. I haven't given up on catching this bastard yet.'

CHAPTER 93

Mansfield Police Station –
December 16th 1984

Danny knocked on the door of Superintendent Jackson's office.

He was waiting outside, holding clear evidence bags that contained the car keys, the epaulette, the nylon cord, the blonde wig and a clear plastic wallet that contained the typewritten note from Jimmy Wade.

Jackson's voice boomed out from within the office, 'Enter!'

Danny walked in and placed the articles recovered from the safety deposit box on the desk.

'What's all this Inspector?' asked a bemused Jackson.

'Read the note', said Danny tersely.

Danny handed him the typewritten note.

Jackson slowly read the note, glancing up every now and then to look at the individual articles on the desk.

'Where's this Jimmy Wade character now?' he said.

'I don't know, but this bastard has killed a miner, two women, and a police sergeant. He also attacked a police woman, leaving her for dead. We need to find him as a matter of urgency, sir.'

'And just how do you propose to do that Inspector?'

'I want to set up a small task force to follow any leads we can find. There are things we can do to trace him.'

'What exactly can you do? Exactly what leads have you got?'

'Well we think he's left the UK, we can check the ports, the airports.'

'Looking for who? Do you have a name to check against passenger manifests?'

'No, not yet.'

'How, exactly, are you going to get that name Danny?'

'I don't know sir, but I can't give up looking. This man's a psychopath, a stone cold killer and where ever he does end up, he'll definitely kill again.'

Ken Jackson was silent for a full five minutes while he thought over the information that Danny had given him. During that time, he occasionally picked up various items that had been placed on his desk as if trying to obtain an inspiration from the inanimate objects.

Finally, he leaned back in his chair and said, 'This is what's going to happen Inspector. You'll draft a report of your findings, everything you have on this individual Jimmy Wade. Description, age, medical history, dental records, anything you can get. You'll then write up a full synopsis of all the crimes he's suspected of committing here in the UK. I'll then ensure that this is passed on to every other Police Force in the world via Interpol.'

'Is that it sir?'

'That's it, I can't afford to waste manpower on chasing a shadow, however abhorrent the monster is who casts that shadow.'

Slowly Danny shook his head, before picking up all the exhibits from the desk. He turned and walked out of the office without saying a word.

In all his career he had never felt so bad.

He was having serious doubts about carrying on, he felt so low. He was struggling to accept the fact that his enquiries had been hampered from the start by cost and budgets.

The decision not to pursue the second killer theory had been plain wrong and had almost cost Rachel Moore her life, Danny knew only too well that nobody would ever be taken to task over that wrong decision.

The chief officers at headquarters would simply hide behind their mantra of budget restraint and manpower shortages.

As he approached the CID office he could hear hooting and hollering and happy laughing voices. The mood from within the office was completely at odds with how he felt personally.

Wondering what was happening he opened the door.

Rob, smiling broadly, gripped Danny's shoulders and said, 'Fantastic news Danny. We've just had a message from Joe at the hospital, it's Rachel, she's finally come out of the coma.'

'That's brilliant news Rob.'

'It gets better Danny, Rachel's already sitting up and talking. She can't remember a thing about that night, but her brother Joe's told us the doctors think she'll go on to make a full recovery.'

'That really is the best news I could've heard today Rob.'

Rob picked up on the muted greeting to the great news.

'Is everything ok Danny?' he asked quietly.

'I've just come from Jackson's office. He isn't going to allow us to follow up on Jimmy Wade. I know it would've been a difficult, nigh on impossible task to track the bastard down, but all Jackson wants me to do, is write a fucking report and pass it on.'

'Bloody hell Danny, no wonder you're feeling down.'

'I just feel like that bastard Wade has got away with murder.'

Rob put his arm around Danny's shoulder, 'Come on Danny, forget all that for now. We'll make a start on the report tomorrow, we can do it together and curse that wanker Jackson under our breath as we're writing it.'

Danny grinned and said, 'Don't let that wanker Jackson hear you calling him a wanker! It could seriously jeopardise your chances of promotion!'

'That's more like it Danny, come on we're all going to The Railway to celebrate Rachel's recovery. Joe's meeting us there in half an hour. Come on Danny let's get shitfaced tonight, we can worry about all this other shit tomorrow.'

'I'll come for a drink Rob, we do need to celebrate Rachel's recovery, but I just want to get home to Sue tonight. I've got some serious thinking to do.'

'Serious thinking about what exactly?'

'I need to re-assess my future Rob, at this moment in time I don't know if I even want to carry on doing this job anymore. Being told what I can and can't investigate properly, depending on how much it's going to fucking cost. I'm sick of the penny pinching Rob!'

'Danny, don't be daft. You'd chased Wade down, he knew you were closing in behind him, and would get him eventually, that's why he's fucked off out of it. You were right all along, your detective intuition was spot on. You can't quit Danny. This is what you do, this is what you're bloody good at.'

'We'll see Rob, we'll see. Come on let's get to the pub and celebrate the good news.'

CHAPTER 94

Mansfield, Nottinghamshire –
December 20th 1985

The letter box in the front door rattled as the postman pushed through that day's delivery of letters.

Sitting in the kitchen, sipping a cup of tea Louise Smedley said, 'That's the post love, are you going to get it?'

Dave Smedley had built his hopes up too many times before. He shook his head saying, 'Nah love. You go and get it if you want, there won't be anything out there for me.'

Ever since he'd resigned from his Deputy's job at British Coal he had struggled to find any work. He had written to countless firms up and down the country, all to no avail. As a last resort he'd written out the job application that was advertised in the press. He was a realist and didn't hold out too much hope of success.

This was the reason for his apathy.

Dave Smedley was also a haunted man.

He had spiralled down into a dark depression ever since his acrimonious meeting with Detective Inspector Flint. The detective had made him feel somehow responsible for the death of Albie Jones.

That scheming bastard Jimmy Wade had tricked him easily, and now he was struggling to come to terms with the fact, that deep down, he knew it was his conduct that had made it easy for Wade to get away with killing Albie Jones.

The hardest thing for him to accept was that he had behaved that way for purely selfish reasons.

At the time, Smedley had based his decisions on money. Albie Jones had died because he, Dave Smedley, could only think about money.

He had also allowed Wade to get away with it, because of money, he'd been so intent on safeguarding his own job and wages as a deputy, that he gladly went along with Wade's deception.

He buttered another slice of toast and was just dipping the knife into the marmalade jar when his wife Louise rushed back into the dining room.

'There's a letter for you Dave, love. It's got an Australian postmark on', she said excitedly.

Dave almost dropped the knife, he grabbed the letter from his wife and ripped it open. Quickly he scanned the document. There it was in black and white on the page.

Louise was beside herself with excitement, 'Come on love, don't keep me in suspense, what does it say?'

In a trembling voice Dave Smedley read the letter aloud to his wife.

Dear Mr Smedley

We are pleased to offer you the position of Mines Supervisor at the Beltana Mine, Singleton, New South Wales.

This offer is subject to your attendance at Canberra House, London for a medical and also subject to the granting of a 12-month work Visa.

Should the Medical and Visa Application be successful your employment will start from March 1st 1985.

The company will not assist you to travel to Australia and this will have to be undertaken at your own expense.

Please notify this office at your earliest convenience if you intend to take up this offer of employment.

I look forward to hearing from you in the very near future.

Yours sincerely

Royce Goudy

Head of Development

The Baluga Coal Management Company

He put the letter down and looked at his wife who was beaming.

'Looks like we are off to Australia sweetheart', he said as tears welled in his eyes.

His wife was equally as excited, 'It's fantastic news love, we need to get cracking. We've got to get the house sold, make arrangements to get the medical passed as well as getting the Visa and making travel arrangements.'

The Smedley's had always remained childless, so they only had themselves to worry about. This bolt out of the blue job offer was in every way a lifeline.

It was a chance for Dave Smedley to start a new life, away from the memories of Albie Jones and Jimmy Wade.

A new beginning in every sense, he could feel his mood lifting already. He grabbed his wife and they hugged each other tightly.

They began to dance around the breakfast table singing together, 'We're on our way to Australia!'

CHAPTER 95

Singleton, New South Wales, Australia – December 31st 1984

The new tenant looked around the spacious living room. He had rented the second floor apartment above Randall's Hardware shop on Main Street, Singleton, New South Wales.

Walking over to the window he looked down over the busy street and watched people rushing home, ready to celebrate New Year's Eve with their loved ones. In the distance he could see the orange hues of the rapidly setting sun glistening off the still waters of the vast Lake St Clair.

Singleton was picturesque, nothing like the grey drab mining towns he had left back in the UK.

The pretty town was just over a hundred kilometres from Sydney, and lay on the banks of the Hunter River.

From the very first moment he'd arrived in the town he knew immediately this would be where he settled.

He'd only rented this apartment for a couple of months, he wanted a base he could settle into, before starting work at the Beltana Mine.

The huge mine was nineteen kilometres from Singleton.

It was nothing like the antiquated mine he had been used to back in the UK. Beltana Mine was modern, vast and employed almost five thousand men.

After arriving at the town and renting the apartment he'd spent a week at the mine getting used to where everything was and being introduced to his new workmates.

A lot of the other miners were also British. They too had emigrated to Australia intent on starting a new life, after becoming disillusioned with the UK mining industry following the long, bitter strike.

He was due to start his first working shift on the 1st January 1985. He felt it was poetic, a new year, a new job, a new life, a new identity.

He walked to the large refrigerator and took out a cold can of Castlemaine beer. Flicking open the ring pull he opened the ice cold can and took a long drink. The cold lager burned his throat as he swallowed. The sun had now dipped below the horizon, and below his flat street lights were beginning to come on.

As he looked out of the window he reflected on the journey he'd taken, as well as the careful preparations he'd made that enabled him to eventually arrive here.

The whole idea had come to him as a result of seeing an advert in the Sunday Telegraph. He'd read the paper after spending the morning in the Welfare, listening to other miners moaning about the state of the coal industry in the UK.

The advert he saw had been placed by The Baluga Coal Management Company. They were specifically advertising for British mineworkers to move out to Australia to help develop the new mine at Beltana, that had opened in June 1983.

After reading the advert, the very next day he'd travelled to a country church in North Yorkshire and searched until he found a gravestone that marked the death of a male infant named Lee Chivers.

Chivers had been born the same year as he had, but had died aged only three months. He went into the small church and checked the parish register. He soon found the entry relating to the death of Lee Chivers. He made a note of the names and details of the dead infants' parents.

Using these details, he had applied for and received a duplicate birth certificate in the name of the dead infant.

He then completed a passport application also in the name of Lee Chivers. He forged the signatures of the counter signers and posted off the passport application and the duplicate birth certificate, not really sure if it would work.

Much to his surprise his new passport arrived shortly after.

He had then made the decision to go back to work as a scab. One of the main reasons he made the decision to go back to work was because he needed to gain access to his own personnel file. It took him almost two weeks before an opportunity arose that allowed him to get into the Personnel Office and remove his own file.

Taking the file home, he painstakingly copied and forged references in his new name of Lee Chivers. He then sent these forged and copied documents together with a copy of his new passport off with the job application.

Again he was somewhat pleasantly surprised when the letter had arrived offering him a job at the Beltana Mine in New South Wales, Australia.

He had travelled down to Canberra House in London for the day to undergo a medical. He passed the medical easily and was granted a twelve month Visa. The Visa was issued with an option to apply for dual citizenship at a later date.

After obtaining the visa and passing the medical he immediately placed his house on the market for a ridiculous amount of money.

The house was quickly sold, almost too quickly, he was forced to ask his solicitor to slow things down a little so he could complete everything else he needed to do.

As soon as the house was sold and the money had been cleared into his bank account at the Nat West Bank, he immediately went into the bank and personally withdrew all the money from his account. The next stop was a travel agent where he purchased a one-way ticket to Australia flying from London Heathrow to Sydney. The ticket was purchased in his new name of Lee Chivers.

His flight left Heathrow airport in London at eleven o'clock on the morning of the 15th November. He'd abandoned the blue Datsun Cherry car in the long stay car park at the airport, never intending to go back for it.

Arriving in Australia, he enjoyed Sydney for a week before travelling on the overland coach out to Singleton.

After arriving at Singleton, he rented the apartment and took his driving test with the Australian Police. Having passed the driving test, he was granted an Australian Driving Licence in the name of Lee Chivers.

He then purchased a second hand Holden hatchback car.

Armed with his Australian Driving Licence and his new passport to confirm his identity, he opened a bank account at The First National Bank of Australia in the name of Lee Chivers.

Before leaving England he had converted the money from the sale of 56 Marples Avenue into Australian dollars. He had hidden the Australian banknotes in the lining of one of his large suitcases. It was a risk bringing cash into the country but it had proved to be a worthwhile gamble.

As soon as the Customs Officer at Sydney airport saw the twelve month work Visa and the letter confirming the job offer he had waived him straight through customs.

He was now sitting pretty with over fifty thousand dollars in the bank, a new job at the mine, a new car and a nice apartment.

Later in the New Year he intended to look for a bigger house to settle down in.

He took another long pull on the ice cold lager and again looked down from his window. The street below was full of people bustling along, getting on with their lives.

He reflected on the fact that getting to this point had been no easy task, it had taken months of careful planning.

As Jimmy Wade, he had easily outwitted the police in England. He was always one step ahead and managed to get away with murder time after time.

Now reinvented as Lee Chivers he felt confident, invisible and untouchable. He'd learned many lessons from the insane Mick Reynolds and now felt even better equipped to outwit law enforcement.

He would be patient and take three or four months to establish and orientate himself. After killing with Reynolds he now realised he no longer had to rely on the urges to guide him. He was now the master of his own destiny. When he killed and who he killed, was completely a matter of his own choosing.

He knew the time would come soon enough for Australia to witness the arrival of Lee Chivers. There was nothing to stand in his way, the killing would soon begin again.

EPILOGUE

Beltana Mine, New South Wales – April 20th 1985

Dave Smedley was now a very happy man.

The depression he had felt back in England now seemed a dim and distant memory. After arriving in Australia, he'd started his new job at the Beltana Mine, right on schedule on the 1st of March. He felt it was apt that he started his new job and effectively his new life on St David's day.

His wife Louise quickly settled in to her new surroundings and soon found a lovely home just outside Singleton.

The pay from the mine was very good and his new employers were extremely happy with his work.

Settling down to their new life in New South Wales had been relatively easy. Dave and Louise had quickly made friends with people in their community.

The sale of their house in the UK had been the only sticking point. It had not sold as quickly as they'd hoped and after passing the medical and being granted the twelve month work Visa, they had gambled and travelled out to Australia using their savings.

Having arrived in Australia with very little money, they had been overjoyed to finally get a buyer for their house almost immediately after their arrival. The house in Berry Hill, Mansfield was purchased by a first time buyer for the full asking price.

As soon as the money from the house sale was transferred over to their new bank account in The First National Bank they were in a position to purchase the small house outside Singleton.

They had quickly settled into their beautiful new home and life could not be better for Dave Smedley.

It was now approaching ten o'clock at night, Dave reflected on a hard afternoon shift as he walked across the large floodlit car park at the Beltana mine.

He was walking with Jeff Evans, another of the Mines Supervisors. Jeff was a born and bred Australian and had been one of the first people Dave became friends with after his move down under. The two men walked slowly across the car park towards their respective cars.

As they walked across the huge car park Dave saw a group of men approaching them.

His eyes were immediately drawn to a tall, blonde haired man at the centre of the group who was laughing.

Dave quickly looked away as he passed the group of men who were heading in for the night shift.

Turning to Jeff he asked, 'Did you see that tall, blonde guy who just walked past?'

Jeff quickly glanced over his shoulder, then replied, 'Yeah, he's another Pom like you mate. He started back in January, just after the new year.'

'Do you know his name Jeff?'

'Why, do you know him from back home mate?'

'I think I do, yeah.'

'Let me think. Yeah, I've got it mate. His name's Lee Chivers. I reckon he lives near you, over in Singleton somewhere.'

Dave was totally shocked, he knew exactly who the tall, blonde haired miner was and it definitely wasn't Lee Chivers.

'Tell you what Dave, the shift I've just had was a proper bastard. Do you fancy a couple of cold ones on the way home?' asked Jeff.

'I'd love to mate, but there's something I've got to do urgently tonight. You ok to have that beer tomorrow?'

'Of course mate, no worries. See you tomorrow.'

Dave Smedley jumped in his car and raced out of the car park. As he drove his car along the twisting roads from the Beltana Mine to his house in Singleton he was desperately trying to remember a name. As he pulled onto the driveway of his house, the name suddenly came into his head.

He ran straight into the house.

'Louise love, what time is it in England?'

'What time is it now?' she shouted from upstairs

'It's about half past ten love.'

'Well then it's about half past nine in the morning over there, why?'

'Never mind love, I'll be up in a minute. I just need to make a quick call.'

He dialled the operator. After a short wait the operator came on the line.

'I'd like to be put through to Mansfield Police Station, Mansfield, Nottinghamshire, England. Thanks', said Dave quietly.

A minute or so went by, all Dave could hear were clicks and other strange noises.

Patiently he waited.

Suddenly a voice came on the line, 'Hello, Mansfield Police, how can I help?'

'I need to speak to Detective Inspector Flint please.'

'Just a second, I'll put you through to the CID.'

Another delay, then a voice answered, 'Detective Inspector Flint, how can I help you?'

'Detective Inspector Flint, It's Dave Smedley.'

'What can I do for you Mr Smedley?'

'I don't know if you remember me Inspector, I came to see you about the death of Albie Jones.'

'I remember you Mr Smedley.'

'Inspector, I'm living in Australia now, at a small town called Singleton not far from Sydney in New South Wales. I thought you'd want to know, I've just seen Jimmy Wade at the Beltana Mine!'

THE END

About the author

Trevor Negus is a retired Police Officer who spent 30 years working with Nottinghamshire Police.

He worked both inner city and rural beats in uniform and spent the entire duration of the Miners' Strike of 1984 on a Police Support Unit.

He then spent six years as an authorised firearms officer and was a sniper on the Force's Special Operations Unit. The last eleven years of his Police career were spent as a detective on the CID, where he was involved in numerous murder enquiries. During his time on the CID he was trained as a specialist interviewer, involved in the planning and interviews of murder suspects.

The Exodus Murders

Nottinghamshire 1986

Two brutal murders are discovered on the same day at different ends of the county.

Both the victims are men, both have been mutilated and tortured before having their throats cut and being left to bleed to death.

The killer has daubed a strange code on the walls at both scenes using the blood of the victims.

Detective Chief Inspector Flint is now in charge of the newly formed Major Crime Investigation Unit.

He and his fledgling team are tasked with finding the killer. After discovering the meaning of the code, Flint and his team know they are in a race against time before the cold-blooded killer strikes again.

He must find the link that ties the victims together, then as the pieces fall into place and the reason for the slaughter becomes apparent, it becomes clear to Det Ch Insp Flint that one of their own is in mortal danger of becoming the final victim.